THE WORLD OF KATE ROBERTS

In the series

BORDER LINES: WORKS IN TRANSLATION

A Project of the Creative Writing Program at Temple University

Lawrence Venuti, General Editor

THE WORLD OF KATE ROBERTS

Selected Stories 1925–19 81

Translated from the Welsh by
Joseph P. Clancy

Temple University Press
Philadelphia

Temple University Press,
Philadelphia 19122
Copyright © 1991 by Temple University
All rights reserved. Published 1991
Printed in the United States of America
The paper used in this publication meets the
minimum requirements of American
National Standard for Information
Sciences—Permanence of Paper for Printed
Library Materials,
ANSI Z39.48-1984 ∞

Library of Congress
Cataloging-in-Publication Data
Roberts, Kate, 1891–1985
[Selections. English. 1991]
The world of Kate Roberts : selected stories
1925–1981 / translated from the Welsh by
Joseph P. Clancy.   p.   cm.
Stories translated from the Welsh.
Includes bibliographical references.
ISBN 0-87722-794-2 (alk. paper). —
ISBN 0-87722-795-0 (pbk. : alk. paper)
1. Roberts, Kate, 1891–1985
—Translations into English.
I. Title.
PB2298.R63A24 1991
891.6′632—dc20   90-41874
                                    CIP

Contents

CONTENTS

Introduction

Kate Roberts (1891–1985) was born and raised in the slate-quarrying village of Rhosgadfan, within the mountainous region of North Wales known as "Arfon," facing west across the Menai Straits to the island of Anglesey. Her father was a quarryman who also, as was common, rented a small farm, where much of the daily labor was of necessity borne by her mother.

When asked what she had inherited from her parents and her community as a person and a writer, she answered: "As a writer, the Welsh language in its purity on their lips. Going to the Sunday School and the means of grace in the chapel; learning the Scripture and hymns by heart, with my parents taking care that I did. Monolingual parents and a monolingual Welsh society. As a person, I can't say whether I have inherited my parents' traits of character: their power to carry on in spite of everything, their outcry against every injustice, their compassion for people who were down and out, their readiness to help a neighbour, their ability to talk entertainingly (on the hearth but not outside), their sense of humour, their honesty. . . . One thing I am certain I have inherited from my mother is speaking plainly, or as she would say, 'speaking the plain truth.' Perhaps one other characteristic: I have tried to show compassion for the characters in my stories; I can't say whether I've succeeded or not. I believe also that I have inherited a bit of my parents' bravery, but I'm not sure."

"I was fortunate in my parents," she wrote in her autobiography. "Perhaps if I had been less fortunate I would have had more themes for novels, but for me as a person, I can look back with delight today, not because of the smoothness of life in earlier days—it was difficult and stormy, it wasn't always peaceful—but because it left no bitter taste."

"It's the impressions of childhood that stay deepest in us," she once said, adding, "I was a child who felt everything to the quick." I have included the first chapter, "Pictures," from her autobiography, both for its literary art and as the best entrance for non-Welsh readers to the world of her stories.

In 1904 Kate Roberts won a scholarship to the County School in Caernarfon. As was standard at the time, all courses were taught in English, and most of the teaching staff was English. "I was hurled," she said, "from a home and a district where no one knew English into the midst of this Englishness. . . . At the end of my first week, I felt that my tongue was swollen in trying to speak English." Although she remembered having an excellent teacher for Welsh courses, she recalled also that of some fifty hymns in the school hymnal, only two were in Welsh. "Two very suitable hymns in so English a school. 'O agor fy llygaid i weled' [Oh open my eyes to see] and 'Arglwydd, arwain trwy'r anialwch' [Lord, guide through the wilderness]. There was a need of eyes being opened, and a need of guidance, for the people who devised such a system of education at a school in the middle of so Welsh-speaking a district."

She went in 1910 to the University College of North Wales in Bangor, where she read Welsh with two of the great scholars of the period, John Morris-Jones and Ifor Williams. After taking her degree, she taught elementary school for a year at Llanberis before going south to teach Welsh at grammar schools in Glamorgan; she remembered the journey as long and strange, and the Welsh of southerners as initially foreign. She married Morris Williams, a master printer and like herself a member of the newly formed Welsh Nationalist Party, in 1928, and they lived in Cardiff and Tonypandy through the early years of the Depression. Of her long stay in South Wales, she said: "It was a rich experience for one who was raised amid the rocks of Arfon, but I had seen enough of poverty myself to be able to appreciate the Southerner's capacity for suffering."

In 1935 Kate Roberts and Morris Williams purchased Gwasg Gee, a long-established publishing house noted for its contributions to Welsh learning and literature, and moved to the town of Denbigh, in North Wales. She would live there for the remainder of her long life.

Kate Roberts began to write short stories in 1921. Her first collection, published in 1925, was followed by two more in the next ten years. This first period of her work produced also two books of children's stories, a play, and the novel *Traed mewn Cyffion* (Feet in chains), published in 1936.

INTRODUCTION

It was the experience of World War I and its impact on Wales, she said on several occasions, that first impelled her to write. She recalled "the terrible injustice I have felt personally, that a government took the children of monolingual Welsh smallholders to fight the battles of the Empire, and sent an official letter to say those children had been killed in a language that the parents couldn't understand."

What particularly stirred her to write was "the death of my youngest brother in the 1914–18 war, failing to understand things and being forced to write lest I smother. (Politically, it drove me to the Welsh Nationalist Party.) . . . Death pulls the scales off one's eyes, gives a shock to the person and gives, as in a lightning flash, a new look at character, or at society, or indeed, at life as a whole."

She did not, however, deal directly with the effects of the war on Welsh society until her novel of 1936. Rather, she said, "in reflecting on the sorrow of the First World War I saw that sorrow was the lot of my ancestors as well, and events from their lives came into my mind." Her concern was to record, to examine, and to celebrate without sentimentality the life of the close-knit society in which she had grown up, "a poor society at a poor time in our history. . . . But one should notice that the characters haven't reached the bottom of that poverty; they struggle against it, fear it." She would note, complementarily, in her autobiography: "We never saw riches, but we had riches that no one can take away from us, the riches of a language and a culture. We had it at home, on the hearth, and that hearth was part of the community." What she meant by this is often an assumed background to the stories—the Sunday School for adults as well as children, the quarrymen's intense Monday discussions of the Sunday sermons, the weekly *seiat* (fellowship meeting), the annual "literary meeting." (Because they are referred to in a number of the stories, I have quoted Kate Roberts' recollections of the last two in the notes to this introduction.)

"When I began to write," she said, "it wasn't that I had an idea for a story, I had an idea about life. When an author has an idea for a story, he finishes there and then, until another idea comes. But if you have a vision of life, another story will be pushing itself forward before you finish writing the first." Kate Roberts' "vision of life" is, I think, better experienced as it grows from, is incarnate in, the world of her fiction than reduced to abstractions. Nevertheless, it is worth citing Saunders Lewis's description "unfashionable classicism," associating Kate Roberts not with modern writers but with Hesiod and Homer in her treatment of "common events of daily life," particularly what the struggle against poverty reveals of human nature and the human condition, so that these events "turn into symbols because they give us a vision of the life of man on earth."

In discussing her earliest work with Kate Roberts, Saunders Lewis remarked: "In 1924 with your story 'The Widow' and the story 'Old Age' we all saw that the Welsh-language short story had taken a new step in its history, a definite step into the world of artistic creation." Although the non-Welsh reader is not likely to be aware of this, it serves as a reminder of Walter Allen's observation that "the short story as we think of it today is both an international form and a recent one, essentially a modern form." We are likely, perhaps, to take its characteristics for granted—literary historian R. M. Jones refers to Kate Roberts' first stories as "a new adventure in Welsh literature," as a "revolution"; and if we recall that James Joyce's *Dubliners* and D. H. Lawrence's *The Prussian Officer* were published in 1914, Katherine Mansfield's *Prelude* in 1918, Sherwood Anderson's *Winesburg, Ohio* in 1919, this will suggest the literary context in which Kate Roberts began to write, as well as the masters of the genre with whom she would earn an equal place. She noted an early taste for Maupassant in Welsh translation, her lifelong delight in Chekhov's stories, and Mansfield's "new way of writing a short story" as early influences. But she added: "What reading short stories from other languages did for me was, not make me wish to imitate their manner, or to borrow anything from them in any way, but show me that there was the stuff of literature in the life of my own district, especially after reading authors who didn't insist on the technique of closing a story with a clever ending."

She came to talk harshly of the stories in her first collection as too much influenced by the then fashionable taste for striking, unexpected endings (though she made an exception of "Old Age" as having more substance in the body of the story itself). This is a verdict Welsh critics in general have found too severe, and I have included a group of these stories in the present selection as of interest in themselves as well as in the light of her later work. While one may agree with the reviewer she remembered well who said that despite his praise, one could not write "perfect" on this first volume, these stories already possess her characteristic power to focus on a small incident that illuminates an ordinary life; to use what from the beginning she found most attractive in the short story form, "its lyrical manner of expression", in economically selecting evocative details of setting and behavior; to restrict narrative perspective so that the character's experience is immediately present to the reader.

INTRODUCTION

Kate Roberts' third collection of short stories was published in 1937. It would be twelve years before her next work of fiction, the long story *Stryd y Glep* (Gossip Row), appeared. We have more reason to wonder at an author's ability to write imaginatively at all than to be surprised at a temporary or permanent cessation of this creativity, but this long hiatus for an otherwise prolific author has inevitably aroused speculation. Derec Llwyd Morgan reports that in a letter to him she once dismissed the cause as perhaps "laziness." He goes on to remark that these were in fact busy years for her as her husband's partner in the printing shop and publishing house of Gwasg Gee.

The press had long published the influential weekly newspaper *Y Faner* (The Banner), which they now firmly committed to the cause of Welsh nationalism, most clearly expressed in a statement by Saunders Lewis, then president of Plaid Cymru, the Nationalist Party: "We do need a government of our own. Not independence. Not even an unconditional freedom. But exactly that degree of freedom which is necessary in order to make civilization secure in Wales." Kate Roberts was to write later: "If a writer is a genuine Welsh writer, he cannot fail to be at one with his nation's past and at one with his nation's future as well, and so he strives to the best of his ability to keep his nation's literature and culture alive. Thus, he divides his life, interests, and energy, and he cannot give his whole life to literature." She herself regularly contributed social and political as well as literary articles and reviews not only to *Y Faner* but to the Nationalist Party's monthly newspaper, *Y Ddraig Goch* (The Red Dragon).

The years between 1937 and 1949 were the disruptive years, one must also note, of the prelude to World War II, the war itself, and its aftermath. This is not the place to attempt an exploration of the complex relationships between Wales and England at that time, but one episode that is now constantly referred to as a turningpoint in the history of Welsh literature as well as politics must be cited: "the Fire in Llŷn." On September 7, 1936, three Welsh Nationalists—Saunders Lewis, Lewis Valentine, and D. J. Williams—set fire to the RAF Bombing School under construction at Pen-y-berth on the Llŷn peninsula and then surrendered to the police. The action was taken to protest the indifference of the English government to widespread Welsh objections to establishing a bombing school in a rural Welsh-speaking community with strong historical associations— particularly since the government had earlier yielded to *English* objections to basing such facilities on sites with historical importance or where fishing or wildlife would be endangered. "Our action," Saunders Lewis said at the trial in Caernarfon, "was a protest against the ruthless refusal of the English state even to discuss the rights of the Welsh nation in Llŷn." A jury in Caernarfon was unable to agree on a verdict; at a subsequent trial in London the three were sentenced to nine months' imprisonment. At neither trial were they permitted to plead their cases in Welsh. After his release from prison, and the refusal of the University College of Wales, Swansea, to reinstate him as a lecturer, Saunders Lewis was given a forum by Kate Roberts and her husband in the pages of *Y Faner*, for which he wrote a weekly column on world affairs from 1939 to 1951.

As one further and final note on the interim between Kate Roberts' earlier and later periods of creative writing, I would suggest that it probably took some while for so reflective a writer to absorb the experiences of living in Denbigh at a time of great changes in Welsh life, and to be prepared to convert these into fiction.

Emyr Humphreys, in his 1988 television dramatization of Kate Roberts' life, has her begin by saying: "The great Irish writer James Joyce wrote about escaping the triple net of nationality, language, religion in order to pursue his artistic vision with total freedom. I never escaped. Never wanted to."

But it has often been remarked of Kate Roberts' fiction that for so committed a person politically, she kept it, unlike the work of many of her contemporaries and her juniors, remarkably free of direct political commentary. In part, surely, this was because in depicting the past or present condition of life in Wales, she could assume that her readers could place them in the context of the effects of a centralized English government, most of whose members either did not believe that Wales had a separate and distinctive reality or did not value that reality when it was weighed against English concerns. The recent comment of poet Bobi Jones that "to use a Welsh word is still a revolutionary action" is relevant here. To continue creating a living literature in a language that was declining in Wales from somewhat more than 50 percent Welsh-speakers in the year of Kate Roberts' birth to 18.9 percent shortly before her death was as much a political act as her vigorous and successful struggle for the Welsh-medium Primary School established in Denbigh in 1968.

She did not, however, see imaginative literature as something to be produced by patriotism; rather it came from "something much greater, a yearning that spurs us to express ourselves on matters that relate to creation as a whole, things that are dark to us or disturb us, or things that interest us without being at all dark. . . . We cry out, cry out at Life, very often because we do not understand it."

When her impetus to write fiction returned, its source was again in a deeply painful event. "At the end of the war, in January 1946, I suddenly lost my husband, and that was the blackest hour in my history. I felt that it was impossible for me to gather the pieces of my life together. I had a brief battle over whether I should go back to being a schoolteacher or carry on Gwasg Gee and *Y Faner*. It was the latter resolve that won. [She was to continue in the business for ten more years.] . . . I believe it was my unhappiness that gave birth to my practice of literature during this time. My distress caused, not a darkening of my mind, but an opening of doors on Life, and a seeing of things and people more clearly. But instead of looking back at the past, I began to look into myself and at my experiences."

When *Gossip Row* was published in 1949, one reviewer commented that it was so different from her previous work that one was impelled to think it belonged to a new author. One reason, certainly, was the small-town setting, which would recur thereafter in many of her stories; another was the use of a deeply introspective first-person narrator (though introspection and retrospection are the typical actions of a Kate Roberts story, early or late). What is most marked in this story as in the decades of stories to follow, most notably in *Dark Tonight*, is that while the experience of poverty remains the vital center of her fiction, it is not material but cultural, moral, spiritual impoverishment—in essence, what Emily Dickinson called "the abdication of belief" which "makes the behavior small"—that defines the experiences and tests the resources of her characters in the Wales (and, by implication, the world) of the later twentieth century. Some of them, one feels, would agree with Dickinson: "Better an ignis fatuus / Than no illume at all."

If Saunders Lewis could invoke the name of Homer for her earlier fiction, one critic would invoke Samuel Beckett for the later. But there is no ultimate despair for her characters—they are more apt to discover that they possess, when hardest pressed, less faith perhaps than a hope for faith in the meaningfulness of existence. And what remains most characteristically Welsh in the vision of Kate Roberts is that membership in a community, fellowship, is not accidental or detrimental but essential to the realization of the human self. However dark and isolated the individual's experience of life may be in her later stories, and however flawed the community, there is no room in her fictions for celebration of romantic rebellion or modernist individualism as heroic. In reading her, I have often been reminded of G. K. Chesterton's dictum: "We make our enemies, we make our friends, but God made our next door neighbour."

Related to these changes in setting and experience, surely, is the most marked change in the technique of her later stories. Derec Llwyd Morgan has noted that the early stories "seem to have the power of tales written after years of oral transmission"—and indeed the external narrating "voice" in most of them, inherited as much perhaps from nineteenth-century traditions as from the experiences of storytelling she recalls on the hearth at home, is something the reader is conscious of in even the most sympathetic story as firmly and effectively distancing and objectifying the characters' thoughts and actions. "The later stories," Professor Morgan observes, "are more intense, and in them the author is more intent on coming to grips with things." The reader experiences, in third-person as well as first-person narratives, the characters' experiences exclusively through their own perspectives—one is hardly aware of an external narrating voice at all in stories like "Two Old Men" and "Family."

Kate Roberts added, after the statement on the loss of her husband, that "looking back to the past is not a bad thing; it is not old-fashioned, as some maintain, since life repeats itself. Trying to fathom your experiences isn't a new thing either. . . . Since 1946 I have been writing both kinds of stories, and I will not apologize for that."

There is, indeed, a kind of contrapuntal effect to her later work. Her novel *Y Byw sy'n Cysgu* (The living sleep, 1956), which deals with a wife deserted by her veteran husband after World War II, was followed by *Tegwch y Bore* (The beauty of the morning, serially published in *Y Faner* in 1957–58 but not published as a book until 1967), which treated a young schoolteacher's experiences on the home front during World War I. The linked stories of childhood in turn-of-the-century Arfon that make up *Tea in the Heather* (1959) were succeeded by the long story, *Dark Tonight* (1962), of the breakdown and recovery of a minister's middle-aged wife in the small-town Wales of the 1960s.

There is much the same contrapuntal effect when one moves through the five collections of shorter stories published after 1964—not simply in the juxtaposition of stories set in different periods but in the frequent use of older characters who themselves juxtapose the organic Welsh world of their youth with its fragmentation and loss of roots in the present day. Her last volume, published four years before her death at the age of ninety-four, concluded with a story that carries a central character from *Tea in the Heather* one step further on. Her final unsentimental record and celebration of the Wales of her childhood, it is both an end and a beginning, and makes a fitting close for this selection as well.

One of Kate Roberts' strengths is her prose style. John Rowlands calls it "spare," "unspectacularly plain and unadorned." Derec Llwyd Morgan, on the other hand, emphasizes her "mastery of idiom and syntax." She herself remarked that "the great thing is economy," and that she "paid great attention to sentences and words, trying to find the right word to express what I wanted," adding that this wasn't necessarily "an uncommon word." She said also that she had made no conscious effort to develop a special style, which she thought "could become a stumbling-block"—"my style depends on the Welsh we spoke at home, and on the books I've read whose manner sank into my unconscious without my realizing it." One interviewer, late in Kate Roberts' life, commented on her use of "idioms and constructions that are fast disappearing" and asked whether she went out of her way to look for them. She answered: "They come quite naturally to me. My parents and the majority of the people of Rhosgadfan knew no English at that time. The Welsh idioms were like wine on their lips. I had the Welsh of the Bible as well in chapel and Sunday school."

It would be pointless to dwell on how much must be lost of such a style in translation, including local dialect and differences between northern and southern Welsh. I have tried to devise an English style that would suggest something of the easy conversational flow and the distinctive rhythms and tones of the Welsh. While I have tried also to avoid the impression of "quaintness" that has sometimes marred attempts to convey Welsh-speaking in English, I have experienced the contrary danger of producing something much too brisk and bland often enough to take what risks seemed necessary to avoid this.

There is a unique challenge for translators, and not least an American translator, in the bilingualism of modern Wales. While I have used British English when clearly appropriate and tried to shun blatant Americanisms (for example, the characters go on British holidays rather than take American vacations), I have not considered myself bound always to render either narrator or character voices in the English a Welsh-speaker would use (when necessary) in daily life.

Because of the frequency of Welsh personal and place names, I have supplied a simplified guide to the pronunciation of Welsh. What may strike a non-Welsh reader as strange, the inconsistent use of Welsh and English forms of the same name (such as "Ifans" and "Evans"), mirrors Kate Roberts' practice, itself a mirroring of the reality in modern Wales. When a Welsh place name also has a well-known English name, I have reluctantly thought it best to use the latter (for example, "Sir Fôn" is always "Anglesey").

Although Kate Roberts' stories are in general easily accessible to the common reader, and this selection as a whole should offer a sufficient context to clarify the world of any particular story, I have provided notes on matters unlikely to be familiar to the non-Welsh reader. In a very few instances, where it could be done unobtrusively, I have incorporated the clarification of a reference into the translation itself.

In this regard, it is easier to explain one Welsh practice here, since it is constant throughout the stories. Because of the relatively few surnames in Wales, persons are regularly referred to by their full names or in terms of residence, profession (or husband's profession), or some individual characteristic. It is the most practical way to distinguish teacher from postal worker, one neighbor from another, when all are named Jones, or Lewis, or Roberts.

I must thank Emlyn Evans, Managing Director of Gwasg Gee, for permission to undertake and publish these translations.

This project has been supported by a major fellowship grant from the U.S. National Endowment for the Arts, which enabled me to spend more than a year of concentrated work to complete it.

I am grateful to Sister Raymunde McKay, President of Marymount Manhattan College, for approving a teaching schedule that permitted me to make maximum use of this time. I am happy to recall, with both of us on the brink of retirement, that it was her enthusiastic support thirty years ago, during her initial tenure as president, that made my first Welsh translations possible.

Professor R. M. Jones of the University College of Wales, Aberystwyth, has been, as always, most generous in his encouragement and advice. My wife has acted as my Welshless first reader, diligent, sympathetic, and demanding—I am greatly indebted to her for whatever I have achieved of a plausible and effective style. For whatever errors or infelicities remain, I alone am responsible.

On my first visit to Wales, in 1961, Sir Thomas Parry—then Principal of the University College of Wales, Aberystwyth, and recent editor of Dafydd ap Gwilym—gave a cordial welcome to the brash young American who appeared unexpectedly in his office and announced his intention of translating that greatest of medieval Welsh poets. He took a warm interest in my further ventures and visits, and I regret that he did not live to see and comment on these translations of his Arfon countrywoman. To his memory as poet, translator, scholar, and generous host I dedicate this book.

Joseph P. Clancy

The Pronunciation of Welsh

The Welsh alphabet uses 28 letters: a, b, c, ch, d, dd, e, f, ff, g, ng, h, i, l, ll, m, n, o, p, ph, r, rh, s, t, th, u, w, y.

In general, the consonants represent the same sound-values as in English spelling, with these exceptions.

c: always the sound in *cat,* never the sound in *cease.*

ch: as in the Scottish word *loch.*

dd: the sound represented by the *-the* in *breathe;* Welsh uses *th* only for the sound in *breath.*

f: as in *of.*

ff: as in *off.*

g: always the sound in *give,* never the sound in *germ.*

ll: there is no equivalent sound in English; the usual advice is to pronounce *tl* rapidly as if it were a single sound, or to put the tip of the tongue on the roof of the mouth and hiss.

ph: as in *physic.*

r: the sound is always trilled.

rh: the trilled *r* followed by aspiration.

s: always the sound in *sea,* never the sound in *does; si* is used for the sound represented in English spelling by *sh*—English *shop* becomes Welsh *siop.*

Welsh vowels stand always for pure vowel-sounds, never as in English spelling for diphthongs. The vowels can be long or short; a circumflex accent is sometimes used to distinguish the long vowel.

a: the vowel-sounds in *father* and (American) *hot.*

e: the vowel-sounds in *pale* and *pet.*

i: the vowel-sounds in *green* and *grin;* also the consonantal sound represented in English spelling by *y*—English *yard* becomes Welsh *iard.*

o: the vowel-sounds in *roll* and (British) *hot.*

u: pronounced like the Welsh *i;* never used as in English spelling.

w: the vowel-sounds in *tool* and *took*—English *fool* becomes

Welsh *ffwl;* also used consonantally as in English, *dwell-ing, Gwen.*

y: in most monosyllables and in final syllables pronounced like the Welsh *i;* in other syllables it stands for the vowel-sound in *up,* and this is also its sound in a few monosyllables like *y* and *yr.*

The following diphthongs are used in Welsh; the chief vowel comes first.

ae, ai, au:	the diphthong sound in *write.*
ei, eu, ey:	*uh-ee.*
aw:	the diphthong sound in *prowl.*
ew:	the short Welsh *e* followed by *oo.*
iw, yw:	*ee-oo.*
wy:	*oo-ee.*
oe, oi, ou:	the sound in *oil.*

The accent in Welsh is placed, with few exceptions, on the penult: Llýwarch, Llywélyn.

I

Autobiography

(1960)

Pictures

The doctor's horse is tied to the gate, and the doctor comes along the path down to the house. He is a small man and has a red beard, he is wearing leather leggings that gleam like glass. He comes into the house and puts his hat and his gloves on the table. There's a very worried look on mam as the doctor goes into the room where my brother, younger than I, is very sick. I am afraid of the doctor, he is so strange and so much of a gentleman, there are no marks of toil on his hands. But he is the one who is going to cure my brother. He leaves medicine smells after him.

In a few days I am rolling Marie biscuits like a hoop along the floor of the room, without fear of being scolded, because my brother is lying on his side in the bed looking at me and at the biscuits. He's laughing and mam is smiling.

.   .   .

It's a fine evening in May, and I can go hand in hand with my father to Bryn Gro. There's a sick man there, Robert Jones is his name, and dad shaves him while he's sick. He is a brother of Glasynys my father says, but I am none the wiser. Dad goes into the house and is swallowed up in its darkness. I wait outside, and Nel, Robert Jones' grand-daughter, comes out to play with me. She has long, thick hair that reaches down below the middle of her back. We go to the pig pen, and look at the pigs. There's one tiny little pig there, and I'm mad about him. Going home I talk to dad about the little pig, and dad says that it's a "cull" or "runt of the litter", that's what they call such little pigs.

.   .   .

I am four and a half years old and we are moving from Bryn Gwyrfai to Cae'r Gors, across the fields. Mary Williams, who comes to help mam sometimes, is carrying Evan, the baby, in the shawl, she has Richard, my other brother, three years old, by the hand, and I am walking beside them and carrying a saucepan. That's my help in the moving. People are going ahead of us carrying the furniture. Just in front of me two men are carrying the bottom of the china cabinet. The cabinet is bouncing up and down in perfect rhythm. I don't remember reaching Cae'r Gors or going to bed for the first time in our new house. From darkness to darkness.

.   .   .

It's a cold, wet Saturday morning, my birthday, six years old. Mam has just cleaned around the fire, and there's a low glowing fire in the grate. I stand by it, and despite the warmth, I have a chill because of the nasty weather. I am crying and crying, and I don't know why, maybe just because it's a miserable day. I am certain that it isn't because I didn't get a present, since we never get birthday presents. Mam says that God Almighty takes care to send rain on Saturday because there's no school.

.   .   .

The wind is moaning around the house and crying like a child. The branches of the trees beside the rickyard are creaking and I hear some of them crack and break. A big, quiet gasp, and a slate comes loose from the roof of the cowshed and falls somewhere. I'm afraid the roof of the house will go. But we needn't be afraid, we're snug in bed and dad and mam are by the fire under the big chimney. God in Heaven is lying flat on His back on the woolly clouds, and His beard is just like the wool. It's He forgives us for doing bad things and makes sure that we won't go to the big fire. But it's dad and mam give us food and a roof that doesn't fall.

.   .   .

I am seven and a half, sitting in the road beside the gate. There's a big flat rock there, and that's where I sit tending my youngest brother, Dafydd, in a shawl. I sit there so much that I've made a convenient hole for my feet. It's a nice day. In front of me are Anglesey and the Menai Straits, the Irish Sea stretches to the horizon, Caernarfon Castle stretches its nose into the straits, with the town a small body behind it. There are little white sailboats going through the Bar, and the sands of Niwbwrch and the Estuary gleam like yellow coltskin in the sun. There's nobody going along the road, it's perfectly still. Presently the shop's big old dray, somewhat lighter than a cart, will come carrying goods from town, as it does every day. The geese belonging to Jane Roberts, Glanrafon Hen, are grazing on the bank and they stretch out their necks in going by to show their authority. But my little brother and I are perfectly quiet and happy, doing nothing but looking down at the sea and peering around and ruminating. We keep on ruminating for a long while so that mam can get ahead with her work, but ruminating is no bother to us, because it's so nice in the quiet. My brother's silky yellow hair tickles my forehead, and his soft flesh is so pleasant on my cheek. Sometimes he gives my face a slap in fun, and he crinkles his nose as he keeps on looking at the world, the world that's only something to look at to a baby and a child of seven.

.   .   .

I am nine years old, sitting at the desk in school doing sums. The teacher has just shown us how to do sums, and we have books with examples, a dozen to a page. Now we have to work these problems in our writing books. The first half dozen are exactly the same as each other and easy enough. The seventh seems different and I don't know what to do. I'm afraid to try a different way than the first half dozen, for fear of making a mistake, I'm in a great quandary. My reason says that this sum is not the same kind as the others, but I fail to see why it was necessary to put a different sum in the middle of things of the same kind. I decide to follow my reason in spite of being afraid. I was the only one to get this sum right. I'm proud, not because of this but because I decided for the first time ever to follow my reason and found I was right.

.   .   .

I am going to Pantycelyn, my grandmother's, my mother's mother's house, during the summer holidays. There is a pool of water before coming to the house, where gran cools the milk pitchers after milking. On the left in turning towards the house is a small flower garden with Adam and Eves, early purple orchids, growing in it, and cream-coloured roses climbing around the door. On the right is a slate cistern made by my grandfather to hold rain water. Grandad is not alive. The brass knobs of the dresser face me like a row of bright eyes. From the wall two uncles look at me under heavy eyebrows. I think they're frowning at me. There's a red coverlet on the table with a big Bible open on it, spectacles on the Bible with their arms crossed like an insect's legs. Gran is sitting on the settle in the same clothing as she always wears. She has a small black straw hat on her head with a black frilled cap under it, and a small puce ribbon on the frill above the ears. She's wearing a black bodice fastened by a row of tiny buttons, over a coarse petticoat. She wears a black apron. She's busy making tea and reaches for a loaf from the cupboard of the big table that's by the window. There are holes in the loaf and it isn't as white as our bread at home. Mam says that gran buys cheap flour. But I like it. Gran says that she has no cake for tea, only cheese. And I say that I'm very fond of cheese, especially the kind with a red crust. This pleases her. She goes past the back of the settle to go to the milkshed and fetch the butter. Her body is very trim, considering her age. I go after her, but not without peeking at the Bible first to see what she's reading. "In my Father's house there are many mansions." She's thinking about dying, for sure. The milkshed is pleasantly cold and its slate floors are damp. There are smells of butter and buttermilk and dampness there, smells I will remember forever. Gran takes a pound of hard butter from the slate and puts it on a plate. We go back to the kitchen and have tea. Grandmother's bread-and-butter is quite wonderful. She reaches for a pot of gooseberry jam from the cupboard. "I'd forgotten this," she says, "Kate Bryncelyn made it." There are smells of "Uncle John's Vinolia Soap" coming from the partition. When gran puts the things away after eating, I go into the bedroom to take a peek. She has a wainscot bed there, and white curtains with red flowers on them around the bed. It was gran spun the material from flax, mam said. There's an old oak chest in the room and a small spinning-wheel. When I come back into the kitchen I squat down to look at the pictures of fish that grandfather carved on the side of the slate platform that's under the furniture.

I ask gran may I go to see the garden. A strange garden, closed in with walls and tall trees and a high door so that nobody can look inside. There are beehives on one side like a number of neat little houses, but I'm not supposed to go near them. I turn to the left and go to the fountain. I look for a long time into its clear bottom, I toss a small stone in and then suddenly there's moving, and I see something like the green brooch that I've seen in the shop window in town moving cleanly through the water. A newt. I don't like it. But it's safely in the water. There isn't a garden like this anywhere. It's like a book locked with a clasp.

After going into the house I ask gran, "Why do you keep a silly newt in the fountain?"

"To purify the water."

I reflect on this.

"How old are you now?"

"I'm just ten."

"Your mother went into service at your age."

I change the subject, because I know what's coming.

"That spinning-wheel in the bedroom, is it the one mam tried to spin with, and got a clout from you for meddling?"

"I don't remember the clout, yes, that's the spinning-wheel."

"Mam still remembers. It must have hurt."

"She deserved it for sure. Do you help your mother?"

I don't like to say "Yes" for fear I don't do enough.

"I did housework to help the other day."

Gran looks at me with eyes like two blades of blue steel.

"What did you do?"

"Washed the mixing bowl with a dishrag and all the dough went into the rag and made it as if it was full of slugs."

"You know by now that you need to use your nails to scrape a mixing bowl."

"Yes."

I am downhearted as I walk home—thinking gran thinks that I don't help mam enough.

.　　■　　.

It's a short day at the end of the year and becomes night before the people reach home from the quarry. I go out to the road half afraid, half curious. A rumour had come by word of mouth that there's been an accident at Cors y Bryniau quarry. I go timidly, warily through the gate and as soon as I've opened it a cart is going past with a man's body on it. There are sacks over the body but the man's big hobnailed boots, covered with clay, are not hidden. A quarryman is leading the horse and other men are walking on either side of the cart with their heads down. I run into the house frightened. The man was alive passing our house to the quarry this morning; he's going home tonight on a cart, dead. It's too terrible.

We're all quiet over our quarry supper. Mam talks about "the poor creature" compassionately and talks about his wife. But dad is solemn and brooding and sighing. I wonder will he be afraid to go to the quarry tomorrow? I cannot sleep tonight. I see the big, clay-clogged hobnailed boots sticking out, and try to imagine how the body and the still face looked beneath the sacks.

.   .   .

We're at the fellowship meeting and our noses are running. One of the deacons is speaking. We've said our Bible verses a good while ago, and the deacon has been on the floor hearing the experiences of the grown-ups. Their experiences are somewhat similar every time, the feeling they are great sinners. Some cry in saying that and the others are dry-eyed. The deacon is talking now about the experiences and saying they have all been blessed. One side of his face is in the light and there is shadow on the other. We children are quiet as mice, but our feet are cold, because there's no heat in the chapel, and I'm longing to be able to go home to a warm fire. But another deacon rises from his chair beneath the pulpit—Owen Pritchard y Gaerddu. He doesn't move towards the lamp like the other deacon, but stands near his chair. He has on a black topcoat with a velvet collar, and he looks like a preacher, but he doesn't speak like a preacher. He has a pretty face, and hair and beard like gold. He speaks quietly. "Refined" is the word for him, everybody says. It's as though he were talking to himself, his eyes not on the congregation, but as if they were looking towards somewhere that we do not see. I know he is speaking well though I don't understand him.

The moon is bright when we go outside, but there's a light brighter than the moonlight ahead of us. There's a man selling dishes at the side of the road with a small circle of people in front of him. He has a noisy flaming torch beside him, and his whole face is in the light. He's talking like a mill and tossing plates into the air in a circle, one after the other, and catching them before they fall.

"How much for them?" the man says, "they're fresh hot from the oven, they'll warm your hands on a cold night."

"Heigh," to me, "here, hold one of them, you look quite peaked."

I think he wants to make me buy one and I flee from the circle.

I wonder will my brothers try this trick of tossing plates without break-ing them tomorrow, just like the trick of tossing eggs the length of the field without breaking them, with mam, frying eggs, unable to understand where the addled eggs have come from and throwing them away thinking that they're bad eggs. But tossing plates isn't as easy as tossing eggs in a field, and in our house there are more eggs in a year than plates.

But it's too cold to stand still even to look at the feats and listen to the clever patter of the peddler. We run home and the road echoes with our footsteps. There's a warm hearth and a cheerful table waiting for us, and on a cold night that's better than a fellowship meeting or a sale of dishes.

.   .   .

The lesson on geography is over and the class is standing in a semicircle around the desks instead of sitting in them. The headmaster, who has taken us for the lesson, is starting to leave the room (which we call a *clasdrwm*) for the big school to sound his pipe and say that it's time to change lessons. He asks me, since I'm at the top of the circle, to stand in front of the class and keep them cowed while he's at the big school. When he's in the dark porch between the two rooms, one of the boys tosses a pea at me. The schoolmaster turns back and asks me in English who threw it. I say that I don't know, and put my lips tightly together. "You ought to know," he says, and gives me two brutal strokes of the cane, one on each hand, as hard as he can. But I don't cry. My lips stay tightly together. The next lesson is sewing and there is a weal on one of my hands and it hurts awfully. The mistress who teaches us sewing suspects that something is wrong and she is kind. But it's not proper for her to say anything, and it's not proper for me to tattle on the headmaster when I go home. That's the rule at our house. But my innards are shouting with rage against injustice. I've deserved to be beaten many times, but not this time. What can a child do against undeserved punishment? Nothing, is the answer, at the moment. But a day of vengeance will come, as the story in the newspaper would say.

.   .   .

It's a fine Saturday morning in September. All of us, except those who are working at the quarry, are in the courtyard in front of the house. I've just finished scrubbing the ladder, and I'm busy now cleaning the knives by wiping them back and forth on a leather-covered plank, with a brick on the leather, a task I do not like: it sets my teeth on edge. There's a broad slate atop the dyke, and my brothers are cracking nuts on it. They've been in Y Bicall this morning gathering nuts and blackberries. Mam has put the blackberries on a big tray on top of the wall. She's wearing her spectacles to examine them, the way she examines my head sometimes. There are so many blackberries they swell into reddish-black hills in the sun. We'll have pudding for supper tonight.

At that moment there's a sound I know well, a man shouting at the top of his lungs, something like "Cra-a-a". The effect on us is stunning. We scatter away from our tasks as if someone had thrown boiling water on our heads, us children to the road and mam into the house to fetch a dish and her purse. It's Hugh Williams, Pen Lan, with his little cart, selling fruits and vegetables. He comes like this every Saturday, and what he shouts is "Carrots", but it sounds like "Cra-a-a" from a distance. The kindest man in the world, too poor in health to work, and going around with his fruit cart. But mam says that he doesn't make much of a profit because he's too kind and there are many bad payers in the world. Mam buys a passel of things— bunches of carrots, two baskets of plums (dad will be pleased), and pounds of apples, and she pays for them. Then we children each have plums and an apple from Hugh Williams, besides the overflow from the baskets of fruit mam bought. "This old chest is the trouble, Catrin," he says to mam. "Poor Hugh," mam says. The world is full of good things in September.

"There's no time to make a proper dinner today," mam says, and to me, "Run to the shop and fetch two ounces of coffee." I come home with cheering just-ground coffee. Mam puts it in a tall jug and pours boiling water from the kettle over it and puts it on the hob to keep warm. Next to it is a saucepan with water in it on the boil. She puts a lot of milk in another jug and puts that jug to stand in the saucepan of hot water. Then she goes on to fry bacon and eggs. By the time they're ready the milk will be warmed enough to be put in the cups on top of the coffee, and the men will have come home from the quarry. All's well.

.   .   .

This is the stormiest day of my life, there's never been such wind and rain. We're allowed to come home early from school. Mam is very uneasy, thinking about dad working "in the teeth of the rocks". To mam, dad's working "in the teeth of the rocks" whether he works in the shed or in the hole. And indeed, today she has reason to worry. Dad comes home with his head wrapped in white cloths. Someone's come to accompany him, and in a little while the doctor comes to treat him. When the bandages were pulled off, there was a big gash in his forehead about two inches long and very very deep, about three-quarters of an inch, I'm sure. Mam is having a fit, a very uncommon thing for her, and we're all crying. Dad's face is like chalk, but he remains brave. There's no pattern to our quarry supper tonight, and dad prefers to have a cup of tea before going to bed.

PICTURES

The powerful big wind had blown a top layer loose and it had hit my father in the forehead when he was in his trimming hut. But something worse had happened in the pit—my father's partner, Wil Tom from Pen-y-Groes, had been seriously injured in his back. "He's had it bad," dad says, "I'm afraid he'll be a cripple the rest of his life." (This proved to be true.)

As I say my prayers, I ask for father to get better. Then I give thanks that he wasn't hurt like his partner, William Thomas, and that he hasn't come home on a cart like William Michael.

.   .   .

We're all playing swings behind the house in the trees next to the rickyard. Jane Cadwaladr, my first cousin, who is living in Rhostryfan now, has come up to us. She's very pretty, her hair is like gold, her skin like the lily, and her eyes blue like my grandmother's. She's just lost her mother and she's getting a great deal of attention. The rope of the swing is tied to two trees, and our aim is to hit the wooden window high up on the gable-end of the yard. I enjoy playing swings, and the further I go the better, because the fear in taking chances sends a thrill of pleasure down my back as I catch my breath. Jane gets to go on the swing more often than me and I'm jealous of her because she's getting such attention. When my turn comes to go on the swing, my brother and my cousin give me a sudden shove, and as I try to aim at the target on the gable-end of the yard, the rope gives a twist and I fall on a pile of roofing slates that are on the ground, leaning against the wall of the yard. I think I'm terribly hurt, and I run to the house shouting and crying. Mam takes pity, more than usual, and gives me tea by myself, as a favour, before the others come into the house. But I'm not much hurt, and my jealousy is less now that mam has taken my part.

.   .   .

I'm home sick, beginning to get better after severe influenza. Our neighbour, and the owner of our smallholding, Mary Jones, Bod Elen, comes into the house with traces of much crying on her. Her brother, Dafydd Thomas, Pen Rhos, has died suddenly. He was taken ill on the way to the quarry, went to the mess hut to lie down, and died there. I'm very sad. He's my teacher in Sunday school, and he's a good teacher, I like him very much. He asks questions with a lot of brainwork to them.

The class is supposed to go to the funeral, and mam is worrying whether

I should go when I haven't finished getting better. But she intends to wrap me warmly—it's cold weather at the beginning of the year. She goes to buy me a black tam-o'-shanter, a cheap one. But I don't like it as well as the white one I have already. It doesn't look good on my head, my hair is too dark. As the day of the funeral draws near I become excited, and I find a thrill of pleasure in thinking I'm getting to face a thing as terrifying as death, and the death of someone I know so well. I'm being lifted to some strange heights and I look forward to this unusual thing. The singing at the graveside sends a nice shiver down my back. A pity we couldn't sing "Bydd myrdd o ryfeddodau". "There'll be a myriad of wonders", with Dafydd Thomas coming to life again.

But Sunday I am very depressed going to the Sunday School and knowing that our teacher won't be there. He was with us last Sunday.

.   .   .

It's a Saturday night in winter and mam has gone to visit grandmother Pantycelyn. We children and dad are sitting around the fire waiting for her to come home. We've done everything we were expected to do, almost, like bringing heather for starting fires into the house, and have begun to fix supper, but we've jibbed at that job because we don't rightly know what sort of treat we will have, and we're content just to set the dishes on the table and live in hope. Dad makes this hope an excuse not to slice bread-and-butter. But the truth is that we can't abide being without mam at twilight like this, and are sick of our own company. Dad starts singing to us. "Gelert, Llywelyn's hound" is his favourite song, and his only song. He sings it with great feeling, especially towards the end when Llywelyn discovers his mistake, and the "You saved his life and I have slain you" breaks my heart, and it's no use telling me that it's a made-up story, because it's true, my father says. The song doesn't cheer us up much or make the time go by quickly. But there's the sound of the door opening and mam puts her head in past the partition before shutting it as if she were in a hurry to see that we're all right. I'm glad to see her clean, pale face with her hair tightly combed, and I forget all about Llywelyn and his hound. We'll have supper and talk, because we had our "wash all over" in the big pan last night. But mam looks over the table, disappointedly: "Not much fixing of supper's been going on here," she says, "and I'm almost famished." We all run to fetch the loaf and the butter and she produces brawn from somewhere, and quite soon we have supper. Nobody asks how grandmother is, because she's always in good health, but dad wants to know has she heard any news. No, nothing had happened anywhere. We enjoy our supper, and sit for a bit in front of the fire after with our faces red from the heat. We begin to nod, Huwcyn the sandman has come, and another uneventful week has come to an end. But before we go to bed mam says we may have one game of "Snakes and Ladders" (we're tired of "Ludo" by now). Dad and mam play with us. Dad is winning and has reached the top before anyone. There's a big snake there with its mouth ready for the dice. I wonder if dad can avoid its mouth. He can't. The dice are on it and poor dad must go right to the bottom. That's a proper excuse for having another game, so that dad can have better luck next time.

. . .

It's a hot morning in July, haymaking day. Dad will come home with friends from the quarry around mid-day, and a few neighbours have already come and begun to turn the hay. I hear the sound of the rakes all going at the same time and the hay making a sound like tissue paper. Before going out to the field I go to the milkshed once more to have a peek at the delicacies. There's a long row of red dishes on the table full of rice pudding with plenty of eggs in it, and the surface of the pudding is yellow and smooth, like the breast of the canary who's in his cage at the head of the table. The smell and the look of it make my mouth water. I wonder will there be enough for everybody. We aren't supposed to ask for more in front of strangers. After going to the field I try to turn with a rake, but the rake is too big for me, and my turning is messy. The women's arms are all alike and move together, and they go down and down to the bottom of the field before turning and coming up and up again, in the same way and at the same time with always the same huh-huh sound. I sit on top of the wall near the bilberry bushes and look at them. Suddenly, pain. I remember last year. A morning just like this, haymaking morning, and the calf being taken sick and dying before dad reached home from the quarry. Mam had tried everything, had given him warm milk, and sent for John Jones y Gaerwen, but he died, and mam cried. She talked about the loss, he was a fine, big calf. I thought about the poor calf dying in a dark cowshed while we were having fun and making merry in the hay. But he was too big a calf, everybody said, and his mother as well, too delicate for mountain land. His mother would have to be sold. But we don't have a little calf this year.

We have dinner and the haymaking begins in earnest, with everybody hard at it making the hay that was turned in rows this morning. Tŷ Hen's cart comes here, and the men and some of the women lift the hay into the cart with pitchforks. My brothers get to carry loads on their heads with a white apron on each one's head: they are like the prophets in the Bible pictures. The smallest children get to go on top of the cart. The stack in the shed grows higher and higher, and with the other children I get to go on top to dance on it so it goes down and makes room for more hay. We're almost near the roof, and the world is down below us. In spite of our dancing on the hay, and the people talking, it's very quiet on top of the stack. It's like Communion Sunday in chapel. We look beyond at the cart coming, with shreds of hay hanging at its sides, just like my hair when it's messy. We're right at the top and almost smothering, but this is the last load. We go down the ladder and feel relief. The men and women come through the gap to the house to have tea and they're having a great time. My brothers tell me, before we go into the house, that I've lost a good time by being on top of the stack. There'd been a great debate in the field on the best way to make hay, with J.J., who'd been in America for a time, saying over and over, "This is how we do it in the States." "Listen to the Statesman," said K.J., a woman free and easy with her tongue. And J.J. said to the woman, "And listen, everyone, to the Welsh Herald."

The hay is all in the rickyard and good smells come from it to the house. Everybody's gone home and we're sitting out-of-doors in the warmth. We've had leftovers for supper. The sun is like a ball of red fire going down over Anglesey. It's hard to go into the house. "Thank goodness," mam says, "all the hay is in again for this year." "And the best sort of hay," says dad.

.   .   .

Mam and the boys and I are going to Bryn Ffynnon, grandfather's and grandmother's house, to make hay. We climb and climb until we reach Pen 'Rallt Fawr. We stop and look back. There's more of Anglesey to be seen than from our house. We see right to Pont y Borth, but we see something else we can never see from our house—the White Road that goes over Moel Smatho to the Waunfawr and to the Heavens. It goes through the heather and reaches the mountain gate before descending to Alltgoed Mawr. We don't see it after that. There are a great many people in the hay field and many children, my first cousins, boys and girls, and we won't get to go on top of the haystack. We're nobody at this haymaking, and nobody takes any notice of us. The girls go along the dykes to gather bilberries. I take a blade of grass and put the berries on it like beads. When it's full, I put one end in my mouth and eat the berries until my lips are puce. The blade of grass rasps my tongue.

The people are beginning to go to the house to have tea, and I'm hungry. They're a very long time, and another tableful goes in. I look closely at the hay, it's thinner than our hay and the wind is blowing it. They need to hurry or it'll be blown to the mountain. Soon there's a summons to the children to go get tea: the house is dark after being in the sun. There's a big iron kettle singing on the hob and light is coming down through the chimney. There are two tables, covered with starched white tablecloths, a square one in the middle of the floor and a round one in the corner under the corner cupboard. There are two seats like chapel seats around the round table and I make for a place at this table in front of everybody, and know inside that I'm being a little devil. Grandmother is tall and goes right next to the clock to see what o'clock it is, and she gropes for the sugar tongs in putting sugar in the cups. Her sight is bad, and she looks tired. She has cake on a plate that's better than any cake I've ever had. Between the layers there's egg custard and currants and candied lemon. Only grandmother Bryn Ffynnon makes this cake. We eat a lot. "There now, my children," gran says after we've finished. I don't see grandmother the same way in the midst of a crowd of children like this, she's like a strange woman at the head of children at school. Some day I'll come up on my own and have tea with gran under the big chimney, and she'll give me toffee, and tell me tales of long ago. She's worked hard today.

. . .

One day I open the door of the china cabinet, and the cat leaps out past me like a bolt of lightning and runs just like the saying "a cat out of hell". I can't understand how she got into the cabinet; she never did this before. Someone must have opened the cabinet door, and she went inside and someone closed it not knowing she was there. Something is tugging at me; I open the door on the left side to see how my hat is. And Oh! what a sight. My grand best hat is ruined. The cat has been lying on it, and worse. I'm almost heartbroken. A Leghorn hat, with light straw like a narrow ribbon folded double around the brim. It was trimmed with a wide shot-silk ribbon of different shades of yellow. Mam comes into the house and sees the carnage.

"That old villain," she says about the cat.

"No," I say, "what if someone had shut you in a cabinet for hours."

Mam laughs heartily and says, "Never mind, it's only a hat; Jane can go into town and buy you another one."

My half-sister was home for a while at the time. I get a new hat, a white one with a feather in it, but I don't like it, and it would be just the thing for someone forty years old. But I try to look as if I liked it. I'd better not show my disappointment, or someone will put the cat's nose in pepper. That's how it is, you have to hide one thing to avoid another.

.   .   .

Great anxiety has come to our house, it lies over everything and holds each of us in its grip. Dafydd, my youngest brother, who's twenty months old, is very ill with fever. The doctor has been and says he's in great danger. There's a fire in the room, a tin kettle boiling on it, and steam going from it in the direction of the bed. I'm afraid to enter the room to see Dafydd, but I'm able to see the kettle and the steam. The house seems as if it were boiling too, with everybody incapable of knowing what to do. Presently, I'm told to go to the shop in Pen y Ffridd to fetch soda water. It's nine o'clock at night, and though there's a full moon, I'm gripped by fear. Not fear of a bogey, but fear, fear of something happening, fear that I won't get the soda water, fear filling the road and the night, as it filled the house just now. I try running to conquer the fear, but my feet are as if they were going backwards instead of forwards. I reach the hollow of Pen Rhos, and there in the field, on my left, is a row of ghosts in white clothing holding each other's hands. I stop short, and my heart stands still. I'm almost suffocating. I can never pass them and I have to get the soda water. I almost turn back to ask someone else to go, but we'll lose a lot of time, and the soda water is needed at once. What if little Dafydd were to die because I've been long? I take a grip on my throat and try to move. My legs feel as if they wanted to curl up like a concertina, but I move one foot and move the other and see that I'm able to run. After going a few yards, I venture to look behind to see the backs of the ghosts. They have blue backs, and of course, they're a row of pillars of slates bound to each other with wire. It was the moon shining on them made them ghosts. I get the soda water, and I'm not afraid going home. I have the medicine and the ghosts have vanished.

.   .   .

We're walking, a gang of us, along the White Road on an evening in April: we're going for children's choir practice to the little chapel of Alltgoed Mawr. The boys start bonfires in the heather beside the road and choke in going too close to them. We reach the chapel smelling of smoke. Awaiting us there are the conductor and the children of Alltgoed Mawr, almost all children from the same family. They're the second sopranos: sometimes they come to us and another time we go to them, like tonight. They're all exactly alike, each of them has black, curly hair, and eyes black as plums. They sing quite marvellously, and the conductor taunts us children of Rhosgadfan with how much better the children of Alltgoed Mawr are.

"Jeriwsalem fy nghartref gwiw (Jerusalem my proper home)," we sing, "cartrefle Duw a'r Oen (dwelling-place of God and the Lamb)." We're happy shouting,

> *"Bryd, bryd, caf fi orffwys ynddi hi,*
> *Yn ia-a-a-ch" etc.*
> *(When, when, may I rest in that place,*
> *Safe and sou-u-u-nd, etc.)*

We understand the words all right, but we don't think at all about dying. Everybody rushes out of the chapel after we've finished, but I loiter to have a look at the pretty children, here in the dark. I'd like to be able to talk with them, but I'm too shy, and I run after the others.

After reaching the White Road again, we scent the smell of the bonfires that have gone out by now and left black patches in the heather, with white borders. The road has white borders as well, of gravel. The smell follows us, as we sing,

> *"Bryd, bryd, caf fi orffwys ynddi hi?"*

The conductor is far behind. It's almost finished getting dark by now, but Menai Straits are a bright strip between the darkness of Anglesey and our county, and the lights of Caernarfon are winking. Then, one of the biggest boys starts to pester the girls and run after us. I don't like this boy at all, and when he tries to take hold of me I give him a push and run for my life. He shouts something spiteful after me, that I think I'm better than he is, and too stuck-up to have fun. I take no notice of him but keep on running. I don't want to go to practice when it's at Alltgoed Mawr again, and I know now why mam doesn't much like us going so far. I feel as if I'd been drinking wormwood water. I want to stay with the girls who are friends of mine, but I'm afraid they'll make fun of me. It wouldn't do for me to tell at home why I've arrived ahead of the others. I have to make up a story. It was so nice when we were walking over the mountain two hours ago.

.   .   .

I'm restless, discontented, moving from chair to chair, from one corner of the table to the other. I can't memorize. I'm fifteen years old and in the County School, and I'm trying to memorize the fourteenth chapter of the *Hyfforddwr* (the Guide), in preparation for being accepted as a member of the chapel. Our minister has told us how interesting it is, and I feel that. Partaking of first Communion weighs heavily on me. I am entering a new world, a serious world, without play; I can't shoot marbles on the road again, or play hopscotch, or run a race to the sheep-washing pool. My skirt will be lower, and my hair will be higher on my head. I can't say my Bible verse or the headings of the sermons with the smallest children at the meeting ever again. I will have to take things seriously. But at this moment it's the chapter that's bothering me, I can't get it into my head. The words won't go from the page into my mind, and they frighten me. "For he that eateth and drinketh unworthily, eateth and drinketh damnation to himself, not discerning the Lord's body." Five years ago I would have learned that by rote and remembered it without understanding it or thinking about it. But today, I understand the word "unworthily", and it pricks me somewhere. I try to make an excuse for myself, that I have a great deal of memorization in school. But perhaps in beginning to *think* about things, I'm not able to remember as well. I give it one more try, but I can't memorize. I get up on the table and sit down on it with my legs crossed like a tailor. It's better like this, and the words begin to get into my head. But things won't be the same. I'm ceasing to be a child and beginning to become a woman. It's terrible to feel that anything ceases to exist, forever.

The Last Picture

I am old—if I can live a few months longer I will have reached the promised age. I sit by the fire reflecting on what I have written, and thinking how much of myself there is in it. I've been in Denbigh for a quarter of a century, living in a town where I don't hear very much Welsh: what there is here is poor Welsh, even in the chapel. The standard of public speaking is low here. Across the years from what I have written come the voices of people who could speak publicly in sumptuous Welsh, who could pray in a refined vocabulary, "Cymer ni i Dy nawdd ac i'th amddiffyn sylw. Rhagora ar ein dymuniadau gwael ac annheilwng (Take us to Thy refuge and to Thy safeguarding notice. Surpass our base and unworthy desires)."

When I was writing these things the dead rose from their graves for a spell to talk to me. They've gone back to sleep again. I have written about my family and called it autobiography, but I'm right. The history of my family is my own history. It was they wove my destiny in the distant past. They were simple people. And here the fear comes back again, the fear that the readers will scoff that I write about such unimportant things. But they're not unimportant to me, that is my life, that is the society I was born into. I was alive then, able to enjoy the feeling of my first fur boa around my neck in winter, enjoy going through the gate to the road because it was there the big wide world was. I enjoyed fighting with boys, enjoyed skating on a brook, enjoyed saying my Bible verse in fellowship-meeting. A day was long and short then, with its fill of things, and when it came to its end it was like pulling the drawstring on a pouch with its fill of marbles and putting it in the cupboard for safekeeping. There was pain in the pouch as well, and shame, and they would come out next day before the happy things.

I had a brown sailor's cap with a silk tassel on its crown, and H.M.S. Such-and-Such on the front. I put it on backwards to go to chapel without knowing it. The hateful boy who would pester girls on the way home from choir practice said to me on my way out, "Do you know your cap was backwards in chapel?" Perhaps I wouldn't have known if it weren't for him. I was ashamed. The shame came back and made me blush for years. Today, I wouldn't be upset. Indeed I wouldn't be upset if I went to the Great Chapel with three hats on my head backwards. I have died to shame.

I had a cat when I was nine years old. She went astray and was poisoned. She came back to die. It was Sunday. There was a prayer meeting in the chapel at night, and every time we put our heads down to pray, I would weep for my cat. I would do the same thing today. I have not died to the loss of a friend.

A little time back in going through my books I came across a little book of the story of Saint Francis that I had from my history teacher on leaving Caernarfon County School. A well-made book, with good paper. In it was the skeleton of a dragonfly. I remembered. My brother, when he was in convalescent hospital in Malta, had sent me this insect's body pinned on silk paper, and had written, "Watch Out", underneath it. It was much bigger than our dragonfly. I gave it to mam, and it was she had put it in the Saint Francis book to preserve it and flatten it. It had been there since 1917. Its wings and its body perfect, but its head had come loose. The veins of its wings were there, fretwork as thin as gossamer. They have kept perfectly. They are dead. They are old.

Everything important had happened to me before 1917, everything that made a deep impression. Hewn stone and the rag to clean the school writing-slate were important. In looking at the insect, and thinking of writing my reminiscences, I thought that they would be like the skeleton, something that had been, but was dead, still there between the pages of the book.

But the veins of the dead body trembled a little. It came to life. I felt the pain, I felt the joy, I felt the disappointment. I laughed, I wept, I was angry. I chatted on the hearth of Maes-teg, I heard the accents, I heard the Welsh in its beauty.

And here I am, back on my hearth in Denbigh, the insect has gone back between the pages of the book. The voices have fallen silent. But just as when I was a child, I reflect and worry. Have I told the truth? No. I have comforted myself that it's impossible to tell the truth in an autobiography. I have left unpleasant things out. There were horrid things in my old district, there were evil things, there were disagreeable people. But if I'd spoken of them, their families would be out for my blood, and I'd find myself in a court of law. I refrained because I was afraid. Fear is our greatest enemy, young and old.

Voices come across the embers of bonfires on Moel Smatho and in waves along the White Road. "Bryd, bryd, caf fi orffwys ynddi hi? (When, when may I rest in that place?)" But I'm not worrying about that, though I'm closer to it. I have remembered and have forgotten. I wonder, will I be like my old aunt, Neli 'Regal, who forgot everything but the past, and as dead as the dragonfly in the book—here without being here? Did Aunt Neli forget her fear? Was she ever afraid? I ask the emptiness of my house the questions. I am a child again, reflecting and asking questions. But I can't solve the problem of playing five-stones.

The fire is going down in the grate. I will go to bed. Tomorrow will come once more, and I can keep asking questions.

II

Stories

(1925–1937)

The Letter

A Saturday afternoon in November 1917, at a lodging house in Liverpool. Dic, Ifan, and Wil were sitting at the table writing letters. Wmffra was sitting by the fire, his chin on his waistcoat, with his hands in his pockets, his feet under the chair, and his eyes on the bars of the grate, looking between them into the fire and through the fire into a small house in a small village in Caernarfonshire. Outside was November haze, inside was a clean kitchen, as clean as town smoke and the drowsy insects of autumn allowed it to be. It was an extremely comfortable kitchen, as comfortable as many fire-irons on a hearth could make it. The fire itself had a good deal of a past and something of a future, and in the middle, between its past and its future, Wmffra was seeing visions. He was seeing his own kitchen at home, not quite as neat as this, yet as neat as six children and two greyhounds and wet weather allowed it to be; no irons in front of the fire, but a long low wooden stool that you could put your feet on without fear of hearing a sermon from your wife, with your two knees up against the bars of the grate. Ann, his wife, was busy washing the mid-day Saturday dishes, Robin the smallest child pulling at her apron while she shouted "Don't". Then shouting at Meri the oldest girl to come into the house, for her to run on an errand to the shop. Meri too deaf to listen and keeping on playing jump rope. Ann losing her temper and shouting enough for the people in the next house to hear her, and Meri for shame coming into the house. Sam and Bob, the two greyhounds sitting one on each side of Wmffra, looking scowlingly at him as much as to say,

"Come on, let's go for rabbits."

Then Wmffra getting up, and going to the back for the two ferrets.

"I want to go for a rabbit or two for tomorrow, Ann," he'd say. Starting off whistling happily, though it was the Saturday afternoon following Friday pay night, the most uncomfortable evening in the month for Wmffra, when he'd be afraid to give his wages to Ann because they were so small. Not that Ann was one of those women who'll be grieving and groaning on Friday pay night. But somehow Wmffra would be fairly uncomfortable until Ann came home from the shop. If there was a happy look on Ann's face, that was proof of the shopkeeper's cordiality, and then Wmffra would be happy, until the next Friday pay night. It was one of those Saturday afternoons Wmffra was seeing now in the fire in Liverpool, when his happiness was at its highest, because of the shopkeeper's smile, and his own distance from the next Friday pay night. Then he'd start off with Sam and Bob, his hands in his pockets, with the smooth fur of the two ferrets tickling them, and the two greyhounds at his heel.

"How're things, Wmffra?" this one and the other would say on the road. No one would ask him where he was going. The two dogs were the answer.

Then leaving the road and crossing Foty'r Wern sheep-walk, Sam and Bob with their noses close to the ground, and Wmffra's eyes darting farther to the right and the left than they'd been. Then going through a field, Sam walking behind Bob, and Bob behind Wmffra, a trinity all of one mind. Over the stile like three greyhounds into Cae'r Boncan, and sitting down for a bit. Then releasing the ferrets, and three pairs of eyes looking in the same direction. Here comes the white-tail out, and in a wink, Sam's on its neck. "Well done, boy," Wmffra says under his breath in his chair in Liverpool, threatening to jump out of it. But he remembered that his hands were in his pockets and his feet under the chair, and he settled himself back.

"Come away from there, you're nodding off, Wmffra," Dic said.

"Yes," Ifan said, "write home to your wife, or she'll think you're dead."

"No danger of that," Wmffra said. "It'd be easier for Ann to believe I was dead if I *did* write."

"Is there an *h* in passionate?" asked Wil, who was writing to his sweetheart.

"No," Ifan said, licking an envelope.

"Yes," Dic said.

"She's sure to understand what you mean if you put fifteen *h*'s in it," Wmffra said.

"Since you're so sure," Ifan said, "come to the table here and write to Ann."

"No, I won't," Wmffra said in the tone with which a disobedient boy answers his mother.

"Ann is sure to understand that I was working overtime this afternoon, and that that's what's kept me from being home today. Blast that old over-time work." He spat into the heart of the fire.

The four were working on the railway in Liverpool, and they had a free ticket to go home every three weeks. Since three weeks is less than a month, and since Wmffra didn't feel uncomfortable now in presenting his wages to Ann, he didn't send his wages home every week as Dic and Ifan did, but Ann got three weeks' wages every time he went home, and neither of them took the trouble to write to the other in the meantime.

None of the lads had ever seen Wmffra write. But the truth, that he couldn't write at all, never crossed their minds. If they had gone to the same school with him as a child, perhaps they would have known. Wmffra was only some thirty-five years old, and a man of thirty-five in 1917 ought to be able to write a scrap of a letter, at least. Dic and Ifan, who were the same age as he, could do that readily. Though the four were working at the same quarry before the War, they hadn't gone to the same school as children. The other three knew that Wmffra could do his reckoning at the end of the month as well as any teacher who ever wore spectacles. But old William Jôs, who was going on eighty, could do his reckoning with-out putting a halfpenny too much in the company's pocket or in his own pocket, in a way that would send the accountants of the present age into fits. But it never entered their minds to put Wmffra on the same plane as old people.

If, however, they'd gone to Ysgol Pen Ffordd Wen with Wmffra, they'd have known that every teacher in that school had given up all hope of teach-ing Wmffra to write. Gabriel himself couldn't have done it, presuming that Wmffra was in school every day, and presuming that Gabriel is as good a teacher as he is an angel. At times Wmffra would come to school, the times between the times of playing truant. I don't rightly know which of the two times was the longest, but Eos Twrog, the truant officer, would swear that Wmffra spent more of his time sitting on the bank by the Gwylif river than he ever did on the benches of Pen Ffordd Wen school.

"Now, come on," Dic said, "write to Ann, and don't be so stubborn. Wil will write the directions like copperplate for you."

Dic was thinking perhaps it was the slovenliness of his writing that could account for Wmffra's letterless life.

"All right," Wmffra said, for fear of being less than a man, and gave a resolute turn in his chair. Wil wrote the address on an envelope and handed paper and pencil to Wmffra. Then he went upstairs to change, and the other two were wise enough to be fully occupied and leave Wmffra by himself to make the best use he could of his pencil and the paper, and to do what many do in writing a letter, namely, put his soul on paper.

Monday morning Ann, Wmffra's wife, was sitting by the fire, just finished getting the five oldest children ready and sending them to school. That was so much of an undertaking that she didn't find fault with herself for taking a spell before dressing Robin, the youngest child, who was playing with the cat on the hearth. She wanted a bit of time for herself as well, to reflect on why Wmffra hadn't come home Saturday night. This was the first time it had happened since he'd been in Liverpool.

Suddenly there was a knock on the door, and her heart leapt into her throat when she saw it was the postman there with a letter for her. When she saw a Liverpool postmark, her face turned pale, and she thought for certain that something had happened to Wmffra. She saw thousands of things in that second, and the clearest thing of all was that a train had run over Wmffra. She was able, however, to open the letter somehow, and the expression on her face changed completely. You couldn't tell what was about to happen. Her forehead wrinkled, her eyes opened very wide, then a faint smile came to the corners of her mouth. But the next minute she was crying the house down. In her hand was a sheet of paper, and in the centre of it, a clear picture drawn in pencil of a greyhound gripping the neck of a rabbit. There was not a word or a letter on the paper, only the picture. She poked into the envelope again, in case. No, there wasn't a scrap of writing in it. The mother cried a long time. Robin couldn't understand why she was crying. His mother didn't understand why herself. She sat on the chair and let the paper fall to the floor.

Robin snatched the paper, and the cat ran for her freedom and her life.

As soon as Robin's eyes fell on the picture of the greyhound and the rabbit, he shouted:

"Oo-oo-daddy!" and tugging at his mother's apron, "Mammy, daddy oo-oo!!"

Provoking

"Selfish old villains, that's what men are," Meri Ifans said, taking a gulp of tea, as if she were washing all the weaknesses of men down her throat with that mouthful.

"Yes, *some* of them," Catrin Owen said, in an innocent tone, as if she'd seen nothing but kindness from the hands of men all her life.

"There isn't much of a choice among them," Meri Ifans said, "the best of them don't think of anyone more than themselves."

"*You* haven't any room to complain," Catrin Owen said. "*I* would have reason to say a thing like that."

"I don't know, indeed," Meri Ifans said, "all one knows is one's own life. The gable-end of my house is to the mountain and the gable-end of your house is the back of the chimney for next door. You can shut the mouths of sheep and ponies, but you can't ever shut the mouths of people who are living on the other side of the partition from you."

Catrin Owen opened her eyes in surprise. John and Meri Ifans' life had always been to her an ideal of felicity. So many times she'd wished that she and her husband Wil could be as happy as John and Meri Ifans.

"Some people can be cruel on the quiet," Meri Ifans said, "and some people's cruelty stirs up a fuss, and it's your misfortune that you're living in the middle of a row."

"Wil isn't cruel," Catrin Owen said, as heatedly as her innocent nature allowed her to say it, "only provoking."

"What's more nasty than provoking," Meri Ifans said. "When you think you've got your life a bit in order, Wil stays home to loaf, and you're forced to turn out to work like today." She finished her cup of tea emphatically.

"But Wil's never laid a fingertip on me the way Robin Huws next door does."

"Well, and to tell the honest truth, I'd rather have a man give me a pair of black eyes now and then, than have a man who spends his life taunting. And take advice from me, Catrin Owen, turn a lip to him, and be as provoking as he is. There's nothing wrong with paying men in their own coin."

"I must be starting home," Catrin Owen said. "I left him in bed this morning, and he'll have raised the street there if I don't go home to make dinner for him; and there isn't much coal in the house there either."

"I'd let him suffer a bit from hunger and cold," Meri Ifans said.

Catrin Owen got up and took the money, and the small print of spare butter that Meri Ifans had given her for doing the churning, from the table.

It was a heavy day in September. Mist on the sea, and everyone's smoke almost jibbing as it went out through the chimney. There was an unnatural heaviness in the air, and a strange silence everywhere: that silence one feels in the country when school has re-opened after the summer holidays. On a day like this, Catrin Owen wasn't in the mood to begin working in her own house, after working in someone else's house. On a light day, when the wind was blowing, and especially if Wil wasn't home, she'd be all set to begin on another day of work in her own house. She felt depressed today, not that she had more reason to be this way than usual. This wasn't the first time she'd gone out to churn because Wil was in the middle of one of his fits of being provoking. He'd done that many times before. One might think she would cheer up after hearing Meri Ifans' emphatic words on men in general. But Catrin Owen wasn't feeling so pleased, never mind happy, after hearing suggestions of this kind. In her own opinion, she was the only martyr of a wife in the district. And having the privilege of being the only martyr in a district is an inspiration to a particular type of person. It was so with Catrin Owen.

Then she began to think about her life since she had married thirty years ago. It was strange enough, so that some women would have left him rather than put up with any more from him. In the same row with her, there were people living who did nothing from one end of a year to the other but work, the husband in the quarry and the wife in the house, eating, sleeping, and raising children, without ever any change at home. Whatever the case with Catrin Owen's felicity, her life was not as monotonous as that. She'd never had anything as monotonous as a month's wages altogether from her husband, since he'd never worked a full month. And Wil didn't always sleep at home. He'd sleep in the lock-up almost every Saturday pay night, and the policeman would visit the house the week after, when Wil was invariably at the quarry. The street had that much more variety in their lives on account of Wil Owen. In truth, it was Wil Owen, and only Wil

Owen, provided all the variety in the street. If Wil Owen would rather toss his weeds over the wall into Robin Huws' garden instead of into his own garden, he'd do it while Robin Huws was lifting a spadeful of potatoes. If Wil Owen would rather fling the waggon over the tip at the quarry than not, he'd do it, if there were a hundred stewards there shouting at him not to.

But Catrin Owen would have preferred the monotonous life of her neighbours to all the variety of her own life. How two so unlike had married is a question for heaven to answer. Such an ill-matched yoking would make you believe that marriages *are* made in heaven. Wil was born to carpet (according to his own way of thinking) and had tiles. Catrin was born to tiles and with no wish for anything better. She put up with all her husband's provoking, not because she had a Christian spirit, but because she was Catrin Owen, with no energy at all as far as her tongue was in question, but plenty of energy where housework was concerned. Sometimes the energy she'd thought of putting into her tongue went into her arms. The way she scrubbed the work clothes on some Monday mornings after having a quarrel with Wil bore good witness to that.

This morning, however, after hearing Meri Ifans, something came into her mind that had never come before. She grasped her shawl and tightened it around her arms with the force of a woman who has made up her mind.

As she was going up to the row houses where she lived, she noticed the stack of their chimney. There were great coils of smoke going up through it, grey to begin with, and then pitch-black. Here was one of Wil's tricks again. She knew that there wasn't much coal in the house, and she knew that Wil would never go to gather kindling. As she neared the house, she saw her husband talking to Ann Huws next door. Obvious from the look of the latter that they were quarrelling. Her eyes were flashing lightning, but Wil Owen was looking completely undisturbed, his hands in his pockets, and his eyes looking this way and that, as though Ann Huws weren't there at all. It was this attitude of Wil Owen's that his neighbours deplored. It had no effect on him. He'd whistle when his neighbour was foaming in his rage.

"Are your clothes whiter than anyone else's clothes, I wonder?" Wil Owen said, and his wife understood in a minute that her neighbour had come there to complain about setting the chimney on fire, when her clothes were outside.

Ann Huws turned on her heel, she knew it was totally useless to argue with adamant.

"It's a shame that anybody's forced to live in the same street with a man like this," she said loudly to herself, without realizing that Catrin Owen was close to her.

"That's the disadvantage of living in a row," the latter said, though she thought of saying, "What if you were living in the same house with him?"

With no more than that, she went into the house more rapidly than usual. There was her husband, by this time, sitting by a big blazing fire of wood, long planks stretching into the chimney, with the flames competing in a race along them.

"Where did you find that wood?" was Catrin Owen's first question.

"It's the wood from the bed."

"What wood?"

"The wood from the bed. The loveliest furniture in the house is a fire. Yes. The loveliest furniture in the house is a fire," he said, as if he were reciting a piece of poetry.

When Catrin Owen realized that her bed, her only bed since her children had married, the bed she'd had from Meri Ifans at the time Huw, her oldest child, was born, though it was only part of a wainscot bed, had gone to the fire to feed her husband's passion for provoking, her heart sank to the bottom of her being, but she remembered her decision on the mountain.

"I'm going," she said, as if she'd spoken half of her decision before.

"Where?" her husband said, without turning his head.

"To drown myself," she said.

"They say that Llyn yr Hafod is the best for a thing like that. There's more depth in it, I should think," he said.

His wife bit her tongue, threw off her shawl and her apron, and put on a coat and hat. She started off towards Llyn yr Hafod. This was the lake where everybody in the district went to put an end to their lives, when they were tired of living, or thought they were tired of living.

It wasn't the same intention she'd had on the mountain that she had now. On the mountain, she hadn't been thinking of the possibility that her only bed would be firewood. She'd thought about paying Wil "in his own coin" on the mountain. But this had been too much for her, and the first thought that came to her was to go drown herself, without considering what that meant. But to the lake she went, and she stood on its bank. She didn't know that Wil had been following her at a distance and had sat down on a small hillock not far away to watch her. Catrin was on the bank of the lake for some moments without knowing her own mind, when she heard her husband's voice shouting,

"Dive, Cadi, dive. Don't be afraid. Dive. It isn't cold."

Catrin Owen stared at the bottom of the lake, and she saw something there that none of those who dared to dive had seen, no matter what they saw after opening their eyes in another world. She saw herself at the bottom of that lake, in a sentence beginning with "if", and she saw, if that "if" were to be true, the glad spiteful smile of her husband Wil if her body were brought home from the lake.

So, instead of throwing herself in, she turned on her heel, and went home.

But the Devil himself was in her face on her way home.

The Widow

Dora Lloyd was standing in front of her mirror in her bedroom. She had just put the last hairpin in her hair. Before her in the mirror was an oval face, straight nose and warm brown eyes, broad forehead with the hair resting on it in russet curls. She put on a white silk blouse, and she didn't button it to the top; she left a little of the whiteness of her neck in view. A year before to the day, namely Whit Monday last year, she wore a white blouse with black stripes, and she had buttoned it all the way to the top.

Dora Lloyd had been a widow for five years now, and ever since the death of her husband she had spent every Whit Monday afternoon with her sister-in-law, Ned's sister, to talk about the late husband and brother over a cup of tea. During her married life she'd spent every Whit Monday in town. Ned would walk with his club, a red ribbon with two yellow bands across his chest. Dora would spend the morning in strolling the street, waiting for the club. Her heart would give a turn when she heard the band coming, and it would keep throbbing until she saw Ned. Then, after she'd seen him and felt prouder of him than she'd ever felt, her heart would begin beating properly, and she would walk back and forth again to wait until he left the dinner. Afterwards the two of them would go together across the river, and then back to a restaurant in Hole-in-the-Wall Street to have tea. The two of them would always walk home if the weather was fine, and they'd arrive at the brink of nightfall by milking time. And the sun would be sinking over Menai when Dora was putting the milk pitchers to cool in the pool beneath the waterspout. That was the Whit Monday of their married life, and she looked back on it as something beautiful, beautiful by now because it wasn't possible to have it back. The first Whit Mondays after her husband's death were very strange ones. In her first grief she was delighted to go to her sister-in-law's house, and she couldn't have too much of talking about Ned, though she knew that the talk was an entirely conventional thing to Nel. But as the years went on, the day that Ned was brought home from the quarry on a stretcher went further and further away from her. She didn't remember with the same clarity the distorting of his friend Morys Pen y Braich's face in trying to break the news to her. She could remember every line on that face in its travail in the first years, but it was becoming less distinct each year. At the beginning she couldn't bear hearing quarrymen pass the house, and she would shut herself in the house every day after the hooter sounded. And in spite of shutting the door, she would imagine hearing the click of the gate opening and Ned's footsteps on the stone pavement in front of the house. But the click of the gate became fainter, and by now it had fallen silent altogether.

Still and all she kept on going to her sister-in-law's house on this holiday. The thing had become as much a ritual as going to town formerly, and she didn't want to lose it. But this year she had no eagerness at all to go there, and still she wouldn't take the whole world to go anywhere else. The cause of the change was Bob Ifans y Rhandir. How he had come into her life, she didn't know. But one day she felt that Bob Ifans was part of her life, and that it wasn't possible to live without him.

Bob Ifans was a widower, and his kindness to the people of the district in need of assistance was proverbial. He wouldn't ask anyone for permission to help them, but he'd walk past your door and he'd put "indoor hay" in the cowshed before you knew it. And it was on one of these occasions that Dora felt differently towards him. Bob Ifans had come there early on Saturday afternoon, and he'd gone past the door to the rickyard without Dora seeing him. It was a bit before the hay harvest, and Bob took it into his head to carry what was left of hay in the rickyard into the cowshed so as to start making a foundation for the stack. At the very moment Dora was coming into the cowshed through one door, he was coming down the slate steps and in through the other door opposite her. And that was the sight she would see for days and months afterwards. A man not too tall, his legs perhaps too long for his body, handsome face just shaved, hair gone grey, black hat and black waistcoat grey with slate dust, white corduroy trousers with greyish-blue patches from the marks of the slate on them, and two grey eyes looking past the arm to see his way. The dust from the hay was falling grey on his face, and a haystalk lingered here and there on his moustache. Everything in the picture was grey. In a word, it was a single patch of greyness, but the picture and the man who was at the centre of it entered her heart.

Bob Ifans came there more often afterwards, and he missed a whole shift to help her with the hay harvest. The memory of that day had been with her now as she dressed. A hot day, like today. She was in the milkshed slicing bread-and-butter for tea-time, and she could hear a sound coming from the rickyard through the open window in back of her. It was the light sound of the hay, and it was falling on her ear, as the hay was tossed from the cart to the stack, like the whisper of a woman's silk petticoat as she walked. Then came Bob Ifans' voice:

"This corner now, boys, jump on it, can you, so we'll have room for the next cartload."

"When will we be at the roof, Robat Ifans?" one of the boys said.

"Oh, we'll have a little stack outside before that," said the head stacker.

Dora was smiling at the loaf with pleasure as she thought of his tenderness and his patience with the children.

Another scene came before her eyes.

Bob Ifans pegging the pig on a cold day in winter. He was as skillful as a pig-pegger as he was as the head stacker in hay harvest, and he wasn't at it a minute. That minute was a dreadful one for the pig, for the pegger, and for the onlooker. It was a delight to Dora Lloyd's feelings that Bob Ifans was able to keep control of his face and his temper. And if a woman can still think the same of a man after seeing him peg a pig, when there's so much temptation for him to twist his face into all sorts of shapes, it bodes well.

But why was Dora dreaming like this, with the time running away? She had still only put her skirt on. Nel would be tired of waiting for her. As she looked at herself in the mirror in her white blouse and her black skirt, she thought that the black skirt didn't suit her state of mind. She might as well not be hypocritical, she would have to talk to Nel about Bob Ifans some time, and perhaps wearing a blue skirt would be a help to break the ice and begin a conversation about the thing. So she went to the wardrobe to fetch the blue skirt, spent time in warming it in front of what was left of a fire, and put it on. She dilly-dallied further by going to look for a basket and an old kid glove to gather hot nettles for the pig. They were very good things to rouse a pig's appetite, hot nettles. By now she was ready to start out.

Who was facing her after she opened the gate but Marged Jones y Pant, who had been at the parish cemetery washing her husband's gravestone? There was a bucket on her arm, and Dora knew there was a scrubbing brush, a thick apron, and a piece of soap inside the bucket. It was on high days and holidays Marged Jones y Pant would go to perform this operation. As soon as she saw Dora, she sat down on the big stone by the gate as if beginning to have a long conversation. The other woman by now was impatient. She was quite satisfied to dilly-dally with her own quiet reflections, but not with the loud reflections of other people.

"Been at the cemetery, Margiad Jôs?" Dora said, looking at the bucket.

"Yes," she said, "and I'm worn out. It's a considerable step to the bottom of the parish on a hot day."

"Yes," Dora said listlessly.

"And it's a considerable bit of work keeping a grave in trim. You never saw old weeds and wilderness grow so fast."

"Yes, don't they?"

"But some people don't care how many weeds grow on the graves of their family."

"No," Dora said, just as apathetically. She knew that cap didn't fit her. But she couldn't understand why Marged Jones' talk was taking that direction.

"And some people are worse than that," the latter added, "you can walk on graves in Llanadwn without knowing you're doing it."

"Oh."

"And I'm surprised at some people too, people you'd expect better things from. There's Bob Ifans y Rhandir now. There isn't a stump of a gravestone at his wife's head."

Dora turned red, and then turned pale.

"Well, I must go," she said, "or Nel will have long since given up expecting me."

"Click," something said at the same time in her heart, like a door closing and locking by itself. And Dora Lloyd knew, that moment, that Bob Ifans was on the outside of that door. She didn't know why, but she could never think of Bob Ifans as a husband when he'd neglected to remember his first wife. To her, a gravestone wasn't something to put a curb on talk in the district, but something you couldn't not put up in your first grief. She had put a blue stone with gold letters on Ned's grave. The blue stone was what Ned had wanted. That's what he'd say should be on every quarryman's grave. And she'd put the blue stone for Ned's sake, but the gold letters for the sake of her neighbours. Still, it wasn't all pride. There was a considerable bit of feeling connected to that gravestone. And she was failing to understand how Bob Ifans would not have done the same thing when he had the means.

After going a few yards, she said:

"I must go back for a minute, Margiad Jôs; I've left something behind."

She went back to the house and changed the blue skirt for the black skirt. As she was going up to Nel's house, she saw her standing at the open door with her hand on her forehead.

"You've been dilly-dallying somewhere," her sister-in-law said.

"Yes, Margiad Jôs y Pant caught me on the way."

"Where had she been, I wonder? At the cemetery, I suppose."

"Yes," Dora said, and sighed.

In her mind, Nel mistook the sigh. To Nel, there was only one reason connected to the cemetery that would cause Dora to sigh. That was Ned. Dora saw that before Nel could say anything, and she said:

"How are your pigs coming on now, Nel?"

"In top form, they're champion feeders."

"Indeed, mine there has clean lost his appetite. I want to fetch a bit of hot nettles for him on my way home."

And the talk was of pigs and cows and calves almost all afternoon. There was no mention of Ned or of Bob Ifans. But in talking about Dora's calf that was grazing at Gwastad Faes at the bottom of the parish, an idea came into its owner's head, and she perked up from then till the time to start home. In that district, pasture was scarce in spring and the beginning of summer, and it was necessary to drive the cattle to some of the more size-able farms at the bottom of the parish to graze. Dora had a calf, and since the cows were at their full yield of milk, the calf had been sent to graze at this time. And indeed, Dora had longed for him after he'd gone, because he wasn't quite like other calves somehow. She'd raised him on the bucket from the start, and he was just like a pet lamb. And the calf was a grand calf, a red calf with a white star on his forehead. His body was in proportion all the way through like his mother's. That was how old Tomos Huws, Bryn Rhedyn, would always speak of a beautiful cow, "a grand cow", just as if he were talking about his daughter Annie's best frock. Wil the Calves had put his head over the wall several times since this calf had first gone out to the field. And if Wil poked his head over the wall more than once, that meant he had his eye on the calf, to buy it. But he didn't succeed in this case, and the butcher had never had a calf from her. According to Dora Lloyd, that saying, "Better the evil you know than the evil you don't know," didn't apply to selling a calf to a butcher. But she wanted to raise this calf come what may, and before very long the little calf became a part of her life. He'd never go far from the house to graze. He would lift his head and run to the wall of the field each time she'd go past to the spout to fetch water. When the time came for his mash at nightfall, he'd run like a mad thing to the gap, and go leaping and frisking past her to the cowshed. And it was such a pleasure to see him lick his nose after finishing his mash and stretch his head over the edge of the rack to look after her, rolling his big bulging eyes! She felt really angry with him once. He broke into the field with the clothesline one day, and he wreaked havoc there. He passed everything cheap, but he chewed everything dear until it was riddled like a pepper-pot, including a white silk blouse, the first bright blouse that Dora Lloyd had bought after burying her husband. She was angry to the point of tears with him in the beginning, and she was hoping his teeth would be on edge till the end of his life. But she pardoned him after considering that "a widow's woes" are a widow's woes after all, and she thought it was a strange thing to call a foolish person a calf.

Now, in talking to Nel about calves and other animals, an idea came to her. She wanted to insist on having the calf back before the appointed time. She was a bit ashamed to confess to Nel that she hadn't seen at all how the calf was coming on. He had been there for a considerable while too, because Whitsun was late that year. If she had the calf back, it would take her mind off other things. And to her mind you must have something to fill your life, or part of it, anyway. And she knew that Bob Ifans would never become part of it again.

Nel came to accompany her part of the way, to the clump of nettles that was growing beside the road. In cutting the nettles Dora looked just as if every jot of her mind were on the stalk of the plant for fear of it pricking her. But instead, her mind was on a picture where she saw Bob Ifans retreating from her, backwards, and the calf returning from Gwastad Faes.

"Are you able to forget things quickly?" she said to Nel.

"Forget what, what do you mean?" the latter said.

"Oh dear, what's wrong with me?" Dora said, because she knew that the question of remembering and forgetting didn't enter Nel's world at all. Took everything as it came, that was what her sister-in-law did.

After the latter went into the house, she said to her husband:

"Wasn't Dora strange today?"

"I always find her strange," he said.

Nel and her husband were as like each other as a pair of toy dogs, but both their heads were turning the same way instead of towards each other.

Next day, Dora sent Joni next door to fetch the calf, and she gave him money to pay in full for his accommodation. She was quite satisfied in her mind that she could manage very well without starving the cows. This year there was more "reaping grass" than usual—that fresh grass which grows as a blue strip in the middle of other grass and makes cows' mouths water.

She could see him coming up the road and she ran to the door to wait for

him. The calf was insisting on passing the gate, and it was with considerable trouble that Joni got him through it. He went past his owner without
showing that he saw her. After entering the field he ran wildly about, and
he didn't take any notice of the other cattle or of his own mother. He would
run away when his mother came towards him to try to sniff him. After
he'd finished running, and being a nuisance to the other cattle, he stood
still at the bottom of the field, with his head over the wall, looking in the
direction of Gwastad Faes.

Dora observed all this, and she went to the field, calling, "Drwia, bach."
But he wasn't taking notice of her.

"Joni," she said, after going back to the house, "won't you go to the
cowshed and fetch the scythe and cut a bit of reaping grass for me."

In ten minutes, she was crossing the field, with the reaping grass in an
old clothes basket under her arm.

The calf wasn't taking notice of her, but when she tossed the contents of
the basket on the ground, he leapt eagerly for them. She took a piece of the
reaping grass and tried to get him to eat it from her hand. But he turned
up his nose at it and pushed her hand aside, grazing from the ground. And
she tossed what was in her hand all around his head.

"You're just like men," she said. "You care more for your place than for
the one who owns the place."

She went back to the house. There was an hour yet until milking time.
But she called the cattle to the cowshed, even though it was so early. They
were unable to understand what was wrong, and they were disobedient
for a spell. But since Dora Lloyd was declaring "Trw, bach" more earnestly
than usual, they felt it was better to obey.

If you'd gone past the cowshed after a while you'd have seen Dora Lloyd
milking with both hands, her head tight against the flank of the cow and
singing, to the music of the milk squirting into the pitcher, this verse:

> *"I have a corner cupboard,*
> *It's full of dishes for tea,*
> *And a dresser in the kitchen,*
> *And everything where it should be.*
> *Fa la la," etc.*

Old Age

As I sit by the fire here tonight, I feel very strange. It isn't often I look back into the past, but the events of these last months have taken me back some thirty-two years in spite of myself. When I turn my thoughts to the past, things there are very indistinct to me. I remember things, of course, but I remember them as a man of forty-four and not as a boy of twelve. But tonight I could tell you, not what happened when young Twm Llain Wen and I were at school, but I could say what sort of smell the old school had and those damp old books in the cupboard by the door. This afternoon, I heard young Twm Llain Wen's teeth gnashing as he scuffled with the schoolmaster thirty-two years ago. And I felt the touch of my teacher's velvet bodice on the side of my face as she marked my sums. Somehow thirty-two years of my life became as nothing, and young Twm and I were at school together, two cubs between twelve and thirteen. Twm is in his grave tonight, a man of forty-four. His mother is alive, an old woman of eighty-eight. She's living in her old house at Llain Wen, with her daughter Gwen; Llain Wen is a quarter of an hour from here. After Twm married Ann y Wern, he found work at Chwarel y Fenlas, and he moved to that district to live. I'm still living in my old home. Twm and I stayed close to each other until he married and went away to live. Then, as it happens, we lost sight of each other, and we never bumped into each other except when Twm would come to his old district for someone's burial, or to visit his mother; or when we'd bump into each other at a fair in town.

At the end of last year I was told that Twm was ailing, and that he wasn't at work half the time. I went to Llain Wen to ask and to get some word of him. But nobody there knew anything at all. The old woman didn't recognize me in the beginning, and I wasn't surprised at that, because it was months since I was there. But after I said who I was, she remembered at once, and asked me about the cows and the animals. She remembered that I'd had a sick cow.

About a month later, I heard that Twm was very ill, and I went back to Llain Wen to know if what I'd heard was true. They'd heard through a letter from Ann that he was very ill, but there wasn't much anxiety there.

"He has a pain in his chest," Gwen said, tossing the matter aside.

The old woman was sitting in her corner by the fire, and she didn't recognize me any more than the previous evening, a month before that. After I said who I was, "Good lord," she said, putting her hand on my shoulder, "I couldn't for the life of me see any likeness at all in you, but I see it now." And she laughed heartily.

I wasn't very easy in my mind about Twm, and next day I went there by train to see for myself. I was greatly surprised when I saw him there sitting by the fire; he had a very sick look on him. His face yellow and thin, and his hands clean. Still, it was the old Twm there, talking about his choir at the quarry with zest.

"I expect that I'll be in pretty fair shape for the meetings this Christmas," he said. "I've had a fairly good day today."

And we chatted about choirs and competitions the whole time. As I started to leave, Ann came to accompany me, and her face was completely different from what it was in the house. There she was cheerful, and you could scarcely have told that anything was worrying her. After she came out I perceived what an effort she was making in the house.

"How does he look to you?" she said.

"Better than I thought he would," I said, lying.

"He's a king today to what he's been," she said. "Some days he has fearful pains."

"And indeed," she said, smothering a sigh, "the doctor is putting a very bad colour on things."

"They don't know everything," I said. "What does he say is the matter?"

"He doesn't say straight out," she said. "But I must go back to the house. Don't be a stranger."

"I'll come again soon," I said as I crossed the stile to the field.

But to my shame I didn't go for a very long time. Strange how a person can forget illness when it's far enough away from him. So it was with me.

When I went there again, I couldn't believe my eyes, so great was the change in Twm. As I went into the house I smelled the good aroma of baking bread. Ann was busy taking the bread from the oven, and Twm was sitting opposite her, with his face thinner and more yellow and his eyes big. If one could have transformed that face, it would have been a cosy picture. He didn't take much notice of me, but kept his eyes on Ann taking the bread from the oven. She knocked it underneath with her knuckles, as if she were knocking a door, to see if it was ready. "Do that again," he said to her, "do that again," with his eyes staring.

And Ann knocked the loaf to satisfy him. "That's how mam did it long ago," he said to me.

And a look came over his face, the same look that I saw on him many a time at a competition, when the adjudicator gave his criticism, and had said enough to show that his choir was the best. That look soon disappeared and he turned his eyes to the fire. That's how he was while I was there, gazing into the fire, without saying much of anything, but answering an occasional question. He asked one question himself without taking his eyes from the fire.

"How is mam?" he said.

"She's quite well as far as her health is concerned," I said, "her memory's going."

"Yes, isn't it?" he said. "Not such a bad thing, I suppose."

Next night I went to Llain Wen. Gwen had asked me to come because she was very worried by now. Just as with the earlier times, the old woman didn't know me. And after she knew who I was, she didn't take any interest in me or my affairs.

It was a hard, moonlit evening, with not a puff of wind anywhere. The frost crunched under my feet along the road to Llain Wen.

"There's a big wind rising, isn't there?" the old woman said without addressing anyone in particular.

"How long is it till Christmas?" she said, before I had a chance to correct her on the question of the wind.

"Two months," I said.

"Dear dear," she said, "I remember as if it were yesterday how I made toffee with my sister Aels the day before Christmas when the two of us were in service at Gwastad Faes. You know what?" she said, tapping her hand on my knee, "we put it outside to cool. As soon as we did, we hear a most frightful screech. And what was it but an old hen who'd run through the toffee, and been burnt. Her claw came off, poor creature." And the old woman laughed.

"Be quiet with your nonsense, mam," Gwen said snappishly.

"How was Twm?" she said to me more gently.

"Very middling," I said, "very middling, has failed badly since I saw him the last time."

"Yes," she said, "he looked to me as if he'd failed badly the day I was there. I'm afraid something's got hold of Twm."

"Dear heaven," the old woman said, "there were funny things happening long ago."

"Be still, mam," Gwen said impatiently, "don't you hear Wil saying how ill Twm is?"

"Twm?" the old woman said. "Yes, isn't he?"

She went off again.

"I remember Aels and me coming home across Gwredog footbridge with our sweethearts, from Holy Rood Fair, and when we were on the bridge, we see a ghost, and back we go, right back to the town, and then around the road home. Aels was a clever girl too. She could have anybody she wanted as a sweetheart."

As I looked at her sitting there, an old old woman, my mind went back to the time when I would call by there for Twm to go to school with him. She was a round, ruddy little woman at that time, like an apple dumpling, darting about the house. She thought the world of Twm. He was the youngest boy, and his mother made a great fuss over him. He had to wear mustard-coated flannel on his chest all winter and almost all summer. And more than that, a flannelette handkerchief around his throat and across his chest under his braces. Twm would need to be close to melting in the heat of July before he could take them off. His mother wouldn't let the wind blow on him. I thought about that diligent mother,—and this old woman, sitting by the fire with her hands folded.

I suppose she had the same clothes now. I never remember her without the white cap under the black straw hat. It wasn't a crimped white cap either, such as I saw Betsan Ifan wear when I was a boy, but a white cap with a little frill, and a small round black hat that turned downwards, with its brim tied with velvet and a feather around the crown. That's the kind I always saw her wear, and I never saw her without it on her head in the house. She wore a coarse homespun petticoat, a flannel bodice, and a blue and white apron; and on her feet a pair of clogs with a bright clasp.

"The same sort of clothes," I said to myself, but not the same face or arms. It wasn't these arms I saw long ago kneading a bowlful of dough until it wobbled like a bog under her fingers. There was little of her face to be seen now, because she tied the strings of her cap under her chin. The little that was to be seen was all furrows, like mud after rain. Her hands were yellow and speckled, like speckled wallpaper in a damp room. In the corner of her eye there was a drop of water. Her head was shaking continually, sometimes up and down, sometimes from left to right.

"There's more wind rising, isn't there?" she said again.

"Yes," I said, "and I must leave." As I opened the door on a calm evening and the moonlight on the doorstep, I heard the old woman:

"There's a big wind rising."

I went home sadly.

I visited Twm often after this, and he looked to me to be getting worse every time.

November Fair Day I was in town early. But early though it was, one of Twm's neighbours, who knew of our friendship, was looking for me. I knew from his face he had bad news. Twm was very ill, he said, worse since the evening before, and he was afraid that he wouldn't be there by the time he came home from the fair. I set off for there at once, leaving the fair to anybody who wanted it. I was bent on having one look at Twm again. But I was too late. He had gone an hour before. To me was given the task of telling the news at Llain Wen.

I walked back, every step, and by the time I reached Llain Wen, the hooters were sounding one o'clock.

As I opened the gate to the path that led to the house, I saw the old woman at the door, with her head stretching past the doorpost. Before I'd opened the gate, a man who was passing by had asked if that was the right road to Llanberis. The old woman had seen him, evidently, because her first question to me was:

"What was that man wanting, tell me?"

"Wanting to know if he was on the right road to Llanberis."

"Good lord."

Then she gazed at me.

"Who are you?" she said.

"Wil," I said, "Wil, a friend of young Twm's."

"Good lord," and I didn't know from her expression if she knew who I was or not. I leaned my back on the wall of the house, thinking about the easiest way to tell her.

"I'd come to the door to look around before it gets dark," she said.

"Yes?" And I hurried on awkwardly. "I've some rather bad news for you, old woman. Twm, poor fellow, has left us."

"Twm," she said, "Twm who?"

"But Twm, your son, your youngest son," I said.

She stared uncomprehendingly, and she said:

"I don't know him, you see."

The Ruts of Life

"Hullo-ee," through the house. Dafydd Gruffyd was waking up to go to work at the quarry at six o'clock on the morning of his birthday, at the age of seventy.

After he answered, his wife Beti went to the kitchen and began to slice bread-and-butter to put in his food tin. She cut eight slices from the loaf, and pressed them into his tin, her ring sinking into the buttered bread as she did that. By the time she was finished putting tea and sugar in the old mustard box, her husband was in the back kitchen washing himself, and she heard the sound of him spluttering suds from his mouth.

After he ate his breakfast he turned his chair to the fire, put his leg over the arm, and reached for his pipe to have a smoke. Then he got up and looked out at the weather.

"Does it mean to rain today?" he said to his wife.

"No, I don't think so, but perhaps you'd better take your coat."

He took it from the back of the door of the back kitchen and came to fetch his food tin and his tea tin and put them in the inside pocket of his jacket.

Beti heard him closing the gate and the voice of his partner Twm Min y Ffordd.

"How's the health today, Dafydd?"

Then she heard the two of them going up past the gable-end of the house and others following them, talking in a low tone as quarrymen do in the morning—a much lower tone than the one they talk in at night.

That is precisely the way Dafydd Gruffydd would go to work every day. He had met his partner at the gate for the last thirty-two years, and neither of them ever failed to set off from Dafydd Gruffydd's house at half-past-six.

But this was the first time it had struck Beti. She was looking at and listening to everything today as if it were new. An idea had come into her head with her husband's arrival at this age that he would have to leave the quarry and live on his pension, and all that he had done this morning and every other morning would come to an end. The government must be shrewd and well-versed in their Bible to think of giving a pension to a man at three score and ten, when it was time for him to die.

After musing like this she went to fetch the cows that were grazing on the wide. She went up to the top of the fields before calling "Trw bach". This was how she would do it in the morning, as if she were afraid of waking the people in the houses. The curtains on the windows of most of them were down, and there was a look on the houses as though everyone in them were dead. She called "Trw bach" quietly for fear of waking them, and the two cows raised their heads together as if they were doing drill, and moved slowly in the direction of the cowshed; their udders swaying like a swing, from one side to the other, and their teats pointing outwards like the spikes on a calf's weaning muzzle. Their drool was hanging like reins on the napes of their necks, and its brightness matched the brightness of their black skins.

"Come closer, my girl," and the collar was on their necks with a click, and the two cows were already gulping the indian corn in their buckets, shaking the handles of the buckets.

Then the beginning of milking, the milk to start with falling blue and thin into the pitcher and sounding thin. Then becoming firmer and sounding thicker. The cow raising her cud and grumbling, then sleeping and twitching in her sleep, with Beti Gruffydd going on milking and going on thinking—a thing she hadn't done for a very long time. Beti Gruffydd's life had been too full to think much. A sleeping tonight for the sake of waking tomorrow was what it had mostly been, and filling the time between waking and sleeping with work. Work, always the same work like a time-table in school, a same thing with many things every day of the week. And Beti Gruffydd had lived long enough for the holidays to take their place in her time-table. If there had been work going on in the quarry on Ascension Thursday, when Dafydd Gruffydd's club would march, that would have disrupted the uniformity of her life. Taking the children to the seaside in summer occurred with the same formality. If you'd asked Beti Gruffydd on which Saturday in summer she'd gone to the seaside with the children, she couldn't have told you exactly. But she would have been quite certain that she'd taken them the same Saturday in July all through the years. The atmosphere of that Saturday would be felt before it came, and when it came, Beti Gruffydd and the children would know that that was *the* Saturday for going to the seaside.

Of course, sometimes things like marrying and dying would come to disrupt this uniformity. There was the time when her child, Meri, had died, at four years of age. God in Heaven! that was a hard ordeal. She thought at the time that it wasn't possible to go on living after losing her. But that saying, that the land of the grave is the land of forgetfulness, was confirmed in her own life. By today she had to make an effort to remember she'd ever given birth to that child. She had a plait of her hair in the drawer upstairs, and a white petticoat of hers with embroidery on its hem. The hair by now had become like a baby doll's hair, and the petticoat yellow with age.

Later there had been the children getting married, they would leave a gap for a little while, in the house and in the purse, but she soon became used to it, and by now she and Dafydd had been living by themselves for so many years that she'd thought there was no way there could be any change in their lives. Beti Gruffydd had always been a proper homebody. There was no room in her life for much besides housework and dealing with milk and butter. Her interest was at home. When she took an interest in something outside of her house, it would come through a book or a newspaper. She read an occasional book like *The Maid of Eithinfynydd* with great pleasure, and her favourite newspaper was the *Red Echo*. If there was no romance about her life, there was plenty in other people's lives as one found them in the *Red Echo*. But she wouldn't go far to find it. She went to chapel sometimes and into town once in a while. According to her own testimony she had never been "at an Association or a 'Steddfod or a Circus"—she always named them in that order, and the three of them conveyed exactly the same thing to her. She'd never been at the quarry. She didn't have the least notion what sort of place her husband was working in. The closest connection between her and the quarry was her husband's food tin, his work clothes, and his wages, all of them covered with quarry dust. Many things like this had come to her mind today.

She took the pitchers outside, and drove the cows into the field. After straining the milk she set about churning. She didn't usually churn on Saturday morning either. But the cows were at their full yield, and there would be too much churning to leave it until Monday. She closed her eyes as she turned the handle of the churn, and on every turn her head came down with her arm. Oh! it was lovely, and the butter was sure to be a single skim on the surface of the milk instead of in positive lumps the way it was in winter. And so it was, and gathered together, clinging to the shallow dish. In winter, Beti Gruffydd could hold the butter on the back of the thin saucer and offer to hit someone with it, but today it had spread across the dish like a pancake. But Beti Gruffydd was not a woman to take her time with soft butter on a hot day. She kept at it, drawing it together and slapping it and making furrows in it with the thin saucer, with the water running drip-drop along the table into the pitcher on the floor.

There were five pounds of butter on the round slate, the churn was drying out in the sun, and the house had been cleaned by the time Dafydd Gruffydd came home at mid-day. After his dinner of new potatoes and buttermilk, he started outside to cut the thorns in the fields. He would do such things every Saturday afternoon, and at nightfall he'd go out to do something around the farm. He was never seen idle. From one aspect the circle of his life was as narrow as that of his wife. It was only mingling with the quarrymen that made it wider.

Today Beti did what she had never done. She suggested that he go to bed after dinner. He looked at her as if she were beginning to lose her senses.

"Yes indeed," Beti said, "better go, here you are, three score and ten today, and I can't say you've ever taken it easy, with your hands folded."

"I have to go and cut those thorns while it's dry weather," he said.

"Dry weather or not, if you died you'd have to let them be."

Beti knew it was no good her chiding him. But she'd been able to give expression to something that had been tossing and turning in her mind throughout the morning.

Presently, after washing the dinner dishes, she went out to fetch water from the spring in the upper field. It was a fine day, and in coming back, she sat down in the field where Dafydd Gruffydd was working. The aftermath was fresh and green, and the sound of the cows at their grazing was pleasant to her ear. Not so the sound of her husband's sickle. The thorn twigs were leaping up like a Jack-in-the-box, and were falling with their arms spread to die in the ditch.

Beti looked for a long while at her husband. She hadn't given him so much thought since before she married. At that time Dafydd Gruffydd was one in a thousand, but by today living with him had made him very much like the rest of the thousand. Beti had too much common sense to fool herself that the romance of courting would continue very long after marrying. She was looking at him now in his work clothes—an old old hat on his head. You wouldn't know what it was for quarry dust. But Beti could see a sweat-stained patch of ribbon at the front of his hat. Part of his coat-sleeve was hanging in a single weary flap, and it swung back and forth as he cut the thorns. This reminded her that she had to mend his clean clothing before she went to bed. A wave of compassion for her husband came over her. He'd once been a very good-looking man. It was a hat a bit blacker than this that he wore for May Fair years ago, and the crease in his grey and black trousers was a bit straighter then than the ridges in his corduroy trousers today. Although he worked many Saturday afternoons with his father, the frame that held the clothing was a bit straighter then. To Beti Gruffydd, he was looking a good deal older today, even older than he'd looked yesterday. She had grown too used to him to think this before. In looking back over the years she could see nothing in his story too but work, work without much rest. What if that work could be seen today, all together, in a single heap? It would have reached to the heavens no doubt, one great monotonous heap. And it was Dafydd Gruffydd, the man who was cutting the thorns here today, who was the author of it all. She gazed at him again, brandishing the sickle like the wind with a moaning coming from his breast like an echo with every stroke.

And she thought to herself, "He'll be lying in the old graveyard there in a little while, with his hands folded forever."

The Loss

The bus's heart was beating quickly, and inside, Annie's heart was beating the same way. Her heart was beating so fast, to her mind, that she was afraid her husband sitting beside her would hear it.

"Isn't it nice, Ted?" she said to her husband.

"Yes," he said, "very nice."

For her, the mountains around Creunant were stretching out before her eyes, and a smile came over her face in thinking of the happiness that could be theirs that day at the lakeside amidst the mountains.

The sun was shining warmly on the window of the bus, and she turned her cheek towards it to get all its warmth and at the same time tried to keep the other cheek as close as she could to her husband to catch every word that came from his mouth. She was thinking only of the afternoon she was to spend with her husband on the mountain. The passing scenery was nothing to the scenery that awaited her, and so she paid no attention to it. She was conscious of the tops of bushes scraping along the glass of the bus, and she shut her eyes for fear they would hit her. She was conscious in the same way of the engine of the bus throbbing under her feet, and her husband beside her bending his head towards her bosom with the smell of tobacco on his clothes.

It was her idea to have this outing to the mountains on Sunday like this to see if she could get back something of her time of courtship. It was a year and a half since their wedding, and she wasn't very happy. According to her poetic way of looking at things, she expected married life to be a continuation of the season of courtship, although she was over thirty when she married. Her husband had become more prosaic after marrying. To him, in the terms of his native town, marrying was a "settling down"; slippers, fire, tobacco, newspaper, with his wife completing the picture by sitting on a chair opposite, knitting. It didn't enter his mind that there was any need to talk the language of courting after marrying. And she felt that she was losing a sweetheart in gaining a husband.

Ted Williams was his name, but it was "Williams" he was called everywhere, except on his medicine bottle, and by his wife. "Mr. Williams" was on his medicine bottle, and "Ted" he was called by his wife. After they were married Ted became "Williams" to her too, in her mind, although he was "Ted" on her tongue. It was as "Williams the Husband" she thought of him.

To try to counteract this feeling, she decided to have a day in one of their favourite haunts during courtship, and make Williams back into Ted again. She was very lucky in her chance to charm him into an outing on Sunday. He was delighted to be able to leave the town, and especially to leave Lloyd and the Teachers' Meeting. Whatever might be treated at a Teachers' Meeting, this Lloyd was sure to oppose him. It was high time for Lloyd to take his leave or to die, it didn't make much difference which. Williams didn't know how the people of the chapel could let him have his own way with everything, when he was only a newcomer. And the previous Sunday, Lloyd had been more contrary than usual. The matter of the Sunday School trip was before them. When everyone else was scratching his head to see which town in North Wales was best for taking the children, Williams ventured to propose Rhyl, so that he could go home shortly to tea. As if struck by a sudden idea, Lloyd proposed that they shouldn't have a trip this year, they should have a tea party instead of a trip. A trip would become very expensive, and more than that, horrible accidents were happening every year with Sunday School trips. And with the tragedy of all the Sunday School trips in the world on his face, he sat down. It was Lloyd's amendment that won, and Williams went home, cursing in his heart and hoping that every child would get the measles, lightly, the day of the tea party. It was the story of the Teachers' Meeting his wife had as cream with her currant tart at tea-time. She would laugh heartily at things like this. But her husband was seriously vexed, and all week, at his job in the post-office, Lloyd was like an eclipse of the sun to him. No wonder, then, that he agreed so readily when his wife suggested Llyn Creunant instead of Sunday School to him the next Sunday. She knew very well how he was feeling, but he knew nothing of her thoughts.

As the bus shook, Lloyd was shaken away from Williams' mind, and in his place came the pleasure of seeing grass rippling in the fields and the varying colours of honeysuckle and roses in the hedgerows. And little by little he came to look forward to sitting on the side of Llyn Creunant again.

The walk from Llanwerful, the place where the bus stopped, up to the lake was hot, and it was good to sit on its bank in spite of the insects that were whirling around their noses. After they came within sight of the lake Annie saw two things to worry her. Three motor cars at the lakeside was the first thing—high and mighty people's cars.

"Why couldn't these people leave their cars at Llanwerful, instead of bringing them to the lakeside?" she said.

"Yes," he said, "it would do double-chinned people like this good to walk, and it would be good for the scenery to be without them and their cars."

The small chapel a few yards from the lake was another thing. It was a small chapel, tiny, some two windows and a door. But Annie was afraid it was enough of a chapel to remind her husband about Lloyd. But to Williams, a chapel in the country wasn't the same thing as in town, and it didn't have the effect his wife feared on him.

They sat lounging on the lake-shore. Before them great mountains were standing like giants between them and the sky, the purple of the heather and the yellow of the gorse melding together on them until they were pale lavender.

At their feet the water of the lake was lapping like a cat constantly tapping her paw on your knee to get your attention. A sight to drink in and not to describe, that's what it was; a sight to intoxicate you and make you light-headed. From the corner of her eye Annie could see the little chapel.

What's going on there, she wondered? Was there a teachers' meeting there and people quarrelling? No, impossible that there was more than one class there or more than one teacher.

"What need have these people to go to chapel in a place like this?" she said to her husband. "One would think that people hereabouts would never stop worshipping in the midst of all this beauty."

"I don't know, unless it's to pray. I should think they'd have to go somewhere to pray on seeing such beauty."

"Yes, to be sure, that's how it is. But they haven't much room to pray in that little old chapel."

"No. It's ferociously small inside. One cough from John Ifans, Eglwys Bach, would be enough of a service for them for a whole month."

She laughed and turned her head towards the chapel. On looking at it, she thought that it didn't look much out of place there. If it had had a chimney, it would have looked very like one of the houses, and it's likely that none of the families saw each other except on Sunday in the chapel.

Shortly, the people came out of it, a small handful, and they went one here and one there to their homes, in every direction, just like the legs of a spider. She followed them in her mind into the kitchens of their homes. What would they have for tea, she wondered? Apple tart or currant tart, for sure, and she could smell a farmhouse kitchen on Sunday afternoon that minute, the mingled smells of farmyard, milkshed, potatoes in the oven, and apple tart. And something like nostalgia came on her in thinking of her old home, broken up by now, as it was when she would come home from Colwyn Bay, where she was in the post-office, to spend the Sunday.

She drew the air into her nostrils. "Isn't it nice here?" she said to her husband.

"It's heaven on earth here," he said, following a bird that was flying above the lake with his eye.

"Do you remember us here that Whitsun long ago?"

"Very well."

"Do you remember what we talked about?"

"Very well. I said that I'd rather have you than the whole world."

"Do you still think the same way?"

"Yes."

"In spite of everything?"

"In spite of damn all."

Williams didn't usually swear, but he was getting Lloyd off his mind with a final kick. And more than that, Annie was looking remarkably beautiful as he looked into her eyes there. She had a very beautiful throat and bosom. Not one flaw anywhere, and a few curls of her hair were coming down from under her hat onto her forehead.

They went to have tea, holding each other's hands. Tea was provided at a small cottage on the bank of the lake by an old woman who lived there with her brother.

As they went towards the house they saw the old woman busy carrying a teapot and hot water out to the people from the cars. And the two of them took another table.

"I'll come to you in two minutes after I finish with these," she said.

"These" had double chins, every single one, and the old woman was a long time carrying hot water to them. They had their own food.

Presently, the old man, her brother, arrived with a pitcher of water, and took it into the house. He looked as though he'd like to throw the water at someone's head. That was his work in summer. God knows what he did in winter.

After taking the water into the house he came out again, and went to sit in a small field in back of them. Annie couldn't stop herself from turning to look at him. She was perfectly certain that there was only one man like this in the whole world. He had a round flat black felt hat, a "Jim Crow hat", on his head, become very rusty. He had sideburns belonging to the Victorian age, and the clothing of that age. The shape of his face looked as if it had been hewn out of marble. His eyes were narrow and without much expression in them. Annie couldn't take her eyes off him, sitting there meditating on nothing.

"What is the old man thinking about, I wonder?" she said to Ted.

"I don't know, unless about religion," Ted said.

"He can't think about religion every minute of his life."

"There's nothing else for him to think about, unless he's thinking about the water he'll have to carry next summer."

She laughed.

"I wonder if he ever had a sweetheart?" Annie said.

"I don't know. It's hard for me to believe. Look at his eyes."

"Eyes aren't anything to judge by."

"No, I could never believe he ever had a sweetheart. He's always been too fond of his own company."

At this the old woman brought them tea. She was a neighbourly old woman, with a motherly look.

"I'm sorry to keep you," she said, "those people were demanding a great deal of service. I haven't seen you for a very long time."

"No," Ted said, "we're married now."

"Well, heavens!" she said. "I would never have known. You're still like two sweethearts."

The two looked at each other.

They greatly enjoyed the tea, especially the currant bread. After they finished they went to sit on top of the dyke in front of the house. The old man was still continuing to meditate in the field, and was closing and opening his eyes like a cat in the sun.

Presently a light grey layer of mist came over the mountains, and after a time it came towards them and curled itself around them. They started down to Llanwerful, and they walked quickly because it was beginning to get cool by now. The moisture fell in tiny drops from Annie's hair.

As they reached the house they saw a man walking back and forth in front of the gate like a policeman on duty. Ted knew him at once. It was Jones the Druggist.

"Where've you been?" was his first greeting to the two of them. "I've been looking for you everywhere since four o'clock."

"For a bit of an outing," Annie said.

"Tuh!" Jones said, "there was quite a fuss at the Teachers' Meeting this afternoon. It would've been worth your while to be there. Wmffras brought this business of the trip up again, and Lloyd became mad as a hornet. He called Wmffras all sorts of names. But the strangest thing, here was that little Morgans, who's apprentice to Wmffras, you know, that shy little fellow who's afraid of his shadow, getting up on his feet and making Lloyd sit down. Somehow or other, terrified at seeing a little pipsqueak like that making him sit down, Lloyd *did* sit down and he couldn't say a thing. Everybody looked surprised, and the Superintendent struck up 'The Grace of Our Lord'."

Annie didn't hear it all, because she ran into the house to prepare supper. She was too happy to ask Jones to come have supper with them.

Her husband came in with a different look on him somehow. As he ate he didn't say a word but looked at his plate of meat. She was looking at the same thing, but her mind was far off in the mountains. She was going over every event and over every word and over every look of Ted's that afternoon. She was very happy. Ted was Ted after all.

After a while, Williams said, "I'd have given the whole world to be at that Teachers' Meeting this afternoon."

She nearly choked. Big tears began to gather in her eyes. But that wasn't for long. After a moment she laughed uncontrollably, at the top of her lungs. Her husband raised his head and looked at her, astonished.

Between Two Pieces of Toffee

"Will you have a piece of toffee, grandad?" his twenty-year-old grand-daughter said to Dafydd Tomos, who was sitting by the fire.

He turned his head and there were his daughter Jane and his grand-daughter Mair in the middle of the floor pulling toffee. The mother held one end of it and her daughter the other end. They pulled and they pulled, always putting one end in back of the other, with the toffee turning colour from brown to gold. Then they would twist it as though they were curling a child's hair and put it on a slate greased with butter.

"Yes," the old man said, and Mair came and put a chew of toffee in his mouth. The act linked his memory to a sight like this that he'd seen sixty years before. He looked at his granddaughter with her short sleeves and her black hair like a cockleshell above her ear and his mind went back to Geini, the girl who'd been in service with him at Dôl yr Hedydd. It was as she was pulling toffee like this that he fell in love with her. She and her mistress were standing in the middle of the floor as his daughter and his grand-daughter were doing now, pulling toffee. She had short sleeves, gathered into a band above her elbow, sleeves high enough to show the round biceps and the dimple in the flesh of her elbow. Her black hair came down over her ears on its way to the back of her head. As she laughed she showed a row of white teeth and a dimple in her cheek.

He fell so deeply in love with her that he became unable to sleep at night, and he would try to be around the house often during the day to get a glimpse of her black eyes. He observed that she understood his state of mind; because she'd pass him shyly in the farmyard, her eyes to the ground, with her eyelashes sweeping the top of her cheek. He declared his love to her one evening as they were feeding the cows when one of the lads was ill and she was taking his place. He remembers now that cowshed at Dôl yr Hedydd as it looked that evening. Its air was warm from the cows' breath, its partitions filthy with dust and cobwebs and dried dung. His shadow and Geini's were moving enlarged on the wall as they moved back and forth between the haymow and the cratch. A row of big eyes turning upon them over the edge of the cratch and necks moving back and forth. Then the heads disappearing and tongues curling around the hay underneath the cratch and the sound of the hay like tissue paper. Dafydd could see Geini's eyelashes turning up past her bonnet as she bent with the hay. He couldn't bear it any longer. The next minute his lips were declaring his heart's passion on her hot lips. They shared one big secret as they went into the house that evening.

The following months were happy months for the two of them. Dafydd didn't need to be close to the house during the day now. He knew that Geini loved him and that was enough for him. He was content with his musings about her as he took the horses to the forge or as he spread manure. He thought about her as he'd seen her that evening pulling toffee, and he thought about her as he would one day see those arms rolling out oat-cakes in their own house.

They spent a great deal of time together, and the more they saw of each other the more the two believed that each had been created for the other. Together they watched the starlings swarming to the field after dung was spread and they smelled the scent of heather bonfires on the mountains as they gathered stones in Spring. On the same occasion they first heard the cuckoo call, together.

"If there's anything in an old wives' tale," Dafydd said, "we'll be together forever."

"And if there's anything in an old wives' tale," she said playfully, "we'll be gathering stones together forever."

Dafydd laughed loud and long.

And that was the time he asked her, since May Day Fair was approaching, when they might marry. Since they were both stooping over gathering stones, he didn't see the sadness that came over her face when he mentioned that.

"Why should we marry so soon?" she said. "Let's be two sweethearts like this for a year anyway, so that together we can watch the grass and the corn growing, and go together to clip ferns and moss. I like being able to be beside you like this."

"All right, but only till All Hallows, mind."

.   .   .

The summer came and went. Their faces and their arms turned brown. Dafydd himself was feeling by now that All Hallows was the time to marry. Because, as he'd say, "I'll have seen her at every season and in every mood by then." And his heart warmed more and more towards her in seeing her always the same, at five o'clock in the morning, milking-time in summer, as at eight at night. They talked of private matters beneath the udders of the cows in the morning and as they bound sheaves of corn by the Indian Summer moon.

One Sunday night, in coming home from church, Dafydd ventured to ask her again to name the day of their wedding, but almost before he finished, her answer was out of her mouth.

"Oh! I don't want to marry."

Dafydd turned her face towards him and towards the moonlight. He looked into those bottomless eyes, and he noticed for the first time ever how sad they were.

"Why, Geini? This is the second time you've refused."

"Oh!" she said, and there was pain in her voice, "I'm afraid."

"Afraid of what? Afraid of me?"

"No, afraid of marrying."

"Afraid that we couldn't live on my wages?"

"No, I'd never be afraid of that, while I had these ten fingers."

"Afraid of the responsibility?" Though he didn't rightly know what that was, but he'd seen it in a book.

"I don't know. No—afraid—afraid we'll come to know each other better than we do."

"I don't understand you, Geini dear."

"Well, like this," she said, with less pain in her voice, "as we are now we know each other well enough to love each other, but I'm afraid if we marry, we'll come to know each other well enough to hate each other."

"That isn't much of a compliment to either one of us. If we're worth knowing it'll take us a bit of time to know each other."

"No," she said, "once we marry, we'll become just like everybody else. My mind will be taken up with the children, and your mind will be taken up with how to get food for them."

Dafydd laughed on hearing twenty talk like eighty.

"So, you won't promise?" he said.

"No," she said, with the same pain in her voice.

He didn't think it wise to argue further with her. All Hallows came and went. Dafydd felt that things couldn't keep going on like this. There would come an end of them some time. He wanted Geini, wanted her to welcome him home at nightfall and wanted her as his very own wife.

A little after All Hallows he ventured to ask the question again. It was a Monday night, when she'd been up since four o'clock in the morning to wash, and busy at five at night chopping up swedes in the cowshed, by candlelight. There were dark lines under her eyes and cracks in her reddened hands.

"Now Geini," he said, and perhaps there was a bit of authority in his voice, "we must marry. It doesn't pay like this. You won't have to get up at four o'clock in the morning after you're married."

"If it won't be getting up early to wash, it will be something else," Geini said.

"Now, now, don't be so snappish, Geini dear. But you're tired," he said more gently. "Only we can't keep going on like this."

"Why not?"

"Well, I want you all to myself." And he suddenly asked, "Do you like someone else better, Geini?"

"You know very well that I don't," she said. And with the gleam of victory in her eyes, "There it is, I said that we didn't know each other well enough. You're selfish, and you're suspicious. I didn't know that before."

"If I weren't selfish or suspicious in love, it wouldn't be worth anything."

"No," she said, "we know each other better than ever tonight, and that's how it would be, if we were to marry. We'd keep seeing something, and in the end we'd hate to see each other."

"Well," he said, "I have to leave. I can't stay here like this forever."

Not at all a threat, but an honest statement.

And she softened. Before they left the cowshed that evening, Geini had promised to marry him. It was arranged that they were to go to buy the ring the Saturday of November Fair, and that they were to marry Christmas morning. They would have a small house not far from Dôl yr Hedydd with a pigsty in the corner of the garden—and both began to gather things for it.

But Geini didn't look as happy as before. She struggled to smile when she was with Dafydd but her sweetheart often caught her looking dazed and sad.

He was counting the hours until the Saturday of November Fair and they ran very slowly. To her, they were running much too fast.

They set off together at five o'clock, he in his cord trousers and his bluchers. He had on a cloth pilot coat, a multicoloured silk kerchief around his neck, and a beaver hat on his head. She was wearing a frock of black homespun material with a brown stripe in it, brogues on her feet, a brown coat of homespun, loose, with the hems of its sleeves opening wide, and a little round brown hat on top of her head. It was a dry moonlit evening and the roads were like a pavement. The hoarfrost looked like a layer of snow on the fields, and the trees were standing like so many birch rods worn out in beating generations of children. He strode along and she trotted in tiny steps beside him, with only the tips of her shoes to be seen beneath her long skirt.

Because she was so silent, Dafydd told her stories. The story of Siôn Dafydd y Goetre going to town with his sweetheart to buy a wedding ring. The two of them quarrelling as they went home and him throwing the ring over the hedge into the field and being unable to find it.

"Did they marry afterwards?" Geini said eagerly.

"Oh! yes."

Geini sighed softly.

They reached the town—narrow streets, mean houses and shops. The people were trampling one another's feet and very many were already drunk. On the field were the stalls for indian rock and fairings, home-made oat-cakes and tarts. The balladeer, Y Bardd Crwst, sang "The Black Blot". Dafydd knew Geini well enough to know that things like this were not to her taste. And when he heard two young fellows asking two young women near The Sign of the Harp "Will you come for a dram, girls?" he said,

"We'll go for the ring, Geini."

He was brimming over with joy. They looked for a bit outside the watch-maker's window. The rings were looking very dull in the light of the candles but they had the brightness of the king's crown to Dafydd.

They went in warily. The watchmaker was considerate and almost before he said why he was there, there were a number of rings in front of Dafydd. But he didn't notice that Geini's face was white until he turned quickly on seeing her run for the door. He ran after her insofar as he could run through the crowd. He caught her at the quay, and when he caught her, it was as if he'd caught a little bird. Her whole body was trembling and he could hear her heart throbbing.

"I can't ever take the chance, Dafydd," she said. "I see an end to my happiness, when I put that ring on my finger. You must forgive me."

And he understood something of her mind as he looked at her face.

"All right, Geini dear," he said, "I won't trouble you ever again."

He went on by himself to the Slate Quay. There he lay on his chest on a heap of slates and groaned into the clefts between them. He didn't know how he went home, but he found himself at some time between eleven and midnight looking broodingly out through the window of the stable loft. The moon was in back of the house and quite likely behind a cloud. There was a large dark shadow on the field in front of him and beyond that field stretched the other fields, yellow in the moonlight. You could have sworn they were fields of corn in September. Dafydd went to bed with the cornfield before his eyes.

He got up the next morning, and packed his clothing in his wooden chest. He went to the kitchen to have a chance to talk to his mistress, and to explain to her why he was leaving. She took it greatly to heart and she wept on hearing Dafydd's story. He arranged for his chest to be sent in the cart later to his sister's house. Then he set off with a few things in a red kerchief on his shoulder. Before going, he went to the cowshed and opened the door. Then he closed the door and a single tear fell on his cheek. He went on then without looking back. He had to pass the cottage they had taken to live in. He looked through the bedroom window. He saw the wainscot bed and the white curtain with a red flower on it that Geini had sewn. The chaff-bed was there on the frame, clean chaff threshed at Dôl yr Hedydd, in the ticking Geini had sewn. In a little while he passed the church. He remembered it was today their marriage banns were to be published. He wondered would Geini go to the church to stop them?

In her bedroom Geini was watching him go, him and his pack, until he became only a black spot on the horizon. When he went out of sight, she fell on her knees by the chair and wept. Her lashes hung wet and limp on her cheek and the tears fell from them as from the branches of trees in December.

Years afterwards, Dafydd met Jane. He was a hand on another farm by now. It was Jane's similarity to Geini attracted him at the start. But in a little while he saw that she was very dissimilar. She was not as ready in her answers or as warm of heart. He liked her well enough. But somehow as the time came for him to ask for her hand, he began to feel a passionate longing for Geini. And he decided, before he asked, to go look for Geini once again. He went to Dôl yr Hedydd, and there he heard that she was in service in one of "those big towns". No one knew where, and her father and mother were dead by now. He went to friends of hers, but they hadn't heard from her for years.

He married Jane that All Hallows. The Saturday of November Fair after that he was in town, and who did he see crossing the street but Geini.

She was looking towards the ground and she didn't see him. He stood still and watched her passage. He saw her go straight to the watchmaker's window. She gazed into the window for a bit and then went on. Dafydd came close to running after her. But for what? He felt that he'd better not. He couldn't marry her now, and he was afraid that one look at her eyes would be enough to destroy his married life.

He went to a pub and drank enough to numb a little the feelings that were in his heart. In his cups, he told something of his secret to one of his fellow-drinkers.

"Well, yes," the latter said, "that's how it is, you see. Everyone has a yearning for something that he can't have in this world."

That was the last time he saw Geini, and he never heard a word about her.

It was things like that were going through Dafydd Tomos' mind as he chewed the toffee. By today going over the story didn't create any disturbance in his mind. He had no feelings in any way in thinking about Geini. He remembered the whole story and that was all. He'd forgotten hundreds of things that had happened after that. But this story stood out in his memory like black writing on white paper, and the events that he'd forgotten were like white paper with no writing.

"Will you have another piece, grandad?" Mair said.

"Yes," the old man said, and as his grand-daughter put it in his mouth, tiny strands, thin, golden, flowed onto his beard from the toffee.

Sisters

Meri Ifans had married when she was twenty, and had a life that is common to many, working, raising children, and quarrelling inside the walls of her own house. John Ifans, her husband, was a quiet, miserly, amiable man, seeing eye-to-eye with you on every point. He didn't smoke, or drink, or swear, though he kept sheep and ponies. Meri Ifans was a neat, cleanly woman, masterful at every aspect of housework. They had nine children. Meri Ifans' house was as clean when the ninth child was born as it was when the first was born. On every corner of it there was the mark of her strong, tough arms. There wasn't a ruffle in the paper on the walls, which she always papered herself. Along her floors brightness followed brightness in a single line into the farthest corners. The scent of her milkshed was enough to raise you from your sickbed when you were at your worst. Her butter was hard in August and tasted as good a month after it was made as it did the first day. The pressure of her arms on the thin saucer had forced every drop of water out of it. There was a clean smell to her cupboards and her clothes-drawers—a smell like the smell of summer and apples beginning to shrivel. The clothes lay in the cupboards like books stacked with their backs facing you in a well-ordered row. There was such a gloss on her clean clothes that it made you almost feel the heat of the iron rising from them if you put them by your cheek weeks after they were ironed. One look at her house would be enough to convince you that housework was poetry, not drudgery.

And Meri Ifans was clean in her own person. She would always work in a blue cotton frock and leather slippers with thick soles. When she put on clogs to go to the cowshed their soles were as black as their backs and their buckles as bright as the fender. Her hair was always as sleek as the floor of her house, and there was never a ripple or a twist in her stocking. An unruffled woman, indeed, that was Meri Ifans.

But her relation to the living occupants of her house was not so un-ruffled. With her husband she had the upper hand rather easily, and despite all his miserliness she was able to get money from him. Her cupboards were always full, and her table, and her clothes and her children's were good. As for the children, they would quarrel with each other and with their father and herself daily. As children accustomed to too much cleanliness, they would seek to find fault with perfection itself. But they had all married, and they had to come to terms with less in the way of cleanliness.

After her last child was married, Meri Ifans thought that she'd find a bit of happiness. She was beginning to get old, and less work and less noise were acceptable to her. She thought that after all the children had left the nest she could go more often to town and buy things that she didn't need for the house—buy for the pleasure of buying. But somehow after the leisure came, the eagerness to go lessened; her legs and her body felt weaker and her mind less masterful than it had been before.

One day her husband found her in the chair, her arm hanging limply over the edge of the chair and her mouth twisted to one side. That was Meri Ifans' first stroke, and that was the beginning of going downhill for her and the beginning of gaining mastery for her husband. She recovered to some degree. Her face returned to its proper shape, and some of the strength of her arms came back. But not all. She didn't have the same spirit for cleaning the house. Cobwebs began to stand in the corners and dust to lurk at the feet of the beds. And Meri Ifans began roaming off to the houses round about to gossip, a thing she'd never done before. Whatever quarrelling and whatever to-do there might be in her house, there'd never be the mention of it outside, because she was a woman who fussed and fumed in her own house and not in other people's houses. So it was a sur-prise to the whole district to see her going into other houses with her hair a bit untidier than it had been.

Then came the second stroke. But she recovered again, though not just as before. There was a suggestion on her face that her mouth wasn't quite right, her jaw sagged a bit, and her arm was more helpless. She didn't take any great care of the house by now. Dust and dullness settled everywhere. Greasy plates lay on the shelves of the milkshed waiting to be washed. Milk began to curdle at the bottoms of the pitchers. Her floors became like a post road. There was only one thing that Meri Ifans enjoyed doing, and that was washing. She had less to wash, and still she'd wash every day. The back kitchen would be swimming with water every day, with her sloshing in the middle of it. By now it was painful to watch her trying to do something. It was obvious that one of her arms was completely worthless. She would spare it constantly in washing. She'd use the useless arm only to hold the piece of clothing. She'd squeeze with the other hand.

Then the third stroke came, and of necessity Meri Ifans was totally confined to the corner. She had acquired a habit of rushing out into the road, and since motor cars were rushing in both directions, her husband thought it wise to get a large bolt and bolt the door securely. There she was, an absolute prisoner by the fire. Her body seemed to be limp all over, her jaw hanging and her mouth open. But her appetite was excellent.

In this crisis there was an appeal to her daughter Beti, who was living near by, without much work to do. Her father had to appeal to her to put the house a bit in order. As sometimes happens, Meri Ifans had raised daughters quite different from herself. Beti's house was so disorderly that it hadn't entered her mind to begin putting her mother's house in order. In truth she was enjoying her mother's house more since it had begun to become untidy. And her cleaning of her mother's house was a mere excuse for cleaning. "Sloppy" would have been too good a name for it.

Meri Ifans had a sister living some half a mile away from her—Sara—a younger sister and completely of the same character as herself. She came to visit Meri fairly often, and her eyes were not blind to the slow and certain change that had come to her sister's house. But she had plenty of work herself at home, and she failed to see that she should spare Beti, who was living closer to Meri than she, and whose hands were much more idle. She suggested at times that Beti clean the house for her mother. Beti would promise to do that. But by the time Sara went there again there would scarcely be the trace of a brush or a dustrag.

One evening, it was the night before Christmas, Sara called at her sister's house between five and six. There was Beti in the back kitchen, at it by candlelight trying to wash her mother's chemise. Sara thought to herself that she would be there like that doing the washing clean on the brink of darkness! She went on into the other kitchen to her sister. Meri was sitting by the fire, as black as a peat-bog. She had an old knitted cap on her head with her hair pulled any-which-way under it. Her face was black, her hands were black, and her apron was black.

"Well, good heavens!" her sister said, "doesn't anybody here wash you?"

"No," Meri said thickly.

At this Beti ran from the back kitchen, drying her hands on her apron, to excuse herself.

"It's no use washing her," she said, "she's putting her hands in the ash-hole, and then rubbing them on her face and her apron."

"Let me see to you," Sara said, and off she went like a whirlwind to look for a dish and soap and a towel. She found a dish and soap, but she didn't see a towel anywhere.

"Where's the towel?" she said to Beti.

"I don't know," she said, "I had it a while ago drying mam."

Sara went to the cupboard to look for a clean one. And if she'd opened a cupboard on a skeleton she couldn't have been more astonished. There was nothing but a feeble effort where there had been a full, well-stocked cupboard. There wasn't a tablecloth, or a towel, or a sheet, or anything. At this moment John Ifans came into the house and Sara began to boil over.

"A thing like this isn't fitting, John Ifans," she said. "Look at your wife and look at this cupboard."

"I can't help it," he said. "I can't prevent these children from carrying things out of their home. Why should I go buy linens for Beti to take home with her? And I've begged and begged her to wash her mother, but she won't do it."

"Oh villains!" Sara said, "damnable villains too. One taking advantage of her mother's helplessness to strip her house, and the other taking advantage of his daughter's impudence to find an excuse for skimping more." The two vanished from the house.

"And mind you, Beti," she said to her as she was vanishing from the house, "there'll be a clean chemise on your mother tomorrow."

Meri watched it all foolishly, and then broke out laughing, harshly.

"Now, Meri," Sara said, after getting hold of a piece of cloth somewhere, "let me wash you."

She did so with warm water. She took off her bodice, and never in all her life had she seen anyone's chemise look like that. It was seamed with filth. Then she did her hair, and Meri looked much better. Then something else tugged at her. She wondered, was Meri getting enough food? Every time she'd been there since her sister had become worse she hadn't seen any food there at all except bread and butter or potatoes in their skins.

"Are you hungry?" she said to her sister.

"Yes," she said eagerly.

In a few minutes she had a little cup of tea and thin bread-and-butter and a boiled egg on a tray. She'd come upon the last at the other end of the food cupboard, far from everybody's reach. This was the only tasty morsel she'd seen in the cupboard. Meri Ifans gobbled the food as if she'd been without food for weeks.

"I'll come here again tomorrow," Sara said as she left.

"Yes, mind you do," her sister said.

As she went through the back kitchen Sara snatched the chemise that Beti had been negligently washing and took it home with her.

That evening she thought seriously about her sister's plight. She began to see how things were. Meri incapacitated for doing anything. Her children some of those honest people who believe there's nothing wrong with taking things from their own home. The husband miserly by nature, finding the whole way clear for himself to be a miser now because Meri was failing. More than that, finding a splendid excuse to be that way because things were leaving the house. Had such a round ever been sung anywhere? And it troubled her to begin sparing the daughter's laziness or sparing the husband's money. And yet she couldn't bear to see Meri suffer.

Next day she had boiled Meri's chemise three times before breakfast. In the afternoon she finished drying it by the fire and ironed it and aired it. Then at nightfall she took it to her sister's house, and in her pocket was a slice of chicken.

When she arrived Meri and John Ifans were sitting by the fire. The husband got up and went out. As on the evening before, Sara washed her sister and did her hair. Tonight she changed her chemise. Then she made her a cup of tea with the chicken, and as before Meri greatly enjoyed it. Sara didn't ask what her sister had had for dinner. She was too much afraid of hearing the naked truth. She took the dirty chemise home to be washed.

And that is how things went on for some months. She'd go there every day to wash and tidy her sister, and she'd take her clothing, outer clothes and underclothes, home to be washed, and she'd change them every three days, until Meri became clean once more—in herself, in sharp contrast to her surroundings. Cleaning the house was impossible for Sara. She had too much work in her own house to do that. Each time, too, she'd take a morsel of something for her sister to eat, a morsel small enough so that nobody else could have a portion of it, and she'd make her eat it while she was there.

On the last matter she was feeling very bitter. She wasn't wholly unhappy working to keep her sister clean—that wasn't costing her much except her labour, but sparing the husband's money and allowing him to hoard money enraged her sometimes. She became enraged one day when she heard that

John Ifans had taken half of his pension and his wife's to the bank. So he was doubtless living on the other half. Meri had never seen her pension; she'd had the last stroke before the time for her to receive it and it was her husband who was receiving it for her. It was a terrible thing to Sara's mind that she was keeping her sister from starving as well as keeping her clean while the husband kept on hoarding money. She thought once of arguing with John Ifans on the matter, but then she thought that there wouldn't be any point. Hard to turn a man away from his pleasure. And perhaps talking to John Ifans would only keep her away from her sister altogether. So she decided to keep on the same way, keep her sister clean, and take her a morsel of food every time she'd go there. How Meri passed the time between Sara's visits was one of the things that Sara didn't dare think about.

After a little while Beti and her father ventured to come into the house when Sara was there. There'd be an apologetic look on Beti, and her father would be very amiable and docile. The latter suggested that Sara take his own clothes home to be washed.

"No," Sara said firmly, "I'll keep Meri clean as long as she's alive."

Then the time came for Meri to die. She was laid up for a fortnight—not because she had another stroke, but she failed suddenly. Sara would go there every day and tidy her as before, and take her a morsel of food. Now, after seeing her bedclothes, she would take those too home with her to be washed, and bring her own bedclothes to take their place while she washed them. She was up all night every other night.

Some three days before Meri died Sara was unable to get out of bed. Fear came to her on thinking that her sister was going to die. She was feeling strangely ill. But she could get up two days later, and she felt all right in going to visit her sister. She was expecting to see a change in her, but the change she expected was not the one she found. Meri was looking more like herself than she'd seen her since the first stroke. Her mouth was firm and closed, and her eyes were bright.

"Do you know who's here?" Sara said.

"Sister," she said clearly.

And she smiled a happy smile at Sara.

Meri died that evening. Sara was with her to the end.

The scene remained with her for years. The dull light from the lamp. The filthy room. The oilcloth on the floor worn to shreds and ravelling around the edges. The wallpaper brown with age. Tracks of water running down it in zigzag lines. A corner of it hanging in one place. A scrap of plaster hanging from the ceiling by something thinner than a thread and turning and turning. The ceiling terribly black except the part above the lamp.

The bedclothes were like cambric, as was Meri's nightgown, and Meri herself was almost as white as they. The clean clothes would give Sara pleasure if only she didn't turn her eyes far from the bed. She did so, after all, in spite of herself, and she had to see what she didn't want to see—a circle of cleanliness and an outer circle around it of filthiness, just like the lamplight on the ceiling—a white light in the middle of blackness. In the middle of it all Meri was smiling and death gave a beauty to her face.

"Sister been kind," she said before closing her eyes.

Sara said to a neighbour next day, with satisfaction,

"Meri got to die the way she lived—clean."

The Victory of Alaw Jim

This story would not have happened if the wife hadn't got the first word in before her husband. That was quite contrary to Morgan's thoughts when he rushed out of the greyhound racing field with Alaw Jim at his heel. He wasn't afraid to go home today, thanks to Alaw Jim. He could put a ten-shilling note on the table for Ann to do with it as she wished. That would make amends for him neglecting his obligations all week long. More than that, Alaw Jim was beginning to pay for himself. And if he hadn't won the race today, it was worth it, in Morgan's mind, to see him running along the field, his head stretching forward, his skin tightening around his ribs, while he moved as smoothly as a boat on a river.

But seeing that head stretching in front of all the other heads at the end had been almost too much for a man with an empty belly like Morgan. He was reliving that moment now as he walked home, and his heart gave the same turn as it had on the field. He believed that running a greyhound paid better than putting a shilling on a horse, though it was with the money he'd won on a horse that he'd bought this dog. And, to close an eye on the monetary side for a moment, there was more pleasure in keeping a dog for running. What good was there in putting a shilling on a horse when he never saw that horse run? He couldn't curse it when it lost his shilling for him, or praise it when it put a shilling or two in his pocket. That's how Morgan was feeling now after getting a dog. He felt otherwise before he had one. Then, it had been worth putting a shilling on a horse, even though it ran like a hen, if it had a chance of bringing him another shilling for his first shilling.

From the day he'd begun to play the horses, he hadn't stopped hoping that the riches of Rockefeller would come to him some day. A chance like that was constantly befalling some people, and why couldn't Morgan be one of them some time? Ann had been stupid, too, failing to see this, and berating him for his weekly shilling on a horse, instead of continuing to hope as he did. After all, what was a shilling out of the dole money, if there was a chance of doing away with all his dole forever after? Indeed, people were stupid. Morgan had long since been fed up with this endless talk at meetings of the unemployed, protesting against this and protesting against that with nobody much better off. That's what was good about a dog. He couldn't talk, and his silence would bring more money than all the talk of councillors and people who wanted to be councillors.

The object of Morgan's thoughts was trotting beside him, almost as quiet as a cat, with his paws clicking lightly on the hard road. His owner, because of long poverty, was light enough in body, but his heelless shoes were scraping on the pavement. He had a tight cap on his head and a scarf around his neck, but he had no overcoat. He didn't own one. But he was perfectly happy. It came into his mind to buy something to bring home to tea. Ann and Tomi would be pleased. But that would break the ten-shilling note. He wanted Ann to be able to see the worth of Alaw Jim.

At 364 Darwin Road, Ann and Tomi were sitting by an ember of a fire in the "middle room". The room was crowded and close. Clean ironed clothing was hanging on a line below the ceiling, and there was a small bed by the fire. It was impossible to keep it tidy because it was the only room they had to live in since they'd let the parlour. Tomi was beginning to get better after the pneumonia, and was now sitting on the bed where he'd been lying between life and death a few weeks before. He sat restlessly, swinging his feet, with his socks in slack coils on his thin legs. His face was pale and there were patches of yellow on it. Tomi couldn't rightly understand the temper his mother was in this afternoon. Ever since she'd talked to Mrs. Ifans who was living in the parlour, when the latter went through to the back kitchen, his mother hadn't said much to him, only sat by the fire with two spots of red in the middle of her cheeks. Tomi could understand very little about things these days. There were Mrs. Ifans and her husband living in the parlour, and it wasn't proper for him to play hide-and-seek and run around the chairs. It's true that he didn't want to run around and he tired very easily. And he wanted the strangest things. This afternoon he wanted liver, but perhaps he'd better not ask his mother when she was so odd, the way she was doing nothing but staring into the fire. Mrs. Ifans the Parlour had had some for dinner, and the aroma of it came to them in the middle room as she was frying it in the back kitchen. That was the worst of living in part of a house, they could smell one another's smells. Sometimes it was a pleasant aroma, Tomi thought, but another time it wasn't. Anyway, the smell of the liver at mid-day had been pleasant, and his stomach had a hankering for it. Of course, Tomi was fond of cake. There was nothing he liked better than going with his mother to the shop, Y Polyn Melyn, on Friday night, and seeing all the cakes. The one with a layer of jam and cream was what Tomi liked best, the five-pence-a-pound one. But somehow, his appetite for tea on Sunday wasn't quite as big as his eyes on Friday night. Now, he didn't want to see it. It was liver he wanted. Maybe his father would go to fetch it after he came home.

Then there was the business of the dog. That was dark to Tomi. His father had told him before Christmas that he meant to buy him a dog as a present, and he'd dreamt about a little black and white dog, with curly hair, and round eyes. He was totally dismayed when he saw the thin grey old dog with the narrow eyes that came. A dog with a long old tail like this could never wag it to show he was glad. But bit by bit Tomi and the dog became friends, until Tomi ventured to ask his father could he call him "Pero". His father laughed, and said, "Do you think it's a blooming sheep dog I'm going to run? 'Alaw Pero', by heaven, no, it won't do the trick at all." And he laughed again. Tomi had noticed too that his mother never looked pleased when Jim was around. But no matter, Tomi liked Jim, though he followed his father everywhere. They'd gone out together somewhere after dinner, and they were staying a long time. He wondered if he'd better ask his mother now about the liver.

"Mam, may I have liver?"

His mother turned a strange look on him, and then turned her head towards the fire again, with her lips moving as though she were talking to herself. She was answering Mrs. Ifans. It made no difference to her where she went to buy a hat. It was four years since she'd had one. Ann had seen a pretty little hat in Mrs. Griffith's shop for two and eleven. Mrs. Griffith's shop was too expensive for her to go there at another time; but when there was a sale, Mrs. Griffith would lower the prices remarkably, and you were sure of finding a bargain. It wasn't like the Argyle Stores, where things were always cheap. When she said this to Mrs. Ifans, the latter went and smiled hatefully and said: "It's nice that you can afford to go to Mrs. Griffith's shop. But to be sure you're doing well on the dog now after quitting the horses."

And off she went with the frying-pan and the liver.

"Stupid, that's what I was," Ann was thinking to herself now, "not to have said that Morgan lost more than he ever won on horses, and that he hasn't had anything with the dog up to now."

But Ann was one of those who could think of everything to say after the event. To her mind, in truth, it was a nuisance to be forced to have anyone in the house. But there it was! They couldn't afford twelve shillings a week in rent, and it was from the mite extra she got for the rooms that she was going to get the new hat, before the "Means Test" people came to know about it and take it. That wretched Mrs. Ifans! The dog indeed! Her rage came back to her tenant, and then came to rest on Morgan. He'd have to sell Alaw Jim before anyone could taunt her again that it was the dog was paying for her new hat.

"I want liver, mam."

Her anger with her husband grew greater after hearing this cry. It would be much better for Morgan to put the money he was spending on the dog to get a bit of nourishment for Tomi now that he was growing stronger, instead of the boy and the other children never having anything but tea and bread-and-butter. She decided to go fetch liver with some of the hat money. It would do Mrs. Ifans good to see that she didn't get the hat after all. And Ann would be able, that way, to chew the cud of her sacrifice.

When she was putting her coat on, she heard Morgan coming down to the back of the house, whistling and petting Alaw Jim more than ever as he shut the door of the back kitchen. The happy look on Morgan's face added a second flame to Ann's rage, and the look Morgan found on Ann's face was enough to extinguish every jot of the enthusiasm that had kept him from collapsing from hunger on the way home.

"You and your old dog," were Ann's first words, and before Morgan could put an answer together she poured ahead:

"Here he is, the poor lad, crying for liver, and you spending your money and your time on that old dog. It's impossible for him to grow strong on the food he's getting. And there the other children are, out in the cold looking for coal on that old level, and you enjoying yourself at the racing field, and people taunting me that I'm getting new clothes on the back of your old dog."

A strange thing happened at this moment. Suddenly, like a flash, it came to Morgan's mind that he'd won the prize for composing four stanzas "To the Daisy" at a competition in the country when he was eighteen years old. It was dozens of years since then, and almost as long as that too since the last time the thing had come to mind. And to think it was his love for Ann had inspired him to write those stanzas! His wife took his silence as a sign of cowardice and of the righteousness of what she was uttering, and she went on:

"And look here," she said, "if you won't get rid of that old dog, I'll drown him myself."

At this came a heartbreaking scream from the direction of the bed.

"Don't, mam, don't, say that you won't drown Jim. You don't want to drown Jim, do you, do you, mam?"

Morgan escaped from such misery, and as he turned his eyes back, he saw Tomi on his mother's knee with his hands around her neck crying and shouting:

"Say that you won't," and her comforting him.

"There now, there now, I won't."

The two objects of all the commotion went up the hill, with one of them struck dumb, and thinking how in the world was it that he'd ever compared his wife to a daisy. After the event he could gather his thoughts together and think of all the things that he could have said to his wife. The other continued to trot quietly at his side.

There was hoarfrost in the air and a light mist over the face of the land, so that it made it bright grey. The smell of frying bacon and onions was coming from houses that Morgan passed on his way up. After climbing a little he sat on a stone and turned his eyes to the horizon. There was the sun going down over the shoulder of a hillock. The sight was one to remember forever. There the sun was, a great ball of orange, its rim a darker orange, and the whole grey sky a background for it. The ugly houses were hidden in the greyness. One by one the light of the lamps began to dance in the streets and in the houses, and the valley was glorious.

A shiver of emotion came over Morgan and he rose to his feet. Peace came once more into his heart. He meant to go home, and the dog along with him, and put the ten shillings on the table for Ann, even if he had to run out afterwards.

The Quilt

The woman opened her eyes after sleeping soundly all night. She was trying to remember what was wrong. Something was wrong, but for a moment she couldn't remember what; the way it sometimes is with people the first morning after someone dear to them has died in the house. Gradually, they come to remember there is a body in the next room. So it was with Ffebi Wiliams this morning. But it wasn't the death of anyone dear to her that was troubling her subconscious. Gradually (if one should consider gradual an act that takes only a few seconds to happen) she came to remember that this was the day the furniture was to go away to be sold. The pain she'd felt last night came back to the pit of her heart. She gazed in front of her towards the window, trying not to think. Then, she turned her head towards her husband. He was sleeping, and his moustache regularly rose as his breath struck his upper lip. There was blue underneath his eyes and his face was pale, and he looked for a minute as if he were dead. She gazed at him a long while, and by gazing long she was able to pull him awake. John looked bewildered after opening his eyes. The blue of his eyes was bright and he smiled at his wife, as if he were going to tell her his dream. But he put his hands beneath his head and looked in front of him towards the window. For a long while the two of them said nothing.

"We'd better not doze off," he said then, sitting up.

"No," she said, without making any move to rise.

"We'd better get up."

"Yes."

"We'll have to get up."

"Yes."

Since it was his wife who got up first every day, John Wiliams was waiting for her to do it today. But she continued to lie as still as a lump of marble.

Presently, he supposed he had better get up. The movers would be there for the furniture shortly. He got up and slowly put his clothes on, looking out through the window as he buttoned them. He didn't ask his wife why she wasn't getting up.

After he went downstairs, Ffebi Wiliams continued to gaze through the window at the sky that lay on the horizons of her consciousness. She couldn't remember a morning for many years when she'd been able to lie in bed and gaze lazily at the sky, when her mind was empty and the sky filled all her awareness. Today, there was only the one thing on her mind, namely the fact that her husband had gone bankrupt in business, and that all their furniture, except for the few things that were absolutely essential to them, was going to be sold. It was this had been on her mind and on her husband's for months now, in every aspect of it. The two of them had thought so much about all the aspects of it that by this time only the bare fact remained to toss and turn in their minds.

Long years ago, in the first days of their venture, Ffebi Wiliams had been afraid that a day like this would dawn on her. She dreamed many times that it did, and she wouldn't have minded much if it had. There was a reckless spirit in her at that time. It would make no difference to her if she should lose the whole world. She and her husband had plunged into the water, and they had to swim. When currents were sometimes with them and sometimes against them, it was easy to cast worries off. There were too many to begin bothering about them.

But the business prospered, and as it went steadily along, the first fears retreated. It stayed like this for years. However, a few years ago things had begun to go downhill. About a year ago, they were certain they were going down the slope dreadfully fast. The terror of understanding that was like hearing a close relative is ill with no hope of recovering. After the first shock, she had accepted her fate quietly, just as one accepts the sick person's dying. But did she accept it quietly? She couldn't get up today. That was weakness, or stubbornness. She didn't know which. The causes of their going bankrupt began turning in her brain again, as they'd done throughout the months. Those wretched big companies' shops about the town were the trouble, selling cheap foods and carrying them twice a week by now to the doors of people's houses. How abominable it was for her and her husband, who'd given these people credit all through the years, to see them pay cash in hand to the people with the vans. Many a time she had hoped they would be poisoned while eating the wretched food from cheap tins, and that their faces would break out in pimples. How glad she was on reading that one of these big companies had been fined because someone had been poisoned.

She and her husband had become too old to struggle by now. That was the truth. And she, anyway, could not submit to her fate. Losing the whole world was not so easy as she'd once supposed, in her youth. It was no light thing to detach oneself and then go on. The theory of detachment was all very well as a theory, something for people who were secure to debate about. "But try it," Ffebi Wiliams said to herself this morning. Her grip on things was tighter than ever. She remembered all the stories she'd ever heard about misers dying, how they gripped more tightly than ever the world they had to leave. She could understand them somewhat today. She never could before. It was easy enough for her and for every preacher who'd ever preached upon the rich young man who went away sorrowful to say and think that losing was something easy. During her life and her husband's in the business, she'd felt many times that the world was going to come down around her head. Today the world was withdrawing from her and leaving her behind.

She heard the sound of dishes clinking in the kitchen, and her mind turned for a minute to her present need—food. Then she remembered how her husband had said they had to sell *everything* but the few things they would need, in order to pay as much as was possible of their debts. She had agreed at the moment—a moment of turmoil, it's true. But in a moment of turmoil there is always a compulsion to decide quickly. By now she would rather be forced to sell the essential things and keep the things that were luxuries. It was the luxuries had given her pleasure in buying them, things she didn't need to have, but things she loved and bought from year to year as their profits grew—an easy chair, an old chest, a clock, or an ornament.

Then came a time of economizing, and there was a stop to that. No money to buy anything. Living on old things. Staying home.

But there was a time, after they'd begun to go down, she went to an exhibition with her husband, because it was a fine day in summer, and they had no hope of being able to go away for holidays. Though fine weather aroused in her a longing for new clothes, still it raised her spirit too. If the sun showed the rustiness of old clothing, it warmed her heart in spite of that. She met an old friend at the show, looking very prosperous, wearing light silk clothes of the latest fashion, while she, Ffebi, was wearing her three-year-old suit.

"Oh, Ffebi, I'm glad to see you," said the friend, and the influence of the sun on Ffebi's heart made her feel the same way.

"You know what?" said the friend. "There are quite marvellous quilts on that stall. Come see them."

And she took her arm and pulled her over there.

There Ffebi had the greatest temptation of her time of economizing, and she wrestled with it as if she were fighting a battle with her enemy. There were beautiful flannels and quilts there, and in the midst of them one quilt that was making everyone's mouth water. Every woman would take it and finger it in going by and cast a yearning look at it in leaving. It was a quilt of thick white wool, with stripes across it, stripes of every colour, blue and green, yellow and red, not stiff and straight, but undulating. Its fringes were thick and a proof of the thickness and the close weaving of the wool. Ffebi was overcome with a longing to buy it, and the more she considered her poverty, the more intense the longing grew.

"But isn't it pretty?" the friend said.

Ffebi didn't say a word, but stood stunned. She left her friend without saying a word and went to look for her husband. She explained to him that she wanted money to buy the quilt at once, for fear that someone else would buy it. Her husband looked displeased though he said nothing. If he'd looked like this in the old days, when they had plenty of money, it would have been enough to stop her from buying the quilt. Her craving today, the craving of a woman on the brink of death, was stronger than any other feeling. She got the money and she bought the quilt. After bringing it home, she put it on the bed, and she felt it on her face to get an idea of how it felt. She'd almost yearned for winter. She remembered now that the quilt was in the chest ready to be sold, and she experienced as strong a craving to keep it as her craving had been to buy it. She decided that the quilt, anyway, would not go to the auction.

At that moment, her husband entered the room with two trays. Breakfast in bed was an absolute luxury for her, but she took it for granted today, and her husband behaved as though he were quite accustomed to bringing her breakfast in bed.

She sat up, the first movement of this body of hers since her husband had gone downstairs, and he sat at the foot of the bed. Neither of them could say much. Indeed, a strange change came over her. The tea was hot and good, and she enjoyed feeling it going warmly through her throat and down into her chest. The bread-and-butter was good too, and thinly sliced. She turned it on her tongue and chewed it a long while. She looked at her husband.

"It's good," she said.

"Yes," he said, "it is. I was thinking I'd sliced too much bread-and-butter, but I don't think I did."

"No," she said, looking at the plate.

Ffebi was feeling wonderfully happy as she ate. She was happy because her husband was sitting at the foot of the bed. He'd never had leisure while in business to sit and eat his breakfast like this. It was always a boat race. Strange that it was today of all days they had the leisure. She was happy eating her food too, tasting its flavour better than she'd ever tasted it, though it was only bread-and-butter and tea. She could rid herself of the thoughts that were wearying her before her husband came up, and feel as she supposed long years ago that she could feel after losing everything. She didn't mind for a minute anyway, and she felt that all the happiness of her life had been compressed into those minutes of eating her breakfast. She felt as if there were no time before it or after it. Yesterday or tomorrow didn't exist. It was the Eternal Moment. And yet what was life all along but thinking about tomorrow? No one would want to go to work or to business if tomorrow didn't exist. But it didn't exist now, anyway, for Ffebi Wiliams. She had gained the upper hand over her grief in those few glorious minutes.

Then the sound of a heavy motor van at the gate. "There is is, it's come," John said, and he hastily took the trays and rushed downstairs. She lay back, slipping into the same apathy as before. She heard the doors open and footsteps walking. There was the sound of moving heard through the house everywhere at once, as it is with furniture movers. The feet of the furniture scraping along the floor and chairs banging against each other. After a moment the sound of feet running up the stairs and their owners whistling pleasantly. In they went to the next room. Then the bed squeaking in there. Ffebi Wiliams leaped out of bed and over to the chest. She pulled the quilt out and took it back to the bed and sat down. She wrapped it around her, putting it over her head. She could see herself in the mirror of the table that stood in the corner.

She was like an old hag, the quilt tight around her face and rising like a little peak on her head. At this moment the door was opened by one of the furniture movers, a young boy. When he saw Ffebi Wiliams in bed this way, he quickly went back out.

After a few moments she heard laughter coming from the far end of the landing.

Red-Letter Day

The ten-shilling note and the first day of summer arrived together the same morning. In a poor, ugly district, where there are more out of work than in, where winter stretches far into spring, both find a welcome. On one of those mornings when the sun flows in through the window after weeks of thin, cold wind, a morning that makes some rejoice because they can wear their new clothes, and that makes others grieve because they have no new clothes to wear, a ten-shilling note came through the post to No. 187, Philip Street, the home of Wat Watcyn and his daughter Rachel Annie, from Wat's brother Mog. Rachel was turned too cold with astonishment to bring the letter up to her father. Four years of living on short rations had paralysed her feelings. She couldn't feel *deep* joy from receiving something she had great need of. Living for years on a quarter of enough had made her insensible to an occasional kindness like this. It would have given her joy in the first months after her father was out of work. By now, she was feeling that ten shillings, with so many holes gaping at her, was only like a pin in a haystack. It was hopeless to begin spending it on the house. It wouldn't buy paper and paint for a single room. It wouldn't buy curtains on the windows or a suit for herself or her father. Then, what point was there in beginning to spend it on necessities? She had to leave the paper on the walls faded and tattered. She had to leave her clothing and her father's threadbare, and leave the traces of mending on the window curtains. Since one couldn't do it all with ten shillings, it was better not to do anything. So Rachel Annie was reasoning.

Her father came down earlier than usual because of the postman's knock, and all his daughter did was point to the letter with the black-lead brush. He didn't say anything after reading it, but went outside the front door to brood and to wait for his breakfast. She knew that his thoughts were the same, and she felt that it wasn't right for two people to be depressed about something which the rest of the street would consider luck, to be celebrated for a month.

For the first time in a long while, Rachel fried bacon for breakfast, and her father didn't ask the reason for having his dinner in the morning instead of the eternal tea and bread-and-butter. As if she were going on with her father's reasoning from the point where he'd finished, she said,

"We'll clear out of here, today, dad, it will do us good."

"Yes, you go," he said.

"No, we both have to go, come to Cardiff with me."

"No, I haven't much appetite for going to Cardiff."

To be honest, she was glad to hear that. It had come to her suddenly, the notion of going to Cardiff, and in a single moment she saw the possibility of a day of pleasure and leaving the mean surroundings that had been here for four years. Just as suddenly she'd worked out her plans for the day, and her father wasn't in them. She'd like to go to Cardiff on her own. She'd love her father to enjoy himself, but if he came with her, she wouldn't have the same freedom to go places according to her own whim. It wasn't that she grudged her father pleasure, but she grudged constraint on her own arrangements. Nevertheless, she saw her pleasure overclouded if her father stayed home. Her selfishness didn't reach so far as to deprive her father of his share in the ten shillings. Again, her mind worked swiftly.

"Why don't you go to Cwm Nedd and see Dan? A chat with Dan will be as good for you as a bottle of medicine."

Her father turned towards her slowly, and in his hesitation his daughter saw a signal of consent.

"Come now, I'll make haste with my work, and you'll have early dinner, so you can catch the one o'clock bus."

"No," he said, and began making a sound in his throat, like the sound of a broody hen, a sound that says "No" but means "Yes".

She interrupted him, using her strongest weapon.

"You have to go, or I won't go to Cardiff."

It was Cardiff drove her on with her work that morning.

"Blast," she said loudly when she saw the fat, shapeless body of Meri Ann Price at the door.

"You're looking very busy," the latter said.

"Yes," Rachel said, "I'm going to Cardiff this afternoon, and I want to finish everything early."

"Some people are lucky," her neighbour said, "they have plenty of ready money."

"No, not plenty, Meri Ann, but my uncle happened to send us ten shillings this morning."

"That's nice; everyone's having better luck than us. What do you suppose the Master did with our Jac in school yesterday; he gave out shoes from the fund, you see, and he gave a new pair to Jac, but he gave the shoes that were on his feet to another lad, and only the day before I'd paid half a crown to have them soled."

"Yes, but Jac got new shoes," Rachel said. "You can't have your cake and eat it, Meri Ann."

"Quite right, but the shoes Jac had, my girl, were much better than these new ones."

"Oh bother," Rachel said to herself, "why won't she and her gabble go away?"

"Oh dear," her neighbour said, "I'd be glad to see some of these pits starting up again. I'd like to have something around instead of bread and margarine. I owe three months' rent and Jenkins sent the final notice this morning. We'll be out on the street, he says. It's nice for you not to have rent to pay, Rachel."

"The rates are high enough," Rachel said, "and if we failed to pay them, the Council wouldn't wait for long, and you wouldn't find anyone now to put up a loan on an old house like this."

"Quite right, but you're able to make a little bit on the sewing, Rachel."

"Yes, and they've trimmed dad's dole because of that; and for another thing I don't get anything from the dole the way a wife does, and you must remember, Meri Ann, that a lot of women get dresses and never think of paying for the making of them."

"I believe you, indeed, Rachel, but I hope you enjoy yourself in Cardiff. It's ten years since I've been there."

And off went Meri Ann, because Rachel's last sentence had stung her. Rachel considered herself lucky, too, that she'd mentioned going to Cardiff in the beginning, or it's likely that her neighbour would have asked for the ten shillings as a loan.

Wat Watcyn easily caught the one o'clock bus for Cwm Nedd, with four shillings in his pocket. Rachel caught the train for Cardiff without much time to spare, with six shillings in her pocket. She was wearing her dark blue coat and skirt and she looked neat, thanks to her own efforts and the fact that she was a seamstress. The suit was old enough to be in fashion for the second time. It had been long to start with, then short, and now long again. It was the skillful hand of its owner concealed the fact that it had gone through these alterations.

It was nice to be able to sit in the train after all the flurry of the morning, with no need to think about anything or to do anything, just letting her mind slip back almost into unconsciousness, but still knowing she was in the train on her way to Cardiff. In a little while, she revived and began gazing at the endless houses as if she'd never seen their like. Her mind began keeping time to the beat of the train engine. "House below house, house above house, how many houses were there? House above house, house below house, who was it owned the house?"

Rachel knew there were three families living in the majority of these houses, and there were rooms in the lowest ones that didn't see the light of day. She and her father had refused to let part of their house. They would rather have peace and live on less.

These houses rose in three stories above their steep gardens, some tidy and some otherwise; gardens in front of some, a patch of wasteland with hens and dogs scratching in it in front of the others; the backs of some houses whitewashed with the wash basin hanging outside the door; clean, tidy curtains on the windows of some; filthy rags hanging by their corners on others.

Many people from Pen y Cwm went down to Bwlch, with their shopping baskets on their arms, and many women came in at Bwlch with similar shopping baskets on *their* arms. Rachel knew that these were going down to Pont, and it's likely that the people of Pont were going down to Cardiff. Strange how the people of the Valley would go from one place to the other to shop at the end of the week. Rachel herself used to go. They believed they were getting bargains, but they weren't. But they got to change places for a while. It was very much like playing draughts. Some of the women were looking worried and depressed and hot in their winter coats. The others looked lively, in spirit and body, dressed in light summer clothing. Some were carrying babies in a shawl, and the babies looked around at the world that was all the same to them.

After the train left Pont, having let many people off there, the horizons widened and the houses became more infrequent until they reached a quite different region. The valleys disappeared from view. Rachel was feeling as though someone had put a lock on the door to the valleys behind her and she was now free from captivity. Instead of pits, houses, and rubbish tips, green fields came into view, low hills with young green trees on them. Everything was so clean. A cold breeze ran through the carriage. It was running through the grass and the leaves of the trees were turned wrong side out so that the lower side looked silvery-grey, like the belly of a fish in sunlight. Rachel changed her seat and turned her back to the engine. She saw the tail-end of the train on the bend it had left a moment before, and beyond the bend a high mountain, which locked the valleys out of sight. The river flowed smoothly, though filthily, past pleasant farms. Clean sheep and lambs were grazing in the fields (cleaner than the ones that came in the mornings to overturn the ash-buckets on Philip Street). The gardens of the houses ran down to the river, and there were yellow, white, and puce flowers hanging on the walls. At Tre'r Eglwys station many fashionable women came in. You could believe there was plenty of money and work for everyone in the world.

There was the zest of the first day of summer in the streets of Cardiff, people were talking and laughing. Everyone was crowding to the shop windows to see the latest frocks and bathing suits and to see the prices of the first strawberries of the season.

After gazing for a long while at shop windows it was restful to be able to sit at a small table in the Elaine, with no need to hurry or to think about washing dishes after a meal; a carpet underfoot, flowers on the tables, and music.

It was enough to make anyone forget who she was. Beautiful young women, well-dressed, came in with their sweethearts. Other women came who were bordering on middle age and who were taking great pains to conceal it. She saw to her delight that she could get a special meal for eighteen pence—tea and bread-and-butter and her choice of a number of things. She chose fresh salmon and cucumber. Food was much cheaper than when she'd been in Cardiff before. She didn't want to hurry, and she wasn't pleased to see the waitress arrive so soon with the tea. She wanted to look around her, wanted to drink in the atmosphere, wanted to feel it was the life of the restaurant that was permanent and not the life of Philip Street, Pen y Cwm. She ate slowly, looking around her. At the table next to her was a woman in expensive clothing. She was fat, and it was obvious that she was having a good deal of trouble keeping her body in proper shape. She was wearing good stays, to Rachel Annie's mind, and she was eating dry toast now and drinking lemon water. Well, everybody's worries weren't the same. Some were fasting by choice and others from necessity.

At another table sat a couple who were none too young—a farmer and his sweetheart, probably. He didn't have much to say. He looked out of place there somehow, as Rachel Annie did to someone else, to be sure. His sweetheart was trying hard to drag conversation out of him. And he'd answer her, and nothing else. He must have more money than talk, or a "smashing" woman like this couldn't have put up with him.

On their left was a woman by herself, in clothes of perfect cut and of good quality. She was a teacher or a doctor, for sure, to Rachel's mind.

The time came, too soon, for her to leave the restaurant, and she began gazing at the shop windows again. There were silks fit for a queen there, and Rachel thought how she could make a beautiful frock from them; and she thought with a pang that she could after all have had material for a frock for the ten shillings. She had enough need of one. But the pang passed— she was glad to see beautiful materials and fashionable frocks—the latter would give her an idea of how to alter some of her old clothing closer to the fashion. After all, she'd rather see pretty things in the windows than ugly things, even though she couldn't buy them. It would have been a very depressing thing to see things for a jumble sale in the windows of Cardiff.

At the market she spent sixpence for a bunch of flowers. How good the smell of the market was—scents of garden vegetables, flowers, cheese, meats, and all kinds of food! How different from the smell of the market in Pen y Cwm, where every Twm, Dic, and Harri was selling all kinds of things called clothing. Ugh—the nasty smell of cheap clothing!

On the way to the station she spent eighteen pence for a pipe for her father.

On the way home there were faint colours, purple, yellow, and red, in the sky, light colours that were casting a sad look on the land. Her mind slipped back to her childhood, when an evening like this would raise fear in her, fear of dying and fear of hell, and that would make her feel estranged from everyone, even from her own family.

What sort of day had her father had? she wondered. She hoped that the visit with Dan would cheer him up a bit and turn his mind to something besides his garden and the fact that he was out of work. His garden was too small, and he didn't want a piece of land. He spent much of his time in it—he watched everything grow and weeds didn't get a chance to show their heads above the ground. There were stones around every path and every bed, and every stone was whitewashed. When he wasn't in the garden he would sit on his heels by the gate to look at it. Rachel would have been glad if her father had taken an interest in something else, in a book or lectures or even greyhounds, as some of his neighbours did. It's true they spent a lot of money, but they weren't forever depressed the way her father was. It's true as well that you couldn't tell whether their gardens were highways or football fields. But—that's the way they were made, and her father was made otherwise, it's likely. He was a collier, first and last. To work his hardest at hacking coal was his pride and joy, and his garden took second place when he was in work. Working in the pit had been his ambition since he was twelve, and he'd never regretted putting clogs on his feet. He was getting on for sixty by now and he knew very well his chance of work was slim. No wonder, then, he was never free of depression.

Indeed, come to think of it, life was a very strange thing. It's true that Rachel and her father and her mother (when she was alive) had had many a time of plenty. They'd never known what hunger was. But neither had they known the pleasant feeling of squandering without sinning. When her father was earning good money during the War, they had to economize to pay for the house. They had to economize to give her sewing school. They'd never been able to feel that they could spend to their heart's content. By now the effect of their economizing was going against them. Her father was getting less from the dole because he owned a house and because she was earning a bit by sewing. She had no hope of marrying, because Enoc, her sweetheart, was also without work. And she didn't want to marry by now. Waiting and waiting had killed every yearning she'd ever had to be a wife.

Her reflections came to an end when she heard the clang-clang of the trams on the streets of Pen y Cwm. She pushed through the crowds towards her home. There was fresh smoke going up through the chimney. Her father was home before her then. There he was, in his shirtsleeves, sitting on the doorstep. The kettle was simmering by the fire and their supper was ready on the table. A little sign like this of her father's kindness went to her heart. She wanted to weep from happiness.

"Well, how did you enjoy yourself?" she said. "How was Dan and the family?"

"Oh, pretty well, indeed. He's complaining because of the long hours and the small wage. But there it is, wherever you go now, people are complaining. Dan is too tired to take his bath, he says, and at the end of the week Jane doesn't know how in the world to divide the money. It's so little."

"But," her father said then, "Dan's able to work," and a second time, shouting loudly, "Dan's able to work." Rachel almost dropped the teapot on hearing her father raise his voice so earnestly.

He didn't want supper, but went out to sit on the doorstep and brood. Rachel was overcome with depression. She wanted to wail loud and long. She didn't have the heart to give her father the pipe. She knew it would give him no comfort while he was in this depressed mood. She put the flowers in water and went to bed. Before drawing the curtains she looked through the window at the thousands of lights up and down the Valley, like thousands of eyes. There was no darkness to be seen anywhere but the darkness of night. The sky was clear above and the stars were out. The valley was pretty at night. A tram was moving in the distance like an awkward animal. She drew the curtains together and went to bed. There it was again—the clang-clang of the trams.

The Last Payment

Yesterday, there'd been the auction of the stock at the smallholding. Today Gruffydd and Ffanni Rolant had moved to the unpropertied house to finish out their lives. Tonight, Ffanni Rolant was standing directly in front of the clock in the new house, making a bow-knot in the ribbon of her bonnet under her chin. She was looking at the hands as a child does in learning to tell how much o'clock it is, as if she weren't very sure of the time. It wasn't her eyesight that was the reason for her uncertain manner, but the importance of the moment. She'd kept busy dawdling over getting dressed for quite a while and now she was ready, but she persisted in dilly-dallying around the clock as if she'd love to postpone the thing. She didn't have to go tonight, of course; tomorrow would do the trick, or next week for that matter. But it was better to get it over with, and in going tonight, she wouldn't break the custom of years of going to pay the shop on Friday pay night. If she didn't go, she'd have to sit in her new house without hearing a cow stirring on the other side of the wall, and think about the old house that she'd been living in for over half a century, and she somehow had to get used to coming to her new house from different directions.

Her husband was sitting by the fire reading, as comfortable as he'd be by the fire in the old house. It was hard to think that it was only five hours since they'd finished moving and arranging the furniture. He read muttering the words quietly to himself, and he was enjoying the warmth of the fire on his legs. The move didn't mean that much to him. He was glad to leave the smallholding and his work. He'd have more leisure to read, and he was able to be unconcerned in leaving the place he'd lived in since the day of their wedding. It wasn't that way for her. From the day they had decided to leave, she'd gone through various experiences of longing and depression and joy. That joy was the cause of this evening's importance. For the first time in her married life she could finish paying her shop bill. She'd do it with money from yesterday's auction.

"I'm going," she said to her husband, folding her string shopping bag, and putting it under her arm beneath her cape.

"All right," he said, continuing to read without raising his head. Strange how indifferent her husband could be. The importance of this moment was nothing to him. Hard to believe he'd had a single great moment in his life, that he'd felt extreme misery or joy. She shut the door with a bang, and she had leisure to think to herself. Tonight was further proof to her that she could best deal with things by herself. Scarcely anyone could understand her thoughts, none of her neighbours or even her husband. Here she was tonight, being able to do the thing she'd been yearning to do for dozens of years at least—have her accounts book stamped "Paid" across it.

When she first married, only Emwnt's Shop existed, and that was in the Lower Village—two miles from her house, and every Friday night she'd trudge down with her bag and her basket and on the fourth week, after Friday pay night, the shop's cart and horse would bring the bags of flour up.

It was about the half-century of that walk Ffanni Rolant was thinking as she pounded her feet on the hard road. She never missed a week except for the weeks her children were born, always every other year. She went through frost and snowdrift, wind and rain, heat and fair weather. She went when she was expecting, and when some of the children were lying, corpses, in the house. She'd had to go and lock the door on everybody in the family sick in bed except herself. She'd had to go on a Friday night when two fine pigs of hers were buried, Gruffydd Rolant having been forced to knock their heads in because they were diseased, and her failing to know where the next rent was coming from. She'd had to go when her husband's wage wasn't enough for her to bother carrying it with her. It's true that she'd also sometimes gone with a cheerful heart at the end of a good month, when she could pay a substantial amount of her bill. But in looking back, those times were few in comparison with the others. It was the monotonous plain of the short end of the month she remembered best.

It was her biography, this road from her house to Emwnt's Shop. In spite of a good wage sometimes she could never clear the tail-end of the debt at the shop. If she could have, it wasn't to the Lower Village she'd have gone tonight, since by now there was an abundance of shops in the Upper Village, every bit as good as Emwnt's Shop and cheaper, but because she could never pay her debt in full, she'd had to pass them every Friday night. Now, when she was seventy-three, for the first time she could buy at one of them. It's true that both ends had been very close to meeting sometimes, but when they were, then illness would come, or death, and drive them further apart. And, confidentially, it must be said that both ends were very close to each other once or twice, and that she could have finished paying her bill.

But Ffanni Rolant had taste, a damnable thing for those who want to pay their way. She knew what linens and woollens were worth. It was a pleasure to watch her fingering them. There was something in her fingertips and in her knuckles that could sense good wool and linen. Her way of handling and fingering materials would make anyone take notice of her. Once or twice, when she was within a little bit of paying her way, temptation came from Emwnt's in the form of a new tablecloth. And she failed to resist it. She saw that cloth on her table at hay harvest, and she bought it. She was remembering these things as she made her way to the Lower Village tonight. She remembered the joy she'd have from buying new things and the disappointment that would come to her monthly from failing to pay her bill. And here she was tonight, going to pay it, after fifty-two years of failing, and not with the money from wages either. She should have been joyful, because some were forced to leave the world with the tail-end of their debt behind them. Indeed she *was* joyful, she'd been joyful for days in thinking about it. But as she neared the shop, she wasn't so certain.

She opened the latch of the half-door that led into the shop, pushed through it, and descended the single step to the floor of the shop, a slate floor and washed clean, but the edges were bluer than the middle.

The sight and the smells were familiar to her—the mingled smells of lamp oil, soap, and tea, with the soap strongest. There was dull light from the lamp that hung from the ceiling, too weak a light to penetrate the corners of the shop. There was grey steam covering the window. This and the feeble light always made Ffanni Rolant feel that the saddest sight in life was a shop in the country.

As usual on Friday pay night the shop was half full, of women mostly, with everybody quiet and strange and distant, as they were on Friday pay night, different from what they were when they'd run in the morning to fetch a treat for "elevenses".

It was all, the silence and the fear, like the communion service, with the shopkeeper at the far end stooping over the books, a white towel as an apron on the front of him. Ffanni Rolant looked around at the long shadows that were cast on the shelves, the gleaming white counter, dented and knotted, the black scales with their iron weights, the black tea chests with the 1, 2, 3, 4 on them in yellow, and the soap in bars. Next week she'd be buying in a shop where there was a red counter, and brass scales and

weights, and the shopkeeper wore a grey coat. No one was saying anything to anyone after the "How are you tonight?" One woman turned to
look twice at Ffanni Rolant because she was wearing a cape instead of a
homespun shawl. Her turn came, and the shopkeeper said nothing to her
as she paid in full. It was as if he understood. He gave her half a sovereign
discount, which astonished Ffanni Rolant. She was expecting to get half
a crown. One thing that hadn't entered Ffanni Rolant's thoughts on her
way down was the fact that she'd paid over two thousand pounds to the
shopkeeper since she married. She bought a few things and paid for them.

"It's likely I won't come down again," she said.

The shopkeeper nodded his understanding. And she walked out of the
shop. She fumbled for the latch, and she latched it carefully after she
reached outside.

She looked through the grey window, and she saw the shopkeeper with
his head bent down once more over someone else's book.

November Fair

There they were, a train compartmentful, with their faces towards November Fair—what was left of it. It was fate threw them all together there like this, until it made them like one family, with each one having his own pleasure in looking forward to November Fair.

In one corner sat Esra (there is no need to give his surname, since nobody used it), wearing a black bowler that tapered to the front and to the back, and a topcoat that had once been black with the border of its velvet collar curling a bit. He was a tall, thin man, with eyes almost too small for you to be able to tell their colour. This was the first time he would be in the Town for a year. He was a farmhand. You couldn't tell what his age was. He could be fifty-five, and he could be thirty-eight.

Beside him sat Gruffydd Wmffras and his wife Lydia—two people about sixty years old, but he was looking better than she was. There was a healthy look on him—his skin weather-coloured and his cheeks red. He'd show two good rows of his own teeth in laughing. He too was wearing a black bowler, a bit newer than Esra's, and a thick black topcoat with a white hair on it. His wife was thin, and had lost many of her teeth without getting them replaced. The dints where her molars had been made her look old. She was wearing a black coat that was in its fourth winter now, and a new black hat that she'd got this year. But the hat didn't look fashionable, because the stack of her hair raised it off her head. Around her neck was a scarf of white lace fastened in front with a brooch.

In the other corner sat Meri Olwen, a neat, handsome girl, about twenty-five years old, wearing a new suit that she'd got at the end of the season. A blue coat and hat, grey silk stockings, and black morocco shoes.

Opposite her on the other seat sat Ben Rhisiart and his wife Linor—a young couple, just married. They'd been courting when they went to November Fair last year. He was a young farmer, farming a farm that his father left him, and his mother was living with him and his wife. His wife and himself were wearing bright, cheap clothing—he wore a cap that came low on his head. She was fair-skinned but toothy, a fact that made her mouth look as though it belonged to someone with a great idea of herself.

Between them and the other door sat Sam, a six-year-old boy, and grandson of Gruffydd and Lydia Wmffras, getting to go to the fair with his grandfather and grandmother for the first time. But already, on his way to the station, he'd attached himself to John, who at this moment was whistling a folk song in the vestibule. John was a thirteen-year-old boy allowed to go to the fair on his own. He was long accustomed to going everywhere on his own, or for the most part, with someone's animals. But today, no one was taking an animal to the fair, so he could go there in the afternoon just like everyone else. He didn't much care to have Sam trailing after him, but still, Sam's grandmother had given him sixpence on the way to the station, and the hint was enough for John.

The inside of the compartment was warm, the two windows were shut to the top, and the steam from the passengers' breath was shrouding the windows. Outside for miles was a bare countryside of farms—the fields perfectly bare, and the houses looking lonely and unsheltered on the hillsides, and from the train like this looking uninteresting to those who didn't live in them. It was nice in the warm train, with the mist on the windows half concealing the greyness of their daily life on the farms. Only John bothered to rub the window, because the only charm of going in a train to him was being able to look out. Inside, everyone was talking about everything, and Sam got more notice than anyone else because he could recite the name of every station to the Town in the proper order. He got pennies from the other passengers for being so knowledgeable.

After reaching the Town, everyone separated. Lydia Wmffras was very eager to have a talk with her sister, whom she hadn't seen for months, and so she asked John whether Sam could go with him. In a weak moment, she'd promised Sam that he could come with her to the Town for November Fair, and by now she'd regretted it, because her sole purpose in coming to town was to be able to see her sister Elin, who was living too far away for her to see her often.

As for Gruffydd Wmffras, he was coming to the fair to look around and see who he could see. In the time gone by he'd come with cattle in the morning, though he sometimes would have only a barren cow and a calf or two. But now it wasn't worth coming such a distance. No one would ask what a cow was good for at a fair. But he needed to be able to come to the Town, and he began to ramble through the Square. There were plenty of people there, and plenty of motors with their noses all pointed the same way like a lot of greyhounds ready to start a race. He felt fine in being in the midst of plenty of people, and he wanted to talk to everyone. After dawdling and having a word with this man and that, he saw at last the one that he most wanted to see—Huw Robaits.

"Did you catch the fair this morning?" Gruffydd asked.

"Catch what?"

"Catch the fair?"

"You can't possibly catch something if it isn't there."

"There wasn't any fair, then?"

"There wasn't one animal here on this Square today. Do you smell the scent of a horse or a cow here? Not a chance! You have to go to Tom Morgan's sale to see a cow these days."

Gruffydd was surprised.

"I don't know what the world is coming to, indeed," the latter said.

"Well, we'll all go to the Workhouse together, that's a comfort," Huw said.

"Have you begun slaughtering some of your animals?"

"No, not yet. Have you?"

"Yes; I slaughtered two lambs last week, but I won't slaughter any again. The butchers are raising too much of a row."

"You'll come for a pint to cheer up, old boy?"

And they went to a quiet tavern in Tre'r Go.

.   .   .

Elin, Lydia's sister, was waiting for her by the motor. Neither one of them had written to the other to say whether they would be in town or not. Each took it for granted that the other would be there.

"Your train was late," Elin said first thing.

"No, indeed; your motor was early. How are you, tell me?"

"Oh, all right I suppose, considering how poor a world it is. I want to buy a hat. Will you come with me?"

"Yes," Lydia said, with her heart in her boots, because she knew what sort of afternoon she would have with Elin.

"We'll go to the Golden Ewe," the latter said, "there are more hats there to suit someone like me. Tell me, are you getting much of a price for your milk?"

"Sixpence a quart; the same as the summer."

"You're lucky. A groat, that's what we're getting over there."

"How's that?"

"Some foreign old things came there and started selling it for a groat. It isn't worth your taking a horse out of the stable to set out with it."

Within a quarter of an hour Lydia and Elin were in the middle of a sea of hats in "The Golden Ewe".

"That one suits you splendidly, Mrs. Jones," the shop girl said about every hat that Elin tried on, with Lydia on the other side making faces and shaking her head to show that she didn't agree.

After she'd tried about fifteen, there was a somewhat frustrated look on Elin, so that it made you feel sorry for her.

"I don't know who'd ever buy a hat," Elin said. "They're making hats now for some old girls with bold faces, and not thinking of anyone who's beginning to get on in years."

"That's quite a pretty one," Lydia said. "That looks very good on you"— though it didn't look much better than the one before.

"You think so? Look, Miss, don't you have anything like the one my sister has? Where do you get your hats, tell me, Lydia? You have the prettiest hat on."

"You wouldn't need to cut your hair." And the two of them were close to quarrelling. At last Elin found a hat to please her for fifteen and eleven. And Lydia criticized her sister on the quiet for paying so much. Six and eleven her own had cost.

"Oh dear," Lydia said, after leaving the shop, yawning, "I need a cup of tea. Will you come and have it now, Elin?"

"Yes. We'll go to Jane Elis' restaurant in Pen Deits."

And there they went. It was beginning to grow dark by now. The dining-room of the restaurant was perfectly empty. A sluggish fire was burning in the grate. There were clean white cloths on every table, and the pepper-and-salt holder was shining even though it was yellow.

"How are you today, each of you?" Miss Elis said. "A heavy old day, isn't it? Have you been at the fair? If you can call that a fair. November Fair isn't what it was long ago. What would you like? Will you have a bit of hot beef with tea?"

"What do you say, Lyd?"

"Yes; hot beef with gravy would be quite nice."

"I wouldn't give a thank-you for a tea with some old cakes," Elin said. "Tell me, have you heard how Bob's wife Lora is?" (Bob was their brother.)

"I had a letter the day before, saying that she has terrible complaints. Bob's forever the one milking and doing everything outside."

"Bob had the luck of the draw when he had Lora."

They'd finished putting them in their places before Gruffydd and Huw Robaits arrived there.

"Who wants to treat me to tea?" Huw Robaits said playfully.

"Yes," Elin said, "it wouldn't be much for you to treat us all, Huw Robaits. I never get a dram or anything from anyone now."

"Here's someone will treat you, Elin," Gruffydd Wmffras said, on seeing Esra putting his head past the door. "It's the old bachelors have money now."

And the five of them drank tea and ate hot meat and gravy for a long while.

Before going to the restaurant Esra had been walking the streets of the Town aimlessly. That was what he did every November Fair Saturday. He was a man too lacking in conversation to talk to much of anyone. He had neither friends nor sweetheart. Had it been possible to win the latter without talking, he would have tried to win the woman he saw in the Town every November Fair. He didn't rightly know who she was. He had a notion that she was in service somewhere. But once he had ventured to strike up a conversation with her, and it was always the same after that.

"How are you today?"

"Very well, thanks."

"It's a nasty old day, isn't it?"

"Yes."

"Have you been at the fair?"

"No."

"There isn't much of anything at all to see there."

"There isn't, is there? Well, I must go."

And Esra would never have enough heart to ask her to come and have tea with him or for a walk. He'd seen her again this year, and the conversation had been the same. But Esra hadn't gained enough strength to ask her. By the time he reached the restaurant he was quite glad that he wouldn't have to pay for anyone's tea but his own. He had a bit of a fright when Gruffydd Wmffras suggested playfully that he treat them all to tea. He was one of those people who are too tight-fisted to enjoy frivolous talk about money.

.   .   .

After leaving the station Meri Olwen walked straight to Huw Wmffras' old shop, where she was to meet her sweetheart, Tomos Huw. He was a quarryman, living eight miles from the place where she was a maidservant. Meri Olwen preferred that Tomos Huw live as far from her as that, because she had ideals. And one of those ideals was that you had better not see your sweetheart too often—as one would if he were living in the same village. She was a good girl for any mistress. She would work unmercifully between every two turns of courting so that the time would go by swiftly, and because she knew that she'd be sure to enjoy herself when a courtship evening came. It was only work could make her forget her yearning to see Tomos. And yet, she was certain in her mind, should she see Tomos often, this yearning would lessen, and so she would have less pleasure when she was in his company.

All the way on the train she was scarcely able to conceal her craving to see Tomos, and when she walked over the Bont Bridd, she was feeling almost ill for fear that Tomos wouldn't be there.

Yes, he was there, talking and fooling with three girls, with the girls laughing at the top of their voices and drawing everybody's attention to them. Meri Olwen stood still. Something cold went over her. Tomos was enjoying himself enormously. He was trying to steal a card that was in the hand of one of the girls, and she was refusing to give it to him. He was able to catch a glimpse of it at last, but not without the girl tugging at it many times. Tomos laughed loud and long after seeing what was on the card, and as he gave it back to the girl his eyes fell on Meri Olwen, and his face settled down. He left the girls unceremoniously, and came to Meri.

"Hullo, Meri, how are things? Your train was early, wasn't it?"

"No earlier than usual."

"Where shall we go?"

"I don't care in the least where."

"Come for tea now?"

"No, I prefer to have it later."

"We'll go for a stroll to the Quay then."

Meri Olwen's heart was like a piece of ice, and her tongue had stuck to the roof of her mouth.

"You're very quiet today."

"There's need for someone to be quiet, since some can make so much of a row."

"Who's making a row now?"

"You and those girls just now."

"A person has to have a bit of a lark sometimes—if you'd seen the funny postcard someone had sent to Jini."

"I don't want to hear anything about it."

"Tut, you're much too solemn."

"Yes; mercifully, I could never fool with boys like that."

"Oh! jealousy, I see."

And Meri Olwen wasn't able to give him any answer, because he'd spoken the truth.

She went ahead, with him trailing after her.

"You'd better go back to your Jini, with her filthy jokes."

Tomos stood there, bewildered. He'd never heard Meri Olwen talk this way before. She was one of the mildest persons.

She walked on and on. She was pounding her heels heavily on the ground, and she found herself within an hour in a village she didn't know. There she began to feel cold. How much she'd looked forward to this day for a fortnight! It wasn't often she could afford to come to the Town. She'd looked forward not only to seeing Tomos, but also to having tea with him in Marshalls, and being able to show people like Ben and Linor, who had just married, that she too was on the way to doing that. But now her ideal was shattered. She walked back to the Town slowly, crestfallen. She didn't go anywhere to have tea. She went to the waiting room of the station to wait for the seven-o'clock train.

.　∎　.

Ben Rhisiart rushed out of the station and ran directly to the football field. The Town was playing against Holyhead. He was to meet Linor in Marshalls by tea-time. Linor walked slowly along the street and looked at the window of every shop. She had a longing for every grand article of clothing she saw. She'd be on the brink of going in to buy a blouse or a scarf when she'd remember that she couldn't afford them. After reaching the druggist's shop she went straight in without a second thought, and bought face powder and a bottle of scent. She walked on slowly afterwards, expecting to see some of her old friends. She'd looked forward to seeing some of them today; not that she wanted to talk to them as old friends, but because she wanted to make their mouths water as a young married woman. But she saw none of them. She caught a glimpse of Tomos Huw running to catch one of the motors on the Square, with his face very red. But he didn't see her—and that was a pity, because she'd have been glad if he'd seen her.

Tired of walking around, she went into Marshalls to sit down and wait for Ben. She felt contented there. Could walk on carpet and look at nice food and flowers and plenty of people. How different from the food she usually had. Her pastry crust was never a success. It was tough as an old shoe. And how should one expect it to be otherwise with the oven broken? And not a chance of mending it while her mother-in-law kept saying it was fine; that it had baked very well for her that way for the last twenty years. Perhaps it did bake bread; but then, why would anyone go baking bread, with the bread wagon calling every day? But as for pastry crust, you couldn't buy that in the country. But today, anyway, she could have tiny pink and yellow pastries, crusts as if they'd been puffed up, with cream inside them. Oh, she was happy—except when she'd remember her mother-in-law. That was the only thorn. Her words today, before they set off, were grating in her ears. "I don't know what's got into you wanting to go to the fair, indeed, with times so bad. And another thing, there isn't any winter fair now, the way there was long ago. There's no home-made cheese, or seed-buns, or griddle-cakes, or anything like that, or anyone like the Bardd Crwst singing ballads." A nuisance, that's what her mother-in-law was, to tell the truth, always talking about "long ago" and spouting proverbs against the extravagance of this age. What if she knew that her daughter-in-law had face powder in her bag now? And what if she knew that Ben would be paying some four shillings for tea for two? Presently Ben came, and many others with him, until they almost filled the room. The atmosphere was warm, and the electric light was shining dazzlingly on the aluminium teapots.

Ben hadn't much enjoyed himself at the football field. The old fiery spirit that once existed between this town and Holyhead had died.

The two of them enjoyed their tea.

"What do we want to do now?"

"We may as well finish it off, and go to the pictures," Linor said.

"I'd thought to go home with the seven-o'clock train."

"Tut, come to the pictures. Perhaps we won't be down again for a long while."

And so it was agreed.

.   .   .

John wasn't very pleased that Sam's grandmother had attached the latter to him for the entire afternoon. John had his own ideas about spending a day at a fair. Half the fun was getting to be there on his own, without anyone to interfere with him, and being able to test his knowledge of geography where he was completely ignorant of it a few years ago. But now he had to look after Sam, and he was too little to be able to admire John's extensive knowledge of the streets of the Town. The two of them followed their noses until they reached the Square. There was nothing at all new there to John. The only difference between this and any other Saturday was that there was a pull-away stall, and it was for this he was aiming. But Sam wanted to stand at the dish stall so he could see the man rap and fling the plates and yet not break them.

"I want to buy a plate to take home to mam," Sam said.

"You'd much better take her indian rock," John said; "she has plenty of plates." In spite of all his knowledge, John didn't rightly know how to bargain at a sale.

"Look," he said to Sam at the pull-away stall, "try aiming at the biggest piece there."

And Sam took a hot, sweaty penny from the middle of a fistful of pennies and gave it to the woman. Sam's tug was very weak, and the ball fell by a thin, slight piece of indian rock. John tried, and he got a thick piece. Sam insisted on trying again on seeing John's luck, but it was a thin one he got that time.

"Come away," John said, "or you'll spend all your money, and we have to get chips before going home."

They went to the Quay, and Sam was insisting on eating his indian rock that minute.

"Leave it, lad, or you won't have any to take home to your mother."

But Sam didn't listen.

"This is the best shop in town for chips," John said, after they arrived at a shop in ——— Street.

He made Sam sit at a table there as if he were at home, and he took off his cap.

"What do you want?" said the waitress.

"Threepenny worth of chips for me, and two for him," John said.

"No; I want threepenny worth," Sam said, and began acting up.

"Oh, all right," John said. "Mind that you don't leave a single one."

Sam was groaning long before he finished his threepenny worth, and he began to droop. In a little while something strange happened to John's eyes. He was looking at Sam, and he saw his face was green.

"What's the matter with you?" he said to Sam.

"Need to puke," he said.

And at the word there Sam was, throwing up.

"Oh! you bad-mannered little brats," the waitress said when she arrived.

"He couldn't help it, indeed," John said, with Sam crying his eyes out by now.

"Never mind; we'll go look for your grandmother," John said.

And they found her as she was coming out of the restaurant in Pen Deits.

John went off to enjoy the rest of his day as he wished, and you could have seen him after a while gazing at the rabbits and the birds in the market gallery of Llofft yr Hôl.

.   ▪   .

It was a quite worn-out little band that gathered together to meet the seven-o'clock train. Lydia and Gruffydd Wmffras were looking extremely happy; Meri Olwen miserable, and Sam pale and quiet. John was whistling by the book stall. Esra was an entirely different man. He'd had three pints after the pubs re-opened. This was his only luxury in a whole year. He came towards the others mumbling a song, with his hat tipped back and his face sweating.

"Hullo, old love; where's your sweetie this winter fair evening?" he said to Meri Olwen.

Esra grasped her head and turned it towards him. On seeing Esra, the silent man, so talkative, and seeing the strange look on him, Meri Olwen began laughing uncontrollably.

"You have a sweetheart?" Esra said. At that the train came in. Everybody rushed for a place.

And in the rush Esra took hold of Meri Olwen, and pulled her into a compartment apart from the others.

In the moving-picture house, Ben and Linor were slouching together, totally lost in a picture that showed the night life of New York, beautiful women in expensive clothing imbibing drinks whose names Ben and Linor had never heard of, with affectionate men gazing deep into their eyes.

They didn't remember there was such a thing as a train.

The Condemned

He had asked the doctor, and by now he was sorry. He didn't know what had made him ask and insist on knowing. It wasn't courage, certainly, because he loved life and feared dying. He was afraid of the nothingness of dying. When the doctor said he could leave the hospital ten days after coming there, through some perverse instinct, because he was afraid of knowing the worst, Dafydd Parri pressed him to know why. When he heard that his case was hopeless, that the growth inside him had become too bad—if only the doctor could have caught it two years earlier—an empty feeling crept down his body from head to foot. When he came to his senses, he regretted that he hadn't died in that feeling.

The first longing that came to him afterwards was to go home to Laura. The surprise was that he could think at all. How was he able to breathe? How was he able to walk or anything after hearing such news? How could he sleep that night? And yet, he slept. His journey home the next day was worse than a nightmare; it was closer to madness. How different from the journey to Liverpool ten days before! He'd had hope then, despite being afraid. There was one element of pleasure in his journey back. It was towards home he was going, and not away from home. It was the craving to reach home that drove him almost mad when the train would wait for a long time at a station. He supposed his brain was muddled, but he'd be all right again after he got home to Laura. Yes, he'd almost say that everything would be as before, that he himself would be exactly the same, without the knowledge he'd had from the doctor. That was entirely the feeling he'd had when he heard the news, of something filling him and smothering him. He'd feel free, fine, after he reached home, and had the same hope he'd had before, with the visit to Liverpool and the doctor's verdict nothing but a dream.

In the meantime, Laura had been seeing their own doctor. He'd had the verdict of the doctor from Liverpool, and to show Laura his cleverness, he told her straight out that her husband would not recover, and that the specialist's opinion was completely the same as his own. The news had a different effect on Laura than on her husband. She became stubborn, and she was infuriated, and she told herself there was very little doctors could do, and once she had Dafydd in her hands *she* would make him better.

When she saw Dafydd, she was not as certain. She supposed that the doctor could be right. But that feeling soon went away. By the next morning, either Dafydd looked a little better to her, or his wife was deluded into thinking that that was how he was before going away. She still had, in any case, the belief that doctors are fallible beings, and that turned into hope for herself, the only thing that kept her going on as before and accepting life in its uncertainty.

Dafydd came home like a guilty man coming from prison. He didn't want to see anyone, and he didn't want anyone to see him. The kitchen of Bron Eithin was looking as it sometimes did on Sunday, or on the day of someone's funeral, when strangers were expected to tea, the best dishes on the table, and a Sabbath tidiness on everything, though it was Wednesday; and Laura in her best blouse and her white apron as if she were serving at the head of the table at Monthly Meeting. It wasn't to a Wednesday night Bron Eithin Dafydd Parri came, but to a strange Bron Eithin.

Next morning, it was the sound of his two sons talking quietly to their mother as they ate their breakfast that woke him. He couldn't define his feelings. This was something very unnatural, because he would be closer to the quarry than to his house at the time his boys were eating their breakfast. Still it was nice to be at home and wake up at leisure, rather than be in hospital, where a person was awakened suddenly from a nice sleep at half-past-five. After the boys set off, and the scurrying sound of the last laggards among the quarrymen died out on the road, Laura poked her head in at the bedroom door.

"Are you awake?" she said. "I was here before, but you were sleeping then. Did you sleep pretty well?"

"Yes, quite well," he said, and glad to be able to say that to Laura and not to the nurse.

"I'll bring you a cup of tea now," she said cheerfully; and in no time she was back with a cup of tea and a slice of toast on a tray. She stayed there while he ate.

"Does it taste all right?" she said.

"It's very good," he said, looking out through the window to the field. And he greatly enjoyed his breakfast.

This first day after coming home, he felt all day long that nothing special had happened, and that he was home as on Sunday, but that everybody else was working. He was glad to be at home with Laura, instead of being in the confinement of the hospital. This day, he was like a prisoner the first day after coming out of prison, glad of his freedom, and unable to look into the future because of the joy of being free. The doctor in Liverpool and his verdict were far off and insubstantial things. Everything was fine now that he'd come to Bron Eithin and to Laura.

But after a day or two Dafydd Parri returned to being himself, the Dafydd Parri he was when he'd work every day at the quarry, before leaving it for the hospital, and he began to fidget, if a sick man's discontent could be called fidgeting. Before going to Liverpool he'd felt fairly strong, in spite of having pains. He was weaker by now, and his discontent was more yearning than fidgeting.

It was hard on him to be forced to stay in bed, and listen to his friends going to the quarry. He'd hear them climbing the hillside past the gable-end of his house, with their slow, heavy gait, and the low sounds of early morning. He'd hear them again at nightfall with their quick, steady pace and their loud cheerful voices. On quarry days, the discussion would often be unfinished when he'd turn in at his gate from his fellow-workers, but it was a hard thing to find yourself left out of the discussion altogether. He was longing for a chat with the lads in the hut at dinner time. Jac Bach talking about his dogs, and Dafydd Bengwar about his canaries. Dafydd found it most entertaining to hear Wil Elis, who dealt in cattle a bit, telling stories, half of which you could venture to say were lies. But no matter; some people's lies were more interesting than other people's truth. And it was at the quarry he'd get all the news, true and false, about people. One could get more "tales" about people in the quarry than in the house.

Now Dafydd Parri had to spend his time in the house and not the quarry. His world became narrow and new. A house to him before was a house after finishing a day's work, a house warm with the events of the day. He knew it only, except on Saturday afternoon and Sunday, as a place you returned to after a day of work to sit down and eat in and read a newspaper by the fire. And that sort of house was different from the house he must get to know now—a house going through the different states a house goes through from five in the morning till ten at night.

He would most often wake in the morning with a bad taste in his mouth. He'd hear Laura blowing the fire, and as usual in the morning, the gasps of the bellows, long and deep. He'd smell the scent of the heather faggot that was used to light the fire, and he could imagine the soft white smoke going thickly up through the chimney. Presently, he'd hear Laura moving the kettle, and he'd hear it begin singing shortly after, and she'd bring him a cup of tea and a piece of bread-and-butter. She'd move back the window curtains, and then she'd be on the go early. She'd leave the bedroom door open, and he could hear the boys talking as they ate their breakfast. He could see a little of the kitchen too, and as he looked at it over the bedside it looked unnatural, as if he were seeing it in a mirror. Around nine, after finishing with the cows and the pigs, Laura would bring him a little Scotch broth, and she'd have time to sit down and relax with him then. He'd get up a little before dinner, and the hearthstone would be just washed, and the edge of the slate could be seen drying in streaks. Laura took care to have a comfortable hearth for him every day by the time he got up.

Dafydd would wash himself deliberately and carefully on getting up. He had a habit of rubbing the towel between his fingers, and he noticed that his hands became cleaner day by day, and that the seam of grey from the quarry dust was disappearing from between his fingers.

Some days Laura would be busy baking when he got up, and he liked to see the bread rising for the second time in the iron pans by the oven bakehole, and the firelight as it came from the hole striking the dough and making a semicircle of light on it, with a few hot cinders sometimes falling on it and giving it savour.

The atmosphere would change by the afternoon. The whole house would be clean, and more activity could be felt in the air. The tranquillity of the morning was gone, and though the tranquillity of the country was there, yet one could sense more sound even there in the afternoon. Laura would beg him to go for a walk around the fields or along the road. He never wanted to go.

"Go; it'll do you good," Laura said, and she believed it.

And he'd go, little by little, after throwing an old coat around his neck, as he'd sometimes done on coming from the quarry, and fastening it with a sack-pin. Laura would look after him, and see one of his shoulders rising higher than the other because of the coat, and she'd go into the house sighing. He didn't have much pleasure in going for a walk. He'd sit on a pile of stones in the corner of a field under a thorn to shelter from the thin breeze of April, and he'd let the sun fall on his face. On the other side of the dyke he'd hear the cow grazing, by turns munching the hay and snorting, and the smell of its wet nostrils would come through the dyke.

Different corners of fields gave him different feelings. They always had. Without any particular reason some fields made him melancholy, and others cheered him up. He didn't know why. Indeed, there was no reason why, only his state of mind, but that state was always just the same in the same field. He avoided those fields now. The earth was hard and colourless. Stones mixed with lumps of dry dung all over it. Someone would have to gather up the stones, but not him. Though it was such a disagreeable task, he'd have been happy to be able to do it this year. He'd never go to the road for a walk if he could help it. There were people there, and people ask questions that a sick man doesn't want to answer.

In the house with Laura, that's where he liked to be. After a while the house and Laura became an essential part of him, as the quarry was before. He gave up asking his sons how things went at the quarry. When his friends would come there to visit him, mentioning the quarry gave him too much pain at the beginning. But gradually his interest in it lessened, and he stopped asking. He became used to being home.

He began thinking more about Laura. He wondered, did she know the doctor's verdict? He didn't want to ask her, for fear that by some sign she'd betray the fact that she knew. Hearing the verdict for the second time, and in his own home, would have been too much for him. He'd be forced to go through the same feeling as he'd gone through the first time he heard, and he was too cowardly for that. He didn't have any feeling at all about the doctor's verdict by now. The disturbance of that moment had worn off, and he didn't feel sick enough at this time to relive that moment or to think about his end. There was pleasure in life as it was now. Having a cup of tea with Laura around three o'clock, and on baking day a dough cake with currants in it, hot. The doctor had said that he could eat anything.

He wondered, how much did Laura know? She looked as if she didn't know a thing. She went about her work cheerfully, as usual, and she talked to him about things on the farm and things in the district. Sometimes he'd catch her looking at his face and at his eyes in the light, as if she were examining his colour. Laura became closer to him and came to mean more to him than she had since their courting days. She was a pretty little lass, then, with her curly auburn hair, and indeed, she carried her age very well now, though she was fifty-five, the same age as himself. He remembered the time he first saw her, the day of May Fair, when she was changing her situation, and when he was in town with his father selling a cow. He remembered how he made a fool of himself over her till she promised to marry him. He'd go to see her every chance he'd get, and he'd see her before his eyes everywhere all day long. After they were married, the smallholding and putting their lives in order had taken up their time altogether, and as is often customary with country people, they supposed there was no need to show love after marrying. Live was what people did after marrying, not love. She, and he too, would sometimes quarrel, and since they weren't passionate people they'd become friends again in a calm unruffled way, by talking about the pigs or the cows, and there'd be no going back to the cause of their quarrel. There'd never be the place or the time, somehow, to talk affectionately. There was work in the fields after coming from the quarry in spring and summer, and there were endless meetings in chapel in winter, and there was no time for anything but to read a newspaper.

Now, Dafydd was sorry that he hadn't given more time to talking with Laura. How much better it would have been by now; that tenderness would have stayed with her after he'd gone, something to be remembered. In looking back at their life, what had they had? Only a cold unruffled life, reaching the highpoint of pleasure when the end of the month was pretty good. They didn't come closer together when the wages were small. Indeed, a poor month would make them silent and indifferent. He wanted to set the past right now. He wanted to enjoy life at home like this with Laura, to go for a spin around Anglesey by car, the two of them. They'd never got about much after marrying. Always waiting for a better time, and letting life go by without seeing the world. Yes, it was nice in the house with Laura. He loved to look at her; he knew now, what he hadn't known before, how many buttons were on her bodice, what the pattern of her homespun kerchief was, the number of pleats in her apron. A pity it couldn't be like this forever. But he just began to realize this, when his pains began to increase. He couldn't enjoy his food as much; there wasn't as much pleasure in looking at the bread rising by the fire, or in smelling its aroma as it baked. When he was on the brink of losing something, he'd begun to enjoy it. He saw the Indian Summer of his illness slipping away from him. He was unable to get up for dinner, and a longing for the hearth-stone came on him. He'd get up sometimes at nightfall so that he could sleep better. The pains increased. He couldn't take notice of things around him. The doctor came there more often, and gave him medicines to ease his pains. He'd go to sleep, and he'd be sick and depressed after waking up. He'd go into a trance sometimes. He'd forget things around him. What did he care about the doctor from Liverpool by now? It was his sickness was important, not the doctor's verdict. The verdict had nothing to do with his sickness. He had enough to do to think about his sickness without thinking about what the doctor had told him in the hospital. What he wanted was to be rid of a little bit of the pains so he could talk to Laura. She was by his bed every chance she had. Sometimes he'd have a better day, and he'd get up in the afternoon, but he didn't enjoy his tea. But in a little while he became so that he couldn't get up at all, and Laura would leave him only when he slept.

And on that hay harvest day in July he was very ill. Outside, neighbours were carrying his hay, with him too ill to take any interest in that. He didn't care this year whether he had a big rick or a small rick, whether the hay was good or poor. He was conscious of the coming and going of people back and forth to the house to have food. He was more awake than usual, and he had more need of Laura. She was there as often as she could be, continually running back and forth from the dinner-table to the bed. He wanted to speak to her, wanted to talk about their courting days, when they'd go for a walk along the White Road, and see lapwings' nests in the crannies of the mountain. He wanted to talk about the time he first saw her at the fair, when she was so downhearted about changing her place. How happy those days had been when they could hug each other tightly in returning from the Literary Meeting of the Graig! What a good time they'd had in returning from Preaching Meeting, when he'd been on fire from wanting the preacher to finish, and found himself looking more often at Laura than at the preacher! He wanted to tell her all these things. Why hadn't he told them to her those afternoons when they'd have tea together? Why was his shyness lessening as his body weakened? The next time that Laura came to the bedroom he'd insist on telling her.

When she came, the last meal was over, and there was tranquillity in the house. They couldn't hear any of the noise in the rickyard behind the house. The smell of hay was coming into the bedroom through the window. There was the smell of sickness on the bed, and an unpleasant taste in Dafydd's mouth. He was lying back, with pillows behind him. Laura came in.

"Will you have a little bit of something to eat?" she said. "Everybody's cleared out of the house now."

"No," he said, "I can't eat now." And he added: "I'm getting weak, you see."

But after saying that, he observed Laura, and he saw the trace of much crying on her tired face. He looked at her.

"Laura," he said, "what is it?"

"Nothing," she said, turning her face aside.

He took hold of her, and he turned her towards him, and in her look he saw the knowledge the doctor had given him. He couldn't put a sentence together. He couldn't remember what he wanted to tell her, but he held her, and he hugged her to him, and she felt his hot tears running down her cheek.

Protest March

After she finished buttoning her coat, Bronwen looked at her feet. Then she turned her head over her shoulder to see was there a hole in her stocking, and raised her heel to see how long her shoe would hold out without being heeled. Then she looked at the place that had worn thin around the pocket of her coat. She was doing all this in the manner of someone conscious of her poverty and wanting to look neat.

Idris, her husband, was sitting on a hard chair on the hearth, with his head down, looking into the fire the way men do who are on the outs with the whole world. That was to be seen in his profile and in his posture. In talking to his wife he would address the spot where she was standing or the fireplace, not her.

Bronwen was setting out to march with the United Front against the Means Test, her husband having refused to come. She still had hope. His had turned sour. The couple were only twenty-five years old, and they hadn't seen a halfpenny of wages since they'd been married. They were living in an underground kitchen, a kitchen that had once belonged to the house above, and their bedroom was the kitchen pantry. For this they were paying six shillings a week in rent. Bronwen was anxious as she said what she'd always say on leaving the house.

"Well, I'm going, then."

"Yes, I'll bet you are; you're stupid enough to listen to the fools. I'm telling you that it's a fraud, the bloody lot of them, and you're wasting your time and your shoe-leather to go listen to such rubbish. United Front! United like hell! They'd like to break each other's necks. Look at how the Labour Party's looking down their noses at the Communists, and then they go accusing the Labour Party of selling jobs for money, and if they'd half a chance to sell a job themselves, they would. A lot of good your marching will do, I'll tell you. And it's no use your coming back here with a headache after listening to their screaming."

He got up as he said the last sentence. He tightened the belt of the grey trousers that were too big for him and came down over his shoes. He gave himself another shake, turned on his heel and went past the curtain into the next room, and lay down on the bed.

Bronwen stood looking at him. She was close to taking off her coat and staying home. But when she thought of spending Sunday afternoon in this hole, her hope had a second boost. She looked at her husband lying in the black windowless hole that was called a bedroom. He lay coiled like a cat on top of a haystack, and to her the turn in his back was an expression of all his sourness and bitterness against life as a whole. She turned on her heel and walked out, and as she went further away from her husband she cheered up. As she went past the ash heaps and the clutter in the back street her hope was on the increase, and by the time she reached the high street with its larger and cleaner houses she was feeling staunch in her hope in the United Front.

It was a warm, tranquil day at the beginning of October, and its effect on people's hearts was like the effect of a day in Spring. There were many others walking ahead of her on their way to the same place, and she was hoping she wouldn't catch up with them so that she could create dreams of her future with Idris; work, wages, better clothes, a house like the ones that she was passing now, children. In a little while she reached the crest of the hill that separated Little Cwm Du from Big Cwm Du. She leaned on the wall to look at the two valleys—the row houses placed like regiments of soldiers along the sides of the hills, with their windows in the sunlight looking like bright buttons, the river between them like a narrow ditch. If the knowledge had been handed down to her by her family or her school she would have known that it was on this spot her great-grandfather and her great-grandmother stood seventy years before, to have the first look at the place that was home to them and their children the rest of their lives. There they had stood, after travelling in a cart from Carmarthenshire, their furniture and their children lying under sacks in the cart, getting their first look at the promised land they'd heard so much about while living in poverty as farmhands and servant-girls. Bronwen didn't know, as she fondled her own hopes now, anything of the hopes of her ancestors on the threshold of their new world. She knew nothing of their homesickness, their joy and their trials later, or she could have blended her dreams of her own future with those of the past. All she knew was that her own parents had had a better time than she was having now. She couldn't see why better times shouldn't come again, and certainly, to her mind, protesting like this against the injustice of the Means Test was certain to lead somewhere. Things couldn't be like this forever.

She set off again, and walked light-heartedly past houses without signs of poverty on them. She couldn't stop herself from looking into them and gaping at the sideboards' mirrors that were reflecting the silver dishes on their tables. She too would have ones like that sometime. Her eyes turned at times to the trees that surrounded the manager's mansion. What struck her most were the colours of the trees and not the mansion. She didn't envy the manager because of his big house. It was in too lonely a place, and she, who was raised in the neighbourly warmth of Cwm Du, couldn't think of living apart like that. But the trees were pretty. A pity their leaves were falling. They whirled and spun into the corners as she turned into the high street of the other valley.

After reaching the field from which the march was supposed to start she saw a crowd of a size that she'd never seen. She imagined the whole population of the Valley was there, men, women, children, and dogs. It was like a sea in motion, and the talking like its monotonous murmur, except that the carefree laughter of the young sometimes interrupted it. In a little while, a number of men went on top of a dray, and one of them began addressing the crowd. A shiver went down Bronwen's back, that shiver which is an expression of something one can't define, when a person sees a great throng hanging on the words of one man. This man had a narrow chest, and there was a terrible strain on his body in addressing the crowd. His words were coming as though from the depths of his guts, and he was bending and raising his arms as if that would be a help to lift the words up. Every now and then a groan would come from the depths of his being at the tail-end of a word. He stood above the crowd, and he addressed it as though he were its father. Everyone was drinking in his words.

There wasn't as fatherly a look on the next speaker, or as many scars on his face. But the stream of his words ran on unbroken. They ran over Bronwen's head as well. She didn't know what he had to say, but evidently everyone thought the language of the gods was on his lips. The only word that stuck in her mind was the word "proletariat", and she didn't know the meaning of that.

The crowd formed a procession, and pushed itself from the field to the street. Bronwen found herself marching side by side with a number of fat toothless women, much older than she was. They had one thing in common—poor clothing. But these women could laugh pleasantly. Perhaps their husbands were more contented than her husband, or perhaps they didn't have a husband. Her forehead wrinkled as she remembered Idris and the stubborn turn in his back. She forgot him in hearing the tramp of the feet on the hard road. She had a shiver of pleasure again in seeing the great crowd marching so united in its determination against that invisible thing that was responsible for all their poverty—the Government. A pity the Government wasn't seeing this crowd. She believed they would get what they were after, and more. These old pits would be opened again, and she'd have a house like her mother at least. They were going past similar houses now, but they were greyer than her mother's house ever was. And here were cellars again, like her house. Her anger turned for a moment from the Government to the man who placed the cellars in their row. He wasn't in this crowd, for sure. In thinking like this, she gave a kick unconsciously to the heels of the man who was walking in front of her. She steadied herself back, and her attention was drawn from the purpose of the procession to the procession itself. The man who'd been kicked by her had big feet that turned out, one to the east and the other to the west. On seeing him like this, she began laughing inside. Indeed, there were some amusing people in the procession as she looked around. The women in the same row with her were there to have a good time, obviously. Some others, in the row ahead of her, looked as though they were in earnest, and were, like herself, putting their hope in the results of the march. One of them was looking very serious, and she didn't speak a word to anyone else. She had better clothing than the others. She was pursing her lips tightly, and she was marching ostentatiously, picking out where to put her feet on the ground. This was very amusing to the women in Bronwen's row. They made fun of her walk, and went straight from that to the woman's record on women's committees of the political party to which she belonged. To Bronwen's mind they wouldn't have laughed at her way of walking if they hadn't had a bone to pick with her about her behaviour somewhere else; or why would they laugh at her and not at the man? Strange, the worlds she knew nothing about, the world of committees for example.

By now the sun was going down low on the horizon, and one side of the valley was black in its own shadow. It began to get cold, and Bronwen felt in need of food. Her feet were aching, and she felt the outer side of her heel turning more and more. She was feeling greatly in sympathy with the man with the big feet by this time, because obviously he had trouble walking, and she was kicking him more often. The humorous women were talking less. In the silence, she could hear the craving of her own hunger grumble in her side. As the talk decreased, the sound of the crowd marching became like the sound of sheep walking on a hard road. They kept on going, and by now the first part had crossed the bridge over the river and were walking back to the valley on the other side, until the crowd was in the shape of a U.

The crowd itself was looking like something absurd to Bronwen now, and depressing in its absurdity. She thought, if the Government were to see them now what they'd do was laugh at them. After all, what were they marching to?

When her row was within ten yards of the bridge her attention was caught by a woman in a row that was walking on the bridge that moment and so was before her eyes. She hadn't seen her before that. This woman had on an expensive coat of fur. This gave Bronwen a shock, and now the woman next to her was starting in.

"Well, great heavens! look at her in her fur coat. That's cost a penny or two, you can bet."

"Yes, there's something better than catskin in that," the other said.

Bronwen's heart fell lower, and when she understood from the conversation of the others that it was the Member of Parliament's wife who was wearing the fur coat, her heart dropped like a clock pendulum when its cord breaks.

She was in a hurry to leave the procession, and she did so when she had a chance. She wasn't looking forward to going home either. She knew something of Idris' feelings by now. But she couldn't bear to think of his sarcasm when she'd arrive, and the look that would say "I told you".

But she had to go. She was almost collapsing from hunger. Of course there wouldn't be a fire in the grate, and she had only bread-and-butter for tea. But there would have been a relish to that if the march had turned out as it began, and if she could have reported to Idris the enthusiasm and the eloquence. What if she should tell him about the fur coat! There'd be a double edge to his sarcasm. A pity her husband was so dreadfully embittered. She knew it was his back she'd see first after opening the door, and she couldn't bear to remember the meaning of that posture. Between fear and weakness and fatigue her legs were sagging by the time she reached the garden gate. She was glad it was beginning to get dark.

No indeed, Idris wasn't in bed. She could see him through the window, sitting by the fire. She went inside like a dog that had been killing sheep. She saw a clean cloth on the table, with tea things and a pot of jam. A small glowing fire had been made up in the grate, and Idris was toasting a slice of bread at it on the tip of a fork. He turned his eyes from the toast and looked into his wife's face. And those eyes were not without compassion.

III

Gossip Row

(1949)

The story takes place in one of the years just before the 1939–45 war.

May 7

I've been on pins and needles since noon after receiving the note from Enid. The boy brought it from the shop on his way to dinner, and this is all that was in it:

> *Dear Ffebi,*
>   *I'll come by to visit you tomorrow night, while everyone is in chapel. I have something important that I'd like to discuss with you.*
>
>   *Many regards,*
>   *Enid.*

This is the most exciting thing that has happened to me since I became bedridden, three years ago, and since I began keeping this diary a year ago. The most frequent thing in it up to now is, "A nice day", "A rainy day", "A nasty day". And since I'm not able to do anything here in bed but read and knit, suffering from curiosity is almost worse than suffering from the numbness in my legs. It's worse than a girl waiting for her sweetheart. It must be important, or Enid wouldn't be missing chapel. I hope nothing has happened at the shop. John is half-hearted and negligent enough, and the shop could go to the dogs any time. Good that Enid's there, she'll prevent the dogs from getting a final grip, for a while, anyway. Only four o'clock now. Twenty-six hours still to wait. I've been expecting Doli, my cousin, down for a while. A pity she didn't turn up out of the blue as she does some Saturday afternoons, so that Besi could linger longer in town while doing her errands. Poor Besi! It's quite hard on her. She can't go anywhere. Miss Jones who keeps house for Dan would come here in a minute, just for the asking. But neither of us likes her. And we can't put our finger on any fault in her either. Some people are like that. And if Doli had come, the afternoon would have gone like the wind. She talks and talks, and you don't know what on earth she's said except that she said something, and that you enjoyed yourself while she was at it. There's no depth to Doli, indeed, she's like a soap bubble from a clay pipe, but it's diverting to look at her and to listen to her. And she would have made tea for me and for Besi by the time she came from town, anyway. I'll try to go to sleep so that the time will pass. I didn't tell Besi about the contents of the note. Was worried that she'd see the stuff of great tragedy in it. I'll do the imagining on my own.

May 8

Enid's been here, and many other people have been. This house is worse than a chapel house on Sunday night for gossip-mongering. Lusty Liwsi was here, Dan, Enid, old Lowri'r Aden, our John of course, and Besi. But I didn't pay much attention to anything anyone said because I was so brim-full of what Enid had said. The big news they had was that Rhys Glanmor had died before chapel that evening, and as usual, no one, with the exception of old Lowri, was thinking at all about his soul, only about his money. Oh, yes indeed, Liwsi was talking a lot about his daughter, Joanna, and was very spiteful about her; saying that now she'll be running after men more than ever. At another time, for sure, the talk would have been interesting enough to me. It's strange how the living gorge themselves on the dead, going after them as far as they can, pulling the souls out of them and putting them back again, going through their pockets and emptying them and putting their contents back again, and after doing that, letting them alone, and starting in on their families. I tried to get a glimpse of John's face. I don't know why, unless because I thought there'd be a great change in him. But he looked quite as usual. The change was all in my mind, I suppose. John had changed completely for me since he gave this door a bang and went to chapel. I had my ears open at that time for one thing, namely Enid's footstep on the pavement. And presently, after Meri next door went past the window with the baby on her arm, and after the children next-door-again had been let out to play, I heard Enid's firm foot on the pavement. Almost before she sat down she began on her story, just like a child saying his Bible verse at Meeting, with her eyes on the window opposite.

"I may as well come to the point straight away," she said. "Your brother has asked me to marry him."

"He's what?" I asked.

I had imagined a host of things since the evening before that could have been worrying Enid, such as that the apprentice had been stealing from the shop, or that some firm was threatening my brother for debt, but not this.

"He's asked me to marry him."

Before I had time to consider all the things that were implicit in that, I asked, quite as if she were talking about going to America: "And what do you intend to do?"

"Refuse him, to be sure."

"Why the 'to be sure'?"

"Because I couldn't think of marrying anyone without loving him."

At this she blushed to the tips of her ears. Strange how shy we are in talking about love. We get an impression from novels that everyone is quite at home in treating the matter. But perhaps it's only in novels that they're this way.

"Why have you come to tell me this, Enid?"

"Well, I'll tell you, Ffebi," she said, turning her eyes on me for the first time since she entered the room. "It's up to me whether I accept your brother or not, but I have a duty to let you know that your brother is thinking of marrying at all."

"He has his eyes on marrying then?"

"Yes."

Full marks to her, Enid knows what the financial situation is for the three of us, and she knows, if John marries, it will be worse for Besi and me after losing John's payment for his lodging, with me incapable of working like this. Full marks to her common sense as well, far-sighted enough to see that if the marrying fever has got hold of him, he won't stop in spite of her refusing him. Well, everyone's gone, and I've got that off my mind. Thinking now that I wonder if I ought to tell Besi. It will be a great worry to her. Better to let her sleep tonight, anyway, on the good sermon she had in chapel. Tell her tomorrow.

May 9

Washing day. Lusty Liwsi here all morning helping Besi, her cleaning and Besi washing. So, not much of a chance to have a talk with Besi. Liwsi going on eloquently about Rhys Glanmor's daughter. Liwsi goes there to clean and she can't bear the woman. I don't know her at all, because she was away at Liverpool when I was in the shop, and it's since I became laid up that she's come home to tend to her father. But by all reports, she's a silly enough little thing, making a fuss around everyone, especially if they're men; and waiting by the deacons' seat to shake hands with every minister, no matter whether she knows them or not. Thought a great deal all morning about what Enid said. John a completely different man in my eyes, though I don't know why. It's as if I were expecting to see the measles breaking out all over him. Everybody's brother marries sometime or other, with some exceptions. But if a man has waited until he's sixty without doing it, perhaps his sisters expect him to be that way forever. Enid would have made him a good wife, and I'd rather have her as a sister-in-law than anyone in the world, but, to tell the truth, I'm too fond of Enid to wish her to marry John. Brother or not, John is a lazy man, and is able to speak eloquently and even intelligently about work; able to give people outside the impression that he's hard-working. He was able to fool my father for years with his talk, and yet I don't know why my father left him the business either, because he too knew long before his death that John's tongue was more fluent than his brain, and moved faster than his feet. Perhaps that's why he left the house to Besi and me. I've felt thankful a hundred times since I've been confined to bed that a girl with Enid Rhodri's energy is in the shop. I hope this won't make her wish to change her place. And come to think of it, it's good that this house is Besi's and mine, because after all, what if John *did* marry? Liwsi came to sit at the foot of the bed before leaving. I like to look at her, she's a picture of health and contentment; her wrists and her elbows totally lost in the flesh of her arms, and there's a charm to me in looking at the shine of her skirt stretching smoothly over the high plains of her body from the waist down. I like to see her walking through this house like a ship on the waters. She literally splutters when she speaks, but the strangest thing about her to me is her eyes. The pupils of her eyes are somehow placed so that she looks at everything as if it were a wonder. And as she gasps an "Oh", or "My", every now and then, it makes one think she's always seeing and hearing everything in this creation for the first time. She was thinking a bit this afternoon about what was going on at Rhys Glanmor's house, wondering whether the daughter would go back to the office in Liverpool, and the house would be broken up, with herself losing a good place that way. "But maybe she'll marry," she said. The word "marry" brought Enid's story to mind, and I thought, what if I were to tell Liwsi, how the "Oh" and the "My" would come out and how the pupils of her eyes would become smaller and smaller.

I've gone and told Enid's message to Besi. She was dumbfounded, didn't know what to think, but was glad that Enid has refused him. I didn't dare tell her what was on my mind, that he was likely to ask someone else if the fever was on him. But she must have been thinking the same thing, because she said:

"I don't know how we'd live without his money."

"Don't talk nonsense," I said, quite bravely, "I've never seen a door close without another one somewhere opening." After saying that I realized how stupid a cliché it is. There isn't necessarily a particle of truth in it, but then I said something closer to the truth.

"We're sure to get along. What's John's thirty-five shillings, after all? We could get a pound or twenty-five shillings from anyone else, and I'm sure that anyone would be glad to be able to come here."

But there was a look on Besi as if she thought that ten-shilling difference would drive us to the workhouse. I said as well that I would be able to get up quite soon and then I could knit more. But she didn't want to hear a mention of that because I'm knitting too much now for people who'd be glad to see me knit in bulk for a shilling.

"Oh, dear," she said then, "why are we carrying on? We're talking as though his marriage banns were out already."

May 10

A day with nothing happening after a night of failing to sleep. A sleep-less night is a terrible thing. Everything can happen during it. I see myself dying, see the nameplate on my coffin, see my burial and hear what every-one says after I'm gone. But last night that wasn't what I saw, but saw John marrying, saw myself dying (and that didn't in itself much bother me), and saw Besi here alone, and forced to work hard when she should be allowed to rest. She's fifty-three now. I was worrying about Besi. But when the morning came, and Besi came with her cup of tea at half-past-seven, the fears had all gone away, and I saw how foolish I was and how baseless is every fear in the night. After I'd had the cup, I felt as jaunty as the cuckoo; I turned towards the window and went nicely to sleep, so that I didn't hear the noise of the usual crowd that goes past this house to work every morn-ing between half-past-seven and half-past-nine. I hadn't heard Besi bring me water to wash myself, and it was dinner time when I woke up. All the fears have gone by, and tonight I feel as though nothing at all has happened and I'm back in the same still stagnant pond that I was in a week ago, that I was in three years ago.

May 11

Another night of failing to sleep. Once something comes to roil the waters of one's mind, it's hard to get the waters to calm themselves again. Yesterday during the day I was perfectly certain that things were quiet, but last night again a tempest of thoughts. Here's what was worrying me last night. Presuming that my illness isn't one that results in an early death, am I going to endure the monotony of lying here for a great stretch of time? If a change could come to break the monotony, what change would I like? That change wouldn't be of my choosing, it's certain, because I'm at the mercy of every wind. And if a change comes, am I going to endure it better than this monotony? What is my future, in truth? Since I was first laid up, I haven't on the whole given as much time to thinking about my affliction as I did last night. And to tell the truth, I haven't thought much about my illness up to now, except as it affects other people, giving Besi more work and aging her before her time, and the loss to the shop, because, without flattering myself, there *is* a loss to the shop since John is so shiftless. A diary's a place to be plain. For some reason or other, I've been able to keep my mind off my illness, no thanks to me for that, that's just the way it is. I would often read about people who endured their afflictions "calmly and uncomplainingly". They aren't always the ones to thank for that, that's their nature. They don't have the strength of character to rebel. And it's other people's nature to "kick against the pricks". They've always opposed and rebelled on committees and at conferences on seeing the injustice of things, and it's those people we have to thank that things change in this world. If everyone had the nature of the calm and uncomplaining people, injustice would be allowed to remain. I kicked and rebelled in the night last night for the first time in a long while. I saw the injustice of my being forced to lie here, good for nothing but a worry to everyone, and I longed for a change to come, not to anyone else's circumstances, but to my circumstances. That would keep me from floating into the stagnant pond of the calm and uncomplaining. But, to be sure, by this afternoon I will have reached the same contentment as before.

May 12

Rhys Glanmor's burial. My cousin Doli here to tea, and the fluff of her talk going with the wind. She was criticizing Joanna Glanmor harshly. The two of them are related on Doli's mother's side; her father was my father's brother. Doli saying that even a funeral couldn't put a bridle on Joanna's fuss. She was going up to everyone to talk and shake hands and tell everyone to remember to go to the house to have tea. She had a fit when Doli said she was coming here. "She'd do better," Doli said, "to stand in the same spot instead of behaving like a housefly. And I've heard that she was heartily glad to leave that office in Liverpool to come and look after her father, and that everyone was fed up with her old fussing, and that she wasn't much of a hand at her job. But if one listened to Joanna, you would think it was a terrible sacrifice for her to give up the office, and she didn't stop saying that all through her father's illness, and sometimes the poor old creature would catch the tail-end of her complaining. No, it wasn't that she was complaining, of course, but making it known, making it known, pursing her lips: 'You see, Doli, I was in a very nice position.'" And on and on Doli went.

May 14

Have had a nice day today and I can't rightly say why either. But Dan came in at nightfall when I happened to be here by myself, Besi in the kitchen making supper and John gone for a walk. There's a very depressed look on Dan lately, more so than when he buried Annie two years ago, and tonight he was in a mood to share confidences, talking a great deal about Annie and about his grief. "But you know, Ffebi?" he said, "everybody thinks a man, or a woman for that matter, sheds his grief like a cow that's lost her calf, in three days, and that it never comes back again. These fine evenings are terrible, making you feel it's impossible for anyone to be rotting in the ground. And if that Miss Jones were someone fairly what-do-you-call-it, it would be easier to bear." (This was the first time I ever heard him criticize her and I didn't at all welcome it this time.) "She tries to make food without dirtying saucepans, tries to wash without scrubbing the clothes, and tries to work without rolling up her sleeves. But, I may as well not talk. All of them are all right for a while, until they find out they can stay." A pleasant smell of frying eggs and onions was coming from the kitchen. "That's something I haven't had for years," Dan said. I called quickly to Besi and asked her to make supper for the three of us here in the parlour, theirs at the round table and mine on the tray. Besi had thought of it before me, because the tablecloth was in her hand when she came in. I was so happy (I can't say why) that I asked Besi to lock the front door for fear that someone would come in. Everyone comes in without knocking since I've been ill, and I was determined to make an excuse not to see anyone tonight. There are some things in life that you are certain you will remember forever, and I will remember our supper tonight. Seeing Dan enjoy it, and wondering what sort of food the poor fellow was having, and seeing Besi contented fetching and carrying for him. Thinking how good a wife she'd make him, if I were to get out of the way, seeing her look quite wonderfully pretty, with her white hair and her plum-coloured eyes, and the frying had given a flush to her cheeks; and seeing her, though she's a little bit of a thing, sit so dignified at the table, and come morning she'll be scrubbing floors in the back kitchen. Don't know how she's kept on looking so tranquil through everything. Thinking how pleasant a thing it was to see Dan help her carry the dishes into the kitchen after we finished and offer to wash them with her, while she insisted that he stay to talk to me. But at that here John came into the house and I was feeling as though my teeth were on edge because of that. I knew that my happiness was over the minute he came in. I felt as if I'd stolen an hour of happiness under the nose of Fate and as if she'd caught me stealing it. I don't know why, we all grew up with Dan from the time we were children and treat him like one of us and John's arrival shouldn't have made any difference. Presently, Miss Jones came here to look for Dan, wanted to know whether he wanted her to make him something for supper. And that was the finish of the evening. I haven't seen her do this before, but for that matter, I haven't seen Dan stay here for a meal since Annie died, until tonight. But there's something in Miss Jones that makes her repulsive to me. In spite of that, I know that I will be able to look back at tonight because of the jot of happiness I've had, and keep it like a treasure in my memory, and that I'll never have anything in the least like it again, even if the thing were to happen in just the same way some other evening in the future. And yet, what is a jot of happiness like that worth unless one keeps on feeling it? No one can live on the memory of his happy moments. I think of a husband and wife who have lived happily for a number of years, and something comes to disrupt that happiness. The two of them begin to feel hatred for each other, and perhaps they separate. Is remembering the happy time of any value then? Does it have any more value than imagining happiness in the future for someone like me, when that doesn't come? How much better off is a woman in her old age because scores of sensible men made fools of themselves over her beauty when she was young? The only way to preserve a time is for time itself to stop.

May 15

Gossip-mongering as usual after the people came from chapel. Everybody talking about the fellowship meeting and about Rhys Glanmor. Dan raving about anyone saying anything commemorating the dead man at the meeting, since it is God alone who knows people's hearts. Liwsi saying he was a very fine old man, was Rhys Glanmor, she ought to know when she'd been working for him for fifteen years. "Yes," Dan said, "but you and I aren't God." "Some people think they are," she said. Everybody protested, hoping that the cap didn't fit anyone in Gossip Row. No, and she was on the brink of saying something then, but she stopped short as if the cap did fit someone. For once the look of seeing a wonder left her eyes and she was looking depressed. That doesn't suit her. "Those little deacons," said Dan (who turns his nose up in scorn at the seatful of deacons we have in Capel y Twb), "were trying to concoct something to say about Rhys Glanmor tonight, and none of them were within a mile of him. They were scratching their necks for something to say because they couldn't honestly say that Glanmor was faithful in the means of grace. Dear Heavens, the man was better off staying home to read something substantial than coming to listen to the tomfoolery that is preached from that chapel seven Sundays out of every ten. Some of these preachers think it doesn't matter what they say as long as they shout with zeal." "Yes," Enid said, "but the worst of it is that the congregation thinks so too." "I hope," Dan said, "that no one says anything about me after I'm gone." "You needn't worry," I said, "you don't go to chapel often enough." "But everyone ought to show what side he's on," old Lowri'r Aden said. "Not if he's droned to sleep," Dan said. John was very quiet and reflective. Strange how religion always sets people at loggerheads. Liwsi was completely out of her depth.

After everyone had gone, a strange feeling came over me that I can't rightly describe. Thought of us here talking about Meeting and God and men, when we're like some tiny insects weaving through each other, rubbing each other, and yet talking about each other as importantly as if we were the hub of the world. Tonight was wonderfully important to us little insects, measuring and weighing each other as if we were gods, and tomorrow all the talking will have gone with the wind. Hardly anyone will remember it and even the substance of the conversation won't remain in anyone's mind. And I think of every Gossip Row in this world, and every conversation, and all the millions of people in every country in the world, and everyone saying or doing something on Sunday night, and all the millions who have ever been, all their talk and all the things that are and that were worrying them. So what importance did tonight have for us? None, just one more evening with its empty talk gone down with the river to the sea.

May 16

Liwsi here working as usual, and obviously there was something on her mind. "I didn't sleep last night," she said, spreading herself at the foot of my bed. "I came close to putting my foot in it here last night in talking about Joanna. It was to her I was referring when I said that some people think they're God." "But you didn't say that," I said. "I almost did, and I thought that everyone had found out who I was referring to. The little pest! It's strange for me with her father gone. She can look very kind, and run to this place and that with her charity, but she doesn't have a particle of interest in anyone but herself. A tumor on her side, that's what all her kindness is. She doesn't see any value in anything anyone else is doing. If she happens to find me ironing she'll say, 'Doesn't that iron iron beautifully?' She doesn't have enough woman in her to give a bit of praise to my ironing. I mean to say some day that it's the iron that's washing the dishes, washing the floor, and making food, and that it's almost all-powerful. It was on the tip of my tongue to say those things last night, but I remembered that she and Dan were friends." "What?" I said, "never," and I was remembering Dan talking about Annie Saturday night. "Well, that's what people are saying," Liwsi said, "and I know she's mad about him. You didn't get anything from her a few weeks ago but Dan Meidrym every minute. 'Mr. Meidrym *is* a nice man.' But I knew myself that she didn't know him, and that it wouldn't take Dan long to dispose of her with his quips. But I was thinking last night there was something in the talk after all, because the most sensible men go daft as a post when it comes to women." "Yes," I said, "and women the same way when it comes to men. But I don't think Joanna Glanmor has bewitched Dan's eyes as yet." "I hope not, indeed, or I'll go pull the scales off his eyes myself." After she left, I thought about it a lot. I wondered, has Dan in reality been fooling with Joanna Glanmor?

Did I feel a tinge of something like jealousy? Would I have felt the same way if she were someone else? I incline to answer in the affirmative.

May 18

Mr. Jones, the Minister, called here today. He doesn't call often. I've told him not to. The poor fellow is clearly at a loss every time in knowing what to say. There's no use in him saying "Hurry up and get better" to someone like me, and seeing me the next time in bed the same way. And my experience is that you can't gossip with your minister, or tell him anything about your neighbours. Then, since I can't talk about very profound things, I gave him the hint, quite kindly, that he mustn't be afraid of committing a sin by not calling here too often. And Mrs. Jones the same way. It's a very disagreeable life, a minister's life, and his wife's life, I should think. Not proper for you to try discussing any of the flock with them, or them with you, they have to keep every opinion they have of everybody to themselves, and they can't say or do what they please. Quite like the royal family. I think it's healthier for a person's body and spirit to be able to pour everything out. Anyway, today, of his own accord, here Mr. Jones was saying: "Mr. Glanmor went very quickly at the end. You know, he was quite a fine old boy, he wasn't much of a chapel-goer, and he'd criticize us quite caustically there at the chapel, to our faces, and there was a lot of truth in what he said. Some petty and mediocre people get a great deal of attention in Wales, and if anyone were to ask me what is the genius of the Welsh, I would say that it's for putting the wrong people in office. But that's what I was going to tell you, there'll be a bit of hubbub between the two children, I'm afraid, because the father made a will that's very favourable to the son. Left the farms and the money to Melfyn and only the house and the car to Joanna. And Melfyn has a good job and a wealthy wife." "She can go back to the office," I said. "Yes, but if I know anything, I know that Joanna won't go back to Liverpool, they won't want her there, and it isn't so easy to find a position now. Oh, yes, your cousin had a bit as well. I don't know what will become of Joanna, it will be quite hard on her." "The same thing that's become of many of us," I said, "she has to turn out and look for something else." "Yes, but it will be very difficult . . ." He stopped short, he found he was on the brink of making a mistake. I know very well what was on his mind, that it is very difficult for someone in Miss Glanmor's position to turn to a lower-grade job after the experience of being in an office. I wasn't surprised that her father had left money to Doli; he was quite fond of her, because she's able to look after her money. On fire wanting to see Doli. Besi thinking that Miss Glanmor will be running after Dan more than ever now.

May 20

Nothing happening. I almost added "except sun and rain and wind". If I hear that again, I'm sure to scream, because I hear it so often. Sun and rain and wind *are* happenings to those who have been bedridden for years.

May 21

Saturday. Doli's been here. Thought she'd be sure to call. She doesn't know which end is up after getting the two hundred. Doli is an amiable sort, quite selfish basically, able to take everything lightly. Hasn't ever had children or tribulation, living altogether for herself and her husband Ben, but can be quite agreeable and pleasant with us, anyway, and can be quite ready to do a favour, so long as the favour won't mean a sacrifice for her. She can't get over Rhys Glanmor leaving this money to her, and leaving Joanna with so much less than Melfyn. Seeing Doli sitting in the chair here looking so pleased with herself, bending her head and lifting her feet as she laughed, a rebelliousness arose in me and a sympathy with Joanna Glanmor, and I couldn't hold my tongue. "It isn't a laughing matter," I said. "I think it's a great joke," she said. "It isn't a joke to Miss Glanmor," I said. "Tut, don't waste your sympathy on Joanna, Ffebi; she's quite capable of looking after herself." "Perhaps, but you must remember that she has feelings, and her mother had a share in accumulating that money, and it's only some five years since she was buried, and I'm certain she has fully as much of a right to her mother's money as anyone." "Oh, Ffebi, you're never jealous of me?" "Don't talk nonsense," I said. "I'd rather spend the money that I've earned myself than money someone else has accumulated." Oh, it didn't matter to her how the money came, it was nice to have it. She and Ben all for going to Switzerland with the money. Haven't ever got about much, and living a very restricted life. I kept quiet, but in telling the story to Besi after she'd gone, I broke out crying. "Never mind," Besi said—and her voice was so different from Doli's—"something will come for us, but for that matter, we have it, and it will never come to Doli and her sort. It's quite a nice thing that we know our world is fuller than Doli and Ben's world, if we never moved from Gossip Row." And it was very nice that Besi was beside me.

GOSSIP ROW (1949)

May 22

The same old crowd here after chapel, and the chatter naturally about Rhys Glanmor's will. Almost turned into two factions here. Some saying "Serves her right" about the daughter, and the others feeling sorry for her. Very strangely, and interestingly, Dan was among the latter. But he has such a sense of fair play. He maintained that it was spite to ignore Joanna for a greedy-guts like Doli, and that no one would have been able to criticize if her father had left money to some library or scholarship, or to the poor of this town. Obviously Rhys Glanmor has gone down severely in his eyes. Dying is a strange thing: it's like a mirror, with a man standing in front of it, and yourself behind the man. You see the man in the mirror, but he doesn't see you. A week ago tonight Dan was defending Rhys Glanmor and blaming the deacons. Tonight here he is defending the daughter and blaming the father. Does anyone know another? Or, is there consistency in people's lives? Liwsi swearing that Rhys Glanmor was a very fine man, and that there wasn't any spite, but complete merit, in what he did, glad that Doli had got the money, but not knowing what she'll do with it; and not knowing how much better she and Ben will be after being in that distant land, that they'll be just the same as herself after they come back. Suddenly, across the talk, Lowri'r Aden went and said challengingly: "Why did he have so much money?" she said. "He must have done wrong to someone to acquire so much." And as far as I know, that was the wisest observation that was heard all evening.

May 26

Thursday. Nothing happened all week long but nice weather. Good to have that, even when one is in bed, and that bed faces monotonous houses. The window is open, and the sound of the children playing comes in. John has gone to Tre Dywod and Besi is here with me. I felt rather angry with John that he hadn't offered to mind the house so that Besi could sometimes go for the sea air. She's been hard at it finishing her spring cleaning and it would have done her good to go to the seaside. But there's no need for either of them to stay here with me. Loneliness doesn't bother me, especially since I always have someone to expect. It would be a different thing if there was no one I could expect to come to the house. Dan came in for a little talk, but he didn't stay long, for fear Miss Jones would come looking for him again, he said. When he was here, Miss Glanmor went past this house, and Dan said that was who she was. I wouldn't have known her if I'd bumped my nose on her.

May 29

A nice Sunday night again, with the friends here. For once they weren't talking about anything but the sermon. Had had a good sermon, they said, against avarice. Everybody, even misers, can agree that a sermon against avarice is a good one. The talk flat because everybody was in agreement. Somehow, I was glad to see everyone go tonight. It was so hot in the parlour here, and sometimes, like tonight, a person is sick and tired of his best friends. But before they left, Miss Jones came in, and if anyone had a desire to start a discussion, the appearance of Miss Jones was like a pin in a bubble. Dan started out at once, and the company broke up. I was vexed with Miss Jones, not because she broke up the fellowship, but because she'd come here at all. If we wanted to ask Dan to stay for supper, we couldn't, because she'd call. No one who has someone keeping house for him can do as he pleases. You can't live with a stranger or with anyone but the ones you love, because it's only to them that you can speak your mind and with them that you can quarrel. John was out and when everyone was about to set off he came in.

May 30

I woke suddenly in the middle of the night last night. I knew something was wrong, but I couldn't say what, whether it was physical pain, or mental pain, or a dream or whatever, that had awakened me. But I knew that it was pain or anxiety. I was perfectly at ease at the moment, I couldn't remember anything that was bothering me before going to sleep, except for feeling that the company here last night had somehow gone flat. Perhaps it would have been better if they'd had a sermon that they couldn't agree on. Gradually, as though it were rising from my subconscious, the cause of my suffering became clear to me. Somewhere at the bottom of my mind, I was worrying, not because Miss Jones had butted in last night, but because she can do it again every Sunday night, and if so, there's an end to our little company. We can't speak freely when someone from the outside is there. If someone compatible now came in on Sunday night, we wouldn't be the same. Well, if someone as incompatible as Miss Jones comes, there's an end to our company. She can be asked to keep away, it's true, or Dan can ask.

But, will we do it? We're too much afraid of speaking plainly. If one of us did it, she'd probably leave Dan. He could get someone else, probably, but that one could be worse. The thing has been churning in my mind all day, turning round and round. Liwsi came for a chat before going home, and to get rid of the hurdy-gurdy in my head I mentioned my anxiety to her. She had been thinking the same thing, she said, but thinking that it wasn't any of her business, since it wasn't her house. She thought that we wouldn't have much fun if Miss Jones became a regular visitor, and we'd had a good deal of fun around this bed, she said. How glad I was to hear her say that! I felt the same way, and we agreed that one thing against her was that she couldn't laugh at what was said by other people. And she can't talk; it isn't that she's too wise a woman to talk, it's as if her brain were in a vise. Liwsi was supposing that we could talk and not worry about her, except that she could gossip about what she heard in other places. I tried to explain to Liwsi that what was bothering me wasn't that, but seeing the company change, when I can't bear change, want things to stay always the same, especially people. Naturally, I can trust everyone who comes here, or I wouldn't say what I often do. But there's something more than that. Miss Jones isn't one of us, the people of Gossip Row, or the people who are used to meeting in Gossip Row. I couldn't get Liwsi to see that. "But maybe she won't come again," she said. I have my own thoughts about that. She hasn't been here at all except when Dan was here.

May 31

There isn't anything happening these days. Expect that the weather will be nice enough for me to be carried to the garden in back quite soon. Saw Joanna Glanmor go past again today, and yesterday as well. I wonder who she knows up this way?

June 2

A nice Thursday again. Right after coming home from the shop John began to spruce up. He never stays home now on Thursday afternoons. But I don't see much to blame in him. What pleasure is there in staying in a close house in a close street on fine summer days, though you feel you have a duty to stay with an invalid? And yet, Besi is here all day and every day without any change. Talked to her about this, and she says that she doesn't want to go, she's perfectly content as she is. John suggested once that she go away for a week or two, that he'd pay, and that Liwsi come here, but she refused, because she'd rather, for her own sake, be here than be somewhere else longing to be here. She'd have been pleased to be able to whisk away this bed with me in it, with the bags, and place it in lodgings at the seaside. It's a cat's longing, her longing, she said, clinging to a house. "And I think," she said, "should it happen that a change or move came in our history, I would have, anyway, a longing for this time since you've been in bed, fully as much as the time when you were in the shop, and when we were going to the seaside every summer. What I always have is a longing for the things that are nearest me. I could almost rightly say, if you were to get up and go to the shop tomorrow next, I would have a longing for the tranquil evenings we've had together in this parlour, with me knitting and you talking. I don't believe there's so much martyrdom in suffering, or perhaps what I ought to say is, someone can find a lot of happiness in the midst of suffering. Not going to Tre Dywod today isn't a sacrifice to me at all. Mind you, I'm fifty-three and the itch to gad about is done with. When you're twenty-three, it's the being drawn after men that makes you gad about." I could understand what she meant very well. But there was one thing she was forgetting. What if we hated each other, and she were forced to tend to me only from a sister's duty to a sister, then she would suffer. So, when John left, neither of us thought more poorly of him, but looked forward to having tea together in the parlour after Besi came from town, with buns and the first tomatoes of the season. John is quite an untalkative person in the house, he reads a lot. But we didn't have our early tea as planned. Before Besi had taken off her hat, there was a knock at the door, and I heard Besi saying: "Come in, Miss Glanmor," and before I could catch my breath, Miss Glanmor was in the parlour. Neither she nor I knew how to start a conversation, since she's never been in this house before, and we'd only seen each other at times in chapel when she was home on holidays. At last she said: "I'm sorry that I haven't visited you before, but you know, surely, how much trouble I've had with father." "Yes," I said. "We were very sorry to hear of your loss." "Yes, I've had a great loss, it's true, but it was good to see father released from his sufferings; he'd become very trying and I was becoming terribly worn out. But I wouldn't think to complain, of course, because we have a duty to do these things. My motto in life is Service." Well, in hearing a thing like that, my whole body broke out in a sweat. I was feeling as though I'd unexpectedly come upon a man changing his shirt. She went on: "I believe that the highest thing in life is service." I caught a glimpse of Besi's mouth at that moment, and I shut my eyes. Then, she went on to mention how she'd given up a good position to tend to her father, and that it wasn't so easy to find a position like that again, and on and on and on. I couldn't say much after that. I was remembering Besi's discourse on the subject of suffering. And as the talk sagged, Miss Glanmor left. Besi and I didn't say anything to each other, but Besi snatched the things and out to the kitchen she went in a rush to make tea. And she began laughing to herself when she brought the tray in. "It takes all sorts," she said, and that was all. I washed the unpleasant taste of the visit down with the tea. Besi came in afterwards and sat in front of the open window to sew, and I felt that what she'd said was true, that some happiness (an occasional moment of it) can be found, though every sinew of me was craving to get up and go out into the thin air of a summer twilight. Presently we heard Enid coming along the pavement. I knew before I saw her face that it was she. She knew from our faces we had reason for amusement, and after we told her the tale of Joanna Glanmor, Enid put her hand on her eyes: "Oh!" she said, groaning, "she doesn't know she's been born. Liwsi was going there at some point every day, except Mondays, and she had plenty of people to go sit with her father." But Enid had come to talk about John. Said things were worse at the shop. People coming in to ask for things, and they wouldn't be there in stock, when he'd said that he'd ordered them the last time he was at the warehouse in London. A very troubled look on her, failing to understand why they hadn't arrived. Then, the people going to other places to find them. Dan came in before we heard the end of her talk, and though Dan will quite surely get to know this at some point, it's another thing to discuss a matter like this among three parties. After Enid left, I asked his opinion about Miss Jones beginning to come here on Sunday night. He, too, was of the opinion that we could never bear it. But what's to be done he didn't know, and yet he saw it was a problem that someone from outside was disrupting a three-year-old fellowship. He stayed for supper without much urging. Miss Jones had gone to visit her sister, and she wouldn't be back until eleven. He left before that. She's in a bad mood every time that he's been here. No use telling him not to mind. Men are simple creatures, it's always anything for the sake of peace with them.

June 5

The same company here tonight, with Miss Jones added. As if we had a mutual understanding, everybody avoided saying anything. Singing practice in chapel. Though Lowri'r Aden hadn't been here on her own, she too could be seen to feel an awkwardness in the company. It was Dan went home first, and Miss Jones last, and she found herself in an amusing situation. She doesn't have much to say at any time; certainly, she doesn't have anything to say to Besi and me. "Well, I must go, I suppose," she said, with emphasis on the "suppose". The obvious thing for me to say was: "I can't see what else you can do." But I didn't say it. It's impossible to say entirely what is on our minds, or the world would be turned topsy-turvy every now and again. Society is founded on hypocrisy. But I said a stupid thing: "Mr. Meidrym has gone." "Oh, I don't have to go because of him," she said, "this is my evening out." The old cat, why couldn't she have stayed out then?

June 6

Old Lowri came here early this morning, couldn't bear it any longer. Couldn't understand what was wrong last night, everyone quiet and saying nothing. Terribly afraid some of the company were angry with the others. When I explained to her she saw, or she said she saw, that we couldn't speak. She saw it as a detestable thing—an un-Christian thing. Everything is Christian or un-Christian to Lowri, and I knew from her silence she was feeling that it wasn't right. I asked her whether she could welcome Miss Jones with open arms and embrace her. That was putting her in too hard a corner, she said. Doesn't it put every one of us in a hard corner? It's impossible to love everyone, indeed it's impossible to feel a particle of kindness towards some people. But why should I worry? And yet it does worry me. When Liwsi came here after she finished cleaning, she had a good laugh in talking about last night. Saw them making off like mice into their holes because the cat had come here. It's fine for Liwsi, able to laugh cheerfully at everything. Worry slides off her like water off a duck's back. And why need I worry about such a silly thing as a woman keeping house for Dan? I ought to worry more about John's business.

June 7

Doli here today, has been visiting her cousin, Joanna Glanmor, not having been there for the funeral. Felt that she ought to call, though she was afraid; I don't know why people do anything because they feel they *ought* to do it. There's no friendship between the two, indeed I was surprised they were speaking a word to each other after the will. And Doli had been afraid to call there. But Joanna was quite agreeable when Doli said she wanted to call here. She didn't know Doli was related to us, she said, but she knew very well, Doli said, only neither her affairs nor her family was of any interest to her cousin Joanna unless they touched her somewhere. She was asking a good deal about John. Doli also full of her own affairs, getting ready to go away—has been in Liverpool buying clothes. I doubt that she gave a thought to whether I was in bed or on the floor.

June 9

Have been too happy to write in this for two days. The time has come for me to be carried to the back into the garden like every summer. Starting off to the garden is for me like going to Switzerland for Doli; I look forward with the same joy. When I'm in the front, seeing a bunch of flowers in Mari's house, across the road, is an event and gives me happiness. This street is so narrow that the shadows stretch across each other throughout the day; and bird-song doesn't come to mingle with the sound of children. But on the little green patch in the middle of the garden in back, I get the sun throughout the day and the song of the birds, and I can see the blue sky. And though I'm fond of people's company, it's nice sometimes to be able to forget Liwsi and Lowri, Doli and Dan, John and Enid, and enjoy the warmth beating on my face and look through sunshine and gnats at Besi sewing. That's how I was today, with John, for the moment, sitting with Besi, when the woman next door came to the wall to say that someone was knocking on the front door. Besi came back and brought Joanna Glanmor with her. Well, I was surprised. She'd come here to offer to take me to Tre Dywod in her car. I almost had a fit, and I knew from Besi's face that she was feeling the same way, and her face grew flushed. She said quite calmly: "You wouldn't know, Miss Glanmor, that my sister has been bedridden for three years, and that the only moving in her case is to be carried here every nice afternoon in summer." Of all things, Besi was just exactly as if she were beginning to cite a passage from Scripture. "No, I didn't know," the other said, "father was weighing so much on my mind." There was an uncomfortable silence which was broken by John in an apologetic tone: "No, to be sure, you were away when my sister fell in the shop and injured her spine." Some devilish spirit got into me, and I said: "But surely Liwsi has told you that I'm bedridden." "Oh yes, of course," she said, quite uninterested. And without taking more notice of me, she went and turned to

John: "Would you like to come for a run in the car, Mr. Beca?" "Well, since you're being so kind," he said, and he went. Indeed, Besi and I couldn't say a thing after the sound of the car had died away from the street. "Besi," I said, "wouldn't you have liked to go?" "Not in that company, thank you," she said, "I would have had to talk to her." I couldn't get over it, and I stated that to Besi. We came to the conclusion that Miss Glanmor was very bold, or that the both of us were two staid, old-fashioned old maids. We didn't enjoy our tea in the garden today, and nobody came here tonight. We were expecting Dan or Enid. After the man in the next house and Besi carried me back to bed, I felt extremely depressed. The street was perfectly quiet, it being a Thursday, like the day of the Sunday School trip, when you're staying home with everyone gone on the trip. Besi went out to look for someone, and I had a good fit of crying, and then regretted it, because it's a poor thing for someone to feel sorry for himself. Besi put her face against the window before coming into the house, and I knew from her questioning smile that she'd hurried back for fear of being away from me too long. And a pain began to weigh upon my breast and crush me, on thinking that I will have to close my eyes on her for the last time some day. But there I was, beginning to be tearful again. Dan put his head in at the door around ten. "Heigh," he said, "what's this? John and Miss Glanmor together in Tre Dywod?" Stories travel faster than the wind. After I'd told the tale, "Huh!" he said, quite dryly, and back he went, for sure, to Miss Jones and her uninteresting supper. What a day!

June 12

Things are moving in Gossip Row. I wasn't looking forward to today at all. For all purposes our company on Sunday night was finished for me, because of the presence of Miss Jones, but I hadn't bargained for what happened tonight. Everybody was here except Dan. Miss Jones came here as on the previous Sunday night, and I thought her face fell when she saw that Dan wasn't here, but perhaps it was all in my mind. But she left quite soon. In some ten minutes there came a knock at the door, and who was there but Joanna Glanmor. There was quite a strange look on everyone when she came in. I almost laughed out loud on seeing Liwsi's face. The wonder in her eyes had almost turned into alarm. Miss Glanmor asked me how I was with such feeling that everyone else smiled, because it's an unwritten law that none of our crowd asks how I am by now. Everybody had begun to find fault with the sermon in the ten minutes they had after seeing

Miss Jones's back, and when Miss Glanmor began to praise the sermon, everybody smiled. Everybody thought the preacher was quite uninteresting, humming-and-hawing and coughing, instead of coming to the point, rambling round sea and mountain to say something quite simple. Enid of the opinion that he could have said it all in a quarter of an hour, and not three quarters as he did. But Miss Glanmor had enjoyed it, and had gone to him to thank him at the end. She asked John point-blank what he thought of the sermon, and he went and half-apologized and said it was quite good but rather long, when he'd just said he'd been disgusted. The old worm! Even old Lowri found fault with it. After discussing the sermon, Miss Glanmor left, and it was too much for everybody to be polite after her back was turned. "Well, upon my word," Liwsi said, "that one would poke her beak into Heaven." "Only her beak," Enid said; "she'll never get to sit there, she's too foolish." "Don't make jokes with sacred things," Lowri said. How many times have we heard that from Lowri, with no one taking notice of it, though everybody in the company recognizes that she's quite an upstanding old woman and everybody respects her? "But she isn't simply foolish," Liwsi said, "she gets everything that she wants." "Except her father's property," I said. "Well, almost everything," she said. We had supper after everybody left, and John went out for a stroll. Presently, at half-past nine, we heard the weary sound of Dan coming along the pavement, and I was able to draw his attention and beckon him to come in. He was looking sad, and tired. Besi brought a bit of supper on a tray into the parlour for him. He was reluctant to stay for fear Miss Jones would come to look for him. But Besi locked the front door and was determined not to open it to anyone. Since there was no need of the light, nobody could tell that we were up. Thinking that Miss Jones could be here, he had kept away, since he's seeing too much of her in the house, he said. He'd gone for a walk to the cemetery. Annie's birthday today. She would have been fifty-five. He'd been walking along the paths afterwards, since it's so nice. "I'd rather be anywhere than my house by now," he said. "Well, why don't you tell Miss Jones to go?" I said. "To tell the truth," he said, "I'm afraid. There'd be a devil of a row there if I told her to go." At the very word, there came a knock on the front door. But it wasn't answered. Why are we afraid of things like this? Afraid of speaking our mind, afraid of deciding anything, afraid of change, and then drifting on. After he left, Besi and I talked it over a very long time; we can't meddle, and yet, are we to allow him to lose heart like that? Obviously the man is losing heart because he doesn't know what to do.

June 13

A chat with Liwsi after she finished cleaning. Joanna Glanmor had told her that she'd taken John to Tre Dywod Thursday. "Poor Mr. Beca, Liwsi, always there with his two sisters, never going anywhere, and of course he's worrying a lot over the one who's ill." I laughed at the top of my lungs. John never going anywhere and worrying over me! "Joanna is sure to find some excuse to feel pity for people," Liwsi said, "especially for men." I thought afterwards, I wonder whether John had been complaining to her, but it's hard for me to believe that.

June 14

Mr. Jones, the Minister, called here to see me, when I was in the garden bed. He didn't have much to say. He mentioned something about J. Glanmor, that he's sorry for her, that it didn't seem as though she were looking for work, but that she'd have to soon. I almost said that she's looking for anything but work, but I restrained myself. He is my shepherd, and every sheep is the same to him, though it would be natural for it to be otherwise. But I don't know why everybody's looking for a chance to feel sorry. But for that matter, I'm the same way myself, feeling sorry for Dan. It's quite a horrid old habit. Can't understand why Mr. Jones is such great friends with J. Glanmor. Perhaps he too melts under her congratulations.

June 15

Here on my own tonight. Besi gone to the Meeting and John to gallivanting. Enid came down for a minute with a worried look on her. She said she wants to get a firm grip on matters in the shop, that things are going from bad to worse. Has told John she's tired of telling people that things aren't in stock and that she wants to go to the warehouse herself, since he forgets to order things. And she's going tomorrow. We discussed John without mincing matters, seeing him as refusing to make a living and refusing to let anyone else make one either. There's a little empty shop at the top of town, and Enid would like to open her own shop there, she could get a loan of money from her brother, she said, but she's feeling sorry for John (feeling sorry again). And the worst of it is, John doesn't learn his lesson. Some people will still keep on coming to the shop to buy, though they can't find other things there. He has a good name in the town. He's always so pleasant and agreeable, never losing his temper, though he can be quite high and mighty sometimes. According to the English proverb, "Give a dog a bad name and hang him," but my experience is, "Give a dog a good name and hang him." Undiscriminating popularity has often hanged a man before now. And you'll hear people all over this town praising John. Well, if a pleasant man who never raises his voice or says anything disagreeable deserves praise, John deserves it. But how much have I suffered because John is apathetic, and how much is Enid suffering now? I'd prefer it if John cursed me and everybody else to the clouds every now and then, to show that he was awake. I wouldn't have fallen if my nerves hadn't grown weak in working to try and keep the shop going, doing things like sewing prices on clothing, doing a shop-girl's work, to save money. That's the truth. And I see Enid still doing the same thing, but I have my doubts. I think that it's myself I feel sorry for and not for John. I took to her when she came into the shop as a schoolgirl, on seeing she had work in her wrists. Enid didn't stay long tonight, and after a spell Dan came here. In my anxiety, I told him the whole thing. He listened in astonishment. "And I was thinking," he said, "that no one had trouble on his mind but me." It was drawing towards the time for Besi to come from the Meeting. "Look, Ffebi," he said, "try not to worry, and don't tell Besi. The two of us must put our heads together to do something practical. I don't believe in letting grass grow under our feet if we need a place to stand. We must think of a plan for you and Besi to be able to live apart from John. There's a lot of suffering in this world because people shake their heads pityingly and roll their tongues in soft-hearted heavenly fervour in talking about people who are suffering. We must not be concerned with John, so that you and Besi have some degree of happiness the rest of your days. Besi isn't young and you yourself are older still." But somehow I can't see it as possible for us to live apart from John. The three of us are bound together.

June 16

John spruced himself up terribly after dinner today and out he went without mentioning where he was going. He didn't have time to carry me into the garden. Asked the man next door.

June 18

Doli down today breathing fire and smoke, saw John and J. Glanmor going for a walk together the day before yesterday along the paths that go by her house. I had a shock, because I hadn't imagined the outing to Tre Dywod in the car would give birth to anything. Doli thinking this was once again a joke. I lost my temper with her and I said that it wasn't a joke to me that my brother was making a fool of himself in his old days. She didn't see that at all. But, to tell the truth, is that what was bothering me? What would I have felt if the woman were someone else? Up to now, I haven't seen anything in J. Glanmor to like. And Enid's words came to mind, that he wants to marry. If so, she's sure to catch him. It will feed his pride because Enid has refused him. I've been trying all day to put things together. There's the business going downhill. Marrying might solve part of the problem. But John knows that J. Glanmor has nothing but the house. Still, it's a very big house, and worth a bit of money. That will be more than he has now. I've given up the problem and stopped trying to pursue it. Dan called at nightfall and I found a moment to tell him without Besi hearing. No need to worry her. Dan had a chance to tell me it's the best thing that could happen for my sake, though he'd love to see John find someone else. He knows what my feelings are towards John, and he said I'm foolish to worry about losing his money. If I did that, he said, I wasn't the person he thought I was.

June 19

The same ones as a week ago here tonight, except for John. He was out, and Dan came in late. But somehow, there wasn't the same go to things. It was as if we were afraid of someone coming to disrupt our merriment, with my own mind far away. Thinking about where John was.

June 20

Expected to hear Liwsi mention something about John and Joanna today. But she didn't. She came out to the garden to collect the clothes ready for Besi to iron. As she lifted her arms to the line, I felt envious of her. Besi brought tea out for the three of us. Didn't have much appetite. Liwsi ate heartily. I fell into a nice sleep after tea. A pity, I won't be able to sleep tonight.

June 21

I was right, failed to sleep. Worrying about John. He was out again last night. I'm certain in myself that he's pursuing Joanna. (I may as well call her Joanna from now on.) He's never in the house now. I try to remember whether he was gallivanting like this last summer. I can't for the life of me remember. Trying to see in truth what's worrying me. Would I worry the same way if he were pursuing someone suitable like Enid? I put the question to myself to be answered honestly, and I believe I can say impartially that I wouldn't worry, only about the little difference in our financial situation; and that would be a bother, not a worry. I try to analyse my feelings. But I can't. And why do I? Am I not running to meet misfortune? Perhaps not, because if John is in this restless state, whether he's thinking of Joanna or not, his pleasure won't be here, and he won't have any interest in Besi or me, and his interest in the shop will become less than nothing. If he's thinking of marrying, what is he thinking to keep his wife on unless the wife takes over the responsibility of the shop? Enid could do that, but I'm doubtful about Joanna. The way I see things, if someone is a failure in one thing, there isn't much chance of him succeeding in something else either. No, that isn't quite fair. But I've observed that the people who are determined to succeed do so in two entirely different jobs.

June 22

Wonder of wonders! Miss Jones came here to visit me today and brought me a cake. I felt like an absolute Pharisee in accepting it, but I couldn't refuse it. There's the hypocrisy that we can't avoid. Besi thinking if we threw the cake away there would be less hypocrisy. But ingredients Dan paid for are in it. It isn't possible to have a conversation with Miss Jones. You try to make a connection with a trifling remark about something, and she slips like an eel from your grasp. I'd like to know why she came here today. Not from any love for me, surely.

June 23

John went somewhere this afternoon with his raincoat on his arm, though it was a nice day.

June 24

Joanna here today with a bunch of flowers. Surprised that we have such a nice place in the back with so many flowers. Probably she saw that flowers aren't rare things for us. She had been at two other places visiting sick people, she said, in Amos Street; the street that Liwsi lives in. She'd been going for months, very nice people, always glad to see her. Enid came here at nightfall looking a bit less worried than the previous time. Has been at the warehouse in London, and got what she needed. John perfectly happy that she went, as if he were losing his grip on everything, she said. Then I had a chance to speak, since Besi was out, about John and Joanna, and my doubts and my fears. Enid wasn't surprised. She knew that's the sort of person she was. Joanna had begun to telephone the shop, and the next thing, probably, would be that she'd be coming to the shop herself. I haven't slept all night. I must ask the doctor for sleeping tablets. I hate Joanna Glanmor.

June 25

The doctor here. Told me to try to be calm. Who could be? All kinds of thoughts darting through my head. The shock three years ago of discovering that I would have to lie for a long time in this bed was less of a worry to me than the things that weary me today. Decided to ask Besi to tell the friends not to call tomorrow night. Dan here tonight, but I haven't mentioned anything to him. I must first wait until I see that John and Joanna are in earnest. If they are, I hope they'll marry quickly. If they're courting for a long while, I won't be able to bear it, it's a terrible thing, waiting and waiting. My body has been waiting to get better for three years. It would be a dreadful thing for the mind still to dwell and dwell on the problem of my brother's courtship and think, what is going to happen. Rather than have them eke out a courtship, I'd prefer Joanna to whisk John away from here and take him out of my life, instead of him belonging half to her and half to Besi and me.

June 26

Sunday night. Miss Jones came here, after all. Of course, Besi hadn't told her not to come, because she isn't one of the company. She was surprised to see that no one was here. I told her I was quite ill. "But Mr. Meidrym was here last night," she said, "and he didn't say anything." "Yes," I said, "he's one person, not a crowd, and someone who's been dropping in here since he was three years old. He's like one of us." "Strange that he wouldn't have told me you were worse." It's a great thing, blindness.

June 27

Liwsi came to my bed after finishing her work. Came to my bed to ask how I was doing, and looked me in the eye. "Are you worrying?" she said. But I kept my guard up lest Besi hear. Besi went in with the clothes, and then Liwsi said: "I heard that Joanna had been here to visit you." I knew that she was feeling her way. "You needn't fear to tell me anything, Liwsi," I said, "I hear that John and Joanna are going out together. As you know, sick people and people in jail and asylums hear everything before other people, and I'm not ignorant of why Joanna is coming here to visit me." She was listening in wonder. "Of course, she goes to visit people in your street as well, and there's no further motive there." Liwsi had a good laugh. "A pity," she said, "that she couldn't hear what they say about her. They can't bear to see her. You see, Ffebi, people like Joanna who have been brought up on chicken can't ever be natural and at home in bringing chicken soup to poor people." I felt that Liwsi had a good deal more to say, but that she didn't like to do it. But she said as much as this: "She's like a cat ready to give a spring on top of a china cabinet without you knowing. She'll go through the glass and hurt her paws some day."

July 24

A hot Sunday night and I've been outside on my bed in the garden since morning. A month has gone by without me writing anything in this diary. Have been in too much pain of mind. Generally, it's to his diary a person will go when he's in pain of mind, because a diary is like the next thing to oneself. Some talk to their diary as though they were talking to themselves, and some as though they were talking to God. But I couldn't write anything, probably because of the nature of my illness. I've been outside every nice day and I've been content to lie quietly and welcome the light and the sunshine on my face and try to forget things. In that I had help from the doctor with his tablets. It was a dark night for me, without a ray of light from anywhere, not even from the quiet moments that Besi and I had together. I couldn't weep, I couldn't talk about the darkness, only try to eat the food that Besi brought me, try to talk to her, try to show that there wasn't anything worrying me, and try to show that what I needed was rest. I knew that Besi was worried, but I couldn't be hypocritical this time and say I was better. The blackness was there, persisting before my eyes like a black curtain, and for once I could understand the state of mind of the people who put an end to their own lives. Joanna came here often to ask about me but I refused to see her every time, and Miss Jones likewise. The others kept away, except for Liwsi, on Mondays, of course. I was feeling that I had come to the end of the road and that it wasn't possible to turn back or to go on. One day last week Doli came here to see me after coming back from Switzerland. She didn't know I was worse, and as usual, she was like a shower of feathers falling around Besi and myself, full of the things she'd seen in Switzerland and full of the news she'd heard after coming home. She had a good laugh in telling us that John and Joanna are courting ardently. Besi's face went white and then red and I knew it was at that moment even a hint of the thing dawned on her. And it wasn't hearsay, Doli said. Joanna had told her that day, before she came here to see us, that the courtship was in earnest and moving towards marrying. As one could expect from her, she carried the news to us before her mouth was dry. What's strange, I have no dislike for Doli, though she's selfish and lives altogether for herself and Ben. But I must say that she doesn't want to put her finger in anyone else's porridge either or try to take a piece of your life away from you or try to possess you. I'm fond of looking at her. Her skin is pure, her eyes happy, she's buxom without being fat. Her hair is still like gold without one grey hair in it, though she's about forty-five years old. There's not a trace of worry on her. She'll come into a room like March sunshine, and her sympathy is fully as chill as that. When she said the words "in earnest", I felt the black curtain open and begin slowly to withdraw, like a curtain opening on another act in a play, and though I knew there would be great worry on Besi's mind for some time, yet I knew that I could convince her that things would be better for us. The road was clear so that I could walk along it; I knew how to act and the uncertainty was over. I was on the other side of the barrier on the road. I could enjoy the tea with Besi and Doli. (Oh, I almost forgot. Doli brought pocket handkerchiefs from Switzerland for Besi and me, and a tie pin for John.) Doli was laughing, and I didn't trouble to explain to her what John's marriage would mean to us. Explanations only go skin-deep with Doli. After she'd left and I'd been carried into the house, Besi and I talked and I told her that I'd had my doubts for some time, and that I was glad my doubts were at an end, anyway, and that I was certain. She was worried to see the mainstay of our support going, but I was able to persuade her that there was no need to worry about that, that we could certainly get someone to stay here and that we wouldn't starve on the difference in the money.

July 25

Liwsi spluttering more than ever today on seeing me better. Obviously Besi has told her what we heard from Doli. After she left, Besi said what she got from Liwsi was only a confirmation of what Doli had said, and that Joanna was mad about John and talked of nothing else and has said plainly that they were going to marry. Enid here tonight, the thing affecting her more than I would have supposed. Joanna's begun to drop into the shop. Isn't it strange that someone of that sort can have such an effect on us? Liwsi said something else, namely that Joanna's going to Blackpool next Saturday for a fortnight's holidays. Wonder whether John will go? Liwsi didn't mention that.

July 26

Enid down tonight in a very bad mood. John said *today* that he's going away next Saturday for a fortnight and asked her to take charge of the shop, when she's used to taking next week every year, and had arranged to take it this year. It's in September that John usually takes his holidays. Joanna in for a long time Friday, with John in the office. Enid out of her mind.

July 27

Wednesday, and Besi went to the Meeting, the first time for a while. John went out but not to the Meeting. Dan came here and I had an opportunity to finish the conversation we'd begun over a month ago, in the light of the latest developments. I could tell my fears to him better than to Besi because I want the opinion of someone who is not a relative. I was able to explain to him that my greatest fear was that Joanna would possess John, I could see that was the sort she was, that she'd own him, body and soul; and I knew, though John would be satisfied with that for a time, once he objected to that and he saw his mistake, it was Besi and I who would suffer. I knew John well enough to know that he couldn't hide something like that. I couldn't say that I love John, but I was sure to feel for him if that happened to him, probably because our roots are in the same place. Dan saw eye-to-eye with me in my analysis of Joanna and her sense of possession. He also said that she'd been after him, but that Miss Jones had kept her away. Indeed, it was no use for a woman to call at Dan's house, since it was a cold welcome she'd have from Miss Jones. It was perilous, he said, for a man to be near these women between forty and fifty, people like Joanna and Miss Jones. It was in love with the married state these two were, he said. But the deuce was that some women in constantly fishing catch someone in the end, and a weak man like John would be caught in his blindness. And also, it would feed John's pride a bit that a daughter to an attorney was taking notice of him (that was his opinion). She in turn was clinging like a leech to a gumboil because she didn't want to go back to work. Dan agreed that Joanna might go too far, since a weak man is often able to be stubborn and thick-skulled. After Dan left how glad I was that he'd confided in me, and how glad that I'm closer to sixty than to fifty!

July 28

Lowri'r Aden here today; surprised to see her, since she only comes on Sunday night. But she wanted to say how glad she was because I was better. I wasn't expecting her to mention John and Joanna, because she doesn't come into contact with anyone who would have spoken about those things. But she said some things that made me listen. She said Miss Jones was becoming quite strange; she, as far as I know, is the only one of the company who goes to Dan's house, or is allowed to go. She's over seventy-five. And it was as a Christian she went there in the beginning when Miss Jones first came to town; to try to make her feel at home, and she still goes there. Miss Jones watches who is coming to the door, from behind the curtain in the parlour, and she doesn't open to everyone, and Dan is more and more neglected. She isn't washing regularly, only once in a while; she'll have a fit of pulling every article of clean clothing from the drawers and washing them all, and then leaving them flung all about without ironing them. Lowri failing to know why Dan doesn't ask her kindly to go away. She has two sisters, and so she isn't without a home. I said he was afraid, since he thinks that she's behaving just as Enoc Huws' housekeeper did. John went out early this afternoon. Tonight, I had a vision. I must act, and act soon. If John is going to marry, we must get Dan here to lodge. Though I know there are many would be glad to be allowed to come here, I must have someone that I can get on with. Impossible to live with the majority of mankind. But here's another problem. What if Miss Jones were to go away and Dan found someone else before John married or set the date of his wedding? There's the plan overboard then. I won't talk to Besi until I'm more certain of my plan.

July 29

Joanna here today with grapes for me. Her fussing was like a sea spitting its foam over the bed quilt. Had been visiting the people in Amos Street. "So grateful, Miss Beca, or may I call you Ffebi?" (I shut my eyes) "because I went to see them, some of them are very ill." She had seen Mr. Jones the Minister as well. I asked whether he was sick. No, but she liked to call there every now and then, because one had one's mind sharpened in talking to Mr. Jones. So many people in this town had such commonplace minds. I didn't think it was worth my saying that I agreed, since it wasn't the same people she was referring to. I let her swim on the surface of her flurried enthusiasm over the bankers and lawyers and teachers of this town, people of whose mental powers neither Besi nor I, nor John for that matter, has a great opinion.

July 31

Sunday night. The company here in full tonight. Miss Jones away over the Bank Holiday with her sister. Surprised that Dan hadn't taken his holidays the same time as usual. Liwsi let the cat out of the bag that John and Joanna have gone to Blackpool together. Besi blushed and neither of us could hide the fact that we knew nothing of their arrangements. Liwsi saw that she'd blundered and apologized pitifully. Lest the company go flat (it seems as if they'd sworn not to be interesting and happy here lately) I told Liwsi not to mind; that we were very glad to be informed so that we could understand where we were; and since they were going out publicly, that it was only to be expected they would marry, and the sooner they did the better, instead of scraping along as John did with his first sweetheart with nothing coming of it later. Lowri's mouth was like the rim of a bowl, as if she'd seen an apparition. "A dreadful thing," she said earnestly. "A dreadful thing, what, that John is marrying?" "No," she said, "but to think that here we are, having said all sorts of things at the time of Rhys Glanmor's death about his daughter, and now here she's likely to be your sister-in-law. It's exactly the same as if you'd been listening to someone disparaging you in a train carriage." And everybody laughed, as in the old days. "Oh heavens," Liwsi said, "I was the one said the most." And she went mute. I had to say something to assure them that it wouldn't make any difference to us. And what I said was no lie. A change of relationship isn't necessarily a change of opinion, though that opinion could be strengthened or weakened. But I knew deep down inside me that I wouldn't change my opinion of Joanna. I was too happy in the midst of this company that has been of so much comfort to me for the last three years to permit something as small as that to upset it. I laughed happily and Besi couldn't understand, I'm sure. Everybody acted as though they were sure to behave properly in the future, and the discussion was closed. Dan stayed to supper, but I didn't ask him about lodging. I must be certain first that John intends to marry, and have a talk with Besi. He spoke about his difficulties with Miss Jones. I told him plainly (and craftily) to tell her to go; he said just as plainly that he couldn't, that she'd be sure to raise a fuss. There'd be a to-do there, probably, when she came back, because she didn't know that he'd intended to stay home. He'd stayed on purpose so he could have the house to himself, without anyone to stifle him, and could feel that he owned his own house. He had to watch for his opportunity, because Miss Jones was so strange. An odd look on her sometimes, she could be unbalanced. A nice Sunday, except that Besi is worrying, obviously.

August 1

Was woken up today by the footsteps of people and children walking along the pavement to catch the train for Tre Dywod. A fit of longing for the time that Besi and I would go together. Was pained to see Besi working on a holiday. Decided to tell her about my plans, but I must try to create the impression on her that it's for both our sakes I'm planning. Stayed in bed in the parlour. No one here to carry me into the garden. Had a fit of crying before breakfast on thinking that I'd have to stay here today looking out at the windows of houses in a sunless and deserted street; but remembered it was worse for Besi. She, like the cuckoo, had decided not to do a single task today. Looking pretty in this little blue frock with the pink flowers on it. This is the fifth summer she's worn it. Dan came here after dinner in messy old clothes, had been working in the garden all morning, and had enjoyed himself with the house empty. Offered to take me into the garden, but I refused so as not to give Besi trouble carrying food out. Dan stayed here to tea and to supper in his gardening clothes. Besi invited him to come for his meals all through the fortnight. He promised to come if he has a problem with making food.

August 2

Tuesday. Liwsi here today with her face like a tomato, had been at Tre Dywod yesterday. Hadn't moved from the beach, gossiping with her neighbours from the next street. Everybody talking about John and Joanna. Nobody saying much either, just surprised. I had a good laugh in thinking of her changing her pitch just to gossip. But she had the sea air.

August 13

John arrived back from Blackpool and Miss Jones from her sister's house. I'm sorry about that. Have had a nice fortnight—saw Besi taking it easy for once, and Dan in and out every day and chatting. Failed, in spite of that, to venture on my plan; uncertainty, fear of putting my foot in it. What if John and Joanna had decided to part instead of marry? That happens to a great many when they go on their holidays together. John didn't mention who his companion was on his holidays. When I asked him whether he'd enjoyed himself, he said he'd had a great deal of enjoyment.

August 14

Sunday. Everybody here tonight but Dan. Not much to talk about. A so-so sermon in chapel. An August sermon in a place that isn't a holidays town. But then Miss Jones congratulated John on his engagement. Talk about a thunderbolt! Nobody knew what to say. John turned red. Besi's lips were trembling. Myself moonstruck, because I understood in a wink the sweet smile that Miss Jones turned in my direction. I was on the brink of asking her how she knew, but that would have let the cat out of the bag altogether. Had it out with John after supper. It was true they were engaged—admitted that Miss Jones had travelled with them the last part of the journey. They're marrying before Christmas. Asked him plainly how he had allowed us to know through other people, instead of telling us himself. Shyness, failing to speak, and hadn't decided to marry until he went to Blackpool, was worrying a great deal about our circumstances after he left. I told him it was Besi and I had cause to worry about his circumstances. Did Joanna know what his circumstances were, and was he able to support her? And I had one of those answers from him in the manner the outside world knows nothing about. That was his business and Joanna's. His and Joanna's! Such a change in so little time! Besi miserable. I almost told her about my plan. Too cowardly. John looking miserable as well. Indeed, I feel sorry for him.

August 15

Liwsi very amusing today. Joanna had gone straight to her after the sermon yesterday morning, something quite unusual, since it's with the wives of doctors, bankers, and dentists she holds court on Sunday mornings. And then she was greeting Liwsi with a lift in her voice: "I'm going to be married"—exactly the same way as she (Liwsi) might say: "I've been left a hundred pounds by my aunt." Liwsi worrying about Besi and me, she said. I told her to go spend her pity on Joanna. Liwsi didn't understand such a thing, and it's better not to enlighten her about the circumstances of the shop. Thinking how to enlighten Joanna on the matter. Dan here tonight having heard the news. A thoughtful and doubtful look on him. Myself once more too cowardly to ask him to come here. A worse look on Besi, dark furrows under her eyes. I spoke to her about that tonight, after avoiding it on every occasion since last night. It wasn't losing the money was worrying her, she said. Better people than us had been on the parish, but it was thinking how we'd be able to be hypocritical with Joanna. We didn't like her, we felt like shutting our eyes every time she spoke, but for John's sake we would have to keep a friendly face to her. And yet why? Only because John was our brother. John must see something in her that we couldn't see. He's the one is to live with her, and he likes someone fussing around him and paying attention to him. If so, the two of them might be happy, and why should we worry? But every time I see her, I feel that I hate her more and more. If she kept out of my sight, perhaps I could become accustomed to her. But we're living in the same town.

August 16

Enid down tonight, and very undisturbed about the marriage. Saw it coming to that for some time. Nobody would have behaved in the shop as Joanna does unless they were going to be married. If Joanna was going to take things in hand, then it was time for her (Enid) to go. But she didn't want to leave John on the rubbish heap either. Why not? What is this compassion everybody has for John? Lowri'r Aden came here later. "Ffebi dear," she said, with her hands up in the air, "what will you do without John?" She was looking as though she were seeing the cart of the workhouse here fetching us the day after the wedding. The dear old creature saying if she could help us in any way, she would, that she has twenty pounds in the bank and that we could have it all. I thanked her, and how cold my thanks were because the words were choking me! "Come here again," I said, "I'll be better able to talk to you." Besi cried after hearing the story. Dan came here tonight, and sat and talked. I felt, though he didn't say anything about John, nor did I, that that's what was uppermost on his mind, and that our chatting was only a veil over our mutual understanding of the situation. Whatever awaits us, we will have a friend, and friends.

August 18

John went out again today without saying anything. Wonder when Joanna will come down. I'll be glad to have that over.

August 19

Joanna's been here, and I've told her about the business. She was all aflutter when she came, saying she was certain we'd heard they were getting married. That broke the ice for me, and made it easier to speak. I put it to her with no nonsense. I asked her whether John had told her about the state of the business. She didn't say anything, and I pressed on so that I could get to the end before giving her a chance to answer. When I told her that the business wasn't at all flourishing, she turned red for a moment; then, perfectly self-possessed, she wagged her head three or four times, just as some deacons do when they see eye-to-eye with the preacher but lack the courage to respond out loud. A very wise wag of the head. Then, without any agitation at all, she said that she knew that things *could* be better, but such things would change after they were married, if some who were in the shop were removed and they had new-fashioned ways there. I grew heated to her at that point, and I said that there wasn't a better girl alive than Enid, and that new-fashioned ways wouldn't transform anything where there was apathy at the top. She didn't understand me, she said. "You'll understand well enough when you're married and when you've been in the shop a bit yourself," I said. But there's no way of keeping Joanna down; she's like a ball rebounding after it's been hit. Still I felt she was a bit crestfallen when she left here. Well, as an old aunt said to me, at the end of her ninetieth birthday: "There, that's over once again." But the worst is that it's a shorter step to what will happen next.

August 25

Doli's been here, having heard the news. As before, thinking it was a great joke. I thought today that she was more selfish than ever and I lost my temper. She was failing to see that Besi and I had any room to complain at all, that there's anything wrong with the marriage. I asked her why she was laughing then. The news of most people's marriages wasn't a laughing matter. And she answered that it wasn't a tragic matter either, and that it could have been much worse for us if we'd seen John buried. And I answered that some people spare a great deal of suffering in leaving this world. But I didn't mean that, in truth. I was talking in extremes to contradict, and to hurt Doli. But Oh! it's hard to bear selfish people.

August 26

Nothing at all special has happened this week. Besi feeling better after I told Joanna about the shop. Have got a burden off our minds. Joanna came here today with flowers. Very agreeable, and Besi and I tried to be.

August 27

A very nice day. Outside in the garden all day. A note from Enid saying she was coming down while they were in chapel tomorrow night. Imagine something is wrong, but no disquiet in being forced to wait this time.

August 28

Enid's been. More worry. She's decided to leave the shop and take that little shop on the square. Couldn't keep on any longer. Joanna's started to meddle more and more, and last week told Enid to go look for John, when she saw that he wasn't in the office as usual. And she sees, if this happens now, it will become worse after they're married. She spoke to the owner of the shop Thursday, and she has his word. Said that she couldn't sleep with the worry on her mind, afraid that John's business will go under completely, and afraid that she herself won't succeed either. But saw it was necessary to decide something one way or the other. Was more calm after deciding. I told her that it was impossible for her always to be unselfish, and that a person who was too kind was the next thing to a fool. In this case, she must think of herself, or go under. Living under conditions like this would be suicide. And what was John to us, or us to him? And yet, there was something more to it. We couldn't toss him out of our lives altogether. That's the damnable thing.

August 30

Mr. Jones, the Minister, called here, came back from his holidays yesterday. Looking well, walked a great deal. He spoke about John's marriage. Miss Glanmor had written to him to tell the news. He didn't look entirely pleased somehow and I knew there was something on his mind. Presently it came out. Wondering how it would be for us. "The same exactly as if we'd never had a brother, or if John had married at twenty-five," I said. But he remarked that we've been used to John for all these years, and that there would be a feeling of loss in more than one sense. (It's a handy phrase, that "in more than one sense".) I saw what he was thinking and I said that we would have to find someone to stay here. He suggested a new teacher who's coming to the school here next term, but I didn't jump at the bait. Full of hypocrisy, I said that she'd need to have two rooms because of her work. He hadn't foreseen such a thing, and I added just as hypocritically that we would have to find someone we knew well, since it would be hard for two old maids like us to get along with a strange young person. He entirely agreed, and he added: "A pity that Mr. Meidrym wouldn't give up that house, that housekeeper isn't good for anything. It's a question with me whether anyone would do the turn for him in his own house; he and his wife were so happy." I didn't say anything. Before he left, he gave me to understand that we would have to decide before the end of the month, since my brother is marrying in a month's time. I tried to hide my confusion. After Mr. Jones left, I decided to send for Dan. But I didn't have to. He came here with the strangest look on him, dead tired, and the first thing he said was that he was completely fed up. I let him go on without making any comment. Miss Jones reprimanded him today that he comes here too often, and that he would do better to be in his own house instead of giving people occasion to talk. He lost his temper at last and told her to mind her own business, that he's come here since he learned to walk. He came here straightaway after saying that, and between his house and this one, he decided to ask whether he might come here to lodge after John marries. Instead of rushing to answer, I said that it was a matter for Besi. And she was insisting that it was a matter for me, since I am the eldest. But we promised that he could come. How glad I am tonight that it was Dan who mentioned the thing first and that I didn't have to plot! How glad we always are that Fate decides things for us! So glad that I forgot to say that the marriage takes place in a month's time. I'll leave talking to John about that until tomorrow.

August 31

Besi and I thinking that Dan shouldn't give up his house or sell his furniture, lest he regret it. Perhaps he can let it as it is. Asked John was it true that he's being married in a month's time. He said he is, because Enid is leaving. There wasn't too happy a look on him in saying that. He said Joanna wants to come into the shop for a bit and have Liwsi to the house more often. We've told him about our arrangements with Dan; he was very glad and cheered up in thinking that we would have support after he left. Dan here tonight and sees eye-to-eye with our notion of letting his house. That would spare him a great deal of trouble, but he didn't know how he would tell Miss Jones. She was sorry for last night. Oh dear! Such fuss and fury! A few months back I was complaining that nothing was happening here, and here we are now, being forced to rearrange our whole life. Great changes, with myself in the middle of them, helplessly doubting whether I can adapt myself to them.

September 2

Joanna here, full of the wedding, being married here. She was very glad Mr. Meidrym is coming here to stay. "A very nice man, you know; I know him very well." "Well, we ought to know him too," I said, "after going to each other's houses for over fifty years." She turned red. She offers such an opportunity every time she opens her mouth for someone to give her a whack.

September 3

Doli here today, had come down to town to shop and to hear the story of the wedding arrangements from Joanna. Called here as a matter of habit. I told her Dan is coming here to stay, and suddenly her whole expression changed. Instead of the humorous look that's always on her face, she became very serious and pale-faced. She was surprised at us doing such a thing as taking a man in and giving people occasion to talk. I was horrified

that she of all people was acting the Puritan. I asked her what she supposed
we were going to live on. Oh, we could find a woman to stay with us, a
really nice teacher, or someone like that. "A nice teacher won't chop firewood for Besi," I said; "and I don't want any of your advice, when you're
too selfish to offer a particle of help. Advice is a very cheap thing. Get out
of my sight." And out she went. Extremely upset. I've never quarrelled
with Doli before, though I've felt angry with her many times. Ever since
Rhys Glanmor died, there have been nothing but feelings of hatred in my
bosom. But indeed, it was hard to keep from losing my temper with Doli.
She of all people finding fault with us taking in a man to lodge!

September 6

Have been very ill and the doctor's been here twice since Sunday morning. One disturbance after another, until I'm almost too weak to write. But
I must write today to see whether I can get rid of some of the pain that
is on my mind. What happened with Doli was only child's play. Sunday
morning, just after John left for chapel, Dan arrived here with a big bag
in his hand, and his face white as chalk. He had chosen Sunday morning
to tell Miss Jones about his arrangements to come here, and she went insane, so insane that he couldn't do anything but escape from her, packing a
few things in a bag and running here. He was too frightened to remain in
the house with her. Didn't know what to do, Besi and I. Decided the best
thing would be for Besi to go and see whether Lowri'r Aden hadn't gone
to chapel, and ask her to go to Miss Jones, since Lowri could deal with her.
But before she could leave, here was Miss Jones herself, rushing into the
house, through the lobby and into the parlour, like a frenzied cow. Before
anyone could try to do anything, there she was above me, shouting: "You
wicked old bitch, luring men here with your old frills and your bold old
face." Besi hurried here and pulled her away from the bed and made her
sit down on the chair. I passed out. When I came to, Besi was beside me,
with a cup of water and brandy, and was urging me to try taking a little of
it on the tip of a teaspoon. I couldn't see anyone in the room, but after a
second I heard quiet, heartbreaking crying coming from the chair behind
Besi. Miss Jones was there. The next moment I saw Besi's hand tremble in
holding the cup, and she had to sit down and I heard her crying quietly
too. Such a Sunday morning! Even if I'd been strong enough to shout, I
knew there was no point at all in shouting for Dan, unless I shouted that
one of us three was dying. Presently, Besi was saying: "Are you feeling well

enough for me to run and fetch Lowri?" I was able to nod my head. And in the few minutes that Besi was out I found a look on Miss Jones that I'd never found before, the look of a defeated woman, and for that moment, anyway, I could understand something of her misery, and I could feel genuinely sorry. I tried to say something to her, but I couldn't. I wanted to tell her not to cry, that was all. Lowri came here and took her home with her. The doctor came here in the afternoon. I can't write any more today, but it was a release to be able to write as much as that. Perhaps I can sleep tonight.

September 7

I must have the chance to write. Whatever Miss Jones' misery was on Sunday morning, it could never be greater than my misery since then. I can't get rid of the effect her words have had on me. I can't turn them aside and say that they were only words spoken in a fit of lunacy by a spiteful, disappointed woman. The words have been said, have been said to me, and so great is our notion of ourselves that hearing any word that sticks a pin into the bubble of our self-esteem, though it's said by an imbecile or a liar, is an open sore on our skin and makes us toss and turn in our minds: "Are we like that?" And ever since Sunday I ask myself, am I "a wicked bitch"? I have an occasional minute, and an occasional hour, of supposing that that is the purest and most honest thing that has ever been uttered in Gossip Row, and that I *am* a wicked woman. Perhaps it's good for us to get a shock to our souls sometimes, and try to see ourselves and our behaviour as they can appear to others, though others in our opinion misjudge us. But do we judge ourselves correctly? Have my deeds and my words throughout these last months been worthy of what I profess? I have been hating Joanna and have been hating Miss Jones. A week ago I would have said that I was the one who was right, and that it was only natural for me to hate them, since there was something in the characters of the two of them that I couldn't like, just as some foods upset us. I don't know, but I know this, that I never imagined it was possible for anyone to bear as much pain of mind as this. I've been able to bear my bodily pain for three years, and here I am, forced to admit today that my pain of mind is getting the upper hand of me.

September 8

No light from anywhere, nothing but light on my folly. I thought, in planning to have Dan here, that I was making a neat parcel of Besi's life and mine after John leaves us. Everything brought to a finish and no care or worry afterwards. That's what romanticizing is, not seeing the other side of things. I didn't think about anyone else, only my own comfort and Besi's. (Perhaps "comfort" is an inappropriate word there likewise, but comfort is a personal thing, like many things.) I didn't think about Miss Jones, not even about the fact that she would be without a place, and certainly I didn't think about her feelings in connection to Dan. And she had as good a right to those feelings as I had to any feeling that belonged to me. The mere fact that Dan had no fondness for her had nothing to do with the thing. What I'd done was consider myself. And now, bit by bit, I begin to arrive at an understanding of her misery.

September 9

A crowd of thoughts, one on top of the other. Is there any escape from thoughts? Perhaps that is only another way of asking "Is there hope for salvation?" My mind is working day and night and working in a narrow circle, and always coming back to where it started. My reflections during the night fell upon John last night, and I began to think it's he is the cause of all my trouble, his apathy indirectly is the cause of my illness. It was his courtship brought Joanna into my life and gave me such feelings of hatred. And here I was, hating him too, and so it was all day today. Are we destined to hate someone or something throughout our lives? Is it only in the grave can be found an end to all hatred and an end to all these thoughts that are running like wild horses through my head? And yet, in stopping to think how nice a thing it would be to get rid of all these thoughts and all the hating, I ask myself would I be happy then. Aren't we fond of hating? Don't we swim in the bliss of it? I sometimes think that hating gives us a feeling of satisfaction, that through it we give a blow to someone or something that is against us. An attempt to conquer, that's what it is, perhaps. Oh! to be able to breathe and throw off this shell of flesh! I wonder would I be better if I could get up from this bed and go about in the world?

September 10

I yearn to see daylight so that I can write in this diary. There's no one around me means anything to me these days. Besi comes in and out constantly, and Dan and John. I have some recollection of seeing Liwsi in this room one day and Enid, but they weren't of any interest to me. I'm astonished now at the enjoyment I had from their company on Sunday nights, or separately on other occasions. They don't know anything about all the warfare that is going on in my soul, and I can't tell them. They're as far away from me as if they were in Egypt. I thought, after getting Dan here to stay, that I'd be very happy, but his presence in the house isn't giving me any comfort. Man is an unsocial creature, fundamentally; he can't tell all his thoughts to those closest to him, or to the one he loves most. He goes about in society, he lives with himself. If one can reach that state of being able to live with someone else as he lives with himself, one can have a happy marriage. That's why I'm writing in this diary, an eagerness to talk to myself. But I can't say it all in this, any more than to myself, because I can't be totally honest with myself. I've been thinking a great deal today about a little woman from the South who stayed in the same house with Besi and me when we were on holidays in Aberystwyth. She had a saying like this at the end of a story if someone turned out different than he had appeared: "We *see* each other, don't we?" For a long time I failed to understand the comment she made use of so often. But I believe her meaning was that we see the outside of people, but we never see the inside. Does anyone see us as we are, apart from God?

September 11

Feeling a bit better today, stronger in body and more cheerful in spirit. Realized as if through a layer of mist that Besi is looking less depressed. She was asking would I like the old crowd to come and see me tonight. When I told her that I didn't know it was Sunday night, the tears filled her eyes, and a stream of other thoughts came to me, some less disturbing. Realized how much I loved her, even if I hated other people, and realized as well how much worry I gave her. How selfish I was to her, the least selfish person in the world! Realizing that did me good for a time, pulled me out of the other hateful thoughts. I tried to persuade myself it was for Besi's sake that I tried to lure Dan here, and that Miss Jones' suffering was justified because of that, since the intention was such a good one. But I didn't want to see the crowd tonight. I didn't have anything to say to them. But I found a little bit of that contentment I've felt a hundred times since I've been ill in seeing Besi sitting in the room.

September 12

Liwsi came into the room today and I was able to smile at her and say I was better. Her "I *am* glad" sounded so genuine. Mr. Jones the Minister called as well, and I felt closer to him than I've ever felt before. He gripped my hand tightly and asked: "How are you?"—a question that wasn't to be asked, according to the hint that I've given him. But I was glad to hear him ask today, since my spirit is ill. I didn't tell him that either. Thought how much of a sacrifice it is for a man like Mr. Jones to be a minister in a stupid little town like this,—-I don't mean a financial sacrifice, because every minister should be able to be above that consideration, if he's on fire for what he believes. But to think of him, a cultured man, forced to tend and deal with stupid little people like us in Gossip Row, and worse than that, perhaps, forced to preach a gospel of self-denial to people who don't understand the first thing about self-denial, who know about everything but that. But he's cheerful through it all, and tries to see some virtue in us, I'm sure. I wonder does he in truth see through us, and know who are saints and who are not? But he's a man who knows quite surely what his own weaknesses are. But I felt he was very likeable today. Ventured to ask Besi tonight how Miss Jones was, and learned that she's still in Lowri's house, but she's better. Full marks to old Lowri!

September 13

Felt stronger of mind today after hearing Miss Jones is better, though I don't rightly know in what sense "better". No one but herself can say, probably. In the middle of this depression today, I had a fit of laughing to myself, thinking about Dan coming here that Sunday morning with his bag (seems like a year to me since then, though it's only a little over a week). Looking at it from one angle, it was a very funny thing, to see a grown man forced to run out of his house from a woman's hysterics, like a cannonball. A thing like that makes me think the story of Llyn y Fan is completely true, and that you can laugh at a funeral and be quite serious. But it's in looking back and knowing Miss Jones is better I'm able to say that.

September 14

I'm not as well today. Joanna's been here. Instead of simply asking how I was, like Mr. Jones the Minister, she spewed a shower of words around me, but I tried my level best to keep the criticism, the first part of the hatred, from coming to the surface. But I didn't succeed. I think it's that self-satisfaction in her which infuriates me. If she only said silly things, one could give her fool's pardon, but she's always so satisfied with herself, and so, she gets the best of me. And there I was again, to try to get the better of her, revelling in my hatred. Looked completely happy, as though nothing were bothering her, and as though nothing could ever bother her. She's won John, of course, and that is a romance at this time; I'm the one knows about the other side of that.

September 15

All my hatred towards Joanna returned today because of the happy look on her yesterday. Hope Doli won't come here, or she'll have the same effect on me. This sort of thing doesn't pay, I must do something with myself. I can't read, it tires me, but my mind can't be empty either. And I must think of Besi, it isn't right for me to give her such worry. And since John and Joanna are going to marry and since I must see her constantly, there's only one of two things: to get rid of the hatred, by driving it out of my soul, or to get rid of it by getting rid of Joanna. I remember reading that murderers find purification that way. Something like a swoon came over me when I realized that. And I prayed. Things began to dawn on me. The truth is that Joanna has defeated me. She's taken John away from me, and I'm refusing to admit it. She's taken something away from me that I didn't want to keep for myself, and I'm behaving like a child insisting on keeping his toy without wanting it. The same with Miss Jones, I was afraid she too was taking something away from me. But I'm the one who's the conqueror in that case. That doesn't give me any pleasure by now, but my feelings towards her have softened. I feel better after realizing that.

September 16

The thoughts have been churning again and I decided today that I will have to talk to someone. Must get rid of them and I believe that telling all my thoughts will be a help to me. But to whom? I can't tell them to Besi or to Dan, the two I'm fondest of on the face of the earth. They know so much about me that showing all the ugliness of my thoughts would be a shock to them, and my embarrassment and shame would be too great for me to be able to tell them. Decided to tell Mr. Jones the Minister. He doesn't know anything about my state of mind, to my great shame, and to his too a little, perhaps. Found great tranquillity after deciding. There won't be a chance to see him before Monday.

September 17

Enid called tonight and I could take enough interest in her to ask how was her shop. Things shaping up quite well, she said. But I didn't have the same interest in it as before. John's shop and hers are things far away from me by this time. Dead things, that's what they are. It's a far road between the warm company that would meet around this bed and this unhappy solitary soul.

September 18

Besi and John went to the chapel tonight, Besi hadn't been for some time, and Dan stayed as company for me. John is as though he were afraid to stay long with me now, for fear we'll be forced to speak plainly to each other, surely. I don't know why Dan needed to stay either, since I'm able to stretch and reach everything on the table. I wasn't able to talk to him about anything, but he said of his own accord how happy he was here. I was able to say that there wasn't much happiness where someone was ill. "The sick woman will get better," he said, "and there's kindness and conversation and a comfortable room here." I knew he was almost choking as he said it. "Yes, Besi's worth the world," I said. But he didn't say anything. Thinking of Annie perhaps.

September 19

Mr. Jones the Minister came here today. I would have sent for him if he hadn't come. And it was better for him to come like this, like soot into pottage, than for me to have time to prepare. I started in as soon as he sat down for fear I wouldn't be able to start at all. It wasn't hard after beginning, and the first parts of the story were things about which I didn't need to be ashamed. I stated quite honestly that Joanna's manner didn't appeal to me before I knew she was in love with John; and that she didn't become more likeable to me after that, since I saw other things in her, like her eagerness to possess my brother altogether, and how I came gradually to hate her. I made it clear that the difference his marriage would make to us financially wasn't worrying me, though I thought that could be worrying Besi, since the burdens of keeping house were on her. I told him as well how it came into my mind that it was the eagerness to get the better of her was making me hate her; and that I considered it was she who'd got the better of me by now, and that my hatred was increased in seeing her self-satisfaction, and seeing her possess what I didn't want to keep. I gained confidence as I went on, and I slowed down and took my time. I was able to talk about Miss Jones without fear at the beginning, how I knew that Dan didn't have any of the comforts of home in his house, and that it worried Besi and me, since we'd been friends for always. I could say as well that I'd been plotting, after understanding that John would be marrying, to get Dan here to stay, before he, Mr. Jones, suggested it to me, and that I was very glad I hadn't needed to carry out my plan. And even if I'd been forced to plot, that I would have been doing it for Besi's sake, for fear of something happening to me. At that point, I began to stumble. I knew I was telling a lie. I couldn't tell him the whole truth about why I was hating Miss Jones. I mentioned, of course, that I didn't like seeing her come into our company, chiefly because she wasn't an interesting woman and everybody became silent in her company. I was stuttering by the time I finished. I had been too cowardly to confess the *one* thing that was underneath all my hatred towards Miss Jones. My minister listened to me without any expression on his face the entire time. If it caused him surprise he didn't show it. Then a sadness came over his face. "Well, yes," he said, "quite a depressing story, not only as it concerns you, but as it concerns the other two as well. I don't know anything of the history of Miss Jones, but I know about Joanna, that she never had much love at home, perhaps it's herself was to blame for that. But it was Melfyn who was everything to his mother and father. She and Miss Jones should have had homes of their own twenty years ago." And then it was as though he were considering and thinking, and he went on: "You know, forgive me for saying this also, this narrow old street is affecting you, in that you haven't moved from here for three years. You've been very brave, and have suffered without complaining. Perhaps it would have done you good if you'd complained more. Perhaps complaining would have woken your brother up a bit and got him to take you to another specialist, or find someone else here. Remember, doctors make discoveries even in three years, and perhaps something could be done for your back by now. It's hard for your sister to think of this when she has so much work. But it's evident this narrow little life has made you turn your mind too much on yourself. But try to pray." I could hardly say anything to him, only thank him. Confessing what I did had almost been too much for me, and something else had begun to gnaw my conscience by then. The confession was a failure. I was like a bird who'd broken his wing, on his side on the ground.

September 20

Since yesterday, I haven't thought about anything but the minister's words, and about my dishonesty with myself. What he said about the effect of the narrow little world on my mind gave me a bit of comfort, but I couldn't convince myself that that was enough of a reason for my wicked thoughts, and certainly, it wasn't enough of a reason for me to conceal the truth about myself. There's too much hunting an excuse for sin in this world. I owed it to myself to be stronger than the circumstances and to be able to get the better of all this hatred. And more than hatred, my craftiness and my power to deceive myself. I was able to convince myself the whole time that I was plotting to get Dan here for Besi's sake, when I knew very well deep down that what I was doing was getting him here for my own sake. And as I went on and on with my story to Mr. Jones, it rose higher and higher towards the surface, and before I finished, the whole thing was standing clearly before me and accusing me. But I couldn't confess that to him, and by now my sin is double, and the end worse than the beginning.

September 21

There's one comfort from all the suffering since yesterday. I am face to face with myself by now, and forced to admit that all the hateful thoughts and the jealousy are only the consequences of this selfishness that's in me. One thought is mine now, and that has made things simpler, and that thought is that I will have to get rid of this self; and that I will have to get the best of myself to start. I have dropped down from the broad, expansive region of the thoughts, into the narrow pass of the self, and I must go beyond it, and I realize that no human power can help me.

September 22

It's a hard battle, and I can't talk about it. But I know I've gone through a narrow pass and gone beyond the self and its ugly face in the pass. A dawn of light came to sustain me. In that white dawn, I saw how tiny and insignificant are Joanna, Miss Jones, myself, and every one of us, and that we are merely tiny specks in the plan of life and eternity, and I would have gone into oblivion with this. I am not unaware, nonetheless, that perhaps the enemy will come back once more, and that winning this battle is no different from other things in life, and that such things cannot be at an end, and completed, and perfected. But I am happy tonight, anyway. A shaft of light has come from behind me, far out of my past. Suddenly remembered a line I heard in a lecture by a college teacher over a quarter of a century ago:

"I put my hope in what will come."

IV

Tea in the Heather

(1959)

Grief

Begw was sitting on a stool in front of the fire, with her back, to anyone who might look at it, showing all the disaster of the morning. The edges of her three-cornered shawl touched the floor, while the floor was covered with tiny pools flowing from clots of snow which bore the marks of iron-rimmed clogs. Today, unusually, her hair was untidy, and it hung in disordered strands on her shoulders. For some reason unknown to Begw, her mother hadn't plaited her hair last night. That was a nice thing, because her mother would almost pull her hair out by the roots in plaiting it, with all the toughness of her arms and all the strength of the temper she was in. Her head would itch for hours after the treatment, but it was nice in the morning, after undoing the plaits, to be able to feel the wavy thickness falling past her ears and onto her neck. The cold wind was blowing under the doors, blowing the fringes of the shawl and going under her drawers, but the fire warmed her head.

In the four years of her experience on earth this was the most depressing day that Begw had ever known—a black, hopeless day, in spite of every place being white. She held her breath as she tried to keep back her sighs. She was afraid of being scolded by her mother, as she always was for going on crying. But this time her mother's voice became milder than usual.

"There now. Never mind. It was only a cat. What if you'd lost your mother?"

The flood-gate broke then. At the moment she'd rather have lost her mother than lost Sgiatan. Sgiatan was always good-natured, her mother only once in a while. What she'd seen half an hour before came into her mind in all its details and overwhelmed her again.

On getting up that morning, Begw had been looking forward to a different-from-usual-day, because there was deep snow covering the earth, one of those days when she could take down the book with the terrible pictures and put it on the settle, one of the days when she could wear her best shoes, a day like the one when she'd had flannel with goose-grease around her throat and toast soaked in water with sugar and ginger on it, one of the days when her mother would sit by the fire to tell her a story. It had been a preparation for a different-from-usual-day not to have her hair plaited the evening before. It had been a continuation of this to be dressed before she was washed and have a shawl thrown over her.

When she got up, Sgiatan wasn't anywhere around, and though she'd shouted "Puss, Puss", she didn't come out from anywhere. Presently, she ventured to open the back door and there was Sgiatan—not on the door-step raising her tail and ready to rub herself on her legs, but lying in a bucket of water, her four legs stretched out as they sometimes were on the hearth mat, but her teeth snarling like that ugly old animal in "The Children's Treasury", and her fur, her velvet fur, like a greasy old slug on the garden path, and her eyes as still and staring as the glass eyes of her doll. She couldn't believe it was possible for Sgiatan, who'd purred to her before she went to bed last night and winked at her from the iron stool, to be—. She couldn't say the word. It was too terrible. Yes, but dead was what she was, nobody had to tell her this was what dead was. She was like the mouse who'd gone into the trap.

"Shut that door, and come into the house, it's cold."

Her mother calling her, but how was it possible to come into the house? She was mesmerized by the dead body. She was afraid of it and she wanted to run from it, but she was nailed to the earth in looking at it. The sun was shining fiercely on the whiteness of the snow, and the steady drops were falling on her head from the eaves. The glass beads of the snow were reaching out long claws to draw the water from her eyes and her eyes were almost following the tears. But she couldn't move. When her mother's voice came the second time, she shut the door, and behind its darkness she felt the first pang of doors closing in her life later on.

Her first thought was to go back to bed to have a proper cry and put her head under the bedclothes. If she put her head under the clothes and shut her eyes, there would be darkness there and nothing at all and she wouldn't be able to see Sgiatan gnashing her teeth.

"You're not to go into that bedroom in your clogs."

Oh, dear, life was hard. "You're not to do this, you're not to do that." And no Sgiatan to rub her head on her legs. She went to the fire furtively, sat on the stool, and burst out crying.

"Stop squawking," from her father. Squawking—squawking—an ugly old word. Her father using an old word like that when Sgiatan was—was—dead!

She got up to fetch her wooden dolly and wrapped her shawl around it. She cried on it so much that the paint ran and went into its mouth. She tried to snuggle it under her arm, but how could one cuddle a hard old thing like this after cuddling something as soft as Sgiatan, who'd looked so funny with her head sticking out of the shawl? Then, on remembering that, she threw the doll into the heart of the fire. She'd have been glad to see it in flames—the doll could go to "the great fire" and not Begw—her and her ugly old painted face. Her mother snatched it from the flames but not before giving her daughter a proper box on the ear. The crying became screaming.

"Well, indeed, I don't know what I'm to do with this child."

"What she needs is a proper spanking," her father said.

"You could have thought twice before drowning the cat. I don't know what this craze is that you always have to put a cat in a bucket as soon as it does something."

So it was her father had done it. Begw got up and went to the end of the sofa and looked outside. The earth was all beads, and the trees were reaching long white fingers towards them. The hens were crouching in the corner of the garden with their heads in their feathers, exactly the same way she'd stuff her head into her fur boa in chapel on a cold Sunday morning. There was a big black old jackdaw picking a bone in the snow and a lot of white birds like geese everywhere. On top of the dyke were the crisscross footprints of the hens. Her eyes ran after the snow far far away. It was like a big pancake with a lot of holes in it, with a blue steel knife dividing it from Anglesey. But her head was spinning in looking at it and her eyes still wanted to come out of her head. The pancake began to rise around its edges and started towards her. Begw fell, and then she knew only that she was on her mother's knee, her head lying on the rough flannel of her bodice, with the chair rocking back and forth, forth and back. Begw opened the buttons of the bodice, and put her cold hand on her mother's warm breast. From the corner of her eye she could see her father, and on connecting him with her grief she quickly shut her eyes, and soon she went to sleep.

The old grandmother doll was smiling from the china cabinet through her spectacles at the three of them, the ship on the clock went on striking its bow into the sea on one side and curtseying to the sea on the other, and the preacher was staring very surlily from his frame on the wall.

That night, Begw woke in her bed at some time in the middle of the long night. She opened her eyes on the black blanket of darkness. She couldn't see where the window was, or the door. It must be far along in the night, because the firelight wasn't coming in through the bedroom door. Begw could hear nothing but the sound of her mother's breath, "pooh—pooh", continually. But suddenly from the darkness something was jumping from the floor onto the bed, and back again just as suddenly. It touched her toes for a second and then vanished into the silence. Sgiatan's come back, Begw thought to herself. But though she asked and asked next day, she didn't get any explanation of the matter, only everyone making fun of her and refusing to believe her, "because she was imagining things".

The Spout

Begw was standing on the lowest slat of the gate, holding onto the upright slats and swinging herself back and forth and looking out into the road. Her range had been very restricted for the past month, bed, illness, and kitchen. Today it was much wider, she could come out into the courtyard and look at the road. She wanted to see and see, see the road at full length, the shop and the chapel, the familiar things that were new again. She put her nose between the slats of the gate, thinking her face could go through, but it was too narrow. She had to look at a square patch in front of her, and it was like a picture in a frame, the spout that hadn't been quiet for a moment the whole time she was in bed, in its green frame of gorse today, tranquilly casting its bow of water into the pool, and the latter receiving it with a monotonous sound like the sound of a recitation that goes on and on forever and ever. When she'd last seen the spout the water had been coming over like a white horse leaping and neighing, the noise deafening the houses, and the pool spluttering in circles on receiving it. Wil y Fedw had come there with a broody hen and held it by the feet with its head down under the spout, while she cried on seeing his cruelty. Then Wil had put foam from the spout on his face and made himself like an old man with a white beard around his chin to frighten her more . . . Her legs had become stiff in standing on the gate, and her grip on the slats was none too tight.

She wondered, would Mair next door come out to play? She turned her head in the direction of the house, but there was only silence and a closed door there. It was nice to be outside instead of being in bed, but it wasn't nice to be still either. She had been still so long in a stuffy bedroom, constantly throwing up, and afraid of her mother leaving her for a second. She'd try her best not to throw up, but it would come without her meaning to like the spout in the road, with her mother running to put her strong hand on her forehead.

"That's it, it will be over in two minutes."

"I'm not trying to be sick, I'm really not."

"No, to be sure."

"And I thought I'd be better by the time dad came home from the quarry."

"And you will be too, you'll see. Shush, listen. Here he is this minute."

"And how is Begw tonight?"

"Just had an attack again," her mother said quietly.

"Never mind, Begw. You'll be much better after getting rid of the old thing."

"A sip of the water there for her, Wiliam."

"Here you are, look, this will wash out your throat."

"Ugh. A sour old taste!"

"I'll make you toast presently to chase it away."

"Maybe that will come back up then," Begw said more cheerfully.

"No matter. It will stay down sometime, if we just try often enough."

She was sorry for her father standing there without taking his food tin out of his pocket, the mark of his hat a red streak on his forehead and a tired look on him.

That was all over. She wasn't afraid of her mother going out of her sight now, and she wasn't sorry for anyone. She walked slowly along the path, drawing her hand along the stones of the wall, to feel the roughness of the mortar on her fingers. At the corner between this wall and the other wall there was a large smooth stone. She had only to get on top of the stone and she could drop easily into the garden next door. She put the tip of her clog carefully into a hole in the wall, and she was able to lift herself onto the smooth stone and slip over it into the garden next door. The stone was warm from the sun, and it was a nice feeling when a bare part of her leg touched it. But Oh! she'd fallen on Mrs. Huws' rhubarb patch, and one of its stalks broke with a crackle under her foot. That sound was a nice sound too, so nice that a little devil entered her and made her break another stalk and another. The next minute fear came over her. What if Mrs. Huws had seen her? She'd get a proper tongue-lashing from her, if her heart didn't melt on seeing her thin legs. She couldn't go back to her own property, the jump was too high. She sat on the smooth stone to look at her neighbour's garden. It was like a picture with its red and white polyanthus, and a border of little puce flowers for the paths—thousands of them close to each other in thick clusters like a choir on stage, blinding her with their brightness. They didn't have flowers like this, but her father said that a preacher had nothing to do all day but tend to his garden. She was feeling comfortable in the sun, her body light and her clothes loose on her, her shawl wrapping her warmly with her hair snug around her neck beneath it.

She decided to go to the road through the next door's gate, and if Mrs. Huws came to meet her, she could say that what she was doing was coming to call on Mair. But nobody came, and when she came opposite the back door, she decided to go to it and knock. But before she'd given a knock she heard the preacher's voice saying grace; she ran back for her life and through the gate and onto her own property. It was horrid for Mair, Begw supposed, her father saying grace at meals and growing a beard. She'd heard her mother say, in one of those fits she had of running down everyone, and especially Mrs. Huws next door, that it was his wife made Mr. Huws let his beard grow to save the cost of shaving.

She went back to her own house, where the warm smell of ironing met her at the kitchen door, and her mother was on her knees by the fire rolling starched collars around her two fingers and putting them on the lazy-boy to harden in front of the fire, where they looked like snakes' coils. Her mother had put her spectacles on to examine her ironing, and the sun was coming through the door and showing the white strands in her hair.

"Well, what did you see?"

"The garden next door."

"Uh? You've never been there?"

"Yes. And I've broken Mrs. Huws' rhubarb stalks."

"Wait till she gets hold of you."

"Tut, she didn't see me."

"I don't know indeed, she has eyes in back of her head."

"But they were eating. I heard Mr. Huws saying—'through Jesus Christ. Amen.'"

"Yes, I know, their thanksgiving's longer than their meal."

On hearing about the eyes in back of her head, something came back to Begw in spite of herself—something she'd been trying for long months to forget. She'd been supposed to go next door at Mrs. Huws' request to play with Mair on a wet day when Mair had a cold. That was months ago. In her great eagerness at being allowed to go to the preacher's house, she went there earlier than she was due, when they were in the middle of their dinner, not yet started on their pudding. Mrs. Huws went and put pudding on a plate for her, and made her sit on a three-legged stool in front of the settle and eat it there, with her back to the table and the family. She felt that Mrs. Huws' eyes were coming through the back of her neck to the plate and the gooseberry tart. She could still see the clotted cream on the tart in front of her. How unhappy she'd felt with every spoonful she put into her mouth, in thinking that she'd gone there too soon. But her mother had put another look on things after she went home.

"I don't want to go next door ever again."

"What was wrong today then?"

"I went there too soon, and they were busy eating; and I had a gooseberry tart and ate it on the settle. I didn't want it. Mrs. Huws was horrid in giving it to me."

"At the settle, is it? If you were good enough to go to play with her daughter, you were good enough to eat at her table as well."

The heat of shame was coming to her face as she remembered that now, and she could see the clotted cream on the gooseberry tart twinkling at her, but she didn't remember with her mother's bitter memory—she wanted someone to play with her *today,* and Mair was better than no one. Her mother rolled another collar over her two fingers.

"I've never seen a place with so few children. There were too many children years ago."

"Where's Robin?"

"He's in the thick of things at Coedcyll, getting his feet wet for sure. He'll be ill again."

"I'll go with him tomorrow."

"No, you won't, the wind is too sharp and the water's too cold."

Begw listened hard, and she heard the click of the gate next door. Out she went, and there was Mair, but not running to meet her, just standing by her own gate without moving. Begw went to her and shyly clasped her hand, admiring Mair's thick curls and her red cheeks.

"I need to go to the shop for mam," Mair said.

"I'll come with you."

"I haven't asked you. Ask first."

"May I?"

"Yes."

And the two set off, Begw striking her clogs hard on the ground, putting her chin on the lace of her pinafore, the cold wind making water squirt from her eyes, with Mair's curls bouncing like an ocean buoy around her face. In the pasture beside the road, a solitary April flower was struggling to show itself, in the middle of the greyness, with the pasture bare enough for you to be able to spin a top on it. A ewe and a lamb stood shivering on the bank of the earthen wall, the lamb close in front of its mother, continually taking a short step and stopping, a short step and stopping, like two miniatures of themselves on a dresser. Then came the knock-knock sound of a hammer, a sound that Begw hadn't heard for ever so long, with a starry stone on Twm Huws the Road's mound of stones shining in the sun. The stonebreaker was sitting on his mound in his strapped trousers, his "London Yorks", wearing wire spectacles, going on knocking as if he didn't hear anyone's footsteps and not turning his head.

"And here's Begw, all better."

"How did you know it was me?"

"Oh, I have eyes in the back of my head, you know."

"The same as Missis . . ."

"The same as everyone who's grown up. It was very strange without you along this road, but I was getting an account of you every day. Oho, it's like that, is it, Mair, giving sulky looks because Begw's getting attention," Twm Huws said, chanting the rhyme:

> "*Monkey see and monkey do;*
> *When one mule sulks, the others do too.*"

"Where did you learn that?"

"From my grandmother. Are you going to the shop?"

"Yes."

"Who told you we were going to the shop?" Mair said.

"You."

"Yes, but I'm the one who's going, not you."

"I'm going home then," Begw said, almost crying.

"Never mind, Begw, your turn to be mistress will come one day. But don't let her bother you. Look, Begw, *you* go to the shop for *me*, and bring me an ounce of tobacco, and here's a halfpenny for you to spend. And Mair, since you're going to the shop *with* Begw, here's a halfpenny for you, to avoid a fuss."

Begw looked on top of the world, and Mair crestfallen. But Mair was a ball, bouncing back, just like her curls, and she began to gossip afterwards.

"Twm Huws is a horrid old man."

"I think he's a very nice man."

"He's a common old man and wears corduroy trousers."

"My father wears corduroy trousers too, but he doesn't have London Yorks. I'd like him to have London Yorks."

The shop was, as always, full of all sorts of smells on top of each other, just like the goods. The shopkeeper didn't say anything to Begw, only smiled. And Oh! there were sweets of every colour there, the same shape as a saucer turned upside down, with all sorts of things written on them in other colours. A halfpenny's worth apiece, and a scurrying outside to open the paper wrapper and study the loving words like "Kiss me quick" that were on the sweets, and eat them. But not before Mair made sure that Begw didn't have more than she did.

Mair hurried ahead, chewing, and reached the door of the house with the shopping for her mother, Begw at her heels, before she'd finished the sweets. Mrs. Huws had opened the door before Mair could lift the latch. Mrs. Huws was looking more disagreeable than usual, with her hair pulled tight away from her face. Her voice was dry and hard.

"You've been a very long time when I wanted the yeast. Talking to that old man of the road, that's what you've been doing, I'll warrant."

"Begw did, I didn't."

"You shouldn't talk to an old man like that, Begw."

"We had a halfpenny to spend from him."

"*You* didn't, Mair, you never took a halfpenny from him."

"Yes," she said in shame.

"And you spent it for sweets?"

"Yes."

"He said it was to be for spending," Begw said defensively.

"I wasn't speaking to you, Begw. I was speaking to Mair. It's no wonder you're turning red and putting your head down, Mair. Begw, go home, and you come into the house, Mair."

This without looking at Begw. The door shut so suddenly that Begw found herself looking up like a chick for its morsel, with her eyes gaping at the paint bubble on Mrs. Huws' door. For a moment she couldn't move from this position, because it had all happened like a whirlwind. Then she tried to listen hard to know what would become of Mair. She stood there expectantly, nailed to the spot, with a shiver of mingled fear and pleasure going down her back. She was expecting to hear a scream. But the pleasure of thinking that Mair was getting a whipping didn't come, only a distant sound like the sound of insects in the air in hot weather.

She grew tired of waiting for something to happen and went back to her own house for the second time. There was the clinking sound of the tea dishes there by now, with the ironing over.

"Well?"

"Mair's getting a thrashing, I think."

"For what?"

"For spending a halfpenny for sweets without asking her mother."

"She never had a halfpenny from her mother."

"No. Twm Huws gave each of us a halfpenny for bringing him tobacco from the shop."

"I thought so. Where are your sweets?"

"Here they are. Have some."

"No, indeed, I don't want those old coloured things from the tail-end of a paper bag like that. I'd rather have a bull's-eye or a mint, and those things aren't any good for you either. Come and try eating something that's good for you."

"I don't want any food."

"Come now, here's some good bread-and-butter for you. We'll have quarry supper soon. Here comes Robin, dragging his feet."

"Oh, I'm just *starving*."

"You could have come home for your meal, I couldn't bring it after you."

Robin flung his cap on the sofa and began scoffing the bread-and-butter before he sat down.

The kitchen was transformed for Begw. The smell of boy came to her, a smell of corduroy trousers and mud and dirty water. A plume of his hair was falling damply across his forehead, and there was a thin streak left by the water running from his hair to his temple.

"And what have *you* been doing with your holiday?"

"Oh, nothing much. There aren't any nuts or fish or minnows or anything at this time of year."

"Don't try to live your life so fast, my boy, nutting time will come for you quite soon enough. Wait till you come to my age."

"But we've found a pond to fish dry when the time comes."

"Yes, I know, you're sure to find some mischief. Poor Begw hasn't had much joy on her first day out."

Robin didn't know what on earth to say to his sister. He could more easily have talked to a fish.

"Mair had to go into the house for spending a halfpenny, and she can't come out again to play."

"Tut. You're better off, it wouldn't be much of a loss if she never came out."

"Maybe she won't come out, she's been half killed," Begw said, enjoying herself.

"You said just now that you *thought* she'd had a thrashing."

"Well, I heard a noise. I'll come with you to the river the next time, Robin."

"No, you won't, a river's no place for girls."

"Never mind, Begw, you can come to town with me, some day."

"I don't want to go to town."

On feeling the tiredness of her legs and remembering the hot streets of the town, she became stubborn. Nobody wanted to let her have anything she'd like to have, not going for a walk, or being allowed to go to the river, or being allowed to believe her own lie. She was feeling miserable.

Her mother was looking at the clock.

"Goodness! Your father will be here any moment and I haven't put the potatoes in the lobscouse."

She scurried about her work. Robin by now had one foot up on the chair, his head lying on the back of it, and he was looking at the ceiling, nicely tired. Begw had her hand under her head on the table, gazing into the fire, painfully tired otherwise, and longing to go to bed. But it wouldn't be the right thing to tell her mother that, or she'd find herself going there before her father came home, and maybe staying in it the next day. She tried to look cheerful and turned her head to look at Robin. He was so messy, and so unconcerned and so happy. She envied him.

As if he weren't saying anything, just for the sake of saying something, Robin said, as his mother by now was supplying the lobscouse with salt, with her back to him:

"Huws next door was at the river."

"Look here, I'll give you 'Huws', you call the man 'Mister Huws'. He's a good man whatever his wife is."

"Oh, all right then. Mister Huws was down by the river, walking back and forth and muttering to himself."

His mother gave a half turn from the saucepan, like the opening of a fan, and held a spoon up in her hand.

"You little wretch, talking about your nuts and your minnows, and not telling something important like that. There are some boys who'd run home out of breath with news like that."

"Tut, that isn't anything. He has a habit of talking to himself by the river."

"The poor creature. I'm afraid, indeed, that that man will put an end to his life one day."

Silence then, with Begw continuing to gaze into the fire.

"Are preachers good people?"—from Robin.

"Well, they're *supposed* to be good, anyway."

"I don't think Mr. Huws next door is a *very* good man."

"Why do you say that?"

Begw took her hand from under her head and sat up straight.

"Mr. Huws curses sometimes."

"Who said so?"

"I heard him myself, in giving a thrashing to Wil y Fedw."

"He gave a thrashing to Wil y Fedw?"

"Yes, for holding a broody hen under the spout."

"He did the right thing."

"Hooray! Well done, Mr. Huws!" Begw said.

"Perhaps that's the only chance the poor fellow's getting to curse and to give anyone a thrashing, and I should think a *preacher* needs to be able to curse sometimes. It would be a great relief for poor Mister Huws."

"What's 'relief', mam?" Begw said.

"Oh, you know, getting something out that's been inside for a long time."

"Like me throwing up?"

"There you are, you've understood it."

Robin had almost gone to sleep by now, and the end-of-day tranquillity was beginning to close around the kitchen. The sun was on the brink of disappearing over Anglesey, and was looking as though it wanted to raise its head once more before going out of sight. Footsteps again, and the next minute their father came to fill the outer door and hide the sun from sight.

"And how has it been for Begw today?"

"Not much fun."

"What was the matter then?"

"They can't get along, her and that girl next door."

"A pity, but the two of them will soon be wiser. What was the matter then?"

"Oh, as you can imagine. Mair getting dragged into the house for spending a halfpenny without her mother saying she could."

"That's a small thing."

"And Mair got a proper thrashing from her mother until she was screaming all over the house," Begw said.

And she, Begw, got—what had her mother said again? Oh yes—relief, in throwing up her wish as a total lie. She saw her mother give a wink at her father, but she didn't understand the meaning of that wink.

"I want some lobscouse, mam."

"That I can believe. You've got an appetite after being out, anyway."

She could scarcely finish her quarry supper without going to sleep, and though her legs were so weak and tired, it was nice to be able to fall into the welcome softness of the feather bed, and hear the spout keep on pouring its water into the pool and lulling her into forgetting the disappointing day.

.　　.　　.

Hours later, a scream from the back bedroom. Begw shouting at the top of her lungs after having a terrible nightmare. Wil y Fedw holding Mair next door by her feet under the spout, Mister Huws cursing Wil with all his might, with his beard having turned pure white around his face, and Mrs. Huws running from the house and throwing Mister Huws into the pool. But her mother was there in a second, and she woke up.

"They're horrid old people, every one of them. Nasty old people. Robin and everyone."

"There now. There now. It was only a dream."

Death of a Story

Three evenings before Christmas, the evening that Begw had been looking forward to for weeks. Christmas was a horrid old time, especially the
evening before Christmas. There wasn't much pleasure in looking forward
to Christmas when you had to get up on a stage and recite such a silly old
thing as:

> *I am bigger than Dolly,*
> *And Daddy's bigger than me,*
> *But Daddy isn't growing*
> *And neither is Dolly, you see.*

Everybody knew, surely, that she was bigger than any doll (she didn't
have one of her own) and that her father was bigger than her. And she'd
never called her father "daddy". What if she were to forget like the time
before, and got a scolding from her mother, or what if her petticoat were
to come down like Lisi Jên, Pen Lôn's? She could see the people in front
of her gaping at her as if a lion had frightened them, just because she'd
forgotten, and her mother's lips moving and saying the words. But it was
too late, she'd forgotten, and because the adjudicator was so kind, she'd
started to cry. What if that happened again two nights from now?

But tonight was something nice, tonight was her Christmas. She could
stay up late when the other children had to go to bed, and Bilw was coming
there—Bilw who never looked mean, Bilw who was always laughing, Bilw
who'd say "Where's Begw?" as if he'd been searching the earth before finding her. She was sitting by the fire, filled with expectation, chewing her
nails while her mother had her back turned laying the dishes on the table.
The smell of beeswax filled the kitchen, the furniture gleamed and the red

and black tiles on the floor were dark from soap and scrub-cloth. Shadows lay over the far end of the kitchen like a great eagle spreading its wings. Behind the shadows were pictures of grandfathers and grandmothers, uncles and aunts, elegies in frames for members of the family who'd spent many a Christmas in their graves. And behind that, in the dark bedrooms, the smallest children with their dreams, very nebulous, about Christmas and the old man who'd come down the chimney with his sack on his back. They weren't afraid of the literary meeting. They weren't old enough. Above the table and the supper dishes hung the canary's cage, swaying back and forth and moving its latticed pattern from the sugar bowl to the bread-and-butter plate. And Dic, the canary, with his head tilted, looking at them. There was a big glowing fire in the grate, with the redness flowing slowly into the embers that stretched far up the chimney. The brightness of the hearth beneath the great chimney was increased by a white sugar sack which had been placed on the new matting. In the peat-hole beside the oven the cat was coiled up sleeping. On the curtain rod hung two ships, the only toys they were ever able to keep, because they were expensive presents from a relative better off than they were. At times a gust of wind rose outside, and its moan would come into the house like an invalid's feeble groaning.

Dafydd Siôn had arrived and was sitting in the armchair. To Begw, Dafydd Siôn was nothing much, just an old man with a grey beard, without any teeth, telling stories, and looking at her as if she weren't there. At times, he'd look through her without a smile or a frown on his face, just look at her and give her a nudge on the chest, and snarl "Buh" as if he were trying to frighten her. She had long since grown used to this. She wanted to laugh when she'd look at his face, with the tops of his cheeks bobbing up like red apples beneath his eyes as he was chewing his food. But she didn't like to look at the waterdrops that hung at the corners of his eyes, like the waterdrops on the window-frame.

Presently, her Aunt Sara arrived, like a ship, and stood in the middle of the floor. Her face was very clean and her hair was pulled tight under her hat. Begw knew she had a lot of things under her shawl, and here she was, starting to unload them and put them on the table, apples, oranges, pocket handkerchiefs, the same things every year. No indeed, here was something else coming from under the shawl in tissue paper, a scarf for Begw. This was the first time she'd had anything at all like this, she'd always had nothing but a pocket handkerchief, but this was something that would be totally in sight, a white scarf with cross-stitches on it. She put it over her shoulders and smelled it and caressed it.

But at that moment, there was the wind whistling at the door and Bilw standing in the shadows and asking: "How are you tonight? Where's Begw?" And she ran and pulled him to the settle. He stooped in going under the great chimney because he was so tall. He took off his cap with the earflaps and held his hands in front of the fire. Begw gazed at him. He was so handsome in his after-work coat and waistcoat and his corduroy trousers. And his face was so clean, and his eyes so bright, and his teeth so lovely. A pity he chews tobacco, Begw thought.

After they'd had a bite of supper, the table was pushed back and they made a circle around the fire, and Begw knew that Dafydd Siôn would start off.

"A nice bright evening tonight, Sara, you won't be afraid to go home, not like that evening long ago when I was close to losing my life on the mountain there."

"No," Aunt Sara said quite amiably, as if she'd never heard a word of the story before.

"That was the most terrible thing that's ever befallen me," Dafydd Siôn said. "My cousin Gwen was very ill at Twmpath on the side of Moel y Grug, and you know how far and what sort of road it was from that spot to Bryn-cyll, my father's and mother's house. Well, I was sent there after quarry supper one evening like this in winter, to see how Gwen was, and charged not to dawdle since I had to salt the pig, in place of my father because he'd opened up his finger at the quarry. It was dark as a black cow's belly, but I could see the tops of the dykes, and I arrived at Twmpath without much trouble. After I sat for some twenty minutes, you see, it was about nine by this time, I started off home . . ."

"You've forgotten to say how Gwen was," Begw said.

"Hush," from her father.

Laughter from Bilw, with Aunt Sara smiling. Dafydd Siôn went on:

"Oh, yes indeed, I did forget. Gwen was very ill, and the poor thing was moaning at the top of her lungs. It was thinking about that made me fail to realize for a minute that it was darker when I came out than when I'd gone into the house. I couldn't see the tops of the dykes on either side of the gate by now, and I knew that there weren't any dykes until I reached Hafod Ddafydd. You know where that is, Bilw?"

"I know very well."

"Then, you see, I had a piece of mountain to cross without a handrail, as it were. Well, there was nothing to do but follow my nose the best I could without turning to the left or the right; I knew that I'd reach home that way, somehow, and I'd come to the dykes of Hafod. Once I could reach those I could fumble along them to Bryncyll. Nonetheless I was frightened, and to tell the truth, I was glad to hear the sound of the dry heather under my feet and the sound of a penny in my pocket. I kept expecting to walk smack into the dykes of Hafod and I was on guard lest I bump my nose suddenly on the wall. But there wasn't a wall, or a house, or a sty, only me and the earth and the darkness. And here I am, trying to think where I was, whether I was close to Twmpath or to Bryncyll, or somewhere around half way. And then I have a strange feeling, as one sometimes does when one wakes up suddenly, and can't tell whether he's facing the window or the wall. And before I could count two, I had lost my direction and couldn't tell whether I was facing towards Twmpath or towards home. I decided to lie down on that spot till the morning, seeing that it would be safer than getting into a bog, if I should happen to go below Hafod. But I re-membered about the pig, and I started walking again. Well, I walked and I walked, I thought I'd been walking for hours without reaching a bankside anywhere . . ."

"Then I hear the soft sound of a brook," Begw said.

"Don't get ahead of me now; yes, the soft sound of a brook, and then I see there's a chance for me to know whether I had my back, or my face, towards home. Anyway, I bent over there, where I thought the brook was, and put my hand in the water straight with my thumb up. I knew if the water broke on the back of my hand, I had my face towards home, we had a trick like this when we were children, but it didn't come off. And there was nothing to do but start walking again. Walking and walking and walking for ages, like a top failing to stop. After a very long spell, I saw a faint light in a house and I aimed towards it. On approaching it, what was it but a light in Gwen's bedroom at Twmpath. I didn't want to bother them again. I turned my back on the light and my face towards home, and straight home I went in the same amount of time as it had taken me to go there. But one thing happened then before I reached the house—now Begw, I'm the one telling this, not you—you know that three-sided corner by the gate of Bryncyll. After I reached there I went and stumbled over something, and I fell flat with this something swaying under me, and there I was, as if I were floating on the ocean, and what was there but a dozen mountain ponies that had turned in for shelter. Indeed, that was the greatest fright I had that night. Nobody in the house was much upset because I arrived so late—had thought Gwen was worse—and by the time I finished salting the pig it was four o'clock in the morning, and it wasn't worth hitting the hay after that."

"How true," Begw's father said, quite cheerful.

Begw almost said:

> *"Amen, man of wood,*
> *Hit a piggy on his head,"*

but she remembered that Dafydd Siôn had toffee in his pocket.

"Here you are, take it," he said, "for not breaking in too often."

"Thank you very much, Dafydd Siôn, and I know why putting your hand in the water didn't do the trick."

"Why?"

"Because you didn't know which side of the brook you were on, to be sure."

"Look here, you're too clever, and too young to be saying 'to be sure' at the tail-end of a sentence,"

She was hurt for a second, but Bilw was smiling beside her.

"Do you have a story, Bilw?"

"Yes, a fresher one than that, just come out of the oven. There's been a storm at our house."

"Oh," from everyone.

"I don't know why there's a need for old literary meetings."

"Oh! Dear Bilw, thinking the same as me," Begw said to herself.

Bilw spat his chew of tobacco into the middle of the flame.

"Siani went over to Grugfab with the children for recitation practice last night and left me in the house to look after the pudding that was on the boil. She had put a kettleful of boiling water beside the saucepan and I was supposed to put water to the pudding every now and then. But I went to sleep, and the next thing I heard was a crack all over the house." (He couldn't go on, with laughing.) "I didn't know what on earth was the matter, but then I remembered about the pudding. And here I was, looking into the saucepan, and there was nothing but a black cinder in a lump on the bottom of the saucepan, and the saucepan was white."

Bilw was hiccuping with laughter; and how true was her mother's saying that Bilw was the only one you could stand to have laugh at his own story. Everybody else joined in with him, and they laughed and laughed, unable to say anything. Begw thought that something was sure to break in Bilw's chest. She stopped suddenly and asked:

"Did you get a scolding from Siani?"

"No, she started in crying."

"Why?"

"Because she had to make another pudding, and maybe buy a new saucepan."

"Did the pudding give a jump out of the saucepan into the chimney?"

"No."

"Well, yes."

And she began laughing uncontrollably in imagining the pudding leaping up the chimney with the lid in front of it.

"Look here," Dafydd Siôn said, "you're not going to say a thing like that. Keep to the truth. That's how tales get about."

"Yes," Bilw said, giving a wink at the others, "the pudding did leap up the chimney with the lid in front of it, but we won't go after it."

"We can't go up the chimney after it, to be sure."

She turned her eyes away from looking at Dafydd Siôn.

"For bed now," her mother said, "Huwcyn the Sandman is coming."

She went, sighing and looking at Bilw. He put a shilling in her hand.

"I hope you'll get something to add to it at the literary meeting."

Begw couldn't say anything. Bilw was too kind, but Oh! why did he need to mention the old meeting here and now?

After her mother tucked her in bed, she asked again:

"Why was Siani crying?"

"I don't know, poor woman."

"And poor Bilw."

"Yes, poor Bilw, and poor everyone who's tired."

"Is Dafydd Siôn tired?"

"He isn't tired of telling that story, I should think."

"He was tired of walking, for sure."

"Yes, but he was young at that time."

"Is Bilw young?"

"Yes, and Siani, and they'll forget the pudding before next Christmas."

"Why doesn't Dafydd Siôn forget losing the way on the mountain?"

"Oh, Bilw will be retelling the story of the pudding here when he's eighty."

"Will *he* have a drop of water hanging by his eye?"

"Yes, for sure."

"And an apple on top of his cheek?"

"And an apple on top of his cheek."

"He'll be ugly?"

"Now, now, Dafydd Siôn isn't ugly."

She kissed her mother and called "Good night" to the others.

"Good night, Begw."

She couldn't sleep. The sound of the talk was coming from the kitchen like the sound of bees in summer, with an occasional "Ha, ha" from Bilw in the middle of it.

She must have slept some, because every place was quiet. She got up and opened the bedroom door. The chairs were empty in the kitchen and looked as though some people had left them forever. And she went to them and sat on each one in turn and to the settle, where there was the mark of Bilw's corduroy trousers on the cushion. The lamp had been put out, but a little glimmer of light was coming onto the sack from the grate. The cat opened her eyes in the peat-hole, and closed them again. Dic was sleeping with his head in his feathers and his perch swung slightly. But there wasn't a pattern on the table any more. The embers were grey, but there in the middle was Bilw's chew of tobacco, quite like the pudding that had burned. Tomorrow, it would have gone the way of the ashes and Bilw would be in the quarry.

Two nights from now, she herself would be trembling with fear up on the platform, fear of forgetting, fear of her petticoat falling, seeing the hundreds of people in front of her like a grey blanket with a lot of bright beads on it, all looking at her, as if she were wonderful, and ready to swallow her if she forgot. Oh dear! why couldn't every evening be like tonight, with no need of memorizing.

"I am bigger than Dolly . . . ?" She went back to bed, and as she put her head on the pillow, one ember fell with its story into the ash-pit, and there was a great calm.

Tea in the Heather

"May I see it?" Begw said to her mother, and got up on the chair in the milkshed on her knees.

The "it" was jelly, a brand-new thing to Begw's mother and to every other mother in the district. To Begw, it was a marvel, this thing that was water on the milkshed table at night and a solid shiver in the morning, but more than that, something so good to eat. Last night, her mother had made an individual red one in a long-stemmed glass that she could take to the heather mountain for a tea party with Mair next door. Mair's mother intended to make something for her too, she said. Begw was hoping that Mair's mother would keep her word, because her possessive eagerness for the jelly was so great that she couldn't think of sharing it with anyone. Her mother had understood that and made it individually in this pretty glass.

"This is all mine, isn't it, mam?"

"Yes, every bit, you'll have an appetite in the mountain air, and it will do you good."

Doing you good was everything with her mother, not the nice sensation of feeling it slipping down her throat cold. But there was something else as well—she could lord it over Mair on account of the jelly. Mair had lorded it enough in school with her tomatoes, and said that they were the ones who'd had the first tomatoes in the district, and before anyone in town for that matter, and Robin had asked her how she could know that when there were tens of thousands of people living in the town.

"And here's a bit of bread-and-butter for you to eat with it, and cold tea in a bottle. And you may get out your best shoes today for once, instead of you dragging those great clogs."

"Oh, I'll be just the same as Mair next door now."

"Only on your feet, I hope."

Mrs. Huws the Preacher and Mair were at the gate when Begw and her mother went out.

"Indeed," Mrs. Huws said, "I don't know is it wise to let two eight-year-old girls go on their own to the mountain."

"They won't be on their own if they're with each other," her neighbour said, to be contrary.

"But what if some old tramp were to attack them, would two be much better than one?"

"It isn't on the mountain tramps beg for charity, Mrs. Huws."

"There are plenty of them crossing the mountain when their shoes are too bad to walk the roads. And there are a lot of wicked old boys around."

"I've never seen wicked boys," Begw's mother said, as if her son Robin were an angel.

"Oh well, nothing to do but hope for the best. We ought to go with them," Mrs. Huws.

There wouldn't be any fun in that, Begw thought, and for fear Mrs. Huws would carry out her suggestion, she started off, with Mair in her wake. They'd had permission to go bareheaded, since it was to the mountain they were going, with their hair ribbons like butterflies on the sides of their heads. Begw was wearing a pinafore with the two frills on its shoulders opening out like a fan. She noticed that Mair didn't have a sign of food anywhere. She was carrying a baby doll on her arm, and that was all. Now perplexity began for Begw, that perplexity that would time and again become her lot. What was it best to do? She couldn't eat her jelly and her bread-and-butter and look at Mair beside her without anything, and she was determined that she wouldn't get any of her jelly. She could offer her bread-and-butter and a drink.

"I have jelly," she said carefully.

"Tut, there's nothing at all in that. It's a cheap old thing. I'd rather have tomatoes."

"Do you have some with you?"

"No."

Begw's face fell. She was afraid she would have to share her jelly.

A little bit before turning to the mountain, who did they see on the road but Winni Ffinni Hadog, standing with her arms spread as if she were doing drill.

"You can't pass," she said defiantly.

And the other two were trying to escape past her, but Winni's two arms were down on them like the two arms of a wooden soldier. Then she was taking each of them by the free hand and turning them around.

"I'm coming with you to the mountain," she said.

"Who said that you could come?" Mair said.

"How do you know that we're going to the mountain?" was Begw's question.

"If you knew me, you wouldn't be asking such a question."

"Is it true you're a witch?" Begw said.

"A little girl like you shouldn't ask questions."

Begw looked at her. She was wearing an old heavy frock, and a raggedy-looking pinafore with no shape to it, just two armholes and a neck-hole, with a drawstring through it. Her hair in long hanks on her head, and falling into her eyes. They had turned to the mountain by now, and a light breeze was running across the cotton grass, blowing Mair's light frock and showing the needlework on her white petticoat. It flaunted the fallen hem of Winni's frock from side to side like the tail of a cow in heat. Her clog struck a stone.

"Damn," she said quietly, and then more loudly, "isn't it a strange thing that you see stars when you bump your clog on a stone?"

Begw couldn't believe her ears, and as she didn't hear Mair express surprise or protest, she decided that she hadn't heard the swear-word. Moreover, the perplexity about sharing the jelly was becoming urgent. Now she would have to offer something to Winni.

"I'm clean worn out, I need food," Winni said, pulling her hands from the hands of the other two.

"This patch of grass is made for our hide-out." And she sat down on a patch of green grass in the middle of the heather.

"Now sit," she said like an army officer.

The other two could only obey, as if they'd been spellbound.

"Have you ever been to Anglesey?" Winni said, looking towards that island.

"I've been, on the little steamer," Mair said.

"I've never been," Begw said.

"Nor I," Winni said, "but I mean to go some day."

"Where will you find the money?" Mair asked.

"I'm going into service, after I leave school next month."

"Where?" Begw asked.

"I don't know. But I'd like to go to London, quite far away."

"Wouldn't you feel homesick for your father and your mother?"

"No, I don't have a proper mother, and I have a devil of a father."

Mair shut her eyes and then opened them in disdain. Begw made a sound like the sound of laughter in her throat, looking half-admiringly at Winni.

"God is going to put you in the big fire for swearing," Mair said.

"No fear of that. God is kinder than your father, and more sensible than the fool of a father I have."

"Oh," Mair said, frightened, "I'll tell Dada."

"How many da's do you have then?"

"Dada is what she calls her father, and I call mine 'dad'," Begw said.

"And I call mine numbskull," Winni said.

"What's 'numbskull'?"

"A dimwitted man who thinks he has more sense than anyone. If he'd had sense, he wouldn't have married her nibs there."

"She isn't your mother then?"

"No, my mother's dead, and this one's his second wife. My mother was a fool as well. An innocent fool, of course."

"Oh," Begw said, "why are you saying a thing like that about your mother?"

"Well, she was foolish to marry a man like dad to start with, and after she married him, to put up with everything from him. It was good that the poor thing could go to her grave. But Mister Mostyn has a master now."

"Who's Mister Mostyn?"

"I don't know at all. Some quarry steward, for sure."

Begw sighed, and looked at Winni's face. Her face was red by now, and she was looking over the heads of the two smaller ones in the direction of the sea. Her mouth was crooked by nature, and since she was forced to fling her head back to toss her hair away from her eyes, she had a defiant look. As Begw was thinking when they might start on their tea, Winni started in again.

"Do you dream sometimes?"

"Yes, at night," Begw said.

"Oh no, it's in the day I mean."

"You can't dream without sleeping."

"I can," Winni said.

"Don't listen to her telling lies," Mair said.

But Begw was listening with her mouth open, with Winni like a kind of prophet to her by now, looking just like the picture of Daniel in the lions' den.

"I don't do anything but dream all day," Winni said. "That's why I have holes in my stockings, and that's the reason my father's wife complained to him about me before he took his food tin out of his pocket after arriving home from the quarry. And I got my arse whipped before going to bed."

"Oh-oh-oh," Mair said, in horror.

Begw laughed nervously.

"It wasn't a laughing matter to me. But one night I turned on him, and I fetched him a clout on the ear. I'm almost as tall as he is by now."

"And what did he do?"

"Locked me in in the bedroom without a light or anything, and I didn't get any supper. But I'd got to pay him in his own coin. But I didn't sleep much because my stomach was ravenous."

"What's 'ravenous'?"

"Thousands of lions roaring for food in your belly. But I mean to escape some day to London. I've started escaping today, because Lisi Jên threatened me with a thrashing this morning."

"Who is Lisi Jên?"

"Only my father's wife."

"How could I know?"

"There then, you know now."

Mair was looking down at her frock without saying anything, and it was Begw asked the questions. She was hurt by the last answer.

Winni went on.

"Mind you," she said, grinding her teeth, "I'll be going like the breeze some day, and I won't stop until I'm in London. And I'll find a place to serve and I'll make money."

"Maids don't make much money," Mair said.

"Oh, it isn't snobs like you I'm going to serve, but Queen Victoria herself. And I'll have a white starched cap on my chignon, and a white apron, and long strings down to the hem of my skirt to tie it. And I'll have a silk frock for going out at night and a gold bracelet, and a gold watch on my breast fastened to a bow-knot brooch and a great gold chain in two twists around my neck. And I'll have a handsome sweetheart with curly hair, not one like these common old boys around here. And farewell to Twm Ffinni Hadog and his wife forever and ever."

Then she began to pluck a tendril of the stagshorn that was growing tightly twined around the stalks of the heather. She patiently plucked and plucked with her tough hand, and then, when she had enough, she put it around her head like a wreath.

"Here you are—the Queen of Sheba," she said.

At that, here she was, flinging off her two clogs and beginning to dance on the heather, her black heels looking like the heads of two jackdaws through the holes in her stockings. She was dancing like a wild thing, flinging her arms about, and turning her face towards the sun. She grasped the hem of her skirt with one hand and held the other arm up. Begw noticed that there was only the bare skin of her haunches to be seen under her skirt. Presently she stopped, and fell half-sprawling on the ground.

"Oh, I'm dizzy."

"Have a sip of cold tea, Winni," Begw said, "this will do you good."

She had got the word "Winni" out at last, and had moved a step forward in sympathy for her.

At that, Winni sat up.

"Give me that basket, I haven't had a morsel of dinner."

And like a person who's lost her senses, she went and took the jelly glass and the spoon and gulped it all down, and then scoffed the slices of bread-and-butter. Begw was nailed to the earth, and the tears leapt into her eyes. Mair was smiling coldly.

"And now," Winni said, getting up and tossing the glass into the basket, "I mean to thrash you."

Mair ran for her life, and let her doll fall somewhere. Begw couldn't move, only look into Winni's face with her expression pleading for mercy. But Winni carried out her threat unceremoniously. She lifted up her clothes and thrashed her. Begw screamed, and managed to escape. She ran up the mountain crying, turned her eyes back once and saw Winni running with all her might after Mair. On and on Begw went, her body strangely light, until she reached an iron stile. Over the stile, and reaching wide level moorland. Going on running and finding herself going downwards. A valley came in sight, with a river running through it. And she stopped, and sat down on some nice moss. She was still hiccuping and crying, and another great gasp started as she remembered her shame. She was wretched in thinking that someone besides her mother had thrashed her. Then another feeling came, thinking how she'd begun to see something that she could like in Winni, instead of being like everybody in the district, shutting her out like a disreputable dungheap that no one could touch except with a manuring fork. And all of a sudden Winni went and did a thing that proved it was the people of the district who were right. She stopped crying, and a quiet sadness came over her. She lay at full length on the warm earth, and looked at the blue sky that was like a great parasol above her head. From the corner of her eye she could see a corner of Lake Llyncwel like a fragment of the map of Ireland, and she felt angry at the beak of the mountain that was hindering her from seeing more. A nice feeling came over her, how nice it was to be apart, instead of being among people. There was Winni, had started to be likeable, but no, she had to forget her. This silence was nice. Every sound, it was a sound from far away, the sound of stones going down over the quarry tip, the sound of shot-firing from Llanberis, the bleat of a lonely sheep far off somewhere, with all of it making her think of the baby's sigh as he slept in his cradle at home. She went to sleep delighting in her surroundings. Then she heard a noise close by, and someone walking soft as velvet over the earth. She sat up quickly and saw her brother Robin coming towards her, with the food basket in his hand. She was almost cross with him for breaking in on her stillness.

"Well," Robin said, "I had a fright."

"Why?"

"Thinking you were lost. Better come home at once, or mam will start looking for you."

"She isn't expecting me now."

"She will be, because I've sent Mair home on her own. I caught Winni Ffinni Hadog before Mair got a thrashing."

"Where is she?"

"Who?"

"Winni."

"She's gone home."

"I don't think so, because she was saying she'd begun to escape from home today."

"That's an old song with Winni, she's bound to arrive home before night, I can tell you."

Neither of the two said a word on the way home about the trouble, Begw from shame, and Robin for once understanding his sister's feelings. When they arrived, their mother was standing by the gate with Mrs. Huws and Mair, an I-told-you look on Mrs. Huws, and a very anxious look that turned into a welcoming smile on the face of her mother.

"That Winni should be put under lock and key somewhere," Mrs. Huws said. "She's much too old for her age, she isn't fit to be among children."

"Perhaps our own children wouldn't be much better if they'd been raised like her, Mrs. Huws. The girl never had a chance with such a father, her mother was a proper woman."

"Hm," Mrs. Huws said, "they're good-for-nothings, the lot of them. Like goes to like."

"*You* of all people should know, Mrs. Huws," Begw's mother said with her strongest emphasis, "that it was the grace of God sent you to Trefriw Wells to meet Mr. Huws, and not Twm Ffinni Hadog."

Then she took hold of Begw's hand and pulled her through the gate, and she told Robin when Mrs. Huws and Mair were turning towards their house:

"Better thank Mrs. Huws for the privilege of saving Mair from the clutches of Twm Ffinni Hadog's daughter."

And the doors of the two houses were shut.

But after she reached the house and could sit in the chair, Begw's mind began working on what she'd heard her mother say about Winni's mother. "A proper woman." The same sympathy for Winni as she'd had on the mountain came back to her, when she was talking about her day-dreams. A dream came to her too. She would like to go looking for Winni and have her mother ask her to come to tea with plenty of jelly, so that she could hear her talk. Her mother would be pleased as well to hear her talk and call people snobs. She could still see Winni's face as it was when she talked about getting to go into service to the Queen. She couldn't forget that face.

A Visitor for Tea

"Do you like Winni, mam?" Begw said, a few days after that strange tea party up on the mountain.

"Which Winni?"

"You know, Winni who went and ate my jelly up on the mountain that day."

"Oh, Winni Ffinni Hadog."

"Yes."

Begw hadn't been certain enough of her mother's mood to take a chance on using the nickname.

"No, I don't rightly know Winni. I knew her mother quite well. Why, what was it?"

"I've been thinking."

"Thinking about what?"

"About Winni."

"What about her?"

"I don't know. Thinking I would—I would—. What are good-for-nothings, mam?"

"Oh, disreputable sort of people."

"What's 'disreputable'? "

"Oh dear, what's plaguing the girl? Do you think that I'm Charles's Dictionary?"

Begw was silent for a while, brooding into the grate while her mother was mending work clothes. On seeing her like this, her mother began to think she had better try to get to the bottom of these perplexing questions, and in doing so, she perceived that she didn't rightly know herself what "disreputable" and "good-for-nothings" were. Before she found a definition to satisfy her, here was another question, like a thunderbolt.

"Are we good-for-nothings, mam?"

"Dear Lord, I should hope not."

"Is Winni good-for-nothings?"

"She can't be good-for-nothings, only a good-for-nothing. No, I don't think Winni is a good-for-nothing."

"Mrs. Huws the Minister said she was, and her family."

"Everybody's good-for-nothings to Mrs. Huws, except herself and her husband and Mair."

"We are good-for-nothings then?"

"Perhaps to Mrs. Huws. But nobody else would call us good-for-nothings or disreputable."

"Would people call Winni's family disreputable?"

"Some people perhaps, but it isn't for people to say."

"Who then?"

"Well, godly people like Mrs. Huws next door are the ones who say, but it's God should say. It's He that knows and rules the world."

"What's 'rules'?"

"Looking after things."

"Well, God isn't looking after things very well, is He?"

"Don't talk that way, the fault is with people."

"Who?"

"People like Mrs. Huws, next door, for being too good, and people like Twm Ffinni Hadog and his second wife for being lazy, and mean."

"Why doesn't God tell them to be the other way?"

"They don't listen."

"Are we good people, mam?"

"We're trying to be."

"Why do we want to try and be like Mrs. Huws then?"

"Drat it," her mother said, "there you've made me plant this needle in my finger."

Silence then, with only the hard sound of the needle going through the corduroy. But Begw hadn't been able to square things in her mind. She didn't know at all whether Winni was disreputable in her mother's eyes or not, and because of that she wasn't certain whether it would be a wise thing to ask her if Winni might come there to tea. She decided to venture on the hardest thing first.

"Mam?"

"Well?"

"May Winni come here to have tea some day?"

"I wouldn't mind. Why do you want to have her?"

"I like Winni."

"After she thrashed you and ate your food?"

"Yes, but you see, mam, I liked her before that. And there were lions in her stomach, she said. They're the ones ate the food, aren't they?"

"Poor creature! There mustn't be any regular meals there."

After she had the promise, Begw felt it was safe enough to warn her mother about other things. She was very much afraid of her mother being disappointed in Winni.

"She swears like a cat, mind. She did on the mountain."

"I'm sure she hears nothing else at home."

"A pity, isn't it?"

"A great pity."

"She wants to go away, into service to Queen Victoria, she said."

Her mother laughed without raising her head from the corduroy trousers.

"Where on earth would the little creature find clothes to go into service in town, not to mention London?"

"Oh, she doesn't want to go to the town, she wants to go far away."

"Well, in case she goes, you'd better try to get hold of her as soon as you can."

This problem hadn't dawned on Begw. It wasn't possible to get hold of Winni at one of the meetings in chapel. She was like an eclipse of the sun in Robert Roberts of Holyhead's almanac, "visible in this land every now and then". Begw decided to go in the direction of her home. She wasn't going to knock on the door. That would be just like going into a lions' den. She might not come out of there alive. Next day she ventured as far as Winni's house. It was an easy enough place to dawdle around without anyone seeing you, since there were some fifty yards of cart road between the gate and the house. Shivers of pleasure and fear were going down her back in turn as she neared the gate; she wanted to see Winni, and at the same time she was hoping that she wouldn't see her this time, but that she'd see her the next time. But, indeed, after she reached the gate, she saw Winni close to the door of the house, holding a small child by the hand. She didn't know what it would be best to do, whether to go towards her or call from the gate. Either one could upset Winni and send her into a flood of swear-words. She decided that her skin would stay healthier by standing at the gate.

"Oo—Oo—," she shouted.

Winni raised her head, and gave it another toss back, to get her hair out of her eyes. She gazed in Begw's direction for a long while, and then moved slowly towards her, pulling the baby by his hand—he was not too steady on his feet, and kept the far side of his body turned towards Winni as he walked pigeon-toed. Begw noticed there was a great heap of dung in front of the door of the cowshed, rising higher than the door, and she remembered her father's description of a lazy man, "his dung-heap is taller than his cowshed door."

"What do you want?" was Winni's greeting from inside the gate.

"Mam is asking will you come for tea to our house tomorrow."

Winni looked down her crooked mouth at Begw, as if she had asked her if she would come to Meeting. Then, quite majestically, as if she were Lord Newborough's daughter, she asked:

"Where do you live?"

For a second Begw felt it was she who was living behind the dung-heap, and that Winni had changed places with Mair next door. But she took heart:

"Along the road that goes the other way from the chapel."

"Close by the preacher's house?"

"Yes, next door."

Winni took time to consider, quite as if those houses were too low for her to accept an invitation to them.

"Is the preacher's woman likely to come there, while we're having tea?"

"That's the last thing she would do."

"All right, I'll come then. But I don't have any grand clothes," she said patronizingly.

"There's no need for grand clothes," Begw said, unable to conceal her gladness or put on an act like Winni.

The baby began to push a filthy crust through the gate and offer it to Begw.

"No thanks, love," Begw said. "Is he your brother?"

"Half-brother," Winni answered, "but he's quite a dear little thing."

"What's your name?"

"Sionyn," he said and looked at his feet, shyly.

"Can Sionyn come with you tomorrow?" Begw asked.

"I don't want him to come," Winni said shortly. "When I go for a visit, I don't want babies at my tail."

Winni had the same clothes on as she'd had on the mountain. Perhaps the pinafore had been washed, but it hadn't been ironed. The baby had exactly the same sort of clothes, a frock and a shapeless pinafore, with the same raggedy look.

"Ta-ta, Sionyn." She searched in her pocket, but there wasn't a single lump of a sweet to give him.

And he smiled good-naturedly between the slats of the gate, and silently flung his crust to the other side.

"Ta-ta, Winni, and mind, we'll be expecting you around three."

"All right." And quite unceremoniously Winni turned back without so much as a smile or a thank-you.

Next day Begw was on pins and needles all morning for fear her mother's mood would change, and she'd say that Winni couldn't come, fear that they wouldn't have jelly, fear that Winni would swear so much that it would shock her mother. In a word, fear that she'd made a mistake in asking that she could come. She went to look around the milkshed in the morning when her mother was feeding the pigs, and found the jelly in a bowl on the floor, solidified, with a plate over it. When she saw her mother putting a cloth on the table after dinner, and taking out the griddle to get ready for making pancakes, she knew that everything was all right on that side. She had one terrible moment when her mother said, to herself more than anyone:

"Lobscouse would be a better meal for that girl, indeed, when she's always famished."

"You're not going to make lobscouse for tea, are you?" Begw said, frightened, because she felt that even Winni Ffinni Hadog ought to have a tea like anyone else.

"Oh no, but I was thinking that it would do her more good than a tad of jelly, and nobody can eat much bread-and-butter with pancakes."

"Wait until you see Winni eat," Begw said to herself.

She didn't leave her mother's knee all the time she was making the pancakes. Robin said that he didn't want to stay and have tea with Winni Ffinni Hadog, and Rhys began crying when he heard him say that. So Robin disappeared and took his little brother with him, a very unusual thing. The baby was sleeping in his cradle with his arms up in the warmth.

Presently they heard the sound of clogs on the doorstep, and Begw's mother was there before her, saying:

"Come in, Winni," welcomingly.

Winni was wearing the same clothes except that the pinafore was different, and the heels of her stockings were as if they'd been drawn together with thread. Her face was very clean and shone, but the clean place ended precisely under her chin, in a black boundary line. The hanks of hair that were falling into her eyes on the mountain had been tied back with a scrap of calico. She stood on tiptoe on the doorstep, and then walked on tiptoe into the house.

"God, you have a clean place here," she said. "Our house is like a stable."

"You'd better come to the table now," Begw's mother said, interrupting her.

"You have jelly again—you must be having a tea party every day."

"No," Begw said, "this was made for you."

"We never have a thing, we're like Job on the dunghill . . ."

"Tut, there isn't much of anything in it besides water," Elin Gruffydd said.

"I haven't had a pancake since mam was alive," Winni said. "Lisi Jên never makes treats."

"Who is Lisi Jên?" Begw's mother asked.

"My father's wife. She isn't my mother, mercifully. I'd be ashamed to be related to her."

"Well, you ought to respect her," Elin Gruffydd said, "since she married your father."

"Respect, indeed. How can you respect a slut? She's an old devil . . ."

Begw began to tremble, for fear the swearing would get worse.

Winni went ahead.

"I'd be able to live with her all right, if she'd let me clean. But the house is so filthy that she's afraid of my getting a good look at it, and she won't let me. The pigsty is cleaner than the house."

"But Winni, can't you tidy yourself up a bit?"

"I'm the one washed this pinafore this morning, and put it on the gorse to dry, but I had to do it on the sly, or I wouldn't have had soap. Oh, these pancakes are good."

"Have some more." And Elin Gruffydd lifted another three on the fork. That's the ninth, Begw said to herself.

"And my father's a real numbskull. He's besotted with Lisi Jên. If mam had been filthy like that she'd have got a thrashing from him. But Lisi Jên can do no wrong."

"How long is it since they were married?"

"Some two years. It wasn't much more than a year after mam died."

"Come, one more helping, Winni."

And she took another three pancakes.

"Lisi Jên won't get up to make breakfast for him before he goes to the quarry. She'll lie nicely in bed until nine. And he doesn't complain that he has to make his breakfast. Mam got up until she wasn't able, and she'd moan in pain as she sliced bread-and-butter to put in his food tin, with him saying: 'What the devil's wrong with you?' I'd get up sometimes and make a fire but I couldn't slice bread-and-butter."

The talk was going in a different direction than Begw had hoped. Winni wasn't defiant as she'd been on the mountain, and there wasn't a sign of dancing on her today.

"Can't you come to chapel sometimes, Winni?" Begw's mother asked.

"I haven't any clothes, and I don't want to come near any old snobs like this woman next door."

"Everybody isn't a snob, you know."

"Everybody turns their noses up at me as if I were dirt. Their houses are dovecotes, a lot of them, too."

"You want to come and pay them no mind. They aren't any better than you."

"No, honest to God, I wouldn't look through a quill at some of them. There's Lisi Jên's aunt, with her feather boa and her morocco shoes and jewels like pegs for pigs in her ears, and she's living in debt."

"And she goes to town every Saturday," Begw said.

"How do you know?" Winni said.

"I get a halfpenny from her for carrying her parcels from the brake."

"That's her to a T, a halfpenny for you, nothing for the shop in the village here, and everything to the shops in town. That's what you mean by a 'lady'."

Elin Gruffydd laughed.

"That's the only time I like Lisi Jên, when her aunt turns up her nose at her. Taking a photo of Lisi Jên and her together would make a good picture."

Winni laughed, for the first time since she'd arrived.

"Snobs, that's what most of the people are here, and they can look quite respectable on Sunday in chapel. But it's a pity you couldn't see them up on that mountain at night."

Elin Gruffydd thought that she'd better interrupt at this point.

"When will you be leaving school, Winni?"

"A bit before Christmas, I'll be thirteen then. And I want to go to London into service—go quite far away."

"Wouldn't you rather go to town or somewhere closer to home? You need to have very grand clothes to go to London."

"London or nothing for me. I could wash dishes with a starched white cap on my head. There are great cellars in London with gas lighting them, and things like a box carrying the food up to the high-and-mighty without anyone carrying it. And I'd have an evening off, and I'd go to chapel then. Nobody would know me there, and nobody would know I'm Twm Ffinni Hadog's daughter."

"How do you know all these stories about London, Winni?" Begw's mother said, putting another spoonful of jelly on her plate.

"I've read about them, on the sly. I'd know more if Lisi Jên weren't after me like a leech. It's in bed at five in the morning I have the best chance, and I hide the book under the chaff-bed. No danger of Lisi Jên finding it there. She never makes the bed."

"Can you read English?" Begw asked.

"A little bit, enough to understand what sort of place London is."

Begw was staring at her with admiration, and her mother with compassion.

"You see," Winni went on, "if I were to go into service in town, I know how it would be. My father would be coming down to borrow my wages shilling by shilling to get drink for that hogshead of a belly of his, and I wouldn't see a halfpenny. Another thing, they're snobs in the town as well. Flies hatched from a dung-heap, that's what they are, the same as Lisi Jên's aunt."

"Maybe you'll be homesick after going to London," Begw ventured cautiously. Winni was silent for a moment, gazing earnestly at her plate.

"Yes, I'd be homesick for someone, that's Sionyn. He's a dear little old thing, but no one takes any notice of him but me. Your little baby is heavenly clean, and Sionyn's like a dung-heap. He never gets to go to the road; I'd be able to see him sometimes if I went to the town."

"You want to insist on being allowed to wash his clothes and your own clothes, Winni, no matter what your mother says, so that you can go around looking nice. Will you have more pancakes?"

"I'll finish with bread-and-butter. This will make a feast for me for a month. A pity that Sionyn couldn't have had a bite."

"I did ask you to bring him," Begw said.

"I'll give you a few pancakes to take to him," Elin Gruffydd said.

"I don't dare," Winni said, "or I'll get a thrashing from Lisi Jên for going around gossiping."

Then she raised her head suddenly, as they heard footsteps in the courtyard. Before they could clear their throats, there was Winni's stepmother, Lisi Jên, inside the house, shouting without taking notice of anyone.

"Here's where you are, yes, going around filling your belly, when I had nobody to look after this child." (Sionyn was on her arm.) "Come home this minute, so you can empty the chamber pots. Shame on you, Elin Gruffydd, for letting a thing like this into your house."

"Sit down," Elin Gruffydd said quite deliberately, taking hold of her, and steering her towards a chair. "You'll have a cup of tea and a pancake now. I'll make fresh tea in the teapot."

Lisi Jên went like a lamb and sat on the chair.

"Winni," Sionyn shouted, and ran to his half-sister. And she placed him on her knee, and began to feed him from her own plate. In no time they were beginning once again to have tea, but the atmosphere was quite different. Everybody looking very serious, except for Sionyn, who was getting his food from Winni's hand like a chick. It was obvious that her stepmother's blackguarding had had no effect on the latter, because she was looking quite happy as she dandled Sionyn and fed him. She couldn't bring the pancakes to his mouth fast enough for him.

After they finished eating, everybody got up.

"Thank you," Lisi Jên said, quite brusquely.

Begw thought from her bearing that Winni meant to make a prophetic speech before leaving, but all that she said was:

"Thank you very much, Elin Gruffydd, that was the best meal I ever had. It will have to do us for a long while."

She said this looking at her stepmother, whose own look said: "Wait till you reach home, you'll get 'the best meal'."

As they turned from the door, Elin Gruffydd thought that "slut" was the proper word for Lisi Jên. On seeing Sionyn's good-natured smile, she remembered that she had sweets in the drawer, and ran to fetch them and give them to him.

Elin Gruffydd went to escort them to the gate, and of course, Mrs. Huws the Minister had to be in the garden, weeding where there weren't weeds and seeing who the visitors were. But Elin Gruffydd paid no mind. There was something besides pleased or displeased thoughts in her heart, they were depressed thoughts as she saw the three turn towards the road. "Why?" she said to herself, "why?" She waved her hand at Sionyn.

After going into the house Begw held inquest on the visit. It hadn't been quite as she'd thought it would be. She had thought that Winni's eloquence would rise to the same heights as it had on the mountain, or higher. But Winni had been very flat. Perhaps she had made her depressed in talking about homesickness. Leaving home wasn't an easy thing, even for Winni who hated it. She wondered if she dared ask her mother a question.

Elin Gruffydd too was sitting, reflecting, with the baby on her knee suckling.

"Did you like Winni, mam?"

"Yes, the girl is all right, if she could get fair play. And that little Sionyn, dear lad."

"Winni's nice to him, isn't she?"

"Yes, nobody else is, obviously. But Mrs. Huws next door is right about one thing."

"What's that?"

"Winni is much older than her age. But it's easy enough for us to talk. She's never been a child, obviously. It will be an achievement for her to get free from the clutches of Lisi Jên and her father. But if I know people, Winni is sure to find a way of being able to look after herself some day."

"And after Sionyn, won't she, mam?"

"Yes."

"Maybe God looks after them better than we think."

"Maybe."

But the great thing to Begw was that her mother liked Winni. She hadn't made a mistake in asking if Winni might come to tea.

Escape to London

Begw was standing by the gate, out of sorts because she couldn't go to pick blackberries with her brother Robin after dinner. He'd said that an eight-year-old girl wasn't up to going through brambles hanging over streams after the big blackberries, and that little ones weren't worth carrying a small quarry pitcher so far. She'd gone to the back bedroom to act up, and on seeing that that didn't pay, went to her doll to look for comfort, and she was holding the doll by her leg now as she looked up and down the road in search of some further comfort.

Then she saw something like a great crow coming by the chapel. The crow made a straight path to Begw and said:

"I'm escaping for real this time. I've come to the end of my tether. Come, Begw, we'll go."

Begw gave the doll a toss over the garden wall, and leapt to the hand of Winni Ffinni Hadog, who took hold of her hand limply, without looking at her or looking anywhere but on the ground, walking as though she were on crusade.

"The devil in Lisi Jên has gone on a rampage, and my father like a stupid mule is listening to her. But he won't give me a thrashing this time. I was through the door in a flash. Say something." All this without moving her head.

"I haven't anything to say."

"Say 'Lisi Jên is an old bitch'."

"Lisi Jên is an old bitch."

"There you are. Hearing someone else say it is a help."

Guto Snot-Nose and Wil Bandy-Legs appeared, coming past the corner.

"Winni Ffi-nni—Winni Ffi-nni," they sang in a drawn-out tone.

"Get along, crookshanks. My father's never been out at night stealing potatoes," Winni said without turning her head, and in the same tone as if she were inquiring about the health of the owner of the bandy legs.

The two of them turned to the mountain and walked one behind the other like two sheep, with the rear of Winni's ample frock flaunting like that creature's tail. The morning mist had retreated, but some threads of gossamer still lingered on the rushes at the corners. The sun was warm on their necks and cast its light into the tiny pools in the bog. There wasn't enough of a breeze to shake the cotton grass, and everywhere was quiet, without so much as the sound of a slate falling on the quarry tip. It was Saturday afternoon.

"Where are you going, Winni?"

"To London, into service."

"But you don't have a tin box with clothing in it."

"Never mind about that; if I go down to London, someone will take pity on me, I won't get any pity from anyone here."

Winni was flinging these words behind her towards Begw, without turning her head at all.

"That Lisi Jên will see then. She'll have to get cracking, and not laze about and drink tea in front of the fire all day."

She was silent for a while, and began again, as if to herself, between her teeth:

"And Twm Ffinni Hadog will see as well, I'll show him, taking Lisi Jên's side about everything, and there wouldn't be a semblance of quarry supper for him save for me. But my lord thinks it's she who does everything."

"Do you know the way, Winni?"

"What? The way to make food?"

"No, the way to London."

"Never mind about that now. It will be soon enough for us to ask when we reach the post road."

"But there isn't any post road here."

"We're sure to find one. There's a post road everywhere."

"Not on the mountain."

"We won't be on the mountain all day. We'll come out somewhere."

"Will we be going past Lake Llyncwel?"

"What do I know? We'll follow our noses the same as sheep. And don't talk so much. You have a lot to say for your age. Lisi Jên would have whipped your arse long since for chattering."

"Everybody has a right to talk."

"Not in front of Lisi Jên. 'Shut your mouth' is one of her scriptures."

"That isn't Scripture."

"Don't be too sure, for fear you'll come across it in the Bible. That would put a pin in your bubble."

Begw didn't know what that meant. But they came to the stile and went over it into the hill country and caught a glimpse of the corner of Lake Llyncwel.

"Oh, there it is," Begw said, and clapped her hands.

"What?"

"Lake Llyncwel."

"You sounded as though you'd found a sovereign on the ground."

"I'd like to see all of it."

"It isn't good for anything to anyone except the high-and-mighty who go on it in their boats to catch fish. And you or I will never in our lives see a boat."

"But it's pretty."

"Lisi Jên is pretty too, but she's good for nothing but to kick. I'm tired. We'll lie down here."

Begw was glad to get a rest. Winni's long legs had moved over quite a bit of ground since they'd started. They looked into the clear blue sky, Winni straight up. The blue sky was making Begw dizzy and she sat up. There was only the grey hill country around, with a crooked wall full of holes running from one end to the other, and an occasional thorn-tree between them and the mountain they had left. To Begw it was all just as though someone had put a brand-new blue hat on Winni's head, with her raggedy pinafore and wrinkled frock. She looked at Winni, who hadn't moved her head since she'd lain on the earth, just looked at the sky. Her face was pale, but her crooked mouth was determined.

"Do you pray?" Winni asked, without moving her head.

"Yes, I say my 'Our Father'."

"That isn't praying, just reciting. Do you ask Jesus Christ for something that you want terribly?"

"Yes," Begw said shyly, "at the end of my 'Our Father'."

"For what?"

"I ask Jesus Christ not to let my father be killed in the quarry."

"And your prayer has been answered up to now."

"Do you pray, Winni?"

"Not now. I did at one time, prayed like the devil."

Begw was horrified, and let out a timid "Oh".

"Why are you horrified? Are you just like the preacher's girl?"

"No—but—"

"There it is, no matter. I asked and I asked Jesus Christ to make mam better, for months, but He didn't do a thing. And mind you, perhaps your father will be killed in the quarry some day."

Begw began to cry quietly, but she didn't want Winni to see it. After all, Winni had no mother, and she wasn't crying. She ventured to say:

"Maybe she's better off, Winni."

"Who did you hear say that?"

"Mam."

"Yes, the old song. They haven't anything else to say. What does anybody know about where mam is? I liked her terribly, and she told me everything, and kept me clean, washed my head every Saturday night, and washed me all over, and put a warm nightgown on me and carried me to bed, so my feet wouldn't get cold. And I'd have a clean blouse and clean drawers every Sunday morning to go to chapel, and a red crocheted woollen petticoat."

"Why won't you come to chapel now, Winni?"

"I'm too shabby. I haven't any clothes at all. And think how the preacher's woman would look at me. She'd climb into the harmonium before she'd sit next to me, and sniff all over the chapel."

She began to chant:

> *"Setting seats for all the big folks,*
> *Leaving poor folks on the floor."*

"What does that mean?"

"I don't know at all. Don't ask. Just that the people in the chapel treat the poor as if they were dirt."

"They don't treat us that way."

"Well, no, sure to God. You're one of the big folks."

"No indeed. We haven't any money."

"Well, you're neat and clean and respectable, and there isn't much of a difference between that and being big folks. Filthy people, that's Twm Ffinni Hadog's family. You know what was the cause of the to-do this morning?"

"No."

"Sionyn, the dear little thing, sleeps with me, and he wets the bed, more's the shame to his mother that she hasn't trained him. And Lisi Jên never thinks of washing the bed clothes until they're stinking. And I said this morning that I'd wash them. I can wash just fine, and I can squeeze tight. Look at my arms."

"And you didn't get to do it?"

"No indeed! In place of getting to do it—when it was such a nice morning, think how they'd swish in the sun—here I was getting a tongue-lashing and being sworn at, and being called one of the big folks. Think of it, *me* one of the big folks."

She laughed at the top of her lungs.

"Me and the preacher's woman together! And the steward's wife! And the lady with the bogus smile!"

"Who is she?"

"You know, that widow woman, that nobody knows where she comes from, her or her money. Her mouth is too prim to speak."

"You know more about the people in the chapel than I do, Winni."

"There you are, chattering again. It isn't in the chapel you come to know people."

"We'll never get to London like this, Winni, talking about the people in the chapel."

Winni sat up and brooded.

"No."

"Hadn't we better go back?"

"To Twm Ffinni Hadog and his wife Lisi Jên! Not a chance."

"But you were praising your father before."

"Who to?"

"To those boys. You did say that your father wasn't going out to steal potatoes."

"Silly chump! I was saying that the other one's father did go. There are worse things than stealing potatoes. God, my father was mean to mam. Saying disgusting old things that went to the bone, and her saying nothing. I'd like to hear him start on his tricks with Lisi Jên. He'd get the poker on his head in a second. But mam was foolish, of course."

The two of them got up and began walking again. Winni started back along the same way as they had come.

"London isn't that way," Begw said.

"I don't want to go to London," Winni said, and broke out sobbing, "I want to go back to Sionyn. What will he do without me? And there'll be another one joining him soon."

Begw was wide-eyed. It wasn't possible to understand anyone. Here Winni had lured her here, and then turned upside-down like a cup in water. Winni dried her tears with her pinafore, and there were two filthy streaks next to her eyes.

"And don't ask anything more," she said dryly, "you're too young to know things like that."

It was Begw's turn to be stubborn now.

"I'm going," she said, "I have to get to see all of that lake."

And she turned on her heel. Winni looked foolish and in a quandary. But she followed Begw furtively, and caught up with her after a spell. They came in full view of the lake, and Begw was enchanted. The sun was gleaming on its tiny waves and making them shimmer, and she couldn't take her eyes off it.

"There, you've seen enough of it now. You'll never get rich while daydreaming."

Begw turned at last and suddenly shouted:

"There it is."

"What now?"

"The post road."

"A post road isn't any good to me now. Once you come upon something, you have your fill of it."

"I didn't get time to have my fill of the lake."

Winni didn't say anything, but both of them were glad to see the post road, though they didn't know where on earth it went. It was their luck that Griffith Jones, Tŷ Llwyd, was starting home from the forge that minute.

"Hi," he said, "where are you going this road?"

"We don't know where on earth," Begw said, "we're lost. Winni started out for London."

"Don't listen to her, Griffith Jones," Winni said, quite respectfully, "we were going for a stroll to see Lake Llyncwel, and lost the way."

Begw was old enough to know she had best go along with Winni.

"Jump into the cart," Griffith Jones said, with a flick of the whip to the horse.

Robin had just reached the house with his blackberries when they arrived, and the fuss had started to be raised about Begw on seeing that she wasn't with her brother. Winni said emphatically that she didn't mean to go home because she knew what would be waiting for her. No one had to puzzle over that problem for long, because Twm Ffinni Hadog himself came to the door, with his look enough to frighten the strongest. He hadn't shaved for a week, and his hair hadn't seen a comb for days. There was no collar on his neck, and no cap on his head.

"Come out of there, you—," were his first words. But before he'd finished his sentence Begw's father had interrupted him.

"None of your swear-words here, Twm."

"I'll kill her, I will—"

"No, you won't."

"Come into the house so we can see you properly, Tomos," Begw's mother said.

And he obeyed like a lamb. And then Begw's mother began to show everybody that she was mistress. She made them a proper meal, and made Twm and his daughter sit side by side so that they weren't forced to look at each other. Nobody said a word during the meal, except for Begw's mother urging them to eat, and everybody obeyed, without looking as though they were enjoying it.

"Now," she said, very authoritatively, "go home, Tomos, to cool off your temper a bit."

Winni began shouting, "I don't want to go with him, I don't want to go home."

And there was a look on her like an animal caught after being harried all day by dogs.

"Let me finish, Winni," Begw's mother said. "You may stay here tonight, I'll make a bed on the sofa for you, and perhaps we can do something so that you find a fairly handy little place to go into service here in town."

"But Lisi Jên will need her help more than ever now."

"Lisi Jên is capable enough of working, Tomos, and if something doesn't happen to remove Winni from there, you'll have killed her."

"But she's so fond of Sionyn."

"She can see Sionyn every week if she goes into service in town."

Twm went out as he'd come in, without showing any sign of temper, quelled by someone else's wife.

Becoming Strangers

"Keep your feet still, Begw. Winni won't come sooner when you swing your feet."

"Do you think that she *will* come, mam?"

"I don't know, she might and she mightn't."

There it was again, there was no assurance to be had from anyone for her doubts. Her mother's answer was a stupid answer, saying words for the sake of saying something and that something was nothing. It wasn't possible to go outside to see if Winni was coming, because of the drizzle with the mist filling it to the door. There was no use looking through the window.

"The wonder to me," her mother said then, "is that she's stayed a whole week in her first place, they'd have heard something if she'd run home."

It had been an empty week for Begw after Winni went into service in town, when she'd had her company every night for some weeks while she was coming there to get her clothes ready. How Winni's father and her stepmother had allowed her mother to arrange everything for the change Begw's childish mind could not comprehend. Her mother had been quite shameless, she said, taking possession of Winni, making her clothes and everything, and even discovering a tin box to put the clothes in. Yes, and she'd found the place and gone to speak to the mistress for her.

These last weeks for Begw had been like living in a land of enchantment. The chests in the bedrooms had been turned inside out, and their contents strewn on the hearth, to find material for Winni's clothes. The clothes were like colourful treasures from a far-off land with the scent of another land on them, old lavender. A black silk cape overlaid with lace, trimmed with tiny beads, with a red silk lining. It was a waste, to Begw's mind, to wear the black outside and the red inside. But there it was, people years ago were so strange, doing everything inside out. And then that black silk skirt with green stripes, stiff silk that rustled, grand things that weren't good for anything to Winni. But her mother got hold of an old black three-quarter-length coat with a curling cloth collar, and she began to take it apart, saying it would make a fine full-length coat for Winni. (Come to think of it, Begw had never seen Winni wearing a coat.) She came across an old grey cloth skirt with yards of room in it, and she made a frock for her out of that. She bought calico, at a groat a yard, and made chemises for her, and drawers with flannelette that was almost as cheap. The little sewing machine was going like a horsefly every night after the children went to bed, and Begw got to stay up late to make a show of helping by fetching and carrying for her mother and threading the needle.

But the great pleasure was that her mother had said Winni herself should sew the lace on the chemises and sew buttons on the other things, and that the only way for her to do that cleanly was for her to come down to their house, and wash her hands first thing. Elin Gruffydd pulled Winni's hair together with a hairpin, so that she could see her work, and to Begw Winni looked as if she had already begun to put up her hair and become a woman. She couldn't take her eyes off her, her face was so different, and the side of her cheek beneath her ear so pretty and so smooth. There was such an earnest look on her as she kept on sewing, stitch after stitch, without saying anything. But perhaps Winni couldn't talk and sew at the same time; it was only her mother she'd seen do two things at once.

After Winni went home every night, her mother would say that Winni had "thoroughly sobered up". Begw was delighted to hear the words "thoroughly sobered up", they were like the sound of a lot of marbles in a pouch, but somehow she didn't like to see Winni herself sobered up. She'd rather hear her railing against her father and Lisi Jên. But her mother had said that she didn't want to encourage Winni to talk about Lisi Jên, especially since another thing had arisen, and Elin Gruffydd didn't want to risk drawing Twm's frown, she said. The girl must have blue-and-white-striped cotton frocks, for the mornings in her new place, and white aprons for the afternoon, and she couldn't afford to buy those—she was ready enough to make the frocks.

The solution came in a way unintelligible to Begw, but quite intelligible to her father and mother. His fellow-quarrymen began to taunt Twm at the quarry, that he was too miserly to buy clothes for his daughter to start her out in service. He was struck on his weak spot, and soon the material was at Elin Gruffydd's house.

One evening when everything was ready, Elin Gruffydd realized that

Winni didn't have anything to put on her head, but she remembered that she'd seen a grey and red tam-o'-shanter at Siop yr Haul for half a crown, and the next night that was on Winni's head, and there was a supper to celebrate the finish before she started home. Elin Gruffydd was satisfied with her work, and said that Winni wasn't starting in service as if she were in mourning, thanks to the tam-o'-shanter.

And then, Saturday morning a week ago, she had called there on her way to the brake, and her father with her, and to Begw, Winni was like a strange girl whom she didn't recognize, just the same as the other girls in the district, her eyes like herrings from crying. There was such a dreadful look to her eyes, between swelling and reddening, that Begw was afraid the rest of her body had turned into one big tear. There was a great emptiness in her life after she'd gone, and she felt, after the weeks of Winni's company, as if she'd gone outside in her frock and pinafore, without her coat, in March.

"She's very long," Begw said, lifting her feet and putting them up on the sofa, where she'd been sitting for a good while on pins and needles, waiting.

"Perhaps she had to wait until the last brake."

"Perhaps she couldn't come at all, or perhaps she's escaped to London."

"You won't get anywhere without money."

"Or perhaps she's become a stuck-up woman and she won't come here to ask how we are."

"Hard to believe that, in so little time."

"She looked like a lady, didn't she, mam?"

"Indeed, she was quite pretty, but she'll need to have a new frock in no time."

"She'll have money to buy some now."

"Perhaps, if her father doesn't get hold of it."

"I wonder, does she answer her mistress back?"

"It will be a great temptation to Winni, because answering each other back is how they've been living at her house."

At that, there were footsteps in the courtyard and a light knock on the door, and Begw's feet and legs turned in a semi-circle before coming down on the floor. Winni came inside, smiling, and the kitchen was filled with a pleasant smell.

"You smell very nice, Winni," was Elin Gruffydd's greeting, to conceal the awkwardness, and to avoid taking notice of the traces of crying on Winni—clean crying, this time.

"Mistress put scent on my pocket handkerchief," she said, "and look, she gave me a red ribbon for tying my hair back that goes with my cap, and I had a shilling from Mister to pay for my brake."

"Very good. Do you like your place?"

"Yes, I suppose, as well as I like anywhere. I was almost dying with homesickness this week. It choked me when I went to bed."

"Everybody's the same way, Winni, it's the same as breaking a horse, you mustn't give in."

"I was homesick for Sionyn," she said, beginning to sniffle.

"Was he glad to see you?" Begw asked.

"He was shy at the start, hiding his face in his mother's apron, but he insisted on having his tea on my knee."

She became cheerful for a moment and began to laugh.

"I have news for you, Lisi Jên had cleaned the whole house, and Sionyn had a clean frock and pinafore."

"Full marks to her," Elin Gruffydd said.

"You see, Elin Gruffydd, I believe she was jealous of me a week ago, on seeing me so pretty starting off, she'd thought that I couldn't ever look like anything but a ragamuffin all my life."

"Well, if jealousy is going to make her spruce herself up, then it's a good thing. Perhaps it will help her stand on her own two feet as well. Quite a hard job for everyone."

"Yes indeed, but I have plenty of work down there, and the little boy is a very lovable thing. 'Robert' is his name, 'Robert' they call him, not 'Robat'."

"A bit of style, I should think."

"Oh yes, there's plenty of that there. But the town is a strange old place. The sound of an old coal cart with a bell on it, and horses' hooves going clip-clop all day on the cobblestones, and it's quite a funny thing to be in the cellar, and see people's feet going by your head. I'd give the world at times to hear a hen cluck."

"There are plenty in the market, Winni."

"Yes, of dead ones, and some on the brink of dying. It's a live hen in the middle of a field I mean. Well, I must get back. It's nice for you that you can sit by that nice fire," Winni said, sighing and getting up.

"Remember, Winni, try not to answer your mistress back," Elin Gruffydd said.

"I'll try my best. But it's very hard to do that all the time, if you think it's you that's right and not her. Why do people have to hold their tongues?"

"Because money is master, Winni, that's why, and it's the people with money have the means to keep maids. They can leave you high and dry in a minute."

"Yes, but it's the maids with a tongue to them can often do more work as well."

Elin Gruffydd couldn't answer that.

"Yes, but it's hard to know what is right and what isn't," said John Gruffydd, who'd come in from the cowshed during the conversation.

"Not so hard in the world of mistress and maid, but it's a proper question for you men to treat in Sunday School," his wife said.

"I can go to the Chapel this Sunday night," Winni said, "I was the one minded the house last Sunday night."

"I'll come see you to the brake," John Gruffydd said, "it's beginning to get dark and it's hard to see in this old drizzle."

"Didn't you want to go see Winni off?" her mother said to Begw after they'd gone.

"Not really," she said, very listlessly.

"Why? What's wrong?"

"She isn't the same Winni."

Her mother raised her head from the potatoes she was peeling for Sunday.

"Yes, to be sure, she's just the same, she's quite like her own mother."

"I liked her better the way she was before—as a good-for-nothing."

"What's come over the girl, when we've been trying for weeks to find clothes fit for her to wear in public, and I was thinking she looked pretty tonight."

"Yes, but she wasn't Winni. We'll never have fun with her again."

"We will, to be sure, after she gets used to the town."

"The mountain's where Winni belongs."

"Utter nonsense, and don't you try to stuff that into her head, or she'll be back like a bullet. She has to think about making her living, as all of us have had to, and as you too will have to some day. That's how the world goes on."

"Why does it need to go on? It might just as well stay as it is."

"With everyone poor? And eating someone else's food up here on the mountain?"

"Winni is eating someone else's food tonight."

"Yes, but she has a right to that."

"I'll wager a herring that Winni likes being a good-for-nothing better than being a lady."

"Yes, now, perhaps, but some day she won't."

"A pity, isn't it, mam?"

"What's a pity?"

"A pity we have to change."

"Don't brood over it, there's nothing exists in this world but change."

But Begw did brood, thinking about Winni in the cellar with the legs above her head, thinking about her homesickness for Sionyn, thinking about Winni going to chapel tomorrow in the middle of the big people of the town, forced to hold her tongue and be nice. Thinking about Winni thoroughly sobered up. No, indeed, she'd shown once tonight that she hadn't completed the sobering up, in talking about answering her mistress back. There'd been a speck of the old Winni there.

And a shiver came over her in thinking that she could see Winni again only on an occasional Saturday afternoon, and if she should go further away, she wouldn't be able ever to see her, when she'd liked her so much. And what had her mother said as well? She too would have to stand on her own two feet some day. She was feeling cold and lonely, and she moved her chair near her mother to crouch by the fire.

The Card Christmas

"Keep your feet still, and don't wriggle."

Rhys gave one more jump, and a clap of his hands. His chin barely reached to the table, and he'd set it on the edge, like a dog begging for a scrap. The sun was sparkling from his eyes after the heavy shower of teardrops a minute earlier.

Begw alone was supposed to take things for Christmas to old Nanw Siôn on top of Mynydd Grug. But Rhys had cried and bawled, like the Shop's old mule years ago her mother said, so that she had to give in, and let him go. Doing quite a foolish thing in nine-year-old Begw's judgment, letting a little six-year-old boy go up Mynydd Grug through the snow, instead of letting her go by herself, and be a companionless hero, as in a story.

It was a very sour face watched the mother wrap the things for Nanw Siôn. Life was very hard on a child. Christmas cards coming every year with a picture of a little girl in cloak and bonnet going by herself through the snow, with nobody near her. And there had never been a Christmas like that for her since she could remember, just a nasty old Christmas of drizzle and mud with darkness falling in the afternoon. But this year, here it was, a Christmas just like the card (it wasn't likely to thaw before the day after), and here was her brother, by acting up, getting the better of his mother, and spoiling her romance. But on seeing Rhys' chin on the table and the redness of his nose and eyes, her small heart melted.

"Mind you tell Nanw Siôn to boil the pudding in the cloth just as it is for two hours, and tell her to keep the toffee in the tin just as it is, so it doesn't melt. Here's a piece of currant bread for her, too, a little print of butter, and a small rib of pork. Tell her it won't be worth her heating the oven for it. Have her put it in the frying pan."

"Is Nanw Siôn very poor?"—from Rhys.

"She's pretty strapped, and she's living in a very cold place."

"I'd like to live in a cold place."

"You're not living in an oven now," Begw said.

Rhys's runny nose confirmed that.

"And here's a chew of toffee for each of you, to oil your jaws."

The two of them opened their mouths like two chicks, and in a second the chews were pinking out their cheeks, and their jaws were aching as they munched.

"There you are now, and say I was asking for her, and that I'll be expecting her down after this freeze is over."

Rhys was about to grab the basket when Begw beat him to it, but Rhys didn't care this time, since he had one victory already.

"May I tell Nanw Siôn it's me who's giving the toffee?"—to see could he win one more victory over his sister.

"Yes."

Begw didn't rise to the bait and look for another victory. It was enough for her that the basket was safely hers.

The two of them set off, both wrapped to the nose like a roly-poly, clogs on their feet, and big scarves tied about their heads. The snow was in heaps along the sides of the road, and the footpath in the middle gleamed hard in the wake of the carts. There were footprints going and footprints coming, toe print trampling on heel. Small paths going to the houses, with mountains of snow on either side. It was a funny thing to the children, hearing voices talking without hearing footsteps walking. It was like a tree without roots. The snow was collecting in the hollows of their iron-rimmed clogs, and Rhys felt as if he were standing on "bandy legs" above everybody. They gave their feet a kick on the wall as they turned towards the mountain path, and a hot pain went from their feet to their heads.

"Oh," Rhys said, making a whimpering noise.

"Tut," Begw said, "that's not much. Wait till you're at Nanw Siôn's house."

But the mountain path wasn't there, only level undented ground. Not a trace of sheep or pony, no hole of a lapwing's nest, nor trace of a cow's hooves, nothing but a smooth plain, with the tip of an occasional rush stalk poking through it.

There came a gasp of thin wind, and the snow drifted into corners in the zigzag mountain dyke, where there was already a sloping heap of snow, and before it slipped and rested on the heap, it would twist like a curl of white hair. There was no sign of the stream, but the two children knew it was there, with a cover built up from different whitenesses of frost.

"The little river of the Foty is dead," Begw said, "listen, there isn't a sound."

But there was a small hole in the ice higher up, and Rhys insisted on removing his scarf and putting his ear to it.

"No, its heart is beating very softly," he said, thinking a good deal of himself for being able to enter Begw's world.

"Look," she said, "there it is."

"What?"

"Nanw Siôn's house."

And there it was, the place where her house was crouching in the shadow of a hillock, with Mynydd Grug behind it, like white flour dumped from a big bowl.

But the snow was deeper and more slippery, and they were having trouble staying on their feet, Rhys holding tight by now to Begw's free hand. By the time they reached the gate of Nanw Siôn's house the snow had got into their clogs, and Rhys was feeling he had a hundredweight of coal hanging on each shoe. They had to knock the packed snow from the hollows again and suffer the hot needles piercing their feet.

A little knock by each of them on the door.

"Who's there?"

"Us."

"Come in. What on earth made you come here in this sort of weather?"

"Mam."

"We like coming through the snow."

"You're liking a very foolish thing. Snow is a jail."

"I had to cry to come."

"And I wanted to come by myself."

"It's very lucky you had company. What if you'd fallen and broken your leg? But why am I talking? Take off your clogs, and take off those scarves."

Nanw Siôn had a glowing fire, none too big, in the grate, with a pile of turves above it stretching into the chimney hole. She pulled one of them down closer to the fire, and then the fire responded by putting out its tongue in that direction. Slowly it began to catch.

"Sit on the settle there and put your feet on this stool. They're sopping wet."

The two of them were glad to be able to crouch as close as they could to the fire. But wind was coming from everywhere. Down from the chimney and lifting the flour sack on the hearth, under the outside door, under the door of the larder. Their teeth were chattering, and they could feel the scarves on their heads though they weren't there. But presently the turf began to flame in earnest, and Nanw Siôn moved some others closer to it, and put one lump of coal into the eye of the fire. Smells of soup were coming from a black saucepan on the hob. Nanw went to fetch three bowls and put them on the little round white table, cut a bit of bread for them, and dipped the soup into the bowls with a cup.

"Now, eat your bellies full. This will warm you much better than a drink of tea."

And it did. Bit by bit the warmth was coming back to their feet and their hands and their ears. Nanw Siôn put the poker under the turf and sparks exploded from it, and the glowing fire climbed slowly across it. There was a small flame in the lamp, and Nanw turned it up. Between the fire and the light there was a comfortable look on things, and the children's two heads began to nod. But Nanw Siôn's nose was running, and she dried it with a pocket handkerchief, made from a flour bag, which she kept between her apron-string and her waist. She had a homespun shawl over her shoulders, fastened with a strong safety-pin. A silence came over the kitchen, and in the middle of it one could hear the cat purring, the clock ticking, the two children snoring in their sleep, Nanw Siôn breathing wheezily like a bellows, and an occasional crackle from the fire.

Rhys woke up.

"Do you have a pretty strap?" he said to the old woman.

"Pretty strap? What would I be doing with a pretty strap, in heaven's name?"

"Mam said that you were pretty strapped."

A punch in the ribs from Begw.

"Yes, I am, it's pretty hard to live, but that's the way I've always known it. No matter how much anyone gets, no one can make ends meet."

"Mam sent you a few little things for Christmas," Begw said.

"And I'm giving the toffee," Rhys said.

"I suppose you gave the spoon a stir or two," Nanw Siôn said.

The basket was unpacked, with Nanw Siôn saying "Well! Oh!" about everything that came out. "The kind creature."

"We're going to have an old-fashioned Christmas."

Nanw Siôn looked at Rhys as if there were horns on his head.

"Who said so?"

"Begw."

"What does she know about an old-fashioned Christmas?"

"Well, you see, Nanw Siôn, I get cards every Christmas with pictures of snow and holly on them, and a little girl going through the snow in a bonnet and a cape."

"And you think you're her?"

"Well, we've never had snow at Christmas before."

"And neither have I. The old-fashioned Christmas is a lie, every word of it."

The children took it hard.

"Why do they say that on the cards then?"

"Some day you'll learn it's the people who tell the most lies who make their fortune soonest."

Begw couldn't say a word. She'd been deceived all the time. Had seen a romantic world long ago where little children had a white Christmas every year. Presently she ventured:

"Well, their lie has come true this time anyway, and maybe now is when we start having an old-fashioned Christmas."

"Don't muddle your head, child. That's how people go to the Asylum."

Rhys was completely lost, and said:

"Never mind about old Christmas cards, they're silly old things. I'd rather have proper snow."

"And you've got it now, my boy. If you were living on top of the mountain at my age you wouldn't want it. Snow is a shackle. Here I am up here, not able to move a step, and I can't come down there tomorrow to have dinner with you as usual."

Rhys was almost crying.

"Try to come," he said.

"Try, try, an old woman of my age. What if I were to fall and break my leg? No, I'll have to be here with the mice and the spiders."

"And the cat," Begw said, cruelly.

Nanw Siôn's eyes grew fierce.

"You know what loneliness is? Living without anyone to say a kind word, or a cruel one, to you. Living with thoughts, that's what 'brooding' is. A woman like me begins brooding, because a cat or mice can't answer you—."

"Why don't you buy a poll-parrot?" Begw asked.

"I'll give you poll-parrot, you chattering little vixen! A pity Rhys didn't stay home, so you could have gone through this snow by yourself, to see what loneliness is."

"I'd have been glad."

"Yes, to be sure, you'd have been glad if the Devil had snatched you up on his horns, and dropped you down the hole of that quarry."

Begw laughed, and Rhys trembled. He wanted to get away. But he was in the grip of Nanw Siôn's words.

"And I'll tell you this, I don't want the cat to catch the mice. They're company for me. And the cat sleeps in the bedroom so I can hear something breathing. And I like to hear a spider ticking, though it's an omen of death. But death hasn't come to me yet."

Rhys started crying. He was sorry with all his heart that he had come. This was a nightmare with both eyes open. But Nanw Siôn softened.

"Hush, my boy, Christmas will go by like everything else. Neither a time of suffering nor a time of pleasant things lasts for long. I'll be able to come down again for a chat with your mother, and to turn the handle of the churn. Your mother is the kindest woman in the world. I don't know who this girl belongs to. Remember to thank her very much for all these things."

By the time they went outside the moon had risen, and the countryside was looking as if someone had covered it all with a great white cloth for a tea party. Rhys was feeling miserable in thinking of Nanw Siôn spending Christmas there by herself, and by now, Begw was feeling that a white Christmas wasn't such a great thing after all. It was much less romantic than when she set off from home. Nanw Siôn had stuck a pin in the bubble of the old-fashioned Christmas, and she felt it was her lie had been stuck with a pin, not the lie of the painters of romance. It was she who'd been pricked.

The wind was in their faces by now, and its edge made every bit of them lose feeling. Rhys drew closer to his sister and put his numbed arm through hers. They looked like two little specks on the lonely expanse, and their shadow stretched out long at their side. They didn't see the other speck at the end of the path, until they came up to it, and heard their mother's voice saying from the silence:

"You were a very long time."

"Nanw Siôn was down-hearted."

"Why?"

"Because she has to be by herself tomorrow."

"But she means to try and come down," Rhys said.

"Don't tell a lie," Begw said, "it was you said to her to try."

And she was so glad to be able to prick someone else for telling a lie. But it made no difference to Rhys. All he wanted was to go home and thaw out and go to bed.

V

Dark Tonight

(1962)

I

Before I was fully awake I knew that Sali was overhead, ready to pull my eyes out of their sockets once I opened them. She was like this every morning, like a Gandhi in her short nightgown, with her big feet and her thin legs. Her hair tied in a ponytail, and her toothless mouth chewing an imaginary tea leaf. She came above my head and looked into the depths of my eyes, while I'd be peering, and trying to penetrate the muslin film that hid the pupils of her eyes. Every morning she'd come like this and ask,

"Does the preacher's wife want to curse today?"

She was the devil who tempted me in this place.

Why have I always thought of the devil as a man? The devils are women, and every woman had gone into Sali. So far I'd been able to refuse to satisfy her, but I was sure to lose control some morning, and then going home would be postponed.

"Nurse, make Sali go to bed."

She disappeared like a mouse's tail into a hole, putting her head under the covers and playing peek-a-boo with them, and then laughing like a mischievous child.

Jane in the bed next to mine was like a white image on a tombstone. No one could tell whether she was sleeping or not. She was a single white lump from her hair to the foot of her bed, her ring on the white quilt like a sliver of yellow moon. She was like this day after day.

"Are you awake, Jane?"

"Yes," softly.

"How are you today?"

"Just the same."

"Never mind, your husband will come to visit you."

"Why?"

"I don't know. You know, to visit you, to see how you are."

"Why?"

"To see if you're better, same as me. I'm better."

".I won't get better."

"Don't you want to go home?"

"I haven't any home, Ned's sold it."

"No, you only think he did."

"I can't think, only lie still."

And she continued to lie still, she and everyone else in the ward. Magi in the furthest bed had turned her back on everyone, on the door and on the world. Nobody ever came to visit her. She had done with existing, lying there like a plank, except that her hand under the covers gave a twitch every now and again. Lisi had got out of bed and was sitting on the chair facing the door, as she did every day. Every time someone came through it she would put her head on one side and try to look through to the porch that went on and on, farther and farther like an iron road narrowing to the horizon. This porch made me think of that FOREVER I tried to figure out when I was a child, without ever coming to the end of it. Had the door been wide open, Lisi would have seen only that, and she had no hope she could see of ever going through it. We'd be soaked in the same stench, every morning, the stench of urine with a bit of disinfectant spread over it like scented powder on filthy skin.

Gruff says to Geraint in the kitchen at home,

"I wonder how your mother is today?"

"Oh, she's better."

"Yes, she'll come home any time now."

"She'll be pleased to hear about the little play."

"We have to watch what we say about it. Anything could throw her off balance even though she's better."

I hear them talking as they eat their breakfast, and Nel, the cat, runs into the back kitchen with her tail up to get a saucer of milk. Gruff dries the dishes with the jug on his chest, just like a man, peering into the bottom, the dish towel a lump in his hand. Geraint trips over the chairs in his hurry to start for school; searches for his cap in the lobby; runs to his father's den to fetch a book, and bang goes the door, a bang that leaves the kitchen shaking; the great tranquility in the house with Gruff in the middle of it. He puts coal in the stove; raises his eyes to look around him and see whether there's anything still to be done. Nel mews in the back kitchen and he opens the door for her to go out. He's longing now to go to his den to have a smoke and read his letters. He crosses the patch of worn carpet. How many times have I stared at this patch and longed for a new carpet? He looks at the messiness of his desk and at the pile of letters; looks through them in general without reading them before starting to smoke; tosses the last one on the pile; that casual tossing shows there's nothing of any importance among them. He sits down in the comfortable old rumpled chair; pulls out his tobacco pouch; puts his pipe to the mouth of the pouch and fills it slowly and carefully. He moves his head up and down as he draws on his pipe like a horse eating hay and enjoys the fume that curls whitely into the air. He thinks and thinks, broodingly; wrinkles his forehead worriedly and looks at a spot on the floor without seeing it. I know what's going through his mind.

"Will Bet be better once she comes home?"

B-r-r. There's the telephone.

"Yes . . . Oh. How are you, Mrs. Williams . . . Who's sick? . . . John Huws, Tŷ Canol. In the hospital, you said, in town? Since when? . . . You didn't lose any time if he went this morning. I'll go down to see him now."

Gruff puts the receiver down in a temper. His heart is saying "damn" and "to hell with meddlesome women. Bet was right. You have to be mad to see things properly." But his face is completely expressionless. He goes to fetch his hat and coat, and he has a smile for Annie who's arrived at the house to clean. Within a minute the chairs will be on top of the tables and the whole house will be on the boil as Annie slap-dashes through her work. The tranquillity has gone, the tranquillity I had every morning for years after Geraint began to go to school. I would sail in it.

"Get up out of bed, Mrs. Jones."

The nurse's voice.

"You're lying down too much and brooding. Try laughing."

"What have I to laugh about in this place?"

The nurse had no answer. She was talking for the sake of talking. She wouldn't feel herself in charge otherwise. I put my legs together; raised them and turned them like opening a fan before putting them down. Me, showing off my suppleness in the midst of old women whose limbs had grown stiff. I had to do something instead of think; my thoughts were winding themselves together like snakes, without ever unwinding. I decided to go to Magi and make her turn around.

"Magi."

Not a move.

"Magi."

Still quiet. I went on my knees and I begged her to turn around, begging what I wished for my own sake. And then the heavy body was turning as clumsily as a cow until the bed was creaking. Her face came opposite mine. All these old women had big faces, like men. The cords of her throat were next to my mouth, her throat too was like a cow's throat, but her breast was young. She opened her kind grey eyes, eyes that didn't look straight.

"Who are you?"

"Mrs. Jones."

"What are you doing here? You're too young."

"Same thing as you. Trying to get better."

"I'm all better, but I haven't any home to go to."

I was the one fell silent now. Something was tugging at my hair. It was Sali there, but she didn't coax me to get up.

"Magi, have you a family?"

She looked past me at something invisible, but I knew it was me she saw.

"No, no one very close."

"But you have someone?"

"Yes, a niece somewhere. But I don't in the least know where she is."

"Has she been to visit you?"

"No, never."

Sali took hold of me and flung me away from the bed.

"Get out of here, you damned minister's wife. Why won't you leave us alone instead of meddling?"

Me, meddling! When I had no interest at all in sick people. I went to get dressed with the tears hot in my eyes. I tried to hide them as they fell on my clothing, for fear the nurse would see them and report to the doctor. When I raised my head I saw that Magi had pushed Sali away from her bed and made her sit on a chair. I had thought in asking to be allowed to leave the private residence, Y Wenallt, and come to the public ward, that I was coming to a tranquil place, where the patients had calmed down and it wasn't possible for them to be upset. But this was a hornet's nest as well. Even people like Magi could turn. I was holding my breath again, and my heart was beating unbearably hard, as I tried to keep the agitation back. I attempted to keep Sali in back of me, but she was in front of me, peering under my eyes.

"Crying, yes?"

Then a shout from the furthest bed.

"Leave her alone."

Magi, enraged, when I hadn't heard a sound from her since I came here.

"She's the only one who's taken notice of me."

I pray lest the fire I've started spread and the place become more of a madhouse, and it set me back. Sali lifted my chin, and looked into my eyes again, but I couldn't look at her eyes; their malice was too much.

"*You* won't get to go home."

I shut my lips tight as I tried to overcome the devil.

"Never mind, Mrs. Jones," from quiet Jane.

At that Magi got up and made Sali sit in her chair.

"If you don't leave Mrs. Jones alone, I'm going to call for the nurse."

"Oh no, Magi, for my sake, don't call for the nurse."

By now my tears had gone, and there was a tight pain in my chest. I was someone who'd worried over unreasoning animals that were being wronged, without thinking there were people like Magi hidden in corners in the world, with no one thinking of them. It was no wonder Gruff answered every call.

Tranquillity came to the ward. The struggle was harder by now because the place was more confined. For all purposes Sali had left the world, and yet, there was a devil in her that couldn't leave other people alone.

Gruff was coming to visit me in the afternoon. I sat in the chair and closed my eyes to think and fill the time between then and two o'clock. In the colours before my eyes I saw everything together at the same moment: the chapel, the knots in the panel in the vestry, Gruff in the pulpit, the patient's lounge at Y Wenallt, and the women sitting in the easy chairs, knitting, sewing, flipping through the colourful magazines, talking.

"The daughter of the woman next door to me is getting married next week, to a clerk from the bank, a very nice boy, a white wedding with breakfast at the Blue Bell."

"In chapel or in church?"

"In church, a very nice setting for a white wedding."

"Where do they go on Sunday?" I asked.

"Oh, you know, I don't think they go anywhere now, they used to go to chapel. But getting married in an office isn't a very nice thing."

"It's a quite honest thing," I said then.

"Yes indeed," said Mrs. Hughes who was sitting beside me, "a good many more of them need to get married on the spur of the moment in an office, instead of people being forced to wait for their money to pay for the grandness. My husband is a printer, and some of them don't think of paying for their wedding invitations."

"And some of them are having children before their time."

"Oh," Mrs. Humphreys said, "I consider a wedding in chapel or in church quite a nice thing, no matter what their condition is. Nobody minds a thing like that today."

I kept still, for fear I would lose my temper.

"And Mrs. Lewis here is a grandmother today."

"Yes, my daughter's had a beautiful baby boy."

The others looked as admiringly at Mrs. Lewis as if she were grandmother to the Prince of Wales.

"I want to go lie on my bed," I said to Mrs. Hughes.

"May I come with you to sit for a little?"

I was able to bear Mrs. Hughes. It was nice to be able to lie on the bed and watch her knitting. How beautiful the wrinkles in her face were, more than the smooth flesh of the others' untroubled faces.

"I can't abide listening to their talk," she said presently. "They can't talk about anything but something that has to do with babies. Have you noticed their eyes?"

"No."

"They don't change, whichever way they look; there's nothing in their eyes but contentment."

"Why are they here then?"

"They're in no hurry to go home. They've found here what they failed to find at home."

"What's that?"

"Grandness and luxuries. I happen to know two of them. There wasn't enough grandness on hand for them. This place contents them. I'm here because I had a loss. Am I tiring you?"

"No. I enjoy listening to you."

"I have one boy, and he's become a wicked boy. He's in jail now, I'd rather not tell you how he went there."

My mind went to Geraint.

"Are you less worried about him now?"

"Yes. And I can go home one of these next few days."

"I'm glad."

"I can't say how it is that I've got better, but my husband has come here from far away every week to visit me, and he's determined to take the boy back and give him a second chance. I had thought that he wouldn't do that, he was so angry at the start, and so was I, for that matter."

"Full marks to your husband."

"And now, I've seen that I must make an effort to give this second chance, and thinking about it has given me a lift. I had to rise out of the depression before I could make an effort to raise my child."

"I'm sure you're right."

I felt I would be quite mean if I weren't to say anything about myself.

"I'm here because I lost something too, but it's difficult for me to talk about it."

"You don't need to, unless you'd feel better after talking."

"I lost my faith."

Mrs. Hughes raised her head from her knitting and looked at me.

"I became depressed and low-spirited because I didn't see that there was any meaning to life. I couldn't believe God was ruling the world when I saw all the cruelty that's in it, and I saw that there wasn't any difference between the people of the chapel and the people of the world. You see, I'm a minister's wife."

"So I understand. I've heard your husband preach—well, too. But I can't go as deep as you. I go to chapel and accept everything with no doubts. But somehow I couldn't ask God to help my boy when he went down the slope."

"A pity."

I was very sorry when Mrs. Hughes went home, and that was when I asked to be allowed to come here to the ward. I thought that I'd prefer the company of old women living in a world completely on its own, cut off from the world outside, and maybe happy because of that.

I went to the hall in a hurry before two o'clock, since I knew that Gruff would be there, and this time I ran through the porches and saw them go past me as though I were on a train. I wanted to see him as much as the time we were courting, and just as it was at that time, we sat at a little table having tea together and talking of private matters. The place was full of visitors and patients, some forced to share tables with others. Gruff went to the counter of the canteen to fetch two cups of tea, but before he could go back to buy the bread-and-butter, a woman from one of the tables was crossing over to us, a cheerful-looking woman.

"Here you are, take some of mine. Are you better, Mrs. Jones?"

Gruff was looking embarrassed.

"I didn't have time to slice bread-and-butter before I started out."

"Thank you very much," I said to the woman, and it was a fine thing to feel my appreciation.

"She has a twenty-five-year-old daughter here," Gruff said after she left, "a hopeless case, I'm afraid. I've seen her here many times."

I did my best not to look around me. But later, in looking at the whole room, I saw the entire place like a room in a restaurant in Cardiff, every bit of it on the boil, and yet its atmosphere was like coming into a cold, virginal freedom after the atmosphere of the ward. The next minute it was like a tea party in a vestry, and taken all together its sound was like the sound of merriment. But as I looked at each table, one by one, there was sadness there. A patient and a relative were mouth to mouth, the relative as if he were trying to cross the bridge between himself and the patient, from one mind to the other, as if he meant to insist on drawing the disease out of the sick man by getting as close as he could to his face. A few patients saying nothing and their relatives becoming silent on not getting an answer. Another patient gulping down his bread-and-butter as though he were starving. A few women patients had dressed themselves attractively, some others were in hospital clothes, the strangest mixture of humanity. Some patients were sitting on chairs—no one had come to see them, or they were late in arriving. Gruff produced a table for them, and chairs, and went to fetch them tea and bread-and-butter. They smiled happily.

"What if we knew what's going through everyone's mind here and now," I said.

"God forbid, we couldn't stand it."

There was a strange look to Gruff himself; his shirt bands and his collar were none too clean, he had need of a haircut, his face had a tired look, and yet he looked as though he'd just had good news.

"Isn't Annie washing for you?"

"Yes, after a fashion. I put this shirt on yesterday, it was supposed to be a clean shirt."

"It's high time I came home."

"Not for washing—but for us to have you on the hearth. There's an empty space there."

"That will come. I'm much better."

"When do you go before the doctor again?"

"I don't know. But he isn't the one can tell that I'm better. I know I'm better."

He looked at me as though he were examining my face.

"Yes, I'm better, much better than when I saw him last."

"I've been thinking, I wonder would it be better for me to find a place as a teacher."

The tears leapt into my eyes.

"I can't think of you leaving the ministry."

"I'd do it, for your sake."

"You don't need to now, I can put up with those petty stings. The other thing was important, and I see clearly now."

"Oh, I'm glad, Bet."

"And you wouldn't be any better off in a school. You'd have to live with people there."

"But, I wouldn't have to try to save them."

"We can deal with things like this when I come home. What need is there to worry now?"

An echo, this was, from our talk when we were courting. This moment, that was everything.

"How is Geraint?"

"Splendid. Well, he's very well considering. He misses having you home too, and Nel is constantly searching for you. Geraint's doing the only thing he can to bridge the time—working hard. Something you should know, your little play was performed last night."

The blood rose into my face. I saw someone directing it and murdering it.

"I directed it. I didn't do as well as you would have done, but everybody enjoyed it, and the vestry was full. Geraint and Mr. and Mrs. Bryn worked hard to get the stage right. The children had taken up a collection, and they're the ones who've sent you these flowers this time."

The tears were running down my cheeks by now. I was seeing how dear

Gruff was to have insisted on directing it, was disappointed that I hadn't been there, and was thinking of the loyalty of the children and the majority of the parishioners.

"Aren't you glad?"

"Yes, but I won't get to see it."

"Yes, you will. Everybody's clamouring to have it again. I have other news for you. Melinda's come home."

"No, never."

"Came earlier because you were ill."

"The loyal thing."

I didn't know whether I was glad or not. I wanted to go home to Gruff and Geraint, as though nobody else existed, and be able to be in my own house, and be able to stand on my own again.

"I hope that people won't come to visit me when I come home."

"It will be hard to stop them."

As I spoke of this my mind went straight to Magi, and I told her story to Gruff. Almost before I finished he had gone to see her, and was back in no time knowing who her niece was, and intending to write to her.

"Ta-ta, Gruff dear, and I can never thank you enough for directing the play."

I was feeling at the moment that I'd like to escape and go back with him. But I remembered Magi and Sali and Jane and Lisi in their cramped, hopeless prison. I stood at the door between the hall and the porch, the flowers under my arm, and I kept waving to Gruff and he to me.

The men began sweeping the floor. The last visitors went through the door. The patients disappeared, and in two minutes the hall was completely empty. I was one of a large company walking slowly back to the ward.

"How was the minister?"

"An absolute love, Sali."

I was sorry that I showed such happiness as soon as the words came out of my mouth.

"You saw him," I said then.

"Yes, quite slovenly."

"Shows he needs his wife to come home."

Magi turned of her own accord.

"Come here. Your husband wants to write to my niece, but he may as well not. She won't come."

She turned her back to me.

DARK TONIGHT (1962)

That evening I couldn't sleep. My conversation with Gruff was turning in my head; I was going over every word of it and chewing the cud of every feeling I had, with the feeling of looking forward to being allowed to go home. Doubt came; had I supposed too soon that I was on the mend; would I be disappointed after being in front of the doctor? The doctors were very powerful, and it was their job to trip up someone like me.

Flat on my back in bed, I tried once more to go over what had happened to me during the months before. I looked at the thing like some hall of Cynddylan in the middle of a field on the edge of a wood, with myself going around the owl-haunted ruins, looking into the emptiness with no fire, no bed.

I began at the beginning and went slowly over all the events, and I was able to bear it all as if it had happened to someone else.

II

It came slowly and I don't know how, except that the word *syrffed*, "fed up", was constantly in my head. I would write it on a piece of paper sometimes and try to make a *cynghanedd* of it, a line of consonantal harmony, with the word *seirff*, "serpents", and fail. I was seeing much more than I'd seen before, as if the air were thinner, or as if everyone's head were covered with glass instead of flesh, and I could see through it to the bottom of their minds. There had been a time when I would e_., _ / sitting in the kitchen after washing dinner dishes to read the daily paper when Gruff had gone out to make his visits. It wasn't the news that was the luxury, but the sitting down to read after finishing work. If I read a book instead there would be something missing; the things that were going on in the world, murders, stealing, fatal accidents on the roads, broken marriages, cruelty to children and animals (I would only glance at the last and go on, but I knew by the pain they were there). There was romance in the fact that they had happened. A shiver would go through me, I'd almost say a happy shiver, when I'd read the name of someone I knew in the obituary column, just because I knew them; the interest was in the knowing. But by now it wasn't a luxury to be able to sit and read the paper in front of the fire.

I began to give Gruff a lashing in my mind; things I'd considered virtues had turned into weaknesses. I found fault with him for running to the members of his congregation so much, and being there, like a policeman, ready at every summons. He wasn't reading very much and he was preparing his sermons in a rush. Geraint didn't appreciate his home now; I saw inside his head the eagerness to escape, escape from his work, from the chapel, from the ideas of his parents, escape to a world of persons just like himself; he had his back to me. Before this the empty pews in the chapel hadn't bothered me too much; I would comfort myself by thinking that they were the faithful few, the ones who came to chapel now, that Gruff knew who was who and thought that these would sometime have an influence on others. But now I saw that it wasn't faith brought them there, all sorts of things, but not faith. I didn't find pleasure in the singing because no attention was paid to the words that were being sung. I longed to go home for meal-time; it was the food I thought about all through the service. I was lonely because I was seeing too much. Of the small remnant there was a dear little remnant in whose company I still found comfort. Mr. Bryn, one of the deacons, and his wife, and Melinda.

It was Monday and our summer holidays had begun, but Gruff had had to stay home to marry some couple; the house was in its mourning-clothes of dust sheets, everywhere but the kitchen and Gruff's den. The change in the arrangements had made me feel as if I'd missed one train and was strolling aimlessly to wait for another. Suddenly I felt that I didn't want to go to the cottage near the sea where we usually went every year. I didn't want to stay home either. I could understand Melinda's eagerness to go to the Continent; the next moment I couldn't understand it; I was hanging there, displaced. We'd had a prosaic early supper with the leftovers from the Sunday roast. When Geraint put the radio on I told him snappishly to shut it up.

"May I go out, mam?"

"Go, and don't stay long."

A bolt from Geraint for the door, and silence; Gruff in his chair going through the newspaper, when I knew he'd read it once before.

I went to the back kitchen to fetch the leftover roast.

"Here's some of this still left; perhaps the cat will eat it."

"What about us having a cup of tea with meat and tomato sandwiches, and having it in the den? This kitchen's uncomfortable without the stove."

It was the pinnacle of luxury for me every night to go to the den with

Gruff and warm my toes in front of a small glowing fire before going to bed.

"A capital idea," I said, "I'll turn the electric fire on."

I ran to the den, looking forward to a bit of pleasure. As I raised my head after turning on the fire I saw the light from the room striking the garden and turning it into another garden with its magic wand, and the den wasn't just the same either; it was tidy, with plenty of room to put a large tray on the table. I ran to prepare the snack, the bell rang, and Melinda came in. When we were just about to begin Mr. and Mrs. Bryn arrived, and I ran to fetch more dishes and sandwiches. As we ate, a thrill of comfort went through me; we were all middle-aged people, and here were the people I was fond of.

"This is what's meant by comfort," Melinda said, tucking her feet underneath her on the chair as if she were a cat. Mrs. Bryn's face was the most exquisite thing in the room, with its framework of fine bones, her flawless skin and teeth, her grey-blue eyes, her dark hair, and her sensitive little nose. One had to be close to Mrs. Bryn to see how pretty she was. Melinda's beauty would light a street, her golden hair, her blue-green eyes and her creamy skin and her perfect teeth.

"No one would think I'd just eaten," Mr. Bryn said. "It's a pleasant thing to be able to eat in company one likes."

"We've been in parentheses for quite a while," Gruff said. "This is the second supper for us too."

He was lounging contentedly in his chair, having pulled the slipcover down on the chair and wrinkled it.

"A nice wedding?" Melinda asked.

"Yes, I suppose, I didn't notice. I don't know who either of them was."

"There's familiarity for you," I said, feeling fed up with weddings.

"You'll have peace and quiet now," Bryn said, "for a bit," having second thoughts.

"The best thing will be to be delivered from the Unicorn."

("Unicorn" was our private name for one of the cantankerous deacons, after Gwilym Hiraethog's sheep.)

I heard Geraint come in. He put his head in at the door. Nel the cat came in and jumped on Melinda's knee. She looked at us all and shut her eyes.

"This boy is getting tall," Melinda said. "If he were living in France, he'd be married."

Geraint turned red, took sandwiches on a plate, poured himself tea.

"I'm going to the kitchen to listen to a play that's on the radio."

I was furious with Melinda.

"Are you going away, Melinda?" Mrs. Bryn asked.

"Always in August, when one part of the country has swarmed like bees to go to another part, I like to have the Continent to myself."

"We'll only be able to stretch the leash a bit," I said, "and there'll be a tug on the leash if anyone from the church should happen to die."

"I wouldn't come back to bury them, indeed," Melinda said. "Let them bury themselves."

She took out a cigarette and Mrs. Bryn did the same thing. I went to the kitchen and fetched some. Gruff got up and drew the window curtains together between us and the street. Bryn took his pipe out, and so did Gruff.

"What if the Unicorn were to see us now?" from Bryn.

"It would do him good," Gruff said. "I have this craving to go on a spree and raise a row outside his house at closing-time for the pubs, and dare him to come out for a scrap."

"Why don't you?" Mrs. Bryn said, innocently in earnest.

We all began to laugh.

"It will be very hard for you to say anything about him after he dies," Bryn said.

"There are plenty of ambiguous words in the Welsh language."

Laughter again.

It came time to depart. Gruff and I were standing on the threshold, Gruff with his arm around my waist. The three of them were standing on the garden path with the light from the lobby thrown on them, their faces in the light and their bodies in the darkness, the way pictures in the newspapers show only the face.

"Goodbye. Goodbye."

The gate was shut, hands were waved, the door was shut.

The next moment there was a mask on my eyes and I was cold with fear.

.   .   .

It didn't come back until the end of the holidays. The days had gone by as they did every year. Taking it easy, eating simply, reading, chatting when our families came, roaming here and there, going to the farm to fetch eggs and milk, and luckily without one summons for Gruff to go back and bury someone.

As usual, too, Gruff's friends came, two ministers and one priest. That was the high point of our holidays. We were a close-knit group around the tea table in the cottage, Geraint and his friend Gwilym who was camping with him in the field having gone out in the boat. I could create an illusion about the four men and put them in one of the restaurants I'd read about in the big cities. They were arguing like those literary men and their clothes were just as untidy. No one would have thought they were any different from the debaters in city restaurants. Wil was the thunderer. When he came through the door he was like a heavy-laden ship and the top of his head almost struck the crossbeam, his hat turned up in front, a scarf around his neck, wearing a raincoat, its pockets bulging out like a mule's packs with books, and high boots on his feet. Before asking how anyone was,

"What do you think of this, Gruff?" producing the Steddfod compositions from one of his pockets.

"I enjoyed it very much."

"Enjoyed, enjoyed," Wil shouted, "enjoyed such rubbish. A man looks forward each year to seeing a particle of genius, and there's not a thing there but a bit of talent with some varnish on it."

"What do you hope to find?" Jac the parson asked.

"A little trace of vision. Here we are, living in the most turbulent age the world's ever seen, and these poets don't see anything in it but a chance to describe, describe the horrors of war, describe the effect of the new age on the Welsh way of life, the world changing, nostalgia for the old things and continually lamenting over the loss. There isn't one of them has the guts to open his own soul and see what's there."

"You're right," Jac said, "we've become too peaceable or too torpid. A man needs to battle before he can write. Something has to stir him up."

Huw, the calm little preacher, was listening with his eyes, his thick brindled eyebrows rising every now and then, as if his mind were pushing them up.

"We're battling in a way," he said, "battling against war, a cock-shy that doesn't exist at this point in time."

"You're right, Huw," Wil said, "we talk of peace as if it were possible to have it. The only peace you'll find before you go to your grave is to lie flat on your back in the middle of a field all day long and not think about anything."

"How would you get your food?" I said.

"That's the trouble. It was in gathering food man began to sin."

"I see it the same way with the chapel," said Gruff, who could never leave the chapel alone for long. "It's fools we're fighting against, not against the Devil, and stupidity has no weapons."

"It can do a great deal of harm," I said.

"We've left the chapel for a month," Wil said, "and one looks forward to August every year to see will there be something better in these compositions; the Steddfod compositions are part of summer holidays by now, and what do you find but disappointment every time. And what's terrible is that there's a greasy satisfaction over the entire thing. Nobody speaks his opinion honestly; if the adjudicators were honest, they'd say that all these things aren't worth the match that could burn them."

"Perhaps they don't understand their job," Huw said. "Perhaps the things that lost were better."

"No," Wil said, shaking his head like a dog coming out of a river, "we've become a nation that's easy to please, lazy and unseeing."

"Well," Huw said, "people today don't have time, everybody's writing in his spare time."

"Time, time, genius doesn't know what time is, it demands a hole to go through. You remember Isaiah and the voice that said, 'Cry out.' There's no one being stirred up to cry out today. We've become people too cold to cry out, too peaceful to battle against anything. No one makes history today but the scientists. It was men of letters who made history in times gone by. Williams Pantycelyn made history."

"And preachers," Gruff said.

I began applauding.

"You're speaking the truth, Wil; when we sing Williams' hymns in chapel, with half of us not understanding them, I think it's a shame that such little people have such great things in front of them and feel nothing."

"Some do feel, obviously," Wil said to me.

The tea table was moved and we sat around the hearth.

"Well," Wil said, lighting his pipe, "if the month of August doesn't bring genius at the Eisteddfod it brings us together to set the world to rights, something we can only do in August; we're too busy kicking the arse of a dead mare."

"Yes," Huw said, "we're as much at fault as the literary men. We haven't anything to say either."

"No time," Jac said provocatively.

"Yes, and no audience," Wil said. "The human mind is deteriorating, and how much better off are you from crying out that the world is going to hell to people who are finding their nourishment in television dramas. You may as well shout some gibberish. You can't frighten anyone today."

"No," Huw said, "we in the chapel know more about our congregations, rub up against them more in weekly meetings, and you choke in trying to say something from the pulpit and remembering the things they're doing."

"They can say the same thing about us," Gruff said, "certainly there's plenty of criticizing of us."

"We have the advantage of you in that respect," Jac said, "the form of our service annihilates those things; we forget in worshipping; it's an advantage not to pay too much attention to the sermon and it's an advantage not to have too many meetings in the middle of the week."

"That's true," Huw said, "but it's a sad thing to admit it after all the great preaching there's been in the chapels of Wales."

"Oh, there's the same indifference in the Church," Jac said, "and since we don't count our members the way you do, we don't pay as much attention to the size of our congregations. I'm afraid that it's the 'small remnant' with us too."

"I saw something very amusing outside an English chapel the other day," Wil said, "that they're having a service by the name of 'Farmyard Praise'."

" 'The Barnyard Trio' would be a good item in something like that," I said.

This gave us a chance to laugh and be less serious.

"No, we haven't become quite as bad as that," Huw said, with a gleam in his eye. "And now the winter's work is ahead of us, out every night and all day long, and preparing a sermon in a rush Saturday night. And we're enjoying criticizing our churches here this afternoon, then going to them as if nothing had happened."

"Quite natural," Wil said. "I read something a Papist novelist said, that it's a novelist's privilege that he may be disloyal to the society he belongs to—the Papists in his case—and that he must be allowed to write from the standpoint of the bad as well as the good."

"But we aren't novelists," Gruff interrupted.

"Perhaps. But we deal with people, just as novelists do, and we can't avoid *seeing* that there's bad and good in the churches."

"That isn't the point. Seeing the standpoint of the bad is what novelists do, not denounce it, like us. They give the same fair play to both," Jac said.

"Anyway," Wil said, floored, "we're rebels, just like novelists, and we're rebelling against the chapel because we know it. We don't know anything about the Papists or the Church; then how can we criticize them? Jac could say the same thing."

"Yes. The wisest thing would be for us to go to virgin lands overseas and be missionaries."

"Oh no," I protested, "I don't want to leave Wales."

I looked out and saw the window beginning to turn grey in the darkness. We went outside.

"Here we are," I said, "boiling away in the house, with this outside for us."

We were too far away to hear the lapping of the sea, only saw its grey rippling moving. The little lights were springing into view one by one and reminding me of the lights at the beginning of winter on the street in town. Beyond in the distance the mountains stood, dark-grey, dignified.

"This is always with us," Jac said, spanning the space with his arm.

"Yes, *up to now*," from Wil. "You're lucky you have this cottage."

"Bet's aunt's old house, she left it to us in her will."

"It's worth the world," I said, "though I would have been glad to sell it at that time. We can run off for a day to see our families, and they come here. You can't live for the whole month of August with your family."

Geraint and Gwilym came back, and I ran into the house to make food for them, while the others still kept on looking at the view and dawdling. They came into the house slowly, like people coming into a house on the day of a funeral.

"We must be leaving," Jac said despondently. "Every good thing comes to an end too soon. I feel as though I'd been running down my family all afternoon."

"Quite a healthy thing," Huw said, "we get it out of our systems, same as cursing and spitting. We'll feel better after we get home."

Geraint put a lively record on the gramophone, and as I saw everybody broody a sudden something was taking hold of me and making me move the chairs to the other side.

"Now, come on."

I took hold of Wil, the closest to me, and began to dance; the notion caught everyone's fancy, with Gwilym and Geraint, the only ones who could dance, at the tail-end. Wil's big feet were tripping me every minute, but we whirled round and round, round and round like mad things, with me resting my head on Wil's bosom—I reached no higher than that—and enjoying the experience. Strange how easy it is to love another man in our imagination. We stopped short at the end of the record, everybody puffing, no one saying anything, as though we were ashamed of our moment's madness.

Our friends went away; nothing much was said; Wil stuck his head out of the car.

"Thanks a lot—till next summer."

The sound of the car became fainter and fainter as it went down the hillside. It disappeared altogether; tranquillity came over the kitchen, where, five minutes ago, there was riotous noise. We sat by the fire without anything to say for a while.

"A very final way to say goodbye," Gruff said.

"Goodbye is what it was," I said, looking broodingly into the fire. "A pity we couldn't always live like that."

"I don't know, it's the rarity of something makes us enjoy it. It would be a pretty high price to pay for friendship if Wil were thundering in your house every night."

But I was troubled in mind, I kept on saying in my head the things that I could have said. One thing came to me—I wanted to go ahead with a little play that I'd begun, to be put on with the young people next winter.

· · ·

The last day we went out in the car for a trip through the country and took a basket with us to gather blackberries. The leaves of the trees had lost their young greenness but not yet begun to turn yellow, the fields were green and yellow by turns, the farmhouses and the cottages were very pretty in their wooded coverts. But twenty years had made a great difference in me. As with people, it was their interiors I thought about. What sort of people were living in them? Same as everywhere, for sure. There was plenty of cruelty in farmyards, I knew that. Gel, the farm dog, would come to our house to get food every day. That was what, to my mind, made dogs kill sheep—because they weren't getting enough food. My mind flew to every country and thought of all the cruelty to children and animals. If civilized people could be mean, what about the others? But perhaps they were kinder. I said this to Gruff, and the only answer I had was, "You can't carry the burdens of the world on your back." In the fields as I picked the blackberries the smells of my youth came to my nostrils—the mint, and the mud after I put my foot in the water. Tonight, I would see in my sleep the clusters on the bushes and the dark red surface in the basket.

We went to the cemetery and read the gravestones; some had died young, some had died old. I tried to imagine what their illness was; what their lives had been; had they been forsaken by their sweethearts; had they had their share of calamities? We put the basket down quietly by the door of the church and went inside more quietly. I never walked quietly into our chapel when it was empty. Everything here was as though it were asking for stillness; the smell of old age was on everything and the coloured windows dulled the building. We read the memorial stones on the walls; some of these men had died in wars overseas; many of them had received honours from the kings of the earth. Quite possibly they'd had as many calamities as their poorer fellows in the cemetery. I was certain of one thing, that they hadn't had problems like ours. They had believed everything simply: they'd come here to worship; they'd go home to eat without thinking any more about their credo. We walked over gravestones on the floor and tried to bridge the long time that they'd been lying under the stones; the events in history that they knew nothing about. I remembered the words of the Book of Job, "His sons will come to honour, and he will not know it." They hadn't known the bad things either. They were dust and bones by now, and the resurrection was very long in coming.

And then the mask was coming over my eyes again and the blackness into my heart.

When Gruff was looking at the altar I went to a pew and knelt on a hassock and put my head down. I couldn't pray for the blackness to go, only sigh because it was there; and yet, there was a wish at least in the sigh. I would feel better after I got up. When I raised my head Gruff was kneeling beside me. We went out without saying anything. We didn't know each other's thoughts.

Everything had been put away in the cottage, the big grate was quite empty and the light was coming down through the chimney. The kettle was quiet and the clock was going. There was a book on the table, the Eisteddfod compositions—Wil's copy that he'd left behind that strange afternoon. It was looking sad, its contents pounded to pulp by savage criticism. A pleasant yearning came to me, I put the book in my bag to send it to him. Everything was ready and Gruff and the boys were waiting in the car outside. Suddenly I saw a bright green bead inside the fender and fur moving. I had forgotten about the cat. I had to lift the fender to get her out—she too didn't want to go home.

.   .   .

I expected to see the same sight after I came back, the house still sleeping under its dust sheets, but by the time I arrived Melinda was there, had taken off the sheets, had lit the stove, and had made tea. The kitchen was cleaner than I expected to see it, the table full—Mrs. Bryn had sent us cakes. As Melinda poured the tea I felt I wanted to take my time drinking it too. It was nice to be back. After Gruff, who'd gone to the den to read his letters, was out of the way, Melinda said,

"What's wrong, Bet? Are you ill?"

"No, I'm fine."

"Did you get any rest?"

"Much too much, I'm full of enthusiasm for the winter's work."

"You'd better come to Paris with me. A few new clothes would cheer you up. You look like a haystack, there's no need for you to be like a ragamuffin even if you are a minister's wife."

"I'm not slovenly. I try to be neat."

"I'm sorry, no, you're not slovenly, but you know, the neatness of doing one's best to make ends meet is almost worse than the slovenliness of the well-to-do. But you ought to have holidays in a place entirely unlike this, somewhere without a single chapel in it to make you think about your home. You ought to see people sin."

"I see enough of that here."

"Not in all its splendour."

"There's nothing grand about sin."

I looked guilelessly at her. I couldn't tell her about the fits of depression that I'd had or about the candlelight that entered my heart after I decided to finish my children's play.

III

I was sitting at the table in the kitchen, the smells of coffee and bacon hanging in the air, the newspaper in front of me sprinkled with the black pepper of the examination results: hundreds upon hundreds of the children of Wales had gone through the washing machine and come out in long, medium, and short clothing. There was joy and disappointment like patches of sun and clouds over the heads of the parents of Wales that day; it would be my worry next year. Nel, the cat, jumped on the table and purred; the sun was beating on the two of us through the window, with the tree in the garden next door shifting it from her to me. I would have to go into town and shop presently, look at the dark blue windows of uninteresting school clothes, listen to scraps of more uninteresting conversations. "Didn't So-and-So do well in her 'G.E.C.'?" "A pity about Such-and-Such, he was sure he would pass this year." "My daughter doesn't want to go to school any more, we can afford to keep her at home." "No, we don't intend to have holidays this year—too expensive. We intend to go for a day to the seaside." "Did you have a nice time?" "It will be winter before you know it. I hope we'll have better weather, it will shorten the winter for us." Enough to make anyone cut and run.

My play was engrossing my mind and keeping unpleasant things out, so much so that my breast would shiver and my breath would catch in my throat, and I'd have to run to the back kitchen and do any sort of thing to move and express my enthusiasm. I felt the weights lifting slowly from my bosom like the pendulum of a clock rising as it's wound. I didn't want to write a Christmas play about the nativity. The older children wouldn't take an interest in something like that, it would be too childish for them. But I wanted to insist on making them look at poverty for a little while at least and then come to terms with it. The thing was jumping in my mind— a poor family who'd sacrificed to have an exceptional feast on Christmas, someone breaking into the house and stealing everything three nights before the holiday, and the rest of the play for catching the thieves. Besides keeping the audience on pins and needles it would give them some notion of "righteousness". I was longing to be able to talk to Gruff about it, a bit of a lucky chance for him. I began thinking about Melinda; she was the one responsible for my being able to take it easy on the morning after coming back from holidays. Everybody thought things were fine for her, everybody but me, because she had plenty of money. Her husband had died suddenly in the first year of their marriage, leaving her well-off and heartbroken; she could never be still; she had to be always on the go. She would dash to the Continent the way I'd dash into town. No one got to know a great deal of her thoughts.

She came in as I was thinking about her, like a picture of autumn arriving before its time—she was wearing a skirt and a jumper of light brown that suited her russet hair.

"There now, you're doing a very sensible thing, taking a break after breakfast."

"Not entirely."

"You're looking better this morning. I want to apologize to you for what I said yesterday afternoon."

"For what?"

"For saying you didn't dress properly."

"That didn't bother me. You know how little I think about clothes as long as I'm neat."

"You ought to think about them more. Clothes cheer me up more than anything."

"You can wear them."

"You could too if you'd try."

"A minister's wife has no time to doll up."

"You're too strict about your duties."

"If you said that of Gruff it would be true."

At that moment her presence was like part of the sun that was coming through the window and it gave me confidence to mention my play. A warm smile came over her face from her eyes to her mouth.

"A very good thing. But it will do more good for you than for the children here and the young people. They're hopeless; you can never raise a house without a foundation, and you can never make anything with a machine that causes destruction. You don't have any desire to go back to the school?"

"No, it would be just the same there as well."

"But you'd get money for trying to do good there. Look how nice a thing it would be to have a penny extra."

"I can't do two jobs."

She went back to her house as briskly as she'd come and some of the sun went out with her.

I was rather disappointed in her response; I'd thought that she'd be enthusiastic, and yet I knew that she had no appetite for moving anything forward. The world had stood still for her; I questioned whether she found pleasure in the traces of history she saw throughout the Continent. I thought she didn't, and that what she did was move across history with no interest in its past, just to be able to avoid living with her own history. And yet, she hadn't narrowed her eyes this morning as she did when she disagreed. "It will do you good." She understood what was inside me. Basically, was I concerned for the young people or for myself?

In the den that evening I felt as if I had a boil on my face and the pain was spreading because it was about to burst. I began talking about my play to Gruff as he smoked and gazed into the grate. That is how Gruff, from a long time of listening to people telling their complaints, probably, would listen expressionlessly and let the speaker go ahead. I was so enthusiastic that I felt the play was composing itself as I went on, but suddenly I realized that Gruff wasn't listening and that he was wrinkling his forehead.

"What's wrong, Gruff? Aren't you pleased?"

"Y-y-yes, of course, but . . ."

"But what?"

"I'm afraid there won't be an empty room for you to use. There's something in the School every night and there's only the kitchen. Then the Women's Society is going to have a fair before Christmas to buy a new stove for the kitchen, and they'll want the kitchen to unpack things and get ready."

"But they meet in the daytime."

"They've changed to the night. You didn't know?"

"No. I wasn't at the last meeting."

My inside was like ice and yet about to explode from hatred, towards Gruff for being so cold and towards the women for their capriciousness. I couldn't speak and I burst out sobbing.

"Great heavens! What did I do?"

"It doesn't matter, you can never understand. Oh-Oh-Oh, I've found a new lift in life in thinking about doing this little play, and here you are, throwing cold water on the idea."

"I didn't, I can't help it that those women mean to insist on having that room at night."

I stopped crying on the spot.

"Look, Gruff, do you have so little imagination that you can't see that it doesn't make a damn bit of difference whether we hold rehearsals in the vestry or in the road, and that the thing you needed to do was show a particle of pleasure that the idea came to me? Are you more afraid of angering those women than of angering your wife?"

"I'm terribly sorry, Bet, I didn't think of the thing that way at all, my mind ran ahead to the difficulty before I realized what your idea was."

At that I heard Geraint going through the lobby to open the front door, and before I could wash my eyes Mr. and Mrs. Bryn were in the den. I had to speak—unwise or not. Mrs. Bryn's eyes sparkled and her husband's cordiality was a damning contrast to Gruff's face.

"That's a capital idea, something for the young people here to do instead of having their heads in the air, and we can raise money for the starving children of the world."

I hadn't thought of that. The difference between their enthusiasm and Gruff's cold manner a few minutes earlier was making me feel sorry for Gruff. It was obvious he too felt the difference, and there was a very ineffectual look on him. Before he said anything that would make things worse, I said,

"But Gruff says that there will be a difficulty in my finding a place to rehearse, that the women are going to have a fair for Christmas to get a new grate for the kitchen."

"Let them find a place, you aren't the one should move. I don't know what sort of tomfoolery it is that possesses these women. The grate in the kitchen is perfectly fine. A great pity that they had the majority vote of the officers to go ahead with the thing."

"I know very well what's wrong with them," his wife said. "They want to have something they can't have for their homes; they want to make a house out of the chapel. The next thing we'll see is a washing machine in the deacons' seat."

Everybody was able to laugh except Gruff.

"I don't know," he said. "It's very hard to keep things in balance between people; I almost give up sometimes. Our chapels are too democratic."

"We've never tried living like Christians," I said. "Members of a club, that's what we are, and the thing has become a commercial concern."

"I'm afraid we can't change it," Mr. Bryn said. "One must have money to carry on the cause."

"But not to have a grate," Mrs. Bryn said. "I believe the best thing would be to sell the chapel and go to a hut to worship, so we could see who's in earnest."

"The women would be wanting a grate there then," her husband said.

"None of them would come there," I said.

Gruff was looking at the ceiling and the spiders.

"Agh," he said, "trying to hold a church together is making me forget the feelings of the people who are close to me. I've hurt Bet terribly tonight, when she was trying to help me."

I said, to myself, that he wasn't the one I was trying to help, but that was the most human thing Gruff had said that evening, and I forgot his first coldness.

There was the freshness of the first Sunday after the holidays in chapel the next day. The chapel clean, a tan on many faces, liveliness in the singing (too much for me). We were looking forward to new things, from the women's hats to the new services for winter. Taking hold of things anew, just as in school the first day of the term. "How are you? How are you?" from everyone to each other after the morning sermon. But there was nothing at all new in Gruff's sermon, morning or night. At night the lights were put on in the middle of the service and made me feel winter was coming and also made me think about that day in the cottage with Gruff's friends, standing outside and seeing the lights springing into place one by one. For a moment I was dancing again with my head on Wil's bosom, and a smile came to my lips. I saw them all preaching tonight in their different churches, not remembering how they'd criticized their congregations that day. Gruff was preaching on the light that came into the world and how people loved the darkness more than the light. But with Gruff you could never tell who the people were who loved the darkness; the people outside, to be sure, in the congregation's opinion, not them. How good it would have been for him to say that most of us who were listening to him were in the darkness, and in more darkness than the worldly people because we were listening every Sunday. A pity he couldn't go to extremes like Wil. I didn't listen to every word, my mind was flitting everywhere. How true John Gwilym Jones' stories in *The Plum Tree* were!

At communion I was able to settle my mind, though once I found myself finding something new to say in my play, even there. Only there did I feel I could worship and that the yearnings and the worshipping were going through one proper wire because I was feeling the suffering. I could pray simply with Siôn Cent, "And forgive the sin of the mind." There I was able to forget as well the things and the people around me; there alone I felt that Gruff wasn't related to me, that he was apart, a stranger serving communion, a priest and not a man. After going home I locked the door of the den, and we had, as usual on communion evening, a very plain supper.

I V

What writing the short play did was shift my interests, not remove my doubts. Those would come back every time I became stuck for something to say in the play. The problem of finding a place to rehearse wasn't much on my mind at the time either. Every time a new idea came to me I'd run to dash it down, and the running itself was part of the creating. I felt it was something like this that Goronwy Owen meant in saying, "I feel my heart come alive." A pulling upwards, that's what it was; a help to looking forward to the next day instead of a day being over when I closed my eyes, as it had been for me for weeks.

In sending the compositions back to Wil I ventured to tell him that I was hard at it writing a play. I was able to look forward to the next day in waiting for his answer. Since he was such a disorderly person it was a surprise to me to have a letter by return mail.

"... I'm very glad you're writing a play even though it's to interest your chapel and to give some work to the young people. After this don't think of any further purpose than giving yourself pleasure by putting down your own experience. You don't have to present the story of your life, you can imagine your situations and your people, but you can put what you think about life inside what you write. I see it becoming more and more difficult to enjoy life today; as far as I can see, a talk like the one we had at your cottage that day is the only enjoyment we have now. On the surface that talk was something very amusing, but at bottom it was extremely depressing. People disappointed in the work we'd set out to accomplish, that's what we all were, but mercifully, we haven't despaired, or we wouldn't have returned to our work. Or have we returned because that's the least bother? Christians are so of the world worldly today, and it requires great faith to keep on. But here I am, preaching. What I wanted to tell you was to write about life as you see it and not try to interest anyone. Perhaps you'll find people to listen to you sometimes, and perhaps we will too. But if *I* were to write, I wouldn't find anyone to publish my work—it would be too libellous . . ."

I tossed the letter to Gruff. "There's a lot in Wil's head" was his observation. "There's more in his heart," I said to myself.

I had chosen the ones that I thought would do best in the play, some whose Welsh was quite poor. I left Geraint out to avoid upsetting anyone. The first evening of rehearsals the Women's Society had chosen another evening to meet, so there was no difficulty coming from that quarter. Gruff was away on a committee and had promised to drop in later, and Geraint had gone to the library. I didn't have much incentive, I was going out of obligation, but this was a pleasanter obligation than some.

When I neared the vestry I heard noise like the noise at a fair; by the time I went inside the place was full of teenagers, boys and girls, dancing, running after each other, shouting and flinging things about, with hymn books flying through the air like crows. There were a number of our chapel's children, some from other chapels, and the Teddy Boys I saw along the street every night in coming and going to the chapel. The first thing that came into my mind was that Gruff would get in trouble with the deacons though he wasn't supposed to be there that evening. Some of them realized I was there and everyone rushed through the door and through the lobby, with the thin legs of the Teddy Boys weaving in and out like moths around a candle. I looked at the floor, it was like a field after a show, the pictures had all been turned with their faces to the wall and the most improper things had been chalked beneath the photographs of the old Welsh preachers. I ran to the kitchen for fear that some of the teenaged boys were there; there was a worse shock awaiting me there. Geraint was in a corner with a girl, the daughter of a woman in town whose husband had left her because she went running after men. The girl herself wasn't any better, it was said, though she wasn't much more than a child. Geraint had her as close to the wall as he could and was kissing her like a madman.

"Geraint," I shouted, "go home this minute, I'll talk to you later."

He went out quickly with his head down, but the girl stood there, holding her head up boldly. If her face had been clean, she would have been pretty.

"You'd better go home too," I said to her.

She didn't hurry at all, but walked slowly, holding her swaying rear end far out and smiling spitefully in my face. I grasped her shoulder and took her to the door.

"Hey," she said, "who do you bloody think you are, don't you know that you have no right to put your hands on anybody else's child?"

"A pity someone couldn't have given you a proper thrashing sometime."

She stuck her tongue out at me and ran through the lobby right into Gruff's face. I was almost trembling too much to say a word.

"Did you see Geraint?"

"Yes, and the others."

We went to the children in the play who were crouching in a corner of the vestry like frightened hens; one of the girls was crying. It was obvious that they'd been caught in the commotion and tossed about like a paper boat in a whirlpool. For a moment I gave thanks that children like this could be found, but on thinking about my own child, I thought that the same stuff was in them as well. Gruff told me quietly not to be long, that he wanted to go see some of the deacons before anyone else had the pleasure of telling them. He wiped the chalk from under the pictures before going out.

"Try to forget it," I said to the children, "we'll have a lot of fun in doing this."

The girl dried her tears as she took the typed copy from my hand, and an eager smile came to the faces of each of them.

"We'll just read it tonight to get the emphasis right."

It was read with gusto.

"May we take the copy home, Mrs. Jones?"

"Yes."

"I want to learn my part by next week."

"So do I."

"That's the way. A week from tonight, the same time."

No, these were different.

In walking down to the house I was trying to nurse enough courage to face Geraint, and thinking it was a serious thing for me to admit I was a coward with my own child. He was sitting at the kitchen table, pretending he was reading. He didn't raise his head.

"What do you have to say after what I saw tonight?"

"Nothing."

"Close that book there and look at me."

He closed the book and looked at the table.

"Well, what do you have to say?"

"Nothing, I'll say it again," wearily.

"That's no way to answer your mother."

"If you're expecting me to say I'm sorry, I don't mean to say it."

"You'll be sorry some day."

"I'm not sorry at this moment."

"Do you know who that girl is?"

"Yes."

"And know her family history?"

"Yes."

"Have you kissed her before?"

"No."

"Do you know how all those hooligans came into the vestry?"

"They were running after her along the street and she ran into the vestry."

"It's someone of her reputation boys of that sort run after, and you got hold of her before they did."

"Don't talk like a moral snob."

For the first time he raised his head and looked me in the face.

"Here now, where did you find that expression?"

"In this house."

I couldn't deny it. In looking at him I was looking at someone I didn't know. At this Gruff came into the house.

"I'm letting you deal with him. I'm going out."

I noticed that Gruff's face was white as chalk and his lips were trembling. I went to Melinda's house.

"What's the matter with you?"

"Melinda, do you have a sip of brandy?"

I tried to tell her the story between outbursts of crying.

"And that has made you ill?"

"It was enough to make anyone ill."

"Bet, it's high time for you to wise up and know what's happening in the world. What you saw tonight was merely what's happening everywhere in every country today. You should have called those teenagers back and tried to teach them something."

"You know very well that Gruff has done everything in his power to get those children into more substantial things than hanging about on the streets, through the Welsh League of Youth and things like that, but without getting a grip on them anywhere. There are some people you have to give up on the way shopkeepers do with old debts."

"The trouble with you is that you come between two periods: you're not old enough to belong to the narrow old crowd who were deacons when we were children, and you're too narrow to relate to young people today."

"Yes, mercifully, and I wouldn't be a minister's wife if it weren't for that."

"Ministers sometimes marry people who are quite strange, and we hear of ministers' children having bastards."

Her eyes had narrowed and were searching me to see how I was taking it. And I lost my temper.

"I haven't said Geraint did anything worse than kiss that girl."

"Don't fly off the handle, he's at the age to do worse things. Boys of his age in France are going to live with women, and not to marry them as I said over there the other evening."

"Thank you very much for considering our feelings that evening in front of Mr. and Mrs. Bryn," I said sarcastically.

I hated her for a moment. I got up and said, "Good night." There was less hatred in my heart towards Geraint. Gruff was by himself in the kitchen.

"Where is Geraint?"

"He's gone to bed."

I didn't want to know from Gruff what had been between the two of them. I went upstairs, and as I passed him Gruff put his head on my shoulder; I thought I heard him sob. Geraint was lying on his bed in his clothes and crying into the quilt.

"You'd better come down and have supper."

Not a word.

"Geraint, you'd better come down and have supper with your father and me, we'll forget what has happened."

I went down, Gruff was busy fixing supper. I had a steak and kidney pie in the oven, done slowly while I was out. Geraint came down furtively and sat at the table; and though the atmosphere was quiet and strange, I felt that we were one family and understood each other.

"This pie is good, mam; do you want to keep some for tomorrow?"

"No, we'll eat it all tonight."

"It's capital," Gruff said, "I was almost starving."

The dish was emptied. The meal was prolonged by eating fruit. We weren't in a hurry to leave the table, and the talk came back. Under the lamp Gruff's face was pale and thin but his eyes were happy.

V

By the next day the mask had come back and the blackness was as heavy as ever, shrouding the bottom of my heart. I was quite certain it wasn't the previous evening's trouble that had brought it this time. Concerning that I was feeling as though someone had taken a broom and swept the house clean. It wasn't the conversation with Melinda either. I wasn't ignorant about many of the things she said; it was her crude way of saying them that gave me a shock. I was perfectly certain in myself it was nothing from outside that was causing the depression. It was in me myself, rising from me myself. I saw it in pictures before my eyes, as a mist, as a mask, as frost, as weights on a crane. The blackness was there, that's all, had descended as quietly as mist on the countryside. It didn't go away when I spoke to people; I was able to conceal it even with Gruff. From outside a small candle was shedding light, like the electric light above the front door when the house was dark—that was the play.

That is how I was feeling the following Wednesday night when I made my way to the chapel by seven. I didn't see a purpose to anything, but it was less trouble to go than not. The eagerness of the children when I arrived was a lift.

There was supposed to be another meeting in the vestry and I walked straight through the lobby to the kitchen, leaving the children there. There was a buzz of talk coming from the kitchen, and when I opened the door I saw a number of women there around the grate and I realized it was a meeting of the Women's Society.

"Oh," I said, "I didn't know there was a meeting of the Society here tonight."

"No," said the president, who was sitting at the top of the circle facing me, "we forgot to announce it Sunday night."

She spoke lamely, like a woman caught stealing, with her face gazing into the grate and not at me.

"But the Society has always met in the afternoon."

"Yes, but we've decided to have it at night now."

"Who are 'we' then?"

"The officers decided to call it tonight at half-past-six, and the rest of us have agreed tonight to have it at night from now on."

During this conversation none of them turned her head, and I was seeing the back of a row of heads with the hair on them like symmetrical wigs, and a patch of redness between the neck of each one's blouse and the fringe of her hair.

"Well, I have rehearsal with the children, and it's more important for me to have the kitchen with them, since it's possible for you to meet in the afternoon—they can't come in the afternoon."

Then one of the wavy heads turned to face me, a woman with a nose like a schooner that was taking her somewhere, to America or to a good job.

"Well," she said, "since we were the ones here first, we're the ones should get to stay."

She turned all red as she spoke.

"Yes, you took care that you met at half-past-six instead of at seven; I didn't know there was a meeting here at all, let alone that you were meeting at half-past-six."

"I forgot to tell you," the president said, with a completely false smile.

I knew she was lying.

"Oh, that does it. I suppose I can't move you out of here, but the play will go ahead, and we'll be able to raise money to send to the starving children of the world, something much more necessary than collecting money to get luxuries for a chapel that's hiding its head."

At that a shy woman rose to say something; she gripped the back of her chair to support herself. She began in a mumble and I thought she was on the brink of falling in a faint. But quite suddenly, a phrase shot out of her mouth like a stone from a sling, and that phrase was "Mrs. Jones".

"Mrs. Jones," she said once more, "I'd like you to know that it was only this afternoon I was given to understand by the secretary that I had to come here tonight by half-past-six, and Mrs. Lewis who's sitting here next to me. And neither one of us voted for having the meeting at night, and both of us think there's no need of a new grate in this kitchen, with so many people starving all over the world."

I heard whispering and quiet laughter follow me into the lobby.

"We'll go to the chapel," I said to the children. "It's warm enough for tonight; we'll have rehearsal at our house from now on."

"Oo-oo," said the girl who'd been crying the former evening, as if she were being allowed to go to the Queen's palace. She'd be disappointed when she saw our threadbare carpets.

Gruff wasn't surprised when I told him after going home; he thought I'd gone too far with my last barb to them though it was true. To him, the thing was a coincidence; it was a very handy word, "coincidence", and there was much too much of it in our chapel. I began laughing uncontrollably in thinking about the earnestness of the women's backs and the thin nose of the woman who'd ventured to turn her face to me, the trembling of the shy woman, and all the pettiness of women who wanted to be foremost without the power to be. It was pettiness in me too to think of the victory I'd have when the play was performed. But I didn't let a thing like that worry me.

I thought once about spilling my insides to Gruff. The fits of depression and the lack of hope were becoming more frequent by now; if I talked to Gruff, I knew that at best he'd say it was the plight of the church that was causing it and that we'd get into the ruts of old arguments. I knew as well that what the prickings of the chapel were doing had nothing to do with my depression; if I were merely a member who had faith, and not a member who came into close contact with the other members, I knew deep down that the link that was holding me to my faith would be at the breaking point in exactly the same way. That's what was making it hard to talk about the thing to Gruff. He was so firm, unyielding, kept on going. He wasn't too blind to see that the chapel was becoming empty, that the ones called "the faithful" were apathetic and unsacrificing and that the collections weren't enough to pay the expenses.

The following Monday night I told him that I didn't want to go to the prayer-meeting; it wasn't boredom with prayer-meeting made me say that—a feeling that I could go if someone persuaded me—but savage objection to prayer-meeting; to a meeting that had become like an old cemetery whose gravestones had sunk level with the earth.

"What's wrong? Aren't you well?"

"Yes, I'm fine, but I don't want to go to the prayer-meeting."

"Stay home tonight, perhaps you'll feel better for next week."

"I won't, I hate prayer-meeting; I don't ever want to go to one. I can't listen to people telling the Supreme Being what He ought to do."

"They're asking, not telling."

"No, if they were asking they could do that quietly at home. Delivering an address, that's what they're doing, talking to hear their own voices. The whole thing's hypocrisy."

"Prayer-meeting can be worship."

"Why call it prayer-meeting then; and when one knows how dishonest the majority of those people are who are going before the Throne of Grace, I feel that I'd be better off at home."

"Bet, you're forgetting one thing: it's the most necessary thing in the world for them to pray; we have no right to judge them; we're all sinners."

I had heard the argument many times before.

"There are different kinds of sinners as well; the ones who think and the ones who don't think, and I can't ever believe that those people think."

"You can never tell: there's more of our lives out of sight than in."

I knew that I might as well not go further.

"Perhaps you'll feel differently sometime."

I looked at him going to the lobby to put on his coat. I was feeling sorry for him because I was so horrid. I was admiring him for keeping on believing in humanity; I was questioning whether this was strength, and there was something by now in the bearing of his back that made me think his strength was beginning to falter. Was it his faith or his sense of duty that was driving him on? I was feeling that I had neither.

I would have loved to find a total stranger to confess to. If Wil weren't living so far away I would have gone to him; he had talked of losing faith in his letter, but I would have had to explain to Gruff.

I couldn't be at ease in the house; it wasn't Monday night, to be at home. I decided to go to Melinda's house, but not before telephoning her to explain why I wanted to see her, for fear I'd get a tongue-lashing like the evening of Geraint's trouble. I told her I was depressed, to prepare the way. Her voice was kind as she said, "Come right over."

On my way there I was feeling like a child playing truant from school, as free as a bird one minute with a thrill of pleasure running through my limbs, and the next minute having a pang of conscience that frightened me.

Melinda's carpets were so deep that they were shutting out the world altogether as I walked to her back parlour. She had a small glowing fire in the grate, and I collapsed into a chair like a feather bed. I noticed a wine bottle and two expensive glasses on the table.

"Drink this, and tell your story. Something's been bothering you for quite a while, hasn't it? I could tell that when you came back from the cottage."

"No, there's nothing on my mind, no worry or anything like that."

"Are those women at the chapel upsetting you?"

"They aren't worth noticing."

"You know, I don't think you ought to be a minister's wife."

"It was Gruff I married, not a minister."

"Yes, but you have to accept everything that happens to Gruff in his church. It wouldn't pay for you to keep away from the means of grace and things like that."

"I did tonight."

"Why?"

"Because I'm fed up with prayer-meeting."

"And with other meetings?"

"Oh no. But I think it's a terrible thing when materialistic people pray publicly."

"They can pray for forgiveness."

"That's what Gruff said, and he says that I'm no better than they are."

"I'm afraid you expect to see too much perfection in the world and the church. You know, there's a great poet in France who worships sin. He's a kind and generous man, and Christians find themselves attracted to him, and are ashamed."

"I can easily believe it, we're such sick people. But it isn't those things that are bothering me, those are things outside me. Inside me, there's the trouble. I've begun to think that there's no purpose in life. I've lost my faith."

"You'll come out of it. I've had that many times."

She said it so lightly that I couldn't believe her.

"And you know, we never get a sermon that strengthens one's faith; nothing but some talk about the faults of society, just as if we never read a newspaper."

"I don't know that a sermon can strengthen one's faith, that has to come from your experience."

"And my experience now is that there's nothing at all holding me to life."

"And I'm afraid that I can't do or say anything to help you. The only places I find it easy to pray in are the churches on the Continent. You don't know anybody around you there."

I was feeling a little better after being able to talk, though I saw that all talk and discussion was a waste. Nobody reached shore or came upon the truth by talking. And I ought to have known that Melinda would never tell me her thoughts. As I was walking home through the sad, too early darkness of autumn the thing that was sticking in my mind was that I had to accept everything that was happening to Gruff in his church. For his sake, I would go once more to the prayer-meeting.

As we sat by the fire in the den before going to bed we chatted as usual. The prayer-meeting wasn't mentioned and I was feeling very warmly towards Gruff for letting me alone. He was thinking, probably, that there was nothing more behind the thing than a whim that would fade away. Geraint was in the kitchen working hard. He hadn't shown any desire to roam the streets after the evening of the trouble at the chapel. As if his mind had been roving around Melinda's house Gruff was suddenly asking,

"Is Melinda going abroad this year?"

"She didn't mention anything."

I thought for a moment that this was only a roundabout way of getting to know what the two of us had talked about.

"There are some old stories going around that she's going to those far-away countries so much because she's friends with men."

I turned red, but I waited a moment before answering.

"I can't believe that."

"No, it's very hard for me to believe that too. But some people insist on giving work to their imagination."

On other occasions, I would have flown off the handle and become furious, but the conversation we'd had had prepared me not to be surprised at anything I heard about her.

"But I'm surprised by one thing," Gruff went on, "that she wouldn't spend her money on something that would bring people comfort."

"She parts with a good deal."

"Yes, for things that don't last; if she gave books to the chapel or something of the sort, that would remain."

"Yes, but she's chosen otherwise. She had such a knock when her husband died so soon after she was married; that's where her mind always is, and it's hard for me to believe the other story. I know travelling has had an effect on her ideas, and that she doesn't look at sin the way we do, but that doesn't mean she's living according to her ideas."

"No. You remember how we were as children, trying to do something clever to show off. That's how I think of Melinda and those like her. They want to show that they're very broad-minded, but when it comes time to behave, they're as strict as anyone."

Before going to sleep that night I thought a great deal about the thing. One minute I was despising Melinda when I thought that the story could be true; the next minute I was feeling that I should take no notice of it. I belonged to two worlds, the shackled world of my youth, and the new world that I saw, that I heard and read about in books, where no fault was found with sin. I thought one minute that I should go to see Melinda and tell her of the rumour and the talk about her. But if it wasn't true, what pain I would give her! If it was true, perhaps she wouldn't confess, or confess and not see that she was doing anything out of place. I was the one who'd feel small then. And if it were true, I felt that it couldn't change my feelings towards her, I was so fond of her. I wouldn't leave her if she were a parcel of sin.

Then my mind went to the conversation Gruff and I had had. I wondered whether he had thought that Melinda was influencing me, and he'd been trying to see why I didn't want to go to the prayer-meeting. The two of us had been watching each other like cat and mouse.

VI

So it was the most necessary thing in the world for me to go to the prayer-meeting; I left Melinda alone. When she said that she meant to go to the Continent shortly, a sense of loss came to me in thinking that I wouldn't be able to run to her. I could talk with her about things that had nothing to do with the chapel, and talk about the uncommon things in life. Whether I saw eye-to-eye with her or not, I had to confess that the shock she'd given me had hit me hard enough for me to go on another trail and see other windows opening. That talk wasn't giving me much incentive by now. It was like food refusing to be digested.

I went from talking to reading, reading books that I thought could grant me deliverance. *Llyfr y Tri Aderyn*—Morgan Llwyd's *The Book of the Three Birds*. But the first thing I read there was ". . . let no one grant room to the black thoughts; for when the Heavenly Spirit enters, he will silence (by diminishing) the flood waters which are in your heart, and then you may see the mountain-tops, and the eternal, loving thoughts, appear from within." "The Most High calls the light out of the darkness, turning the shadow of death into daybreak." "The creature crawls after his light . . ." Yes, but how? It was very easy for Morgan Llwyd's style to run smooth and loose-reined and give great satisfaction to its creator as he turned the wonderful words on his tongue. It was easy to say the Most High calls the light out of the darkness. But how? There was more sense by far in the Eagle's question: "But how does the mind of man find peace and quiet?" The Dove's answer gave me no comfort. Going into the secret room (as the Dove said) wasn't going to give me a meaning to life. But there it was, I wasn't a mystic; I was fond of life and fond of its luxuries. I was living in the world, and the world was cruel.

Then I began to read the story of Heledd in Dr. Thomas Parry's book, and her grief for her brother above the ruins of her old home. I knew that her grief wasn't the depression of losing faith, but a naked pagan grief for the dead man, the grief of one without religion as her stay, hopelessly accepting her fate and being hacked to the bone. No wonder she went out of her mind. Still, though the circumstances were so different, I felt I was more closely related to Heledd than to Morgan Llwyd. There were no dainty words as cushions for her grief. I could imagine the Hall of Cynddylan, the turves fallen from the roof; a clod remaining here and there with its stringy beard; the stones that had sheltered the fire blackened, with a few twigs on them, and the room empty. Quite possibly Heledd was fond of the comforts of home.

I cherished comforts too; enjoyed my food, enjoyed new clothes; enjoyed the least little bit of something in the house, something that would liven it up. More than anything I enjoyed peace and quiet after finishing work; being able to sit comfortably in a chair and reflect over a cup of tea. A little while ago that had been entirely a luxury, something to lie on; by now it was a stick to drive something else away.

Gruff had gone away after dinner and he wouldn't be back until late. I was looking forward to having an afternoon of peace and quiet. After washing the dinner dishes I went to spruce up; I put on my best frock and powdered my face. I took out one of my best tablecloths for afternoon tea, a white one with lace crocheted around its borders, and placed it cater-cornered on the table, a table I'd stained black; the contrast between the table and the cloth was a pleasure to the eye. I took care to have each corner of the cloth exactly in the middle of the side of the table. I got the best dishes out, dishes that had a pattern of pale blue and red flowers with a bright gold border. I had made a yellow cake, jam between its two halves and powdered sugar on top. Its pale gold colour was so pretty it was a shame to eat it. At another corner was a small dish of bright red strawberry jam with the strawberries almost whole in it; in the middle of the table bread-and-butter sliced as thin as lace with the butter showing its tears. The kettle was singing sleepily on the stove; I put the water in the teapot and let it brew, and moved the kettle so as not to hear the monotonous sound of its singing. Geraint had left his cap on the chair before going to school and left himself in the cap. I took it to the lobby. There was the trace of Gruff's body on the cushion of another chair; I shook the cushion and turned it on the other side. There was a high wind outside but it was calm inside, and I was feeling the comfort of the kitchen like a fur boa around my neck. I poured the tea slowly and decided that I was going to enjoy every mouthful of it and every bite of the food.

I raised my head and saw that Nel, the cat, was on the window sill outside, opening her mouth in mewless misery. I got up and went to open the door for her; she was there before I called, with her fur turning wrong side out. She sat down on her blanket, then lay down and curled up in the comfort. As I ate, I looked at the tree in the garden next door; one minute its branches were conducting a choir like a mad musician lost in his work; then it was bowing low to me; it was waving at me next with its leaves running away. I was as though I were looking at a picture without taking much interest in it. The food tickled my appetite and made me wish for more; I wanted a cigarette afterwards. At that the kitchen began to tremble and the air to quiver with the sound of the front doorbell. I took the cigarette box to the back kitchen and went to the door unhurriedly. There was the president of the Women's Society.

"Is Mr. Jones in?"

"No."

Disappointment came into her face.

"Will he be in some time today?"

"No."

She moved and leaned against the frame of the door, from which she could see into the den.

"No, Mr. Jones isn't in his den," I said.

And she moved quickly to the middle of the step. I gazed at her. She was a handsome woman, tending to fat; her hair was in perfect waves; her blouse had been glossily ironed and some of her lacy underclothes could be seen through it, its neck low enough to show the swell of her breasts. Did these women try to get Gruff to take an interest in them by their taking an interest in the work of the church?

"Old Robert Hughes is ill," she said.

"Well, my husband isn't here, and it's best to get the doctor when someone is ill. What's wrong with him?"

"Shingles."

"Oh well, he can wait."

"Can't *you* go to see him?"

"No, and I don't see that there's need for anybody to run. I'm trying to
have a moment's rest."

"That's it then. I'll go there and tell him."

She started down the steps but not before giving me one frown that
showed she was thinking there were the makings of a murderer in me.

The tree was inviting me back, with its arm beckoning, "Come". I boiled
the kettle again and put additional tea in the teapot; but it wasn't the same.
I lit a cigarette; that was pretty dry too, but it was a great help to me in
reflecting.

The kitchen was trembling once again. It was Jane Owen, an old woman,
there this time, and she was inside in the lobby almost before I asked her.

"Oh, you have someone here to visit."

"No, no one but myself."

"And you put on all this style for yourself."

"Not every day."

"Are you having your birthday or something?"

"No."

"I can tell the smell of smoking."

At that she went and pulled out a tin of snuff, put a bit between her
finger and her thumb, and put it in her nose, holding her head to one side
like a hen listening. For fear she'd think I was hiding a man in the back
kitchen, I went on smoking. I made tea for her and she continued sniffing
and rubbing the dust off her coat.

" 'Oh how sweet is hidden manna,' " she said.

"It isn't so hidden to me, it's a great comfort, every now and then."

"Yes, but take care about those chapel women coming to know. Is it
true that they turned you out of the kitchen so you couldn't have drama
practice there?"

"No, what they did was change the evening. I'm the one who moved,
it's much nicer having the children at the house."

"I wouldn't have moved for them. I can't bear the devils. You'd think
they're the ones who are holding the world together, and they're as stupid
as mules. Envy is a good manure," gazing into the middle of her bread-
and-butter.

"Some of them haven't any too good a name in the town shops here, and stealing is what I call it, going into debt. And they cut a dash with their old English in chapel and everywhere, pretending to be great friends and running each other down to other people. There's that one who lives in the top house near me; easier to get a devil out of his pit than to get money out of her. And you watch if the women are asked to stay after for something on Sunday night, she's the first one there to preen herself in the pew."

She still had her head down. I let her go on because I had nothing to say.

"Religion has become a laughing-stock, indeed. There isn't anyone suffering anything for religion today; if they give a trifle to the cause and take a bunch of flowers to someone who's ill, they think that they've done enough, when you know they have thousands upon thousands in the bank. And they're so miserly, there's that bearded man in the deacon's seat for you, if that one should happen to be selling monkey nuts (it's only luck that he isn't) he'd cut a monkey nut in half before he'd let the scale go down a jot. And he's everlastingly running down people who take a glass. I take a glass of stout every night, that and this snuff are the only pleasure I have, and I've worked hard enough all my life. This tea is good."

"Have another cup."

"And preachers now aren't as good as the ones long ago."

"Were they very good, or do people only say so?"

"It was a pleasure to listen to them, and that wasn't all, you could remember what they'd said for weeks, and my memory's fully as good as it was then. But today these preachers have nothing to say."

"Mind you, it's a difficult time to try to say anything; people don't understand; your generation could understand when a preacher went into things in depth. What is a preacher to do today but become babyish since it's babies who are listening to him?"

"Maybe you're right. Tell me, you know that woman with the funny name—Mel—Mel—"

"Melinda?"

"Yes, she goes away a lot abroad, doesn't she? Is it true that what she goes away for is to pick up men?"

I was furious.

"No, that isn't true."

"But you don't know either, you don't go with her."

"I know Melinda, and I know that it isn't true. She'd be able to do that at home, if she were that sort of person. She's been roaming about ever since she lost her husband, and she likes those distant countries."

"What's wrong with Wales?"

It would have been useless for me to try to explain.

"It does one good to move one's tent."

"She could help a lot of people with her money."

"How do you know that she isn't doing just that? She's very generous, and it's her business that she enjoys herself as she pleases."

"Is it true that those sideburns boys came into the chapel one evening and turned the place upside down, and that your husband got it good and proper from the deacons because he was late to a meeting?"

"You know more than I do."

"It *is* true then."

She kept on eating without looking at me. I was dying for her to go. There was a bad taste in my mouth when I shut the door after her. Who ever thought that old people are interesting? It didn't make any difference to me by now what anyone was saying about Melinda. If she was sinning, it was a more natural sin than going around spreading gossip. No doubt everything the old woman was saying was true, about religious believers in general, but it was so obvious a truth by now, a thing I saw without the help of anyone else's eyes. I preferred what I saw through Melinda's eyes.

I began crying after I arrived back in the kitchen, and that was how Geraint found me when he came home from school. He was startled for a moment.

"What's wrong, mam?"

"Nothing."

"You've had a stranger to tea, and they've said something . . ."

"No."

Then he looked at the table and at my frock.

"Why—uh—?"

"I thought that I'd like to have these pretty things on the table to have tea, but two chapel members called, not together either."

"Bad luck, but you're worrying about something."

"No, it's just that I'm depressed."

"Nobody's depressed except when they're worried."

"Yes."

"You're not worrying on my account, are you? I haven't seen that girl since."

"No, I've forgotten that."

I thought how undiscerning I'd been about Geraint's situation those last weeks, not trying to help him in any way, just saying "We'll forget it", and leaving the thing alone, as if that were enough to check his instincts. He was sure to get hold of someone else, and one could only hope that he'd come across someone he wouldn't regret being fond of. I got up to fix another tea with him helping me, whistling.

"Have another cup with me, mam, and if the bell rings, we won't open the door."

And we had peace and quiet.

That evening Mr. and Mrs. Bryn called. Their visit on this evening was as though someone had put a cushion behind my back on a hard chair. Geraint had gone out, and I was glad I could talk to someone. But the conversation went in a direction that I hadn't foreseen.

"Forgive me for asking," Mr. Bryn said, "aren't you feeling well? Maggie and I think that you haven't looked well for a while."

"I'm fine, a bit depressed, that's all."

"Things are enough to make anyone depressed," Mrs. Bryn said.

"It isn't *things* that are making me depressed."

"You should go to see the doctor."

"They can't do much."

"Go away with Melinda."

"That wouldn't cure me either."

"How is the play getting on?"

"The play? Oh yes."

I had completely forgotten about it, though it was the only thing about the chapel that was giving me pleasure; it had been washed away from my mind like writing off a slate.

"Oh, it's coming along quite well; the most pleasing thing about it is seeing how the children enjoy acting. They never miss rehearsal."

"We're looking forward terribly to seeing it, and so are a good many people."

"I think," Mrs. Bryn said, "that those women think they've put a stop to you by getting the kitchen for themselves. It was a good stroke to bring them to the house."

"Yes," I said, without any interest.

I was glad to see Gruff arrive. There was no one but Mr. and Mrs. Bryn I would have asked to stay for supper when Gruff had been away for the day. After supper Mr. Bryn and Gruff went to the den; Mrs. Bryn and I washed dishes and Geraint resumed his tasks in the kitchen. As the suds broke on my ring and my ring tinkled on the cup, I was seeing Mr. Bryn talking to Gruff about me in the den.

"Look, Mr. Jones, Maggie and I think that Mrs. Jones isn't half well; forgive me for mentioning it."

Gruff quickly pulls his pipe from his mouth and looks in astonishment at Mr. Bryn.

"Don't you see her changing before your eyes?"

"I haven't thought about it."

"Instead of being a nice cheerful woman, she's begun to look depressed and brooding; there's something heavy on her mind."

"She's fine in the house with me."

"Other people are noticing. Is she worrying about the things that have been happening at the chapel lately?"

"She looks as though she's shrugged them off, and I don't think little things like that would worry her. She appears very happy with that play."

Mr. Bryn isn't aware that I'd forgotten about the play when we were talking just now.

"I'll talk to her," Gruff says, in the same tone as he would say that he meant to talk to the carpenter about coming to repair the floor of the chapel.

"You should have the doctor take a look at her."

Gruff is frightened, and straightens up again in his chair and pulls strongly on his pipe.

"Now that you mention it, she did behave quite strangely one evening, not coming to the prayer-meeting; talking about being fed up and things like that; but she came next time, and I thought the fit had passed. And I'm so busy running to this place and the other. A man doesn't have time to notice what's happening in his own house. I don't know when I've read a book all the way through."

Gruff was very thoughtful when the two of us were sitting in front of the fire in the den before going to bed, gazing into the fire without his pipe.

"Bet, is something wrong; are you feeling ill?"

"No, I feel fine."

"Confess now, you haven't been just like yourself lately, have you?"

"No."

"Are those women at the chapel worrying you?"

"No."

"I asked too much of you when I asked you to marry me, because you had to marry the chapel as well. I've begun to think that the most difficult people to live with are Christians."

"They're often difficult enough, but a person knows what to expect from people wherever they are, Christians or not. But it frightens one to think of what can happen to oneself."

"Has anything happened to you?"

"Yes, it's happened, to me; I've completely lost my faith."

Gruff came to sit on the arm of my chair and took my hand.

"And you're worrying."

"Worrying isn't the word. When someone worries, they have hope. But I've gone into a state of despair."

"Has Melinda been talking about things like this to you,—because she has some very strange ideas?"

"Melinda has nothing to do with my state of mind."

"You can never tell; the influence of one mind on another happens without one knowing."

"No, Melinda believes, and I don't. She sees that there's meaning to life, I don't. I can't explain it to you, Gruff."

"You're thinking, aren't you, that I never have any doubts like that, and that I would never understand."

"No, that isn't what I think, I'd be able to talk better to a stranger. You're too closely related to me."

"I don't know whether this will raise your heart. You talked about despair and losing faith. The despair shows that there's some amount of faith left. There's still a bottom that keeps one from falling through."

"But one can sit a very long time at the bottom."

"Like you, I feel I'm too close to you to be able to say what I'd say to someone else, or from the pulpit. But we must have the doctor here for a look at you; you don't know that it isn't some physical illness that's causing it all."

"I'll go to see him. But before I go I'd like to have an afternoon in the country together, just you and me, by the river. The weather's nice and you can leave your work for one afternoon."

"We must do the afternoon and leave the work; we'll go tomorrow. It's more necessary for you to have a bit of pleasure."

An afternoon in parentheses, that's what it was; it was impossible to have a full day to while away. Work for Gruff in the morning, and work at night. We didn't have time to linger and gaze at the colours of autumn tree by tree, only saw them as a single patch of copper hues running together. The sun was so warm that we didn't feel the car was running through the colours of death; they were the colours of life in middle age with a long-lasting look on them. We sat on old coats on the river bank to eat our sandwiches, and gazed lazily through the brightness of the water at the gravel on the bottom, with the weak sun falling on one stone and making it cast its sparks of light like a star. I lay down at full length after eating and turned my face to the sun and enjoyed its faint heat on my skin; the scent of the earth was a balm to the nose. I had brought *Yr Haf a Cherddi Eraill* with me, R. Williams Parry's *Summer and Other Poems*, and I asked Gruff to read me the sonnet *Dinas Noddfa*, "City of Refuge". He read splendidly and his gentle voice gave me the same pleasure as the little breeze that was playing around my head. But despite being urged by the poet to follow the wise and raise myself a fortress and be the builder of my own heaven, I couldn't. When the sonnet was written, the experience was, certainly, true for the poet; fervently expressed. But for me today, the words were an enjoyment that pleased the senses; I enjoyed them as Gruff was reciting them; their sweetness flowed over me. But when I sat up, I knew that what they were was words; I had raised a fortress, not as a refuge, but as a wall of darkness. I remembered suddenly that Melinda was going away in a few days, and a shiver of cold ran through my flesh. That vanished as the car ran swiftly homewards; I had had a tiny interval of pleasure.

I went to see the doctor the next day; I could tell him only a little bit, that I was depressed and weak. And he gave me pills.

VII

That afternoon on the river bank was the last pleasant afternoon I had before coming here. Melinda came to say goodbye before going away. She was wearing new clothes; a three-quarter-length coat of warm green wool with matching skirt; a felt hat of the same colour. She would come home with bags full of other new clothes. I didn't envy her; that was her pleasure; my pleasure would have been coming back to enjoy the things I'd enjoyed a while ago. She was full of the zest of looking forward; I managed to keep a face that showed I enjoyed the small circle I was living in. She spoke briskly; I felt as she spoke that she was going no further than the shop.

"I'll bring you a new frock from Paris," she said, and went out before I could say thank you. I saw an empty space in my own house after she'd gone. My mind followed her next morning to London, to the airport, and to Paris, though I'd never seen it. We've never lived constantly in each other's houses, but now, since she wasn't at hand, the sense of loss was just as if she'd been living with us forever. I went inside her house in the afternoon; it was as quiet as a church; I was expecting to hear someone ill moaning upstairs. Something moved and I jumped. There was a bucket turned upside down in the kitchen with a floor cloth spread over it; the dish cloth placed on the edge of the sink; the last breakfast dishes had been put neatly on the board beside it. If she'd been coming back that evening these things would have looked different, expectant and cheerful; now they were looking like nothing at all. There was more difference than time between a day and three months. I dawdled around the house; I went upstairs and saw a skirt hanging on the back of the door, the skirt she was wearing when she came over the morning after we returned from the cottage. In passing it I smelled the light scent of Melinda's favourite perfume. There was a tiny bottle of it on the dressing-table. I put a little of it on my pocket handkerchief and regretted it. Melinda's perfume was as much a part of her as her skin; on me it was outlandish.

I went back to my own house; the kettle was singing on the stove; Nel was purring on her blanket; Gruff was writing in his den; I was moving back and forth in the kitchen; the lazy tranquillity of afternoon over everything. How nice an afternoon like this would have been if I'd been able to look forward to the next day, or look back to the day we were by the river. I was standing still in time, and yet forced to move as though I were on the escalators in London's underground stations.

I would have to go to the fellowship meeting that evening; that wasn't as hateful to me as going to the prayer-meeting. A discussion circle, that's what the fellowship meeting was to me; it no longer included confessing sins. How much would anyone take to confess his sin? I wouldn't have taken the world myself to go there and say that I had lost my faith. I didn't believe that anyone confessed his true sin in the past either; made-up sins, that's what they were, and false tears. It was in the houses people washed their dirty linen, not in chapel.

Twelve of us were sitting in a corner at the school. We held meetings in corners by now; old people who'd retired to a corner and huddled there; still waiting for something to happen. The old preachers were looking at us from the walls with contempt, I thought. The walls themselves were enough to make anyone feel down in the dumps, with their mud-coloured paint; the high windows through which one couldn't see so much as a chimney, and the filthy lampshades. In the wooden panel facing me the edges of a knot formed two eyes that didn't quite match. I'd been gazing and gazing at these two eyes for years. They were what tested my interest in a meeting. I scarcely noticed them at an interesting meeting. My eyes would sear through them when someone would try to speak and falter and go on (eloquence wasn't one of our members' high points). The eyes would change their expression as I gazed at them; sometimes they were amused, sometimes sad, sometimes indignant; tonight they were indignant. The subject was the story of the buyers and sellers being turned out of the temple, and instead of discussing it as it was, as a condemnation of defiling the temple, the indignation of Christ turned into an argument for using power and an argument for war. I saw Gruff's mind working: "You lost the thread some time ago; what's here is righteous indignation with no risk to life; but it's better than nothing, it's forcing you to try to think; that's better than having no thoughts at all. I'm having to pull this talk out of you, as if I were pulling a tree from the earth by its roots. I'll try to explain my own thoughts at the end."

Most of the congregation were women, old and middle-aged women; there were no young people there. Everyone was looking pleased, as if what they were saying was going to change the course of the world. To me all the talk was worse than pointless, and I felt as though I were on the brink of exploding in seeing these people looking like unsung heroes, an expression that made me want to vomit. If they were unsung, how did anyone come to know about them? Our innocence was a funny thing. Then an old man got to his feet, a wishy-washy old man whose sincerity no one could doubt. He said there was no need for us to worry or fear; that God was taking care of us. The women were looking angelic, with their heads to one side. As he spoke he rubbed his right arm along the top of the bench as if he were sawing wood. He raised his voice, "No, war will never come; 'the Lord reigns, let the earth rejoice.'" The vestry went dark to me; I saw Gruff's face as if through a veil, as I shouted, "No, you're wrong, it's the petticoats reign, let the earth rejoice." I wasn't conscious of anyone or anything; but I felt Gruff's arm around me as he carried me like a piglet at a fair into the chapel kitchen.

I don't remember how I got home, but I saw the kitchen of my own house through mist with Gruff and Geraint rushing about, one making a cup of tea and the other going to the telephone. Before I drank the tea I jumped on top of a chair and shouted,

"Now listen all of you I want to tell you what's on my mind religion has become a laughing-stock there's no religion today everybody's left it everybody and gone their own way to hell the chapel people are worst of all because they're pretending to be otherwise the worldly people are better and much better because of giving to everything the chapel people are cutting monkey nuts in half charging an exorbitant price for everything just like the worldly people the last penny is their principle they're starving the women who clean for them and going to collect the rents of their condemned houses in fur coats money money is everything piling up money like marbles to put it in the bank people never darkening the chapel coming there to be married because it's nicer and them with their bellies to their noses they're trying to talk cleverly at fellowship meeting and Sunday School about what people should do when they themselves haven't a particle of faith they don't understand the hymns and shout in singing the tenderest things Oh blessed will be the shouting of the day to come I see you Gruff going to tell me I'm as bad as them I know that but I know as well that I know that I know the others don't the world has destroyed itself before war does it this is the end of the world man has killed himself by his selfishness and I see you Gruff going to say there are a very few unselfish people always as the salt of the earth and that they will save the world yet I can't believe that . . ."

I saw Geraint's face as if he were having a convulsion, becoming all shapes, as if he were about to laugh, about to cry, about to be serious. At that, Nel the cat went and jumped on top of the chair and rubbed her body affectionately against my legs. Geraint laughed his head off; I gave him a clout on the side of his face, and I got down from the chair. I went to the den and asked for Melinda's number on the telephone; the cat came in and jumped on the table beside me and purred. I put the telephone receiver down and walked slowly to the foot of the stairs. The cat jumped down and walked alongside the lobby wall. As I put my foot on the first step I saw her walking close to the wall with her tail up, the way you see a criminal in a film walking in the shadow along a dark wall, keeping as close to it as he can so that the police won't catch him. After reaching the far end she turned back and looked at me, but since she found no welcome she went back to the kitchen with her tail limp. Gruff came out of the kitchen and asked,

"Who were you phoning?"

"Melinda."

"But she's away."

"I know, but her house was alive with her presence, the way a dead moth trembles on a person's hand and the trembling makes it look as though it were alive."

I went up the stairs to my bedroom with Gruff coming behind me. Gruff was dazed and silent as I undressed. For the first time in a long while I felt it was a nice thing to be able to lie in bed. Geraint came up with a cup of tea for me. I put my arm around his neck and said I was very sorry but I was very ill. And he began to cry. The doctor came and gave me an injection so I could sleep. The next day I myself insisted on being allowed to enter Y Wenallt.

*   *   *

Here I am then, able to go over my experiences and look at them coldly and without agitation. I've managed to go over them without once stumbling or coming to a halt. I saw myself as if I were going about the Hall of Cynddylan, feeling my way like a blind person towards the end when the floodgate broke. They were ugly enough ruins, these experiences, and looking in at them through the holes called for a bit of courage. But the sun cast its light through a hole at times and made a strip across the grass like the one I saw across the flowers of the garden the evening before we went to the cottage in August. Grass had grown on the floor of the Hall and the bright strip gave it some cheerfulness in spite of the bearded turf. The sun struck the stones where there had once been a fire, and they weren't as grey in the sunlight. It made me feel that fire would be kindled here again and children would come to warm their hands at it and to weave pictures in its flames. But Heledd's hair was in untidy hanks over her eyes; her cloak in tatters around her feet. She saw no hope; she had no family; she turned her back and returned to the forest and to her madness. I turned my own back on her and went in another direction with the sun on my face.

The weeks that I've spent in this place weren't part of the experiences. Calm down was what I did here, take pills, receive letters and visitors as though I were in a waiting room, where I was expecting to be allowed to go inside somewhere to look for someone, and that someone was myself.

VIII

I was as limp as a tadpole after answering the doctor's questions, and there was no sign that he meant to be finished soon. I was having trouble keeping my back straight. Until now it hadn't been hard to answer, they were questions about my family and my background. But when it came to personal questions I felt different. There wasn't anything in the doctor's attitude that made it too easy for me to answer his questions, or anything that made it difficult either. It was as if he were holding himself back; asking questions like a form. In spite of that, I couldn't forget there was a living person in front of me who was receiving into his own consciousness the most secret things in my heart. I had to face him, since it was these secret things that had brought me here, and if I were to be allowed to go home, or rather, if I had recovered, I had to answer a stranger's questions about things I thought were hard for me to understand myself. I might trip in not remembering quite correctly how I was feeling at that time, months ago now; it's hard to catch a flash of feeling and describe it months later. But I supposed the doctor knew about something like this better than I. Moreover, I was tired, but from my experience in the past, I knew there was something like an iron rod in my constitution that would make me keep on going.

"Mrs. Jones, when this depression first came to you, was there anything outside yourself worrying you, anything at the chapel or in the family?"

"No, nothing more than usual. There are always some tiny worries at a chapel or in a family. The depression came suddenly, of itself, like a shower of cold mist."

I stopped.

"Go on and describe it."

"If it had been caused by things from outside, that's what I would have thought about, but I didn't *keep* thinking about those things. To me, the depression was a state that I'd entered; I had no interest in the world around me, no looking forward to the future; never looking back to the past either. I wasn't able to enjoy the things I'd enjoyed at one time."

"What sort of things?"

"The house, my food, going for a trip to the country, the services at the chapel, seeing a play, reading, meeting friends; in a word, I was fed up. But in a little while the depression itself became something I saw in pictures; as a mask on my face; as a patch of blackness; as frost; as mist; as weights on my heart with the weights about to break and fall. I would become better for a fairly long spell, and then it would come back. And then came a change in the depression."

"Yes?"

"I realized one day that this thing wasn't standing on its own, that it was fastened to something else. This change came when I was feeling that the depression was weights and they were about to break and fall; I saw it was my faith that was about to break loose, and the reason I couldn't look forward to the future was that I didn't believe in a future; there was no meaning to life; God wasn't ruling the world; He'd left it to some cruel fate."

I stumbled at this point.

"Can you say anything more?"

"It isn't that I can't speak, but I find it hard to talk about religion to anyone else, even to my husband. I don't like godly talk, but I had faith; Williams Pantycelyn had said everything for me. But that all went; I couldn't believe anything."

"Can you explain what happened to you that last evening you were at the chapel?"

"I went wild and blew up that evening; I have a rather fierce temper at times, and I'm impatient; I went wild on hearing people declare what I couldn't believe by that time, namely that 'the Lord reigns'. I was feeling too that it was hypocrisy in them; they were so complacent; I couldn't believe their faith had cost them anything."

"You were saying just before that your faith has come back. Can you explain how?"

"It came back in just the same way as it went, quietly. Not by degrees or anything like that, but like putting on an electric light. Perhaps my husband's at the back of it somewhere. All I can say is that it's there and I'm not afraid of facing things now. The thing I was most afraid of facing was the thing itself. After coming here, I tried to go over the thing that happened to me and I couldn't; I had to stop thinking about it, but by now I can go over the thing without a tremor at all, look at it as if it had happened to someone else."

I remembered I had left very important things out, and I added somewhat shakily,

"I've put the cart before the horse."

"Never mind about that. Say what it is you want to say. Maybe it was I who led you in the wrong direction."

"I haven't mentioned anything of my story since I came here. But I know why; at the beginning, anyway, nothing happened; I was calm, not objecting to being here, and with no eagerness to see anyone, even my husband. I took no interest in what I'd left behind or in anyone or anything around me here either. I'd listen to the women talk without being able somehow to take it in. Nothing was sinking in. It was all just the same. But bit by bit I came to see there was a great difference between the talk of Mrs. Hughes, the little woman with the marks of suffering on her, and the others'; and I came to like her talk, and dislike the talk of the others. After Mrs. Hughes went home, I asked if I could go to the public ward."

"Why?"

"I was afraid that I'd lose my temper with them for talking so frivolously. Things weren't so happy after I went to the ward either; Sali was so provoking and I had trouble avoiding taking notice of the hateful things she said. But I was able not to, though she tempted me very often. And then . . . ?"

"Yes?"

"I came to look forward to seeing my husband come to see me; I wanted to see *him;* I came to feel that I'd been horrid to him before coming here. At the beginning that hadn't been bothering me at all. But when he'd come here, I didn't want to see much farther than himself; until one day when his friends, two preachers and a parson, came with him. We'd all had a nice afternoon together last summer at the cottage where we go for summer holidays. They had holiday clothes on that day, and an irresponsible holiday spirit as well; they talked quite facetiously and quite depressingly too about their work. But when they came here in their round collars, they looked different and talked differently; more in earnest and more high-heartedly. Somehow, that gave my heart a lift. I can't say how, but it put some enthusiasm for work in me. One of these preachers is a very inventive person, and he was saying, 'What if we were to have a *noson lawen,* a merry evening, at the cottage on New Year's Eve?' And the other three's mouths were watering with enthusiasm over it. Bit by bit, I began thinking the idea was a good one too, and I felt as though my hand were stretching out to reach for something."

"Is the cottage far from where you live?"

"Yes, a good forty miles, but through this, that is, through looking forward to the *noson lawen,* I came to be able to look back at my home and able to come to terms with thinking of going back there. At the beginning I didn't want to hear my husband even mention our house, never mind the chapel, but in a little while it was I myself began asking about the house. And now I can bear to hear my husband talk about the chapel as well. I'm not afraid to face it by now; indeed I'm rather looking forward to being able to begin working there again to help my husband. He's one of the best persons; he can stand people. I ought to have said all that before talking about my faith; because it was bit by bit that that happened, but my faith came back suddenly."

"Well, there we are then, Mrs. Jones. Thank you very much."

DARK TONIGHT (1962)

I came out feeling just the way I did in those dreams I'd have, that I'd gone outside stark naked and wasn't able to find my nightgown. I hadn't confessed as much as that to anybody before. I wanted nothing at that moment but to become no one and nothing, like cuckoo-spit vanishing from the grass.

.   ▪   .

In going back to the ward, I decided, whatever the consequence of this conversation with the doctor would be, that I didn't want to think too much about being allowed to go home. The disappointment wouldn't be as great if it were decided to keep me there longer; and when the word came that I was well enough to be allowed to go home I was able to take the thing quite unexcitedly. For the rest of the time Sali was in another ward, and there was tranquillity in our ward. I walked now and then to the women's tuberculosis ward next door. There were large windows there reaching all the way to the floor, and one could see the fields stretching all the way to the hills. Going into a green world once again would be a strange thing for a little while. Many of these women would never be allowed to go. I would be in prison, too, after going home, but it was a prison where I would have freedom to do battle; but these old women had finished doing battle; were expecting the end whenever it would come. No, it wasn't that they were expecting it, just waiting until it came.

Once the day of departure came, my feelings were running back and forth between my home and the ward. I was trying to curb my eagerness to go back to the old life, and I was trying to kill the tenderness of my feelings for these old women. Here was where they were supposed to be, home where I was supposed to be. They would have every kindness here, more perhaps than they would have with a family. It was myself alone who was seeing the misery of their condition from the standpoint of a middle-aged woman. I learned in those few hours that I had to be cruel if I were to be able to bear the world at all. I went to each of them and gave them a kiss, promising that Gruff and I would come to visit them before long. Magi's face was to the wall and she didn't turn her head; Jane was as quiet as ever but I saw a tear in her eye. Someone else would be in my bed that evening, for sure. The last thing I saw was Lisi's head going from side to side as the door opened, and her stretching to try and see the porch. I didn't turn my head back, and I didn't run along the porch either, this time.

VI

Stories

(1964–1981)

Cats at an Auction

Elen was sitting in her parlour—she was of a mind to go to the auction, and of a mind not to. She felt no urgency about the corner cupboard by this time. The thought of it today was an old yearning that had grown cold, because she'd failed to find one after searching for years. When she'd heard that the late Mrs. Hughes had had one among her furniture, a jot of the yearning had come back. But now, in looking over the old things here in her own parlour, thinking of it didn't give her much pleasure. It would be the same as having a child after all the other children had all grown up, and the corner cupboard would be like an unnatural growth on a tree stump. Her hands had waxed these things over a long stretch of years until their surfaces were as smooth as pure silk, and there was talk that Mrs. Hughes hadn't taken much care of her house. If so, the corner cupboard would be more like an unexpected child than ever. But sometimes one came to love the unexpected child more than the others. She would go to the auction.

She sat back down, and this time she looked at her furniture from the other side of the grave. Some day these pieces would all be parted from each other; the dresser would go to one place, the chest to another, the oak table to yet another, and they'd be like orphaned children divided up and adopted by different families, and her own furniture would be no different from Mrs. Hughes' furniture by then. The next minute she remembered it was from the other side of the grave that she was seeing this, and she didn't mind. The sting that the thought had given her disappeared. To Mrs. Hughes today it made no difference in the least how she had kept her furniture. By night it would be scattered in different directions like mats under the feet of a rampaging dog.

She'd go, she would. But she dawdled again and sat down. She started thinking about Mrs. Hughes. She didn't know her too well, though she'd attended the same chapel. The dead widow had belonged to a set of women who always spoke English though their Welsh was better, helped with sales of work, prepared food for the Monthly Meeting and supper for the Literary Society, did everything that Elen didn't do. It was as one of a clatch that Elen thought of her, without anything special to make her visible in the clatch of these sixty-year-old women. Indeed, the thing about her that was different from the others made her more unnoticed and melded her more and more into the clatch and hid her in it. The others wore smart, colourful clothing; they curled their hair and they coloured their lips— they tried to improve on nature. Mrs. Hughes was colourless, always wore grey, pepper-and-salt-coloured clothing, and her hair, which had begun to turn the least bit grey, blended into her clothes like the water of a stream running into a river. Everything about her made her look worse than she was. Nobody could know when she had new clothes—they'd be the same colour.

She had plenty of money, it was said, and she was miserly, it was said: by now the story was abroad that her house was slovenly, and even worse, though it could have been otherwise, since she had plenty of money to pay for help. Indeed, these tale-mongers said, she shouldn't have died at all. She was found dead in her bed one morning after someone broke into the house because she hadn't been seen for some days and there were a number of milk bottles outside the door. If she'd had the doctor in time they said (there wasn't much wrong with her), she could have been alive today. Then the imagination of the tale-mongers enlarged on the reason she hadn't called anybody in, not her friends or the doctor, when she had a telephone: she didn't want anyone to see how the place was, because, they said, there were signs she'd got up to make herself a bite of food more than once. But that was that, it wasn't her business, detective business, Elen thought. Her concern would be to buy the cupboard, if she did. Yes, if. She realized as well that this woman's dying so unexpectedly was the true reason for her lack of yearning to have the cupboard now. What if she too were to—? She began to feel depressed. But she would go, nevertheless; she'd get to see people, get to see life. An auction was part of life, even an auction of what belonged to the dead. That was life, the living buying the things of the dead, the living living for a while. She'd get to see her friend Margiad as well. She went to every auction without a thought of buying anything, to get to see people in circumstances different from the circumstances of sermon, drama, and concert. People were different at an auction, her friend said.

She aimed for the room where the furniture was, the parlour probably. The corner cupboard was in its place. A very good cupboard, full of possibilities when it was cleaned. More than that would need to be done to the room itself. Old paper on the walls, with traces of rain water and dampness all over it, like a map of Anglesey above the fireplace and a map of the Midland towns under the windows. The tiles of the hearth had come away here and there and made it resemble someone who'd lost some of his false teeth. She'd noticed before coming in that the window curtains looked passable, but from inside they were looking like rotten network ready to collapse. Elen wouldn't be surprised if they fell of themselves, silently, like dew, once some spirit loosed them from its hand. The dust of years had hardened on the edge of the skirting until it was like packthread.

Buyers were coming in from the other rooms. She saw a chair and sat down on it. A young woman was already sitting on another chair as if she'd been nailed to it. She wasn't looking at anyone. She looked as if she were a newlywed, neat from her beige skirt to her thin red lips. There were scores of young women like her all over town at the time: her hair cut in the latest fashion, nothing in the back and a thick clump in the front, making her look like a chicken with its comb clipped. On Elen's left was a small ladder for housework, with a man about sixty years old sitting on top of it, wearing bifocals, and every time someone came in he'd look through the lower half. Presently Margiad arrived, and found a chair so she could sit between Elen and the young woman.

"Do you mean to buy anything?"

"I don't know. Maybe. The corner cupboard."

The young woman turned her head the slightest bit and moved it back. She was tapping her foot nervously on the floor and twisting her ring around her finger.

"Things are going well here in spite of the look on them," Margiad said.

Four women came in, friends of the late Mrs. Hughes, and sat on a bench near by. They had nodded at Elen. The oldest of them, Mrs. Jones, had been Mrs. Hughes' best friend. The two of them would go for holidays together every year. And she was saying:

"I never thought the place was like this. It was no wonder that she never asked me to come here."

"No, other people's houses were preferable," one of the others said.

"And cheaper," said Mrs. Jones.

"Listen," Margiad said.

"Who can avoid it?" Elen said.

Mrs. Jones bent her head back and looked around the walls of the room and the ceiling, as if she were looking at the sky and counting the stars.

"When *I'm* dead," she said, "*my* house won't be filthy like this."

The small man looked at her through the lower part of his glasses, and gave a spiteful "Huh" in his throat.

Elen felt something come over her heart as though someone had put a cold poultice on her. It oppressed her.

"The Judas," Margiad said, under her breath. "The bitch," she added.

"Sh," from Elen.

To her, Mrs. Hughes was more than the late Mrs. Hughes at that moment. She came back to life, part of the clatch of women at the chapel, looking at them and smiling, enjoying herself in their company at another auction. Then she fell from the clatch like a sheaf from a stook of grain.

More people came in, and the young woman was looking more nervous. Other voices were coming from the back, with one louder than the others, the voice and accent of a country woman.

"Mind you, Mrs. Hughes was a very agreeable old thing, with a smile for everybody no matter who. Not much of anything in her head, but she was a real trump to her friends and very faithful. She and her husband were very happy together."

The auctioneer came in, and the young woman began to bite her lips. The corner cupboard was put up first.

"Three pounds," said the small man from the ladder, as if he were glad to get it off his chest.

"Three and a crown," from the young woman softly, bending her head, with the clump of hair moving forward as if she were a ram about to butt the auctioneer.

"Three and ten," Elen said, more spiritedly than she'd have thought she could.

"Three pounds twelve and six," from the small man.

"Three pounds fifteen," Elen said more loudly.

"Four pounds," from the young woman.

"Four and ten," from Elen.

"Whew," said the small man, and that was the end of his bidding.

"Five pounds," said the young woman almost savagely.

"Five guineas," said Elen.

Mrs. Jones leaned her head forward past the other women to look at her, and a new inspiration came to Elen, that she'd like to get the corner cupboard for herself, not as an addition to the old furniture in her parlour, but as something in memory of the colourless dead woman, something to say to her, "I bought this at your auction out of compassion because your friends had deserted you."

"Five and ten," said the young woman.

Elen was on the brink of raising it another crown when the young woman looked at her beseechingly, with her head to one side, as some dogs do on hearing someone whistle close to them. Elen was vanquished, and the auctioneer firmly united cupboard and young woman for five pounds ten. And she went straight out without looking at anyone.

Elen had no interest in the rest of the furniture, but she didn't get up to go out. She began to reflect. On the floor near her was a flimsy old carpet, folded up untidily. She looked at its folds, and bit by bit the folds turned into the shapes of a face, nose, mouth, forehead, and ears. They'd turned into the face of a dead body in a grave, grey as putty, heedless of criticism, the body of a woman parted from the things that were sold in her house today, separated from her friends. Elen gazed at the face a long while, expecting to see the shapes change, and that there'd be one expression of a smile for her in it because she'd given her one kind thought. But she didn't find one. The next minute a man came into the room wearing heavy shoes. He trampled the carpet and the shapes disappeared. He had trampled the face of the dead woman in her coffin.

The sale of the room's contents was finished, and before the small man came down from his ladder, a pretty, cheerful woman came towards him.

"Did you get it, love?"

"No, what chance does a man have against such damned determined women?"

"None. That's why I sent you here. Come home, love. I have salmon for tea."

"Much better. You don't need to have a corner cupboard to keep a tin of salmon."

The two of them went out happily, and the ladder was moved to another room.

"I want to go home," Elen said to her friend.

"Why? Come to the other room so we can see what's there."

"I've seen and heard too much."

"You're disappointed because you didn't get the corner cupboard."

"No. Someone who's just starting out in life has got it."

"A very selfish little thing."

"To be sure. Everybody's selfish at an auction."

They were carried into the next room, where a miscellany of things was to be sold, old ornaments, old pictures, new bedclothes that had never been unfolded, sheets and blankets, with the edges of the folds ruined. Piles of underwear that had never been unwrapped.

"What was wrong with the woman?" Margiad said. "Why didn't she wear them to have a bit of enjoyment?"

"Maybe she was meaning to, sometime."

Mrs. Hughes' friends were there as well.

"She had enough underwear to be able to change more often," Mrs. Jones said.

"Hush," one of the others said, "this man who's walking around is her brother."

"It won't do him any harm to hear. It's obvious that he's the same sort himself, or he would have taken things like this home instead of selling them at auction."

Margiad insisted on staying until the last minute and going through the whole house to have a good look. Elen went into the parlour where the corner cupboard had been. Someone had fetched it; the chairs had gone as well, and nothing was left but the folded carpet in the middle of the floor. Elen tried to see the face in it again; and little by little it came back. Mrs. Hughes' face was looking at an empty room just as indifferently as before, but this time as if she'd gained a victory over everybody. The mouth was shut more tightly. Elen moved to the window and looked at the carpet from that direction. The afternoon sun was coming in through the window and striking the dusky walls and casting the pattern of the window on the floor. This room could be cheerful again some day, Elen thought. She gazed once more at the carpet. A change came into the face, the mouth was smiling.

Margiad came in and caught her gazing.

"What's wrong with you? Are you ill? You're white as chalk. Come home and have a cup of tea with me. I've been through the house. There's nothing left at all but a sliver of soap in the bathroom."

As they went out through the lobby the late Mrs. Hughes' brother was talking to his sister's friends.

"A very good auction," he said, "sold everything and got excellent prices."

Elen turned back to look at the house. The curtains were still on the windows, and the house was looking the same as when the owner was alive. Only those who'd been inside would know it was an empty shell.

"Why are you so quiet?" Margiad asked over the cup of tea.

"I'm thinking."

"Thinking about what?"

"Thinking about Mrs. Hughes."

"Tut, she's stopped existing by now."

"I don't know. She was very much alive to me this afternoon, more alive than she'd ever been in her life."

"You didn't think much of her when she was alive."

"No. Some people have to die before we come to know them."

"Well, she could have been alive today if she'd been less stingy. She had enough means to pay for help."

"Life had become too much for her."

"If it had, there was no need for that to have happened either."

"We don't know. We don't know what is the first thing that gives way in us."

"She could have spent her money. Look how that brother and his wife will squander it."

"Likely enough. But we don't know what that little thing is that starts refusing to work in us, starts becoming too unconcerned even to spend our money. She did spend on some things."

"Yes. That was very strange."

"We'll never know what the little insect was that began to make her decay and sucked out her energy. I don't think it was fear of anyone seeing her house that was wrong with her. The woman had been overcome."

"You're too kind to her."

"As we should be to the dead."

"Perhaps you're right. But I don't see why we have to be depressed because of Mrs. Hughes."

"We're made of the same stuff as Mrs. Hughes."

"Well, we're alive today. Drink your tea. Have some more of this bread-and-butter."

John, Margiad's husband, came home from work.

"How was the auction? Did you buy anything, Elen?"

"No."

"She gave in on the corner cupboard to some snip of a little girl, just married."

"You have plenty of furniture, and there'll be an auction of your things too some day," John said.

Elen left them. The two of them would discuss her once her back was turned, with Margiad as unconcerned as the dead body she'd seen the first time in the carpet, licking her chops as she told John the story of the auction. To Margiad this was an auction like every auction, a place to see people and not to know them, living or dead.

After reaching the house, she sat in her parlour and looked lovingly at her furniture. It was all of a piece, and it would stay all of a piece. It wasn't the word of Margiad's husband John that would be the last word on her furniture. She would write to her attorney that he was to change part of her will—her furniture was to be kept together in a storehouse until it rotted and fell apart like Mrs. Hughes' curtains.

Buying a Doll

She was so glad she'd remembered to put the little frock in her bag this time. At one time the thing had pursued her like a hound, it hadn't let her alone for weeks. Then, after she failed to find a doll in her own town to fit the clothes, she forgot about it, until a little while ago, when she came across the clothes in a drawer while searching for something else. Then the fascination had come back, and since she wanted to go to the Big Town today to buy a hearthrug, she decided to try and find a doll there.

The clothes were well over half a century old, clothes that she'd made, like many other students, when she was in college. They were half the size of the cut-out pattern for a child's clothing, and they would fit a medium-sized doll. The notion had come to her, about two years before, that it would be a good thing to put the clothes on a doll, since they were so old-fashioned, and then place the doll on the blue table, like an ornamental pincushion.

First she went to buy the hearthrug. That didn't take much time, since she found one fairly reasonably priced. She was on fire to get to the toy shop. There was plenty of choice there, hundreds of them, of every sort of colour, and size, and shape. A busy little man came towards her, wearing glasses, and looking like a little bird with a crooked beak. She explained to him hesitantly what she wanted, and shyly drew the frock out of her bag.

"I have the exact thing that you want," he said, darting small and swift into an invisible corner of the shop.

"This is," he said, having reappeared from behind a curtain, "a very special doll. In the world of dolls, she is just like those beautiful women in London who are wearing fashionable clothes to walk in front of women and show the latest fashion. She cost twenty-seven and six at one time, but you can have her for twelve and eleven."

The great thing was, would the frock fit her? It was tried on, and, indeed, she was quite marvellous. Two women who were serving behind another counter came there to see, and they were mad about her. And she liked the doll, too. She could move her head and her arms and her legs up and down, to the right and to the left and every way. She didn't have blonde hair, that sort of hair which makes you give doubtful praise to a woman's beauty by saying that "she's pretty as a doll". Oh no, but light brown hair, as natural as her own hair when she was a child. She had eyebrows of a bit darker brown, and blue eyes that were closing and opening as she was moved.

She decided to buy her, and the little shopkeeper's satisfaction was so great that she felt for a moment there might be something wrong with her. But no matter. She observed that the shopkeeper had written twelve and six on the bill, to *her* great satisfaction.

Before she reached the door, she saw a large mirror on the wall, and she looked into it. There was a cold look to her left eye, it was all watery, and the corner next to her nose had swollen and held a little pool of a tear. What if it were to keep on swelling and become red, like Ugly Wil's eye long ago?

The bus was full, and the conductor said so quite emphatically on seeing her jump onto the platform by the door, where two young women were standing already.

"Well," she said, "I'm not about to get off for you or anyone else. Half of these people will be getting off at the next stop, and I'm going to the end of the line."

She was ready to box the ears of anyone who would dare try to make her get off. The man smiled cravenly, and one of the two women made room for her to pass into the bus, where at least she could stand more comfortably. Opposite her in a seat for three sat two women and a young girl about seven years old holding a big doll in her arm. The child's mother made no move to take the child on her knee and make room for her. She began gazing at the mother, she tried gazing to conjure her into making room for her. But she couldn't charm her. This young woman, she thought, was clothed in an iron coat of selfishness. Then she began gazing at the child and her doll. This doll had clothes on, but it wasn't in the same world as her doll. On remembering about her doll, she drew her bag closer to her for fear of someone hitting it. After some five minutes the three got off, and she could sit down. The bus was half empty the rest of the journey.

As she walked down to her house, she was feeling shaky from fatigue and hunger, and her body was swaying from side to side like an ancient sailing-ship. A car came from in back of her, and threw its gleaming light far in front of her, and made her look like a telegraph pole.

"Oh dear," she said after opening the door, "I was forgetting about him."
"Him" was the dog, who came to her to welcome her, and stretched his
legs and hollowed his back. Then he began jumping all over her and licking
her, more as a sign that he wanted to go out than as a welcome.

"What if you were like that little dog from Russia," she said, "whirling
around space for thousands of miles now, *he* doesn't get to go out." Then
she added: "Well, not on his feet, anyway."

She was used to preaching to the dog like this, to be able to hear the old
forgotten words of the Welsh language roll across her lips, words like *ffali-
gragwd, gyrbibion ulw, straffaglio, newydd sbon danlli grai*. But the dog didn't
understand, any more than the young people of the present age. And he
didn't show any sign of understanding this time, only wagged his tail more
entreatingly.

First she went to put a hot water bottle in her bed, and then took the
dog for a walk. After returning, made a supper of meat sandwiches, and
ate them dry.

Then she took the doll upstairs with her to try the clothes on. She studied
them before putting them on, and wondered how in the world she had ever
been able to make them. Drawers of white calico with the legs gathered by
bands at the top and the bottom, with lace on the bottom. The band at the
top in two parts with four buttonholes, to button them to stays, probably.
All the crimping gathered minutely and at regular intervals with the finest
needle. A white flannel petticoat with a band of calico stitched with blue
thread. Two kinds of stitching, one turning onto the other and one turning
away from the other, made with a running stitch and a cross stitch. A pleat
on its hem, and the top pleated to the band. A row of backstitches on the
band, tinier than any sewing machine could make them.

A dress of pink cotton, in a pattern very like babies' frocks today, with
a split collar, trimmed with lace. Crimping on this too, between the frock
and the waist and at the bands of the sleeves. There were cross stitches for
decoration on this, widening at the hem and narrowing at the waist.

A totally plain cotton pinafore, the like of which had never been seen
since. A white background with a small sprig of a red flower on it. There
was no crimping on this. A narrow white ribbon ran through the hem of
the neck, a false hem that was cut crosswise, and so narrow it was hard
to know how the ribbon went through it and managed to curl and close
tightly around the neck.

Small solid cloth buttons on the whole thing, secured to the clothing
with a short row of buttonhole stitches, with loops made the same way, instead of buttonholes, on the frock and the pinafore. Every opening in every

piece of clothing finished neatly from inside with tape across the fold. They were all stitches to demonstrate stitches, handicraft, and so tiny, except for the cross stitch, that she couldn't see them tonight, even with spectacles.

She put the clothes on the doll, and how happy she was to see her limbs bend and give as she pleased. There was nothing wrong with her at all. She was quite marvellous, and the old-fashioned clothes were so pretty.

Then she began getting ready to have a bath, and she sat the doll on the blue table. The water was pleasantly hot, and it sent shivers of pain through her legs. She looked at herself in the water. She was just like the pictures by these newfangled artists, or pictures by a five-year-old child, her limbs as if they'd been soldered to her body, instead of growing out of it. But up to now . . . they had gone on moving nimbly. There was nothing wrong with the way they were moving, any more than with the movements of the doll.

She put on a warm nightgown, and ran down to the kitchen to make a cup of tea, and took it to bed to drink it. The bed was warm and comfortable, and she was feeling very happy, having done a good day's work. The words of Turgeniev came into her mind:

"Happiness doesn't know about tomorrow, and it has no yesterday. Happiness forgets the past, and it doesn't think of the future. It knows only the present—and that, not for a day, but for a moment."

How true! How true! And this truth gave her a moment of happiness.

She lay back in bed and she could see the doll and her image in the mirror. She enjoyed looking at her. Her head was the least bit to one side with her shoulder tending to rise towards her head, so that it made her look shy. From gazing and gazing and going on gazing, she saw herself in the doll, herself at seven years old, when she'd had her picture taken for the first time ever, with a look half sad, half shy on her, the look of an innocent child. The doll became bigger, and more like herself: she couldn't bear the sight. She was almost losing her mind, and she wanted to get up and go there to throw her out through the window. But it was too comfortable in bed. She put out the light, and at some point, she fell asleep.

It was the church bells woke her next morning. She looked out through the window at the leafless trees and the grey sky. Bit by bit, she turned her head and ventured to look at the doll. But there was nothing there but a small doll, completely expressionless, like every other doll.

Flowers

Someone's footstep on the garden path, the front door bell ringing softly, Leusa opening the door and saying, "Come in" very dryly. The visitor's voice wasn't heard from upstairs, but Leusa's voice was like a bell, saying, "She's quite well," so hale and hearty. The answer to the visitor was surely to a question about her, Gwen Huws, ninety-two years old, in bed with her last illness. The invalid could guess who the visitors were for the most part by the tone of Leusa's voice in the lobby, warmly welcoming, or coldly unwelcoming. She'd never heard her so dry; she was afraid the next thing she'd hear would be the sound of turning the visitor out the door. But here came the sound of walking up the stairs, and here was Leusa with an air of pushing the visitor in front of her, and then telling her curtly to sit on a chair by the bed; then turning on her heel and going down the stairs without so much as presenting her to the invalid. There was no need to present her, except as a matter of courtesy to a sick bed, because it was Mrs. Jones, the coffin-maker's wife, coming to see her for the first time, when she'd been bedridden for five months.

"How are you, Mrs. Huws?"

"Oh, not bad, holding my ground very well; I'll be getting up quite soon."

(Now she saw the significance of Leusa's "She's quite well" a minute ago.)

Mrs. Jones' face was all smiles, from chin to forehead, like pleats in a thin man's waistcoat, hiding her eyes.

"It's good to hear that you're better; you're marvellous, and at such a great age."

"Oh, I don't mean to die soon to please anyone."

"That's the spirit. I've brought you a few flowers. That woman of yours has put them in water."

"Oh, thank you very much. She's Leusa next door; she's let her house go to come here and tend to me while I last. She goes to the same chapel as you and I."

"How long have you been laid up now?"

"The past five months."

"I'm sorry I've been so long in coming to visit you, but you know how it is, there's always something to be done."

"Well, it's nice for you that you're young enough *to* do it."

"The women of the chapel are thinking of you."

"A lot of them have been here from the start, but thank you for carrying the message."

But Mrs. Jones wasn't finding any joy in bedside chat. She tried again.

"It's terribly cold out. It's March, though the sun is shining."

"Yes."

The invalid's face grew flushed, and she closed her eyes. Mrs. Jones saw that it was time for her to go, and walked to the door. Without opening her eyes, Gwen Huws said,

"I've made my will, and Thomas Ryan is to make my coffin."

She didn't see the pleats disappear from the other's face, but she heard the door shut with a bang.

Leusa came upstairs on tiptoe, and the old woman opened her eyes.

"Is the corpse-bird gone?"

"Yes, thank goodness; I didn't pay her much mind. A proper name for her. A coffin-maker's wife is the twentieth century's corpse-bird . . . and so is an insurance agent. And what do you suppose, she's brought you flowers, marvellous; just think, carnations in March; they aren't honest. Stolen, that's what they are, from that crematorium on the seaside. The rest of them will be on the Women's Society's supper table tonight."

"Leusa," the old woman said sharply, "you'll be clapped in jail for slandering people."

"It's perfectly true, I tell you."

"People can go to jail for telling the truth."

"There's chapel people for you."

"A few of them. Grace has left a bit of its mark on the rest."

"Not very much. Most of them will leave this world without grace putting its little finger on them. But I'm telling the truth about that woman. I'll throw her sneaking old flowers out."

"Yes, do. I don't want to see them. But I told her that her husband won't be making my coffin."

"Full marks to you. She's upset you."

"She shouldn't. Death won't come any sooner."

"I'll go and make you a cup of tea."

"Yes, and bring your own here too, so we can drink it together."

As Leusa raised the old woman to sit up, she was glad to feel strong arms under her, and feel health breathe over her face from a breast that was high and solid enough for someone to make a seat of it.

"Does it have a little taste to it?"

"It's wonderfully good."

"I could kill that woman," Leusa said.

"Don't think about her. She doesn't bother me. We'll enjoy this now, and not think about her."

"Quite a difficult thing."

"How many cups of tea have we had like this, Leusa?"

"Hundreds upon hundreds. I'd rather have little chats like this than meetings."

"Yes, they've been nice. Heaven, to me, is something like this."

"You aren't going to heaven. What I mean is, you aren't going to die."

"Of course I'm going to die."

"Would that everyone were so happy in going."

"I'm tired."

"Lie back down then."

"No, that's not what I mean. Sometimes a person comes to the end of his tether, and is ready enough to give up. But I like being able to be at home like this instead of in that hospital. Everybody was very kind there, I had plenty of food and every care. But you know what was depressing there, Leusa?"

"No."

"Waking up every morning and seeing a row of white heads on white pillows; a single white line along the ward, just like a blind man's cane. I can wake up here and see paper on the wall instead of paint."

Leusa began to laugh.

"Forgive me, Gwen Huws—I was thinking of old Tomos the Shop, begging to be allowed to go home from the hospital, he'd rather go to heaven from his home than from there. The old penny-pincher! He won't get there, no matter where he starts from."

"No more than many of us. But I was saying how I've enjoyed being in bed here. Hearing you knocking things about down there, hearing the sound of tea things, and it isn't depressing to think that I don't need to wash them, though it was in washing dishes that I'd find time to think. And I like seeing the old cat come up sometimes and lie on the bed, purring and winking at me. It's quite a nice thing to have the last look at things familiar to one when they were healthy."

"Nonsense! Don't talk about 'the last look'."

"I don't mean now."

"Try to have a little nap."

Leusa went down with the dishes. But sleep didn't come to Gwen Huws. In spite of everything, notwithstanding what she'd said to Leusa, Mrs. Jones the Coffins had upset her; it wasn't that her visit was a portent of dying soon, but she'd had a shock from thinking that people like that could be found, and that they were stupid enough to think that nobody else saw through them. She'd had occasion once more to hate, when she'd thought that would never come to her portion again. In that region between sleep and waking, she was seeing the people of the chapel take shape before her one by one, appearing for a moment to show themselves, and then moving aside, one after the other.

Tomos the Shop, as Leusa had said. Mrs. Pedr who went further than you with everything: if you'd had a cold, she'd had a worse one; if you were tired, she was more tired; if you said you were poor, she was poorer, though her husband was a schoolmaster. Mrs. So-and-So, who spoke eloquently for the Society on platforms, and who'd done her best to hinder the town from getting a Welsh-language school. Mrs. Jones Tenth, who couldn't utter a word in public and who was criticizing everyone who could; won her status in the parish by arranging tea parties. John, the deacon, not speaking a word to his brother for the past fifteen years. Twm the Coal, pure of heart, no malice, not much in his head. That other man who gave a taste of his sharp tongue to people on the telephone, because he was too cowardly to do it anywhere else. Dic Penrhwth, generous of heart, had womanized all his life and not been caught, with nothing worse than that to be said of him. Poor, lovable, godly old Matthew Jones, carrying his godliness naturally, not making anyone feel uncomfortable; listening to everyone's complaint and helping them. And many others, mistier. And there was dear, faithful Leusa, the kindest of the children of women. And there was herself, Gwen Huws, seeing through people too much, hating, hating herself, because it was her own impulsive mistakes had brought all her troubles on her, giving her heart thoughtlessly to everyone, as if she fell in love with everyone the first time she saw them, loving them too much and being disillusioned . . .

The characters disappeared one by one, greyly, over the horizon, herself last, waving to herself as she disappeared.

She went into a light sleep. She was awakened a little later by a well-known voice on the stairs—Mr. Davies, the minister.

"And how is Mrs. Huws today?"

"Quite well, thanks."

"I've woken you from a nice sleep. Your face is flushed."

"No, I'm glad to see you."

"Many people been here today?"

"No, not much of anybody. Leusa and I had a cup of tea together here in the bedroom just now. Leusa has more of a sense of humour than a hundred nurses; and we enjoyed ourselves. I was saying to Leusa that it's like this, in the middle of my things, I'd like to have the last look at this world, not at hospital walls, though it's good to have them. I know some people like to have the last look at a view of nature."

"Like that teacher from Bangor who was begging to have one look at the Menai Straits before he went."

"Well, yes, I've never had much time to gape at the Menai Straits, but I like remembering a nice dishcloth, that was a help to me in getting on with my work, or a nice little supper in front of the fire when I'd finished my work."

"Yes, you did work hard all your life."

"Not always a credit to me. A lot of us work hard to avoid being idle, not for the sake of working, or in my case to forget things."

"You haven't much cause to forget."

"More than you'd think. I've been a very foolish woman, and I have much to regret."

"You're brooding, because you're idle now."

(What if you knew, Gwen Huws thought to herself. Why was she able to tell her thoughts, even about religion, better to Leusa, the half-pagan, than to her minister? Was it because it's easier talking to someone less experienced than trying to express something to someone whose experiences she knew were of a very much higher nature than hers? She wanted to explode, and tell the story of that coffins woman to someone besides Leusa, and talk about her hatred, but she couldn't.)

"Maybe," she said to the minister, "I greatly regret that I've let little things bother me."

"Things like—?"

"Oh, thinking that people were criticizing me for saying or doing something, instead of kicking the thoughts away and saying, 'Damn you, I'm as good as you, and I have a right to say what I like.'"

"Quite true," the minister said.

To Gwen Huws the "damn" was one small kick for the coffins woman.

"Do you, Mr. Davies, regret the things you haven't seen, or anything in the world you haven't learned about? But nonsense, what am I saying, you're still young enough to learn and to get to see things. But I'm leaving this world without being to places, without seeing much and without experiencing many things."

"You haven't been in London at any time?"

"I've never had any urge to go there. I've never gone to Pantycelyn or to Ann Griffiths' home."

"A great loss."

"Yes. Why didn't I go? And there are so many feelings and experiences I know nothing about. I'm leaving this world knowing nothing about the mind of a murderer or the mind of a Teddy Boy."

"There are plenty of doctors could tell you that."

"Yes, second-hand; and that would be guessing. Doctors guess, for the most part. I want to know from the fountainhead, exactly how does a murderer feel when he's busy killing someone."

The minister shivered his shoulders.

"You see," the old woman went on, "we see faults in people without knowing anything of their histories, or any of their thoughts."

"Have you felt like a murderer at any time?"

"Yes, many a time, and I still do. I've felt I could hate people till I squeezed the life out of them, and stopped before I was quite finished. I thought old age had softened that, but it hasn't."

"You surprise me, when I've been thinking you're able to love people."

"Maybe I am; that can turn into hatred too. It's a funny thing that on our sick beds in old age, the grooves of pain and the traces of toil leave our faces, but hateful old feelings come back."

"You know what I always remember," the minister said, "I remember looking at your hands at communion, with so many marks of toil on them, and I thought it was a very beautiful thing, more than seeing ringed white fingers reaching for the bread."

"And to tell you the truth, my hands weren't always clean; had to run to the chapel after milking, without finding time to wash my hands. The smell of milking is a bad old smell on someone's hands, a smell like the smell of oats. I was ashamed."

"You don't think, do you, that Christ's hands were clean when He was taken down from the cross, after all the abuse He'd had?"

"I've never given it a thought—but you're a poet."

Gwen Huws was afraid the question would come now—the reason he'd led the talk towards communion, because that's what he had done.

"I don't mean to ask you to give me communion today, Mr. Davies."

"You know best, Mrs. Huws."

"Don't think that I'm seeing death close by, or anything; there are plenty of signs of that inside me, what the outside doesn't show me. But somehow, I've been running from the pagan world to the Christian world all my life, so that I can't feel the depth of anguish in communion. And somehow one has to be more honest by oneself than in chapel."

"Very few people can feel anguish."

There now, she'd been impulsive again; said exactly what she shouldn't have said. She was regretting it the next minute: the best way for her to be rid of her hatred towards Mrs. Jones the Coffins would be for her to take communion. But as always, she'd made an excuse for herself not to do the thing she should do, and passed by on the other side.

"I'll tell you what I'll do; I'll take it tomorrow if you can come."

"It's all right, you're tired today."

Her face was greatly flushed again.

Down in the kitchen the minister said to Leusa:

"Something has disturbed Mrs. Huws today. Somehow she isn't like herself."

"She'll be herself again in no time."

But she didn't tell him about the visitor; Mrs. Jones, too, was a member of his chapel.

The Journey

Here was the sound at last, the sound that the mother had been fearing for weeks, the harsh sound of the brake stopping at the gate, as though the gate itself were squeaking on its hinges. She pushed her spectacles higher on her nose to have a look once more at her son Dafydd, the last of her children to leave home, before he started for the South. The father took a grip on one handle of the tin box, and before the son could grasp the other, the mother had snatched it, and the two of them took it and placed it in the brake as though they were carrying a sacrifice to an altar, protesting but compelled to offer it. Dafydd turned his head and looked at the kitchen, the comfortable hearth, bright with hope from the lamp, separating itself from the other dark part. He looked as long as he could at the plate and the cup and the saucer on the table. There would be another cup and saucer somewhere tonight.

"Goodbye, my boy. Remember to put the postcard in the post first thing when you arrive."

"I'll be sure to. You'll see, everything will be all right."

He didn't know what to say. He was glad he could start at last. These last minutes had been painful; talking so as not to say what they were truly feeling. The mother made a gesture as if she were going to put away the dishes, but she left them as they were; this way she could keep the last minutes before the parting in front of her and remember them.

The driver cracked his whip; the two horses moved slowly with the feeble little light of the two lamps playing around their feet. Father and son were sitting on either side of the tin box as though they were sitting on either side of a coffin, the father leaning forward, with his eyes piercing the face of the son. The box *was* a coffin to him.

"When will you arrive, I wonder?"

"Oh, it will be after dark."

"Yes, for sure."

They were speaking quietly as though they were afraid of the driver hearing them. The land around them was like a black forest with the houses only darker patches in the midst of it; the sky like a coverlet of blue-black ink meeting the earth at the sea, with the lights of the town like a cluster of stars at the corner. As they went on their eyes grew accustomed to the darkness; the shape of the houses was becoming clearer, and the lamplight behind the curtains was like moonlight behind mist. As the road narrowed, they knew they were going between hedges, and presently they knew there was sea on the horizon.

"Here we are," the father said with an unexpected finality.

There was a large lamp with a gleaming light in the waiting room of the station, and the station-master had his face in the ticket-window as if he were expecting them.

"Come round to here," he said after punching the ticket, "I have a blaze of a fire." The driver of the brake preferred to wait outside. The tin box was pulled out and put by the place where the train would stop. The fire gave a flush to their faces, and they felt comfortable except for thinking about the train. The father would have liked the station-master to go out so he could speak freely with his son.

"You have the postcard safe?"

Dafydd took it out of his inside pocket.

"Remember to post it first thing when you arrive."

"No danger of my forgetting it."

"It's nice for you," the station-master said, "we'll see you back in a little while having made a fortune."

Dafydd was too depressed to argue, only said, "There are things besides money."

"Yes, but you have to have it."

"Yes," the father said, "a pity one has to go so far to fetch it."

"Tut, it pays to go out and see the world instead of staying in a hole of a place like this all your life."

A hole with one's family and one's friends was quite a nice hole, Dafydd thought.

Once more there came a sound, the slow, measured sound of wheels,—the final sound. The tin box was tossed into the van; the door was clapped shut, and the door of the carriage, and Dafydd wasn't sorry to see it close. He waved a long time at his father, and the father turned away when the smoke of the train disappeared under the bridge.

The sky was bluer by now and stars were suddenly swarming into it, one after the other. The houses were visible too with the lights in them clear and full. A quarryman here and there would put his head out the door to look at the weather.

"When will it arrive?" he asked the driver.

"As it's getting dark."

"As early as that. I'd have thought it wouldn't arrive till tomorrow."

"It isn't going with the brakes on."

The driver put his chin inside the collar of his coat, and he didn't speak for the rest of the journey.

Elis Huws decided to get down at Tŷ'n y Gamfa, half a mile before reaching his own house, to have a word with Elin William. He wanted to talk to someone before going home to his wife to get a look at the parting from another standpoint.

The door was open when he arrived and he smelled the aroma of bacon frying.

"I heard you coming, I have a bit of breakfast for you. Owen has just set off for the quarry. I heard you passing just before as well, but I'd rather see a funeral pass than see someone pass on his way to the South. How was Meri before he set off?"

"Down-hearted enough, but one is forced to bear everything. It's hard to understand the ways of providence."

"There's no providence, except the providence we make of it. No, not us, but what those high and mighty rich people make of it. They aren't going to the South to look for work. They keep coming to the quarry in their closed carriage."

"You remember the first year of this century, Elin, how we were looking forward to better days because it was the beginning of a century, and here ten years of it are gone, and if anything, it's worse for us?"

"I don't know why we had to look forward then more than any other year. It's the same on New Year's Day and birthdays—wishing each other well and things not becoming a particle better. But we must keep on hoping or we'll sink into the earth."

"I don't know how much better we are in living apart as Dafydd and us will be now, and being unhappy, just to be able to say we're alive. We're going through life without living it, because we're always expecting something better."

Elis Huws became quite unbelieving at times, waves of unbelief flowing over him and withdrawing, leaving a wet crinkled beach after them. That would dry out and be smooth to walk on when his faith came back.

"I'm a deacon now for a quarter of a century," he went on, "and indeed I must say that I clean lose my faith sometimes in trying to understand the ways of providence."

"Well, Elis, you must remember that faith and lack of faith are very closely related to each other; two neighbouring links in a chain, that's what they are."

Elis Huws looked at her sitting in her chair like a prophetess, watching him eat and twirling her thumbs. He wondered, was she speaking from experience? None of her children were old enough to leave home yet. Their shoes, noses up on the side of the fender, were waiting for them to get up. His own children's clogs had been like that at one time. How few years it was since then!

As he looked at the shoes, he said, "They don't know what's ahead of them. We can only know after it becomes a fact."

"That will come soon enough for them too."

"It's come for me."

"Only part of it, Elis. There's no knowing what on earth will still come. Perhaps the next part will be brighter. But I believe that something very great will have to happen, an explosion, before it becomes brighter in these quarries."

These last words were on Elis Huws' mind when he was looking at the quarry hole later, and seeing the men like tiny insects hanging roped to ladders. Insects they certainly were in its providence.

The majority were laughing and fooling in the hut at dinner time. No one remarked that Elis Huws was there without his son, but no one was talking much except the young people, who were teasing each other about Saturday night's carryings-on in courting, as they'd do on Monday morning. They never stopped teasing Bob Jones, the most innocent among them, and that was cruel, because he'd never had a sweetheart.

"You have a good chance to get a sweetheart, old Bob," one of them said, "now that Dafydd Huws has gone to the South. You can make a run of it with Alis now, she'll need to find someone to keep her warm."

"Be quiet," Elis Huws shouted, "Alis isn't that sort of girl; she's far too true."

A blanket of silence came over the hut, and in the middle of it Lias Roberts, Fronlas, was saying quietly, "A year ago today my boy was killed in that old hole."

If it were possible for silence to become more silent at that moment, it did. Everyone walked out, one by one, after mumbling a word of sympathy, and left only Lias Roberts and Elis Huws behind.

"You have him alive, Elis," Lias Roberts said, and that was all.

After going home that evening Elis Huws had the questions he expected from his wife. How was Dafydd before setting off; she wondered, was he sure to post the card? He had avoided these questions in going straight to work from Elin Wiliam's house. He didn't find they were affecting him so much now after he'd blown up at the quarry and after Lias Roberts' thunderbolt. He was feeling much better.

"A year ago today Lias Roberts' Rhisiart was killed," he said to his wife.

"Is it as much as that? Poor them, just the same age as Dafydd."

She reflected a bit.

"Elis, come, hurry up and eat. We'll go there to look in on them. It will do us all good."

In half an hour the lantern that guided them was casting its moving light on the road, making a quavering pattern, and there was a cheerful lift in their walk as they went to Lias Roberts' house.

.   .   .

After the train started, Dafydd shut his eyes. The parting had been long and tiresome, and he was glad to see it over. He would have loved to sleep for the rest of the journey, and not let his mind wander back and forth. He couldn't see through the misty window of the train. He knew his old district on the slopes of the hills was like something distant and strange when left this way. But he didn't want to see. In spite of that, he rubbed the film of mist with his hand and looked in its direction. There was nothing there but greyness with yellow spots on it, like pimples on a person's face, the spots of the innocent little lights. He closed his eyes again and began to think: his thoughts were going around in a circle and returning to the same place—a small wage or no work at all, burdening his family and worrying, or else going away to look for work; existing or living, living or existing. In the end the scales came down on the side of leaving home. He was trying to remember the host of young men who'd left home since the start of the century: some to the South like him, some to America; some coming back because they were too homesick to make themselves at home; the others coming back after a while for a visit with gold in their teeth and topcoats down to their feet, an accent in their speech, every sign that they'd come on in the world. That was a hiding of homesickness too, perhaps. He preferred the first group who broke their hearts and soon came home.

He couldn't forget Alis' face last night as she said goodbye; her eyes were bright with hope, longing fearlessly to be able to come to him in the South and settle there. In thinking of this his heart became a block of ice; he wasn't going to the South to settle, but going there thinking he could return. But Alis was an orphan, in service at a hard farm for five pounds a half-season. She wouldn't have to tug hard at the roots if she were setting off; it would be her heaven to start over somewhere new. That morning in his bed in the loft, with his nose almost touching the roof, he'd almost changed his mind and stayed home, on considering that he wouldn't still be able to go down the ladder to the warm kitchen, wash in the back, and have breakfast on the bright comfortable hearth.

As the train ran along the seaside it began to grow light; the clouds hanging zigzag like shreds from a sack above the cold grey-blue sea, with the latter brightening all the way to the foam on the edge of the beach. He felt hungry; he had a packet of bread-and-butter in his pocket his mother had sliced for him, putting a white cloth around it like an envelope and using a safety pin from her small shawl to fasten it. He was afraid to open it. His home and everything it represented were in the packet. The string that held him was in it; that thing which would pull him back with a tug; the thing which had held him all through the years and which was giving him so much pain as he gave a tug the other way to break free. He knew, he had only to open the packet, the thing would be there, the knot, there in the bread-and-butter. The roots had burrowed down deep, and home-sickness was sprouting on the branches. When a fellow-passenger offered him a slice of bread-and-butter, he had to refuse and open his own packet. The mark of his mother's thumbs was on the slices, and he almost choked on them.

A whole hour of waiting at Cyffordd y Ffos. There was no cheerfulness in the countryside around there either, though the earth was greener. Occasional white farmhouses looking cold in their distance from each other: animals shivering at the farmyard gate and dogs barking. A glossy look on everything, but the warmth of the quarry districts wasn't there for him. The train came in with no haste and no passengers. His mind began moving now; it had been in a hard, indifferent stretch for hours. This was the last change; his friend Dan would be waiting for him at the station of his new place, and an expectancy entered his heart. He put his hand in his pocket to see was the card safe; he'd almost forgotten it.

The train was running swiftly, and suddenly it came from the bareness of the country into the midst of thousands of houses, rows after rows, dark rubbish heaps, high chimneys, the sound of trams clanking clumsily over streets that he supposed were full of people. The train was running past the backs of houses with gleaming light in their windows: he'd catch a glimpse at times of a woman ironing by the window, or a child at a table doing his schoolwork. The sky was lit up in the distance by fire from furnaces; everything was alive; alive enough to give him a feeling of not heeding anyone at all; a feeling of confidence and daring.

His friend was at the station, and the first thing that he said to him was, "I want to put this card in the post to say I've arrived."

"It's too late," his friend said, "the post for the North has been gone since two o'clock. You'll have to wait till tomorrow morning. You could say how you slept then, and what sort the landlady is."

Dafydd looked at the card. He felt a stab of pain in thinking of his parents' disappointment next morning from not receiving it. Then he realized that the card would have to travel the whole way he had travelled today. He became passive and unconcerned. His father and mother's hearth was far away, and the card couldn't span that distance. He could go back with the card, but for what? The journey had left the quarry and his home behind, perhaps forever.

When Dan opened the door of his lodging, the thing that first struck Dafydd was the gleaming light of the gas lamp that was hanging from the ceiling; it blinded him for a minute. Then the cheerful face of the landlady.

"Come along now, you must be dreadfully hungry; I have fish for you and the chips are close to being ready. Take off your coat and make yourself to home."

There was no need of urging; he sat at the clean table, with its abundance of food, and the light falling on the whiteness.

The Battle of Christmas

Sunday, December 1

There's one thing to be said for a poor sermon, you can let your mind wander where you will, and my mind was in the cellar throughout the sermon tonight, with the scores of toys that are waiting to come out of their shavings tomorrow, be carried up to the shop and placed on the shelves. Talk about a snail! Every other shop in town did that a fortnight ago. And I've been putting it off as long as I could because I'm afraid of a battle, and Christmas is a battle to me now. Another task will be to move the poll-parrot from the shop and try to keep him quiet in the kitchen. I came close to losing all my business because of him last year: it became a howling bedlam after I spoke my mind to a great lady from here in town when she came to buy English-language Christmas cards and said that the poetry in them wasn't classical enough. Polly cursed her ancestors back to Adam.

Decided to enjoy every bite of my supper tonight, for fear I won't have any appetite for food again before my Christmas dinner. Decided that I'm a coward, when I'm afraid of a little thing like a rush. Envied Lloyd the School who's been retired for years.

Meg made an omelet for supper instead of the eternal cold meat, frying potatoes with it and putting onion juice with them. Ate it all slowly and chewed every morsel twice. The trifle slipped down my throat like flummery. "Stop sighing," Meg said, "you won't shorten tomorrow by sighing." Enjoyed a smoke before going to bed. Dreamt I was smothering in the dust and the shavings.

December 2

Put off going to the cellar; heard Meg telling someone, "No, the dolls aren't likely to be seen till this afternoon." She'll be lucky if she sees them at all today. Heard Polly screeching from the kitchen. Carried all the toys up to the shop first. By the afternoon, the shop a chaos of little horses, motorcars, airplanes, doll carriages, cradles, trains, zinc hammers, balls, and thousands of other things. Placed them on the shelves. Leti, the shop next door, came here and asked if I'd been making hay. She gets the first peek at the shop every year; it's so different from her own second-hand shop. "I'll come here again to buy a Christmas card," she said, and out she goes. Just like every year. The shop looking like a hodgepodge of Euston Station, London Airport, the town park here in the afternoons, the post road with its cars at any time. Nobody buying today, just coming "to get a look at what you have, Mr. Ifans."

December 4

Polly's driven Meg mad in the kitchen. Brought him back into the shop, he was pretty quiet till the girls from Ysgol Ifor came in to buy Christmas cards. A gang comes in with one of them to buy some two cards. "No room in the shop," Polly shouted. Lloyd the School came in in his slippers almost at closing time—a pretty nasty old habit. Admired the shop and doubted that I'd sell them all before Christmas. He doesn't know that Mrs. Jones next-door doesn't mean to be second to Mrs. Jones next-door-down. The jealousy of neighbours is meat and drink to a shopkeeper. Polly shouted, "Closing time," but Lloyd didn't take the hint, just stared around him with the crown of his head almost on the nape of his neck. "Where did you get that Mona Lisa," he said, looking at a doll on the shelf. "Look at her crooked mouth; someone's been eating her porridge." I hadn't noticed. Looked around before closing the shop and going into the kitchen. Saw a gallery of dolls; some smiling, some with their feet out as if they were about to give someone a kick, some reaching their arms out to be cuddled in the bosom of an owner; a mischievous look on the black dolls with some half asleep. After putting out all the lights but the last, raised my eyes to the Mona Lisa, didn't like the look of her at all. Quickly put out the light.

December 5

A better start today. A man from the top of the town here came in with a flock of pretty small children; he has ten altogether with the ones who are in school. He's out of work and getting unemployment pay; pays him better than working, he said. Bought two dolls, a train engine, an airplane, a doll carriage, a mule and cart. After I'd packed them, said he could only pay for half of them. "The little things have to have toys," he said. "Perhaps," I said, "but I have to live too." Refused to give him credit, but said I'd hold the rest until next week. The smallest child started screaming, wanting to buy the poll-parrot; his father humoured him. "You'll get that the next time." Polly perfectly silent.

Leti came in after hearing the screaming. "It's people who aren't working do best today," she said, "that man gets everything from the Government, and I get nothing." I don't know how much work Leti does either, besides stand in her shop waiting for a customer. (But it's not a shopkeeper's job to busy himself with other people's business.) I don't know whether Leti is poor or rich. Her clothes are just like clothes bought at a jumble sale. The things she sells in her shop are rubbish from a jumble sale, anyway, and auctions. At least she washes her face as far as her ears. The only fashionable thing on her body is her hair—it's tied with a piece of old ribbon like a pony-tail. She always looks as if she'd just washed her face or just been squeezing a dishrag. "That's a strange old doll," she said and stared at the Mona Lisa. "Look at her crooked old mouth; I wouldn't give her to anyone's child; a child would make a face and start crying in looking at her."

Mrs. J. came in, a woman from the bottom of town, wife of a teacher or a school caretaker, someone in school anyway; and she gazed at the Mona Lisa, but said nothing. "Oh," she said, as if she were waking up from a trance, "may I see a few Christmas cards?" Shuffled through the cards. A very pretty little woman, with perfectly clean hands.

December 8

A bit of rest today, no need to think about fetching the toys into the shop tomorrow; could think about the sermon and listen to it tonight. Enjoyed the cold meat and pickles for supper. Suddenly remembered tonight the two old Misses Huws who were living by the square about twenty years ago—the two of them calling here about seven on Christmas Eve to buy sweets, and carrying a valise. Explained that they'd had the flu and felt quite weak after it, and had asked the doctor if they could go into hospital to spend Christmas Day and the next day; that was the meaning of the valise. The two of them thinking it was quite a good plan to spare folks trouble. Impossible to do it today with every bed full in the hospital. Impossible to develop flu and begin to recover too, in so little time. Reminded Meg, she laughed through the tired lines on her face. Went to bed early, ready for another week of battle.

December 9

Lloyd the School flip-flopped in in his slippers, smoking a pipe, with his glasses halfway down his nose. "The Mona Lisa's still here," was his first observation. "Yes, maybe her face will have changed by next year." "Maybe, it changes from one minute to the next; you don't know what that mocking smile means; spite, self-satisfaction, deceit, revenge, or what; I never see her just the same twice in a row."

Mrs. J. came into the shop and bought three Christmas cards again. Fail to understand why she doesn't buy what she needs and be finished. "I remembered friends I'd forgotten existed," she said; bought nothing else.

December 11

Many people down from the country today; crowded around the Christmas cards. "Will you choose one with a nice verse on it?" said one after the other. Lloyd crammed into the shop as far as he could. "Hi, Lloyd, give these people your literary advice." And he pushed through them to the counter. Selling chocolate at the other end I heard, "There you are, quite a good one with a picture of Mary and Joseph. Here's one with a pretty little dog on it." "I have enough of dogs at home." "A cat then?" "No, a picture of a little house sheltering in a grove of trees in the middle of the snow, with a red robin by the door." "Here it is, the very thing, with holly as a bonus." "They're much too dear at sixpence." "So is your milk," from Lloyd. "Nobody uses milk to make Christmas cards." "You never know; people are very clever today." The shop full of laughter. "There's a pretty one, Miss Humphreys, a picture of two sweethearts kissing." I didn't have to turn around to see if Miss Humphreys was blushing. Polly was screeching "Nonsense, nonsense."

Think I'll hire Lloyd for next Christmas. Peeped at the Mona Lisa before putting out the last light tonight. Lloyd spoke the truth; she *did* look different, as if she were saying, "Take care, you too will be deceived." She was making fun of me. Shut the door on her and her spiteful smile and went into the light of the kitchen and saw Meg's cheerful, unambiguous smile. Went back to the shop and moved the Mona Lisa to a dark corner.

December 14

A real fair of a day. Drizzle all afternoon. The floor worse than the post road with people cramming to the counter as if to a cake stall at a "Bring and Buy". More selling of toys today; the pounds coming off their rolls three and four at a time to pay for the horses and the motor cars. Where do people find the money? But there it is, I'm the one it's rolling in to—it's none of my business—. Mrs. J. in again today buying a little doll with a Welsh dress this time, instead of cards. Children from Ysgol Ifor crowding above the cards again, and buying nothing of value. In the middle of all the fuss and frenzy Polly was shouting, "Doll, doll," and then screeching.

Couldn't move after closing the shop tonight. Groaned after sitting down in my chair. The cat jumped on my knee; pushed her down, too tired to pet her. Decided not to go to chapel tomorrow. Poor Meg trying to tidy up the floor of the shop.

December 15

Got up to make breakfast and brought it upstairs for Meg and myself. Got going slowly and took a stroll into the shop. Much emptier. Found that the Mona Lisa wasn't there; had a proper shock. I know that I didn't sell her to anybody; I don't know whether she was here last night or not, since I didn't look at her as usual. Someone's stolen her. Decided not to tell anyone but Meg, for fear they'd think I suspected them. Brooded about the thing all day.

December 16

A limp, grey Monday morning. Mrs. J. came in and wanted a little doll again, a black one this time—considers her very pretty, she said. The minute she came in Polly began screeching and shouting. "Doll, doll, there she is." I saw Mrs. J. turn pale and totter, but before she fell, I was able to take hold of her and run with her to the little office behind the shop, and I was able to shout to Meg to come into the shop before closing the door. I gave her a sip of water. She came to and started crying. "Oh Mr. Ifans dear," she said, "I've done a terrible thing, I stole a doll from your shop Saturday night, that doll with the crooked smile. She'd bewitched me, and why I had to steal her instead of buy her, I can't say, unless she'd bewitched me into that too. You'll never be able to understand, and I don't want anybody to know; my husband is terribly mean to me in a deaf silent way, and I was thinking that this doll might give him a bit of a scare when I put it on the mantle. That's the way he looks at me every day, and I was thinking that he might see himself in the doll. But he hasn't up to now. He's going to Liverpool to his sister over Christmas, without so much as asking me if I'd like to come." She stopped sobbing.

I told her to keep the doll and that I wouldn't say a word to anybody about it. I also told her to come here to spend Christmas Day. She was almost too grateful to speak.

Talked to Meg about it tonight. "Surprised" isn't a strong enough word to say how we felt, just thinking that you can never judge how anybody lives by the way they look. A problem arising now is how Leti and Mrs. J. may get along with each other Christmas Day. Leti comes here every Christmas; thought of telling her this year that we couldn't ask her because we're too tired. But as Meg said, there'd be more pain on our consciences in *not* asking her than fatigue to our bodies and souls *in* asking her. And it's more of a quandary in that we don't know whether she's poor or miserly. But she hasn't any mother or father, or brother or sister.

December 23

Not much of anything happened during these last days. The late-comers among the customers complaining that I didn't have a selection of toys or cards—the same old song every year. "Try somewhere else" was my answer. Their refusal proving that the other shops have been emptied too. A woman from the end of town came here today; I know about her, she's quite poor, her husband always sick and getting low wages, when he works. Wanted a few Christmas cards, couldn't buy presents, she said, because they're too expensive. She was cursing Christmas. "Hell for poor people" she called it. Gave her what Christmas cards were left, almost all of them— I know some people will be here later tonight. Gave her a doll and a mule to bring home to the smallest children. Her expression was enough to relieve all weariness, and her "Happy holidays" came from the bottom of her heart.

Leti came to buy her annual card. I knew it would come through our letter slot tomorrow morning.

December 24

Mrs. J. came again today. A happy look on her. She apologized because she couldn't come here Christmas Day. Had decided to stay home by herself in the house, since it was such an infrequent thing for her to be able to be in her house without her husband's cruel eyes looking at her. She'd have enough of him afterwards, since he would be back Monday night. She wanted to enjoy her house to the utmost; I saw it made sense and felt quite glad.

Closed the shop door tonight and locked the middle door with a sigh of satisfaction. Brought the parrot into the house. "Closing time forever," he said. Meg hard at it peeling the potatoes and the carrots and putting stuffing in the goose. I felt happy and set about making toffee and fixing supper. Boiled eggs tonight and bread-and-butter but enjoyed it as if it were a meal for a king. Went upstairs feeling good, like someone who's finished a heavy job. Felt sorry too that the children and the grandchildren couldn't come home.

December 25

Got up early and had a plain breakfast so we could have early dinner. Leti arrived at 11:30 in a new frock with a new ribbon in her hair. She'd been thinking for sure that Mrs. J. would be here. She smiled like Mona Lisa, when I explained to her. Leti hadn't much to say at the table, just praised the dinner. "Mrs. J. has lost a feast," she said, "in that place all by herself. They say it's a cold enough life the two of them have together. He's a mean old one, and she has a strange old habit of bringing dolls into the house, making beds for them, trimmed with pink muslin and lace." Meg and I went on eating without raising our eyes from our plates. "They haven't any children," Leti added. Then she asked what had become of the crooked-mouthed doll. "I gave her to that man with a lot of children you saw here one morning." Leti laughed. "His children will straighten out her mouth; there'll be a hammer through her face by tonight."

Leti set about washing the dishes and ordered Meg and me to go sit in the parlour. After she finished she put her head in at the parlour door and said she wanted to go to the house for a bit and that she'd come back to make us tea. The two of us went to sleep, with the cat on my knee, purring.

It was the sound of Leti making tea woke me up; it was like the sound of Kreisler playing the fiddle. Not another sound anywhere. Floated in peace and quiet.

Two Old Men

As the coffin went through the chapel gate on its way to the hearse, the sun came out of the mist and struck the "88 years of age" on the lid, making the 88 look like four wheels. It fell also on a drop of dew on the gossamer thread that was hanging from the hinge of the gate. Nathan Huws observed them both and fixed his gaze on the 88. So that was Wil Dic's age; he, Nathan Huws, still had ten years to reach that.

A number of people came between him and the hearse and went into the first carriage—the dead man's relatives, who'd alighted on the funeral like a crowd of starlings on a field of gleanings. Nathan had never seen them at Wil Dic's house. There'd been a fair-sized little congregation in the chapel, more than he'd expected. Everyone has someone to bury him, he thought: something in humanity always takes care that no one is put away without there being someone's eyes on the coffin, and that some people had something good to say, even about misers like Wil Dic.

It was a calm, quiet finish, which made him feel everybody was distant and apart, as a building that is seen through mist looks higher than it is. He had no feeling about the dead man, not pity, not longing, not loss, not a thing. The dead man in his coffin was like part of a withered tree, that was all. The only feeling he had was anger, because someone in the deacon's seat in doing the commemoration had said that Wil Dic was a gentleman. Nathan had noticed that that was what was said of people who had done nothing at all for anybody during their lives. They were "judicious" or "gentlemen" because they'd kept quiet and stayed clear of injustice. The flawed logic of commemorators! But then it was necessary to say something good about everybody from the deacons' seat. It was he, Nathan Huws, could say what Wil Dic was, who'd come to his house more than once every day. Gentleman indeed, when he'd constantly eaten up his food and his time for the past four years.

He was awakened from his reflections by the undertaker.

"Come into this carriage, Nathan Huws."

"No, I don't want to go to the cemetery."

The thought had come to him that very minute. Looking into the bottom of a grave made him giddy, the same as looking into the bottom of a quarry hole. He decided to go for a glass to The Red Fox: he hadn't had that pleasure for the past ten years. The door of the last carriage was shut with a terribly final bang, and the procession disappeared.

The pub was warm and half dark, with only a few young people there. Opposite him sat a young couple, the girl's skirt halfway up her knees, her hair like a crow's nest turned upside down, a line of black running towards it from her eyes. She made him think of the wooden dolls of his youth, with the colour melting and running when they were held in front of the fire. She was lounging and laughing on her sweetheart's shoulder. His hair and his collar were like Disraeli's. The beer was good, and Nathan felt his heart and his feet growing warmer. Every now and then, the girl would turn towards him and smile, quite nicely, as if she liked to see him enjoying himself. Indeed, there was something very pleasant about her. After smiling at him, she would turn back with a gurgle of mirthful laughter on her sweetheart's shoulder, and say something in his ear. He was somewhat cold, as was fitting for a young man in the image of Disraeli. Everybody of Nathan's age ran down this type of young person today. But come to think of it, they were no worse than servant girls in the middle of the nineteenth century. Looking at this couple, he felt there was a great part of life that he knew nothing about, and it was the life of the majority today. He hadn't included it in his stories. He'd been describing moss with short-stemmed blossoms, grey mountain plants that were a comfort to a child who was dwelling in a teeming countryside and had a taste for beauty, no matter how inconspicuous. But by now cotton grass and heather blossoms didn't matter. Everybody wanted the ugliest in taste, in personal appearance, in language and everything. He'd written about people with backbones, and he'd arrived at a time when eels were trying to hold the world up: and yet, there was a place for eels, in life and in literature.

As he was thinking like this, the door suddenly opened, and a man about sixty years old came rushing in and shouted at the girl.

"Come out of here, a place like this; this isn't a place for you, and you the Sunday School secretary."

The girl blushed, but then she gave a hard-faced laugh, and didn't move. The man moved forward, and he was on the brink of grasping her by the shoulder when Nathan rushed to him and took hold of him.

"Look, it isn't any of your business what the girl is doing; she's her own mistress."

"I'm surprised at you, Nathan Huws. An old man like you tippling in a place like this."

"And that's my business."

He remembered that the man was a deacon in one of the town's chapels. The latter went out quickly, crestfallen. It was the Disraeli boy's turn to laugh now, but the girl was amazed, more amazed than her false eyelashes had made her look before. Nathan Huws rose to go home; the beer had given him a new zest to begin writing again. He was longing to go home to the fire, to his own kitchen, where he hoped there would be a kettle singing on the hob waiting for him. The cat probably wouldn't be there to give him a welcome (her welcome was sometimes a comfort). She'd been out the past three nights, having a high time love-making, for sure.

He wanted to buy cake for tea, and he pulled a clean paper bag from his pocket to put the cake in, a habit he had because he bought so little, seeing that the shopkeeper had to give a pennyworth of paper bag to hold a groatsworth of cake. Suddenly he put the paper bag back in his pocket; what if the shopkeeper mistook his purpose, and supposed it was his miserliness that was causing him to bring the paper bag. The thought of miserliness had become a grief to him, after experiencing four years of the miserliness of his neighbour, Wil Dic. He bought two cakes to make the paper bag pay for itself.

He gave the fire a poke, moved the kettle to it, and in no time there was a nice fire and the kettle was singing. The kitchen was comfortable. He could clean the kitchen and the back kitchen, the lobby and his bedroom every day himself, and he left the rest and the washing to the woman who came once a week. But he didn't have much of an appetite. Instead of craving the cake, he ate it almost one crumb at a time.

The events of these last days had told on him more than he'd supposed. There'd be a change in his life, a change he'd thought would be a great blessing to him, something he'd looked forward to for many days. He gave up on the food half way. He put his slippers on, and sat in an easy chair to reflect.

When Wil Dic had come to live in the neighbouring house four years ago, he'd come to see him one morning just when he was in the middle of writing. The visit interrupted a stream of thoughts that was flowing onto the paper. But he didn't like to be unneighbourly and he made him a cup of tea; and that was his first and most important mistake. It was the same as giving milk to a stray cat and taking him into the house. Wil Dic had the shameless face of a stray cat. After that he came often, at all times of the day, until at last he set his sights on meal-times. That's how it had been, with him feeding Wil Dic and losing money, and Wil Dic boasting of how he was putting part of his pension in the bank every week; he, on the other hand, being forced to borrow money from the bank to be able to live. Sometimes there were funny stories around town about his neighbour. He'd gone up to someone on the street one day and asked for the loan of half a crown to add to the seventeen-and-six he had in his pocket, so that he could put a pound in the bank. He'd paid back the half-crown. It didn't do for Nathan to tease him about something like this; his sense of humour was as scarce as his generosity.

He remembered Wil Dic saying at dinner one day that he'd bought a kipper for supper the evening before.

"Never," said Nathan.

"Yes indeed," said Wil Dic, not seeing the point. "Well, half a one."

Nathan smiled.

"That man in the fish shop on the square is a very nice man. You know what he said? 'How would you like me to cut it in half, across or lengthwise?'"

Nathan laughed at the top of his lungs.

"Why are you laughing?"

"I see the shopkeeper has a sense of humour."

"What's that?"

"The ability to be amusing."

"I don't see anything amusing in that."

He was hopeless.

"Which way did you choose?"

"To cut it across, and take the part next to the head. There's more meat on it."

"You're a scholar."

"Well, one prefers to have the best of everything; so I might as well have more than someone else."

Nathan had once thought of writing a story about Wil Dic. He'd have been the last one ever to see the story because a book and he were never seen together. But he wasn't enough of an interesting character, like a few other misers he'd known. Wil Dic's conversation always ran towards nothing but money, like a man hitting a cock-shy at a fair. Nathan would try talking to him about the old days, but he couldn't be pulled off his track.

In talking of the 1914–18 War what he'd talk about was the big money he'd had for his produce.

"You should be able to put some of your pension in the bank," he said to Nathan one day.

"How can I?"

"What do you spend your money on?"

"On food."

"There's no need of much food for one."

"No, two eat twice as much."

"Why don't you drown the cat?"

"I'd find it easier to drown you. The cat is company for me. I wasn't referring to *her* food."

Wil Dic laughed; he hadn't seen the point. How in the world had such a stupid man been able to pile up money, thought Nathan. They'd been enjoying lamb's neck stew at the time, with plenty of vegetables in it, and had drawn the table near the fire.

"I'm sure you make a lot of money on those stories."

Nathan laughed at the top of his lungs.

"What's amusing about talking of making money on stories?"

"A piece of fiction."

Wil Dic had been in a temper this particular morning because some farmer on the outskirts of town had got twenty thousand pounds for a parcel of land to build houses on, and the farmer had paid only nine thousand for it a few years earlier. He, Wil Dic, had had an offer to buy that land at that time and had refused. That was the only topic over the stew.

Well, there was plenty of land on top of the old skinflint by now, and he, Nathan, was free to write as much as he wished, but he had no urge to begin. He hadn't written a word since that morning six days ago when Wil Dic came to his house before he finished eating his breakfast. When he heard his footstep at the door, he cursed, because this was the only mealtime he could be sure he'd have without Wil Dic's company. But when he opened the door, his attitude changed. There was the old man, half-dressed and tottering. He couldn't say much except that he'd been sick all night. Nathan took hold of him and brought him into the house and put him in an easy chair by the fire. He went to the lobby to fetch his coat and threw it over his shoulders. He hurried to make him a cup of piping hot tea; he couldn't take bread-and-butter; it was obvious he'd thrown up in the night. He began to look better, but the sight of him was enough to cause Nathan to go fetch the doctor. He was indeed sorry for him this morning; this was the only time he could pity him from the bottom of his heart. When he came back, the old man was napping and his face was flushed. He took no notice of Nathan. He was taken to the hospital, and there he died after two days.

Nathan was sorry that he couldn't feel all that genuine pity now. But his heart was cold. In going over these four years, he couldn't feel the anger, the hatred, the bad temper that he'd felt towards his neighbour at the time, only remember them. In the same way, he couldn't feel the warm pity again, only remember that he'd felt pity. If he had any feeling at all, it was a tinge of envy because Wil Dic had been able to go to his grave without the long spells of depression he himself was always having, worry about paying his way, wondering where to go if he failed to carry on, wondering whether he could keep on writing. Wil Dic had had one passion, piling up money, and that passion had shut out every worry about everything else, had even shut out the thought of dying, and the fear. He'd been living in a fool's paradise, it's true, but what difference what sort of paradise, set against the day of death? And he'd been a fool himself, pitying a miser and putting cash in his pocket. Writing was a stupid thing too. How much better off was anyone for seeing on paper what they saw every day in life?

He turned from Wil Dic to himself. At the chapel he'd seen that he had ten years to reach the age of his old neighbour. He kept looking into a future which had no prospect of security for him. He'd done the same thing years before. He wondered if the fact of having life was enough in itself, and an assurance that the years to come would be the same as the present. The weakness and afflictions of old age were heavy. But it was necessary to keep going, and because he'd managed to keep going, people were less kind. If he'd thrown in the towel he'd get more sympathy. In spite of that, he didn't want anybody to coddle him with comfort. The only thing he wanted was strength, strength to run a race with time and to keep on writing. When he was a child he'd been afraid to be left on his own, and he'd scream the house down when his parents weren't close by. He'd longed to be on his own in these last four years. Did he still have the longing? Wasn't it a sense of loss that had made him idle and bewildered for the past four days? Had Wil Dic become part of the pattern of his life, a pattern too solid to be got rid of, as familiar as the noise of the school children who went past his house at the same time every day?

There was a sound at the door just like the sound of Wil Dic. He leapt up in a panic. When he went to open it, there was the cat, like a limp tape-worm. She passed him without taking notice of him. And he continued to reflect and to question himself. The leaves of the trees were falling, and his years and his acquaintances in them were running away from him like a waggon of slates down an incline.

He'd had a fortnight of depression before Wil Dic died, more than de-pression, dejection of spirit. Had reached the bottom, with despair like a large layer of steel on that bottom. He'd been that way for days, when the thrust came. Something came then that he could only call a lift, and he began to find some diversion in his own sadness. Maybe it was refusing to wait for the lift that made suicides put an end to their lives. Hope, to him, was the child of despair. Little things, bit by bit, gave him comfort now; life was morsels of comfort by this time, not one large comfort.

He rose to put more coal on the fire and removed the dishes to the back kitchen. He thought of going to the pub again for a while, but he was too tired. At that there came a knock on the front door. He leapt again. At the door, there was the deacon he'd seen in the pub. Before he finished asking him to come into the house, he said,

"I've come here to apologize to you, Nathan Huws, for what I said to you earlier in The Red Fox. But I was so impatient with that girl. She's the Sunday School secretary and her family is quite poor and has sacri-ficed to give her an education. The young people of this age are living in another world."

"They're no worse than young people a hundred years ago. They went to pubs, girls and boys."

"Yes, but they could do it only twice a year, at the times of hiring fairs. These go pub-crawling every day."

The man sat down and looked around.

"You have a comfortable place here, I understand the place your old friend had was quite uncomfortable. It's sure to be very strange for you with him gone."

"He had enough money to have every comfort."

Nathan Huws was on the brink of asking him to stay to have a bit of sup-per. But he restrained himself: he remembered his first time with Wil Dic; maybe asking him would be to start all over again. The man was pleasant enough. And he too had a passion—guarding young people's morals. That was his soul's passion. As he went out he said:

"Perhaps I'll call to see you from time to time, Nathan Huws. You're very much alone."

"Thanks," Nathan said, as dryly as he could.

He went to the kitchen to fix his supper. He moved the table towards the fire, and when he was beginning to eat his eggs and bread-and-butter, the cat left her bed and rubbed herself on his legs. He decided to go to bed and begin writing again in earnest, tomorrow.

The Treasure

For the fourth time in her life Jane Rhisiart was trying to put the events of that life in their proper place. As she was seventy-two years old, there was more of it to be set in place by this time, more events and persons to be moved and distinguished and classified.

The first time she had stopped to reflect on her life was when she was thirty-five years old, the day after Rolant, her husband, left her, an event that gave a shock to the whole district, but not to her. When Rolant disappeared with his wages one Friday pay night, it wasn't a great surprise to her. She was a woman with eyes to see, but with lips to shut tight lest her tongue talk to everybody indiscriminately. Because of her romantic nature, it's true that she took time to see, but when she saw, she saw more clearly than any realist. That's why her husband's disappearance gave more of a shock to the district than to her. That's also why she didn't do anything to try and find him, or try to get anything to support her. She'd rather work ten times harder than before, even, than suffer the quiet, provoking cruelty she'd been suffering from Rolant for years. Some of his fellow-quarrymen knew of some of this cruelty; it was impossible for his partners, and through them, their wives, not to know that Rolant kept back an unreasonable portion of his wages.

In this crisis, which was very far away by this time, she had the sympathy of the district, but she didn't want it. She decided to keep on with the smallholding without asking help from the parish or anyone else to raise her three children. That wasn't easy, not because of the constant battle against poverty—a person often finds peace of mind in poverty—but because Ann, the oldest child, was old enough at twelve to realize her loss after her father's disappearance, since she was his favourite, and had many times been used by him as a weapon against his wife. The boy, Wiliam, who was her favourite, was ten at the time, and Alis, six, wasn't old enough to realize things.

The second time she sat down to meditate on her life was twenty years later, with her children all married, and herself forced to realize that each one of them had disappointed her through their selfishness. Not one of them ever made a gesture to give her any financial help, which they could easily have done. But it wasn't that which had brought her disappointment, but their ungrateful attitude of taking and accepting everything as if she had money for them and not the other way round. Not one of them, not even Wiliam, showed a single sign of thanks or of appreciation. Unfortunately, the three of them were living close enough to visit her every day, and they'd taken advantage of that to pluck her feathers. Taking her butter and her eggs and sometimes paying for them, and more often forgetting to pay on purpose. And her, because of that, forced to ask her customers to look for butter somewhere else. She'd been able to get along better when they were little, than when they'd married and had homes of their own. Not one of them or the in-laws would offer her a helping hand either, but when they had need of help, to her they'd come, and for years she had been blind enough to give it.

But she had a strong and healthy body, a great help in nourishing independence of spirit.

The third time she took a picture of her life was five years later, just after she moved from the smallholding to a little cottage in the village, a few months after she'd become friends with Martha Huws; she was sixty years old at that time. She'd been completely disillusioned about her children by then; she saw that there was no point in holding on to the farm to feed them and their children, and bear their quarrelling and their envy of each other. She saw that she could be fully as well off on ten shillings a week in an unpropertied house, and she was strong enough to go out to work if there were need. So completely had she been disillusioned that she wasn't deceived by Wiliam, who tried to persuade her to invest the money from the cattle and the stock in something he could recommend. She kept her own counsel, and put the money in the bank, after using enough of it to make her cottage cosy.

And here she was today, at seventy-two, trying for the fourth time to set the events of her life in place and in their proper light, and doing it with a heavy and sorrowful heart; not in bitterness like the former times. She was doing it in a very strange place, at the seaside, the day of the Sunday

School trip. A fortnight ago Martha Huws, her friend for the past twelve years, had died; and this time her grief was so great that she didn't know how to put her life back together and begin again. Indeed, this was the first deep sorrow of her life.

She'd become friendly with Martha Huws a few months before leaving the farm; it was the desire to be closer to her friend that made her decide finally to move from the farm. She had known her forever, knew she'd been disappointed in love, that was a district story, and had gone to England into service, and returned when she was about fifty-five to live in a small house on her earnings and the small pension she'd had from the last family she served. But Martha Huws was only an acquaintance to Jane Rhisiart until the latter went to visit her when she was ill. And from that hour the friendship grew. Jane Rhisiart saw that day quite a different woman than she had supposed her to be; a woman with an open, intelligent face, beautiful blue eyes set far apart, and thick white hair. She hadn't noticed that when she'd caught a glimpse of her on the bus or in the shop. She could talk to her freely, not an easy task for Jane Rhisiart, and when the sick woman said, "Come visit me here again," with such warm earnestness, she decided to go. Talked more freely the second time than the first. By the time Jane Rhisiart moved from the smallholding the foundations of the friendship were down and the two of them were going in and out of each other's houses.

Because she'd been disappointed so many times in those to whom she'd given all her love, Jane didn't rush to pour out her heart to her friend, though she was by nature that kind of person. But she knew by this time what suffering could follow that, when she saw that the taker gave none of the love back. So for a long time she was groping her way tentatively into the heart of Martha Huws, as though she were walking in a tunnel, but Martha's personality soon threw enough light from the other end for her to be able to walk boldly.

The friendship was not without difficulties at the start, but these were from outside. The two of them were going to one another's houses often, and within a year, they found themselves seeing each other at some point every day. It was from Jane Rhisiart's children the difficulties came. They and their children were in and out of her house daily. She couldn't prevent them. And when Martha happened to be there, they would continue to stay and talk in spite of the children's crying and in spite of the taciturnity of the two women. Indeed, Ann and Alis and Wiliam's wife seemed as though they aimed at coming on the afternoons when Martha was visiting Jane. But they had to go home to make quarry supper for their husbands. If Martha came at night, Wiliam or Ann's and Alis's husbands would be sure to come there. That difficulty was overcome by Jane going more often to Martha's house. They wouldn't come there, but once Wiliam succeeded in a plot to go there to fetch his mother, on the excuse that he needed to see her on an important matter. He didn't succeed in getting her out of there the second time.

Then Wiliam went so far as to try weaning his mother from Martha by suggesting vile things about the latter, such as that there was no knowing what her life had been when she was in England. After all, why had her master left her money in his will and a pension? Jane was able to make him look very foolish when she said it was a woman and not a man had been her employer. But, had it been otherwise, it would have made no difference to her by this time. She was too fond of Martha to let any event in the past affect her. All the women could say to reproach her was "that they might as well not come to visit her now, since that Martha Huws was there all the time."

"She's not here every day nor all day," was their mother's answer. They would often find the door locked when the two friends went for a stroll or when Jane went to visit Martha, and that would drive them wild. Wiliam went so far once as to reproach his mother for spending the money she had in reserve to go off with a woman whose history she knew nothing about. And she answered like a shot, that it would be soon enough for him to reproach her for that when she came asking him for something to support her, and that she hoped she could spend it all before she died lest it cause more jealousy among the three of them than there already was.

Wiliam took a great interest in this little sum of money in the bank. He'd suggested many times to his mother that he could have started a little business or raised chickens if he had the money to start, and he was sick of the quarry. "Yes indeed," would be her answer, "a pity you couldn't have saved up when money was easy pickings." Her friendship with Martha was her backbone for these answers.

And in sitting down and analyzing that friendship from time to time it dawned on her that its basis was conversation. She had never before found anybody who could respond intelligently to what she said to them. She'd say something to a neighbour. The other woman wouldn't take any interest or she'd say something stupid, worthless. But with Martha she found from the start a response that had shown intelligence and interest. And that was the beginning of talk, and the beginning of understanding each other, and the beginning of friendship.

Despite that, a good three years went by before Jane could break the ice and could talk about Rolant. He wasn't the uppermost thing on her mind at the time. His disappearance had become something cold and impersonal, and she could talk about him without any feeling at all, not sadness, not bitterness or fondness. Indeed, some of the story seemed amusing by now, such as her knowing what the quarrymen didn't know—namely, that Rolant had used money he kept back to increase his amount for the monthly collection in the chapel, and made himself a laughing-stock to many because his contribution was almost as much as the shopkeepers' and the stewards'.

Martha was able to talk about her own experience of love, but not in as much detail, because there was an element of sadness in what had never reached fulfillment. Martha had had a sudden vision, something like a prophecy, that she would not be able to live with her sweetheart; Jane had seen more slowly and thoroughly. But what Jane liked in Martha was her saying she didn't want to talk about it. And what Martha liked in Jane was that she understood.

They often went for a walk to the mountain, which put the stamp of oddity on them to their neighbours. To them the mountain was only something that their husbands crossed to the quarry and something that was a sign of rain when mist came to wrap its crown. But Jane and Martha didn't weary of climbing it, and the great thing was to have a lie-down in the heather, and a talk, a cup of tea from a flask, and cake from a paper wrapper.

The greatest thing was the talk. When they went for an outing to Llandudno or Colwyn Bay, walking the streets and gaping at shop windows, the highpoint of the day would come when they went to a restaurant and had a proper meal before starting home, and talked. Neither of them had been able to do this with anyone else before. They thought by now that this was the only way life could still be endured, talking about their experiences—not the experiences of the past, there was no life in those, but their opinions and their feelings about the events of the day, in their village and in their country, and about what they read.

They didn't thrash the youth of today with the cudgel of their own youth's good behaviour, but they rejoiced that they'd lived in a pleasanter age. To the youth of the district they were a laughing-stock with their old-fashioned ways of going for a stroll, of dressing so plainly, of such dignified living, but these young people would have been a good deal surprised had they known the pair were in one thing part of modern life. When they went away for the day, both of them had a little powder in their bags to take the shine off their noses after having too high a tea.

But that was all over by now, and Jane was by herself on the Sunday School trip. A fortnight before, quite suddenly, Martha had left the world that had been so full of her for twelve years. Jane had been with her the night before, and had declared that she was looking pale and tired and offered to stay there with her. But her friend didn't want that. The next morning she was found dead in her bed. Jane's world had fallen apart for days.

Today, at the seaside, she was able to look more tranquilly at the events of the last fortnight, though she was constantly remembering that her friend had been with her on the trip last year. Her memories interwove with the colours of the clothing of children who were playing on the beach and with the millions of pearls that danced on the sea and shone on the sand. She had had a treasure in Martha's friendship, a spotless treasure, the only spotless thing in her life, and no one could take it from her. The string had been broken before it reached the end. But who was to say what the end might have been? Perhaps (but she couldn't think of it), something could have happened that might have made this treasure less spotless.

The minister came towards her and sat down on the rock. He spoke of this and that, and at last he said quite indifferently, as if he'd just thought of it, "It will be quite strange for you with Martha Huws gone, won't it?" Neither he nor anyone else could understand that this was the deepest sorrow of her life. She was on the brink of telling him, telling how much she longed for and how much she prized the good friend she'd had for twelve years. She wanted to spill that out to someone, just to be able to say it. But she remembered the lift it had given her heart at the Meeting the evening before when a child had said the verse "And His mother kept all these words in her heart", a verse to which she'd never given a moment's notice. No, she couldn't express to the minister her feelings about what she had lost. Only to Martha could she have spoken of the loss she'd had through the passing of her friend.

Family

Ela was sitting in the back kitchen with a tableful of food in front of her, more than she'd seen for years, a plate of ham, a big plate of bread-and-butter, farm butter at that, and a bowl of salad that was almost too pretty to dig into. A strange happiness came to her heart from seeing the sun beaming on it all, as she relaxed after walking three miles from the station, and relaxed while eating choice things that she hadn't had for years. She was feeling so happy that she turned every morsel over leisurely in her mouth, chewing the ham into tiny pieces. She took time to cut up her bread-and-butter, and she mused pleasantly over it all, forgetting what had brought her there, forgetting her husband John's pointed remark, that had been fretting her mind through the entire journey on the train. From the parlour came whispering, an occasional low cough and an occasional sigh, all unnecessary, as she knew, and silence after them; from the field close by, the bleating of a mournful ewe and silence after her too. She heard Lisa Jên, her first cousin, walk to the lobby and speak quietly to someone there. Then, she heard her coming back and into the back kitchen, and that broke into her musings.

"Are you finished, Ela? Mrs. Jones needs to clear the table before the minister arrives," quite briskly and bossily.

Ela swallowed the jelly without enjoying it and her face became flushed. Yes, here she was, the same Lisi Jên, neither death nor anything else could take the bossiness out of her. Mrs. Jones, the hired help, came to clear the table and gave a wink at Ela, and she went to sit in the parlour, feeling as though she were walking into a preaching meeting a quarter of an hour late. There around the room sat her whole family, aunts, uncles, first cousins (male and female), brothers and sisters, nieces and nephews, looking at each other and at her as if they'd never seen each other. In the armchair by the fire sat Lewis Tomos, Lisi Jên's husband, with his head to one side like a dog. Opposite him sat Uncle Enoc, chewing tobacco, with juice running down his beard, and looking quite unconcerned. Both looking into the fire. The cat was lying inside the fender. These were the only things that could be seen clearly. Everybody else was half in darkness. Lisi Jên kept walking back and forth to the back kitchen and staring at the clock as she went past. Ela turned instinctively to look at the clock, and it said a quarter after one. Another three-quarters of an hour of staring at her family! John's remark came back to her with more of an edge. She'd tried to persuade him to come with her to her aunt's burial.

"No, I won't come," he said emphatically. "A funeral's the place one sees one's family."

And she didn't answer, because she knew what her answer would be: "They're my family, not your family."

She knew it wasn't she who'd have the last word, though she'd have the last word but one. So she kept quiet. It would end in a quarrel if she went on, and going on a journey after a quarrel was worse than going on a journey to face one.

Lisi Jên's authoritative remark about her hurrying began turning over in her mind, in just the same way as John's remark had been turning on the train, pursuing her and turning true at one and the same time. Why had she needed to hurry over that good food with three-quarters of an hour's time to wait?

"Make less of a noise with those dishes." Lisi Jên snapping again at Mrs. Jones. The old bitch! She had to be able to boss someone. No wonder Lewis Tomos stooped perpetually by now. He might as well not straighten up. It was less trouble to hold the neck ready to accept the yoke. Not only did he look like a dog, there by the fire, but like a dog who'd had a thrashing.

The kettle was singing lazily on the hob and the cat was purring, as homely as though her aunt were alive and sitting in the armchair. Some of the family who were sitting on the sofa were whispering, and her Aunt Beca said "Be quiet", quite loud.

Ela was overcome with a need to laugh. What if she had to, lest she explode? She'd get a proper tongue-lashing from Lisi Jên later, for sure. Maybe that would be best, so that she could let it out, and be finished with all the bad temper that had festered inside her since John made that remark about her family. But it would be a terrible thing to quarrel at a funeral, though that was a notorious place for it. Why she had come to her aunt's burial she didn't know, and her aunt, the only one she would have liked to please, wouldn't have known if she'd stayed home. What is it makes people go to one another's burials? Respect, duty, compassion? She couldn't say, as far as her aunt was concerned. The custom of going to a family burial perhaps. She didn't feel any grief; she was perfectly sure of that, only the grief of seeing the old things passing, and seeing each time she came to bury one of her family part of her own youth go down into the grave with them. She might as well not puzzle herself, she wouldn't find an answer, but the puzzling had been a help in keeping her from hearing the awkward unnatural silence that filled the room.

The clock was pounding like a hammer behind her, somewhere in her backbone. Thomas John Cilgerran's clock in Hell. Forever! Forever! This silence would continue like this. Forever! Forever! There came a sigh once more, the one that she'd heard from the back kitchen.

She turned her head to see who it was. Uncle Lias. Who would have thought? The poor old creature! But perhaps it was to see a break in the silence he'd sighed, and not for his sister Deina.

She remembered her mother's words about someone she hadn't cared for, after he died: "She didn't give a sigh after him." There was no need to sigh after Aunt Deina when she'd lived to be so old. But there was nobody there to sigh but Lisi Jên, and she, the only child, would be left very tidy. She'd have a welcome for her money, Ela thought, since it wouldn't stir from the bank. When would the preacher come to quiet Thomas John's clock?

Horseflies came from somewhere and sat on Uncle Enoc's beard, and the next moment he spat a stream of tobacco juice across the bright hob.

"Why won't you look where you're spitting?" said Lisi Jên.

But Uncle Enoc didn't hear her, and Ela gave thanks for that much of a break in the silence. She was on the brink of saying something, when she felt, rather than saw, the two shining eyes of Nesta, her niece, who was smiling at her from the sofa. And she gave thanks, from the bottom of her heart, for something that restrained her from breaking out shouting.

At that moment, the minister came and the service was begun. He was a young man who had known her aunt only at the end of her life. His voice was gentle, his expression clear, and Ela took pleasure in hearing "The days of man are as grass", though the words weren't suitable for her aunt, who was far over her four score. Her days had been as an oak, almost, and in thinking this, she thought for the first time since she'd arrived about the person in the coffin upstairs.

She had a yearning to get up there and sing the praises of the old woman, when he thanked God for her faithfulness in the chapel. It wasn't the chapel had been her passion, but her house and her clothes. She'd like to sing praise to her beauty as she remembered her forty years before. She was remembering two things especially. Coming across her aunt unawares as she was milking in the cowshed, sitting on the stool under the cow, her skirt opening out from her beautiful body like a fan, and her with her head on the cow's flank, as though she were listening to the milk falling into the pitcher. She thought at the time how she'd like to take her picture in that meditative pose, and wondered, was something troubling her when she looked like that. Another time she remembered being allowed to go sit in her pew in the chapel, when her aunt was wearing a new blue suit. A blue hat with a white plume on it, and the light plume falling across the brim and softening the strength of her face. Remembered her frequent favours and her kindness towards her always. Remembered. Remembered—what the minister didn't know.

She began to feel tearful when he read: "For this corruptible must put on incorruption, and this mortal must put on immortality." It was the word "corruptible" made her feel this way every time. Remembered her aunt as a fairly young woman. Remembered how she looked, like Nesta now, and remembered herself when young, and here she was now at that slippery uninteresting place between middle age and old age. But there was peace in these thoughts. They were sad thoughts, flowing across her consciousness without fretting.

As she left the house she took hold of her niece Nesta's arm, and went into the same carriage with her, in spite of the undertaker's orders. She didn't care about the confusion she was causing. She put her arm through Nesta's arm, and clung to her to the graveside because she was the one who'd brought the speck of light into the dark parlour a little while ago.

"When are you being married, Nesta?"

"In a month's time."

"I hope you'll be happy, indeed."

"You needn't worry, Alun is an absolute love."

"I hope he'll stay that way to the grave."

She was sorry, as soon as the word crossed her lips. What right had she to suggest the disappointment of middle age to a young girl on the threshold of her heaven? And such a lovable one as Nesta, never a frown to be seen on her brow or a wrinkle on her forehead. And she'd hurt the one she'd have given the world not to hurt. That's how it always happened—hurting the ones dear to her.

They were back from the cemetery, at the tea table, with everybody talking, just as if the departure of the dead had given them free rein. Uncle Enoc was looking at his plate and eating without stopping, his beard rising up as his toothless mouth chewed the food; and when he spoke, he spoke to himself, more or less, since he was hard of hearing, and nobody troubled to answer him. But here came a cannonball from him:

"What happened to Deina's first love, that one she kept company with for so many years before marrying Wmffra?"

"Don't open old wounds on the day of your sister's funeral," from Aunt Beca.

But Uncle Enoc hadn't heard. He went on.

"He was a good, smart lad—"

Aunt Beca shouted in his ear at the top of her voice:

"Why are you opening old wounds on the day of your sister's funeral?"

"Opening old wounds? It isn't opening old wounds to talk about a lovers' quarrel. I'd call it opening old wounds to talk about them if they'd left each other after getting married."

Aunt Beca scowled, and whispered under her breath:

"With the preacher here and all."

But the preacher was enjoying the whole thing.

This was the first time that Ela had heard the story of a sweetheart before Aunt Deina was married.

"What came between them, Uncle Enoc?" Ela asked loudly.

"Listen to her again, shoving the boat into the water," said Aunt Beca.

"Nobody knows what came between them. But I heard a rumour that that boy had told her lies, and she found out, and began to think that he'd do worse than tell lies after he was married."

"And she was right," Lisi Jên said, out of feeling for her father, "because he deceived the woman he did marry right under her nose, and they left each other."

"No, he died," from her Aunt Beca.

Ela turned to look at Nesta to see what effect this might have on her, but she was still like the sunshine.

Ela had been on the brink of asking for more, but this time she considered in time that it could hurt somebody.

Uncle Lias, the youngest of them, sighed.

"Father in heaven, what's wrong with Lias, always sighing?" Aunt Beca said.

And for the first time Uncle Lias spoke:

"I see that you have all forgotten poor Deina, and forgotten that none of us has much time before we'll be going after her."

And silence came upon everyone.

Nesta came to escort her Aunt Ela some of the way to the station. Ela felt very warm towards her and she was very sorry she'd been so free with her tongue in the carriage on the way to the cemetery.

"I'm very sorry, Nesta, that I hurt you."

"Hurt? When? How?"

"Well, in the car, when I said I hoped that Alun would stay an absolute love to the grave."

"Indeed, I didn't see anything wrong in that. What was wrong with it?"

"Oh, well, that's that then."

She kissed her at the crossroad, and turned back to wave at her afterwards.

On the train, Ela reflected later on the afternoon's events, especially what she'd heard about Aunt Deina's first love. Had she been happy afterwards with Uncle Wmffra? It would seem so. But he'd been a wishy-washy man who wouldn't quarrel with anybody. And in Ela's mind, Aunt Deina had been a woman who needed to have someone her own size to match her before she'd be happy, and perhaps she'd have been happier with the other man for all his lies. But there it was, it hadn't happened that way, and she and her husband had gone beyond being hurt by a lie or anything else by now. And Nesta's great faith in her happiness. She hoped that she, at least, wouldn't be deceived, in her honest innocence. As she was nearing her home, John came to mind again, with his sharp remark. Yes, he was right. He spoke the truth. That's the sort of thing a family was, quarreling in their old age as they buried each other. But it was fretting her mind terribly to think she'd disagreed with him when she was starting out, and had perceived that he was the one who was right. But she decided that she wouldn't say so after she reached home. She'd keep it to herself. And if he asked questions, she'd hide things from him. After all, Nesta had been very lovable—that much was true.

Hope

If someone that minute had offered Sal Huws a hundred pounds for her thoughts, she couldn't have said straight off what they were, since they were running criss-cross over each other in her reflections, and on two planes, the plane of her relationship with her husband Huw, and the plane of her relationship with Iolo, her four-year-old boy, which were two very different planes. A plane of interminable, prickly, petty quarrelling, that was the plane where Huw was; and a plane of peaceful adoration, that was the plane where Iolo was.

The scene where she was thinking these things was a strange one. The little field beside the house, with her sitting there on a bench, holding the leather leash that was around Iolo's waist, Sam the cat beside her, Pero the dog on the ground next to her, and lying in the middle of the field, the pig, his back filthy and his belly white.

The iron sun of July was pouring down on them. She would have been in the village with Iolo were it not for this intense heat. The theme of her reflections was her own life for the past five years and more. Strange how little time it took her to run over the period in her mind, and strange how many important things had happened in that time. She'd had a child after waiting twelve years for him after getting married, and having had him, discovered that he wasn't right, that he was feeble-minded. Her memory of getting the news from the doctor was as clear as the evening she'd had it; the lines stood out like a pattern of gossamer threads. The doctor had given the news candidly but not callously, and added that the child in time could become stronger, in body and mind. He vanished from the house like a shadow after he'd spoken, and Sal felt the blood drain from the roots of her hair down through her face as she fell to the floor. Huw ran to lift her up and fetch a cup of water for her. Then a strange thing happened. A feeling like water rising on a dry course came into her spirit. The baby was there, and alive. She had cherished him since the day he was born, but now she saw him as a treasure to be loved more, to be worshipped as a little god, to be pampered and coddled. She picked him up from his cradle and hugged him in her arms, and kissed him, with her husband staring at her stupidly.

"And this is what we've got after waiting twelve years, a child who isn't all there," Huw said.

"Hush," she said, "don't speak so crudely. Don't talk about a child who isn't all there. You heard what the doctor said—he'll grow stronger in every way, bit by bit. What the little thing needs most in the world is care."

"It would've been better if he'd died at birth."

"No," hotly, "it wouldn't. See how much pleasure he's given us already. He's our treasure."

"Yours, maybe, not mine. He does nothing but cry when I hold him."

"He feels your arms are different."

"I can't be fond of him."

"It will come as he gets stronger."

"He shows no sign of getting stronger."

The months before the child's birth had been happy ones for Sal and Huw. When they first knew that Sal was in the family way, they were like two children themselves. You'd think nobody else had ever expected a child but them. It filled their minds every waking minute of their lives. Sal couldn't stop knitting. She went on displaying her achievement like a child, whenever anyone came there. Huw cleared the grate in the morning before starting for work, and arranged it ready to be kindled, and he took Sal a cup of tea in bed. They would go for a walk together at nightfall like two lovers, and they'd talk about the baby as if it had already arrived. If it was a boy, its name would be Iolo. If a girl, Branwen. Huw thought that it would be a clever child, since they were both fairly old, just like Joni Jones who'd had three first-class honours for his degree; but she imagined that this was an old wives' tale, though she hoped the tale was true. She wanted to dress it as grand as means would permit. "As grand as we can," she would say, "if we have to do without things ourselves." The two of them would go into the house to dream dreams.

Their joy was bubbling over when they had a fairly easy birth and a fine boy. He was called Iolo; Sal had been determined to have a name that didn't exist anywhere at all in the district. But after some two months she noticed that the baby wasn't responding very much to his surroundings. His eyes were tiny, and didn't take a great deal of notice of anything, not even the electric lamp. He had frenzied fits and couldn't be quieted, and this was the time he began to cry when his father took him in his arms. He was very greedy for his bottle too.

Then came the great disappointment a few months later when the doctor told them. Huw changed entirely, and he'd gone to bed that night like a man in the sulks. And he *was* in the sulks, with what or who it was hard to say. Sal decided to sleep on the sofa next to Iolo in his cradle. She didn't sleep. Huw got up next morning, but he didn't say a word as he ate his breakfast.

"Look, Huw, we must accept our fate."

"A very cruel fate, one of us must have sinned."

"We might as well not talk about things that way, with the smell of old hags on them. The doctors know that it's a defect in the body somewhere."

"You're right, and I know what I'm doing is trying to grasp at a reed to find a reason, in talking about these old wives' tales. But why did things like this have to happen to us?"

"We can't ever say, we must accept it. I'm sure the little thing will become as dear in our eyes as if he were like any proper boy."

"I don't know. I'd set my heart on a clever lad."

"Clever children aren't any easier to raise, or more precious."

But Huw changed completely. The corners of his mouth began to turn down, and his moustache too. He looked like a Chinaman and as sour as a pot of clabbered milk. But for Sal, what she'd said turned into truth; Iolo became as precious as any proper child in her eyes, more so, because his weakness was ready to accept the strength of her love. She doubted the love sometimes, more pity perhaps, because she found herself over and over going up against a hard fate, and thinking what if he were like another child, how unblemished her love for him would be. But bit by bit, her pity became so strong that she couldn't call it anything but love.

At the start, she was worried what her neighbours would say. It would be "honey on the fingers" to some, a reason for compassion to the others. But she determined that she didn't mean to pay attention to people's reactions. In keeping with her dream before Iolo was born she decided to have the best things for him. She saw an advertisement in a paper about a second-hand pram, by someone she knew about, a wealthy woman. It was as good as new, no hard old leather inside it, but leather as supple as a kid glove. She bought it and bought a cream-coloured silk sunshade to put over it in summer. When she went down to the village, people would turn to look at her, but she didn't know whether they were looking at the pram or hoping to catch a glimpse of the baby. "A pity it couldn't have died," one said. "You'll see, he'll get better," said another. "He's a very dear little thing, and a comfort," said another. It didn't matter whether they were being hypocritical.

As the baby grew, Huw tried to take an interest in him, but he was still suffering from the first shock. He would look in on him every evening after coming from work. He tried to entice him by making animal noises, but he didn't succeed. Huw would turn away from him, like a cat sniffing his food, and leave him. Not that the baby took much notice of her either, but she loved him as he was, and without expecting a response. He was a child of hers, and that was enough for her. Huw became more frowning and can-tankerous and he was always finding fault somewhere; and it was the baby who was blamed in the long run. One afternoon, Sal had taken the pram for a walk to the mountain. She'd had a notion that wholesome air would make Iolo more like other children. She sat on a rock with Iolo quiet in his pram, drinking in the wholesome air, she imagined. It was so nice, being able to look at the cotton grass wagging. She was hoping that Iolo would notice it. She waited and waited, and by the time she reached home, Huw was there before her. "I went with Iolo for a walk to the mountain" (she would speak of him by now, when he was two years old, as if he were a big boy, full grown and her partner); "this is the first time this has happened."

"This isn't the last time, as long as you idolize this lad."

She hurried to make the food. She knew she was at fault in neglecting Huw, but being in Iolo's company had become too strong for her, between hoping for him to improve and her love for him.

"I'm sorry, Sal."

"What for?"

"For my complaining about the food."

"Tut, forget it."

He began sobbing.

"I'd like to be able to love him as you do, but I can't."

"A pity. Our life could go back to the way it was when we were expecting him. That was a nice time."

"Yes, there was hope in not knowing then."

"There's still hope."

"I don't see any sign of that."

But indeed, a little later, while he was being washed, Iolo showed he was able to stand on his feet, and he walked to his father and leaned on his knee. Huw looked at him and smiled.

"A pity he couldn't talk yet," the father said.

"That will come too."

"If it comes, we'll go to the headmaster of that new school to ask can he go there."

"It will be quite soon enough in another two years. He's only three years old."

She put his night clothes on and walked him up to the bedroom, her heart lighter than it had been through it all. Huw didn't speak very enthusiastically after she came into the kitchen; there wasn't much to be had from him except the wish that Iolo could speak. That's what would show he had intelligence, in his opinion.

Sal went to him and kissed him.

"Huw, try to see further improvement in him."

"I'll be on top of the world when he says something."

It had been a year since then, and she was going over all these things in the small field in the heat this afternoon. Every spot was quiet, except that the pig gave an occasional grunt, and the gorse was clicking. Her mind was very restless. She was worried that she and Huw had become so distant from each other, and yet, she was afraid that Huw might come to win all of Iolo's love and that she would lose him. She was afraid that Iolo might die. What would she do afterwards without his love? She thought what if she herself were to die, and Iolo had to go to a home where he wouldn't have pity or love. She was worried too that Iolo cried so much, was in a bad temper so often, and then was so affectionate. She was worried that he was so long learning to control his body's functions, though that was coming slowly. He was greedy too. But she tried to comfort herself that he'd be able to control himself with these things after a while, just as he'd learned to walk. Her head was a whirlpool of anxious thoughts. She kissed Iolo, the cause of all this. In the middle of this she looked forty years into the future, and she could hear some people passing the house and saying:

"Do you remember Sal Huws living there? She had a little boy who wasn't right. What became of him I wonder?"

Saying it unemphatically, like a fact in a newspaper, when today she was filled to the brim with anxiety and pain that they would know nothing of; her mind like a harrow on a fertilized field. They'd know nothing of her joy either. Then her mind took another track. She'd had long years of happy life after getting married, but it was the unconcerned happiness of a honeymoon. Her love for Iolo was a love that included concern, love with her insides hurting. She could cry out like Jeremiah, "My bowels, my bowels."

Then Iolo began to stir. She thought for a second he was about to have a fit of bad temper. He made a noise in his throat and pointed in the direction of the pig.

"Buh—," he said, and looked at his mother. Then he pointed at the pig.

"Big," he said clearly, and "Big" again and again. Sal cried with joy; he had said something at last. Huw would be pleased. At this, the woman next door came out, with a camera in her hand.

"I saw you looking so happy," she said, "and I thought I'd like to take your picture."

Very strangely, Sal had never thought of taking a picture of Iolo. She'd imagined that after Iolo had grown big he wouldn't like to see himself as he was now.

"Why are you crying, Sali?"

And she explained. The neighbour raised her arms in joy.

"Oh, I'm glad. We must have this picture to celebrate the occasion."

Iolo was continuing to point at the pig, and Sal thought that she'd keep the pig to die a natural death. A pig who'd sparked such an exclamation didn't deserve the butcher's knife. She thought that now the sourness and the bickering between her and Huw would be over, perhaps, unless his jealousy towards Iolo gave birth to another excuse for not loving him. Anyway, she would have to face this and hope. The honeymoon life was over, and even if Huw displayed his jealousy, she would have a concern; something that gave purpose to her life, instead of a monotonous plain of happiness.

Return

She was walking light-heartedly up the road that led from her house, swinging her shopping basket. She was happy because she'd finished her work, and she was looking forward to having an evening of reading by the fire. A large gang of schoolboys came down the road; she went by them without taking notice of them. After they passed her, some of them started mocking her, mimicking the way she would forbid them to ride their bikes on a private road. And she said that she would send to their headmaster to complain about their conduct. At that, they'd begun shouting the filthiest language she'd ever heard, language too filthy to be repeated. She went on, bowing her head, crestfallen. In town the young people in the shops were pleasant, but that couldn't ease her pain. When she arrived home she sat on a chair to reflect. She realized that she wasn't good for anything by now, just a poor old creature who was a laughing-stock to loutish schoolboys. In her days, school had stood for courtesy. By today, it was no better than a home for good-for-nothings, and its language was the language of a country going to the dogs. Instead of reading, she proceeded to feel sorry for herself.

.   .   .

She walked up to the mountain and saw the house with the one window in its gable, like a one-eyed man looking at the long moor. Cotton grass was quivering in the breeze, and the lapwings were flying from hole to hole. And she walked to a green patch by the house and close to a tump of heather where sheep would graze, and lay down there. She heard Leusa Parri walking back and forth in front of her house in her clogs, swinging buckets. From the corner of her eye she could see staghorn growing level with the earth through the heather. She began to pull it slowly, just for the sake of meddling, to see if she could succeed in pulling it up in one piece. She didn't want it; pulled for the sake of pulling. She managed to get a long piece and put it around her neck. She sat up to look for heathberries but she didn't see any. Just as well, because she didn't have a dish to hold them. She walked to the foot of the quarry tip to look for mountain fern or quarry fern. There was a little growing there between the blackish-blue scraps of slate, and looking quite discouraged. Her mother had told her not to pull it up and try growing it in the garden beside the bachelor's buttons. It would die there because it wouldn't like its place, she said. It liked a lonely place, with its roots between the slates. She walked to the stile and climbed over it to have a look at the valley where the river was a single grey lifeless string, as if it had stopped running. She was furious at this valley when she first discovered it. She had thought there was nothing in the world but her mountain, the village, and the sea in front of it as far as she could see. It was a disappointment to her, to see that other places existed. She sat down again, pulled off her shoes and stockings, and put her feet on wet moss.

The snail was in the garden, a fat one with a white belly. She recited above its head:

> *"Snail, snail, stretch your horns out for me*
> *Or I'll toss you to the red cattle in the Red Sea."*

And its four horns came leaping out like wicket stakes. It must like the verse because it looked so jaunty. And she, Annie, had made it obey.

She was coming from the cowshed to the house carrying a kitten in her pinafore, the big cat following her. She put the kitten on the table, and it went and walked sideways to where her mother was making a dough cake on a blue slate. Before it could be stopped it was standing on the cake. As she and her mother shouted, the big cat jumped onto the table. Then she and her mother began laughing. Her mother said that she could keep the kitten since there was only one this time, if she'd look after it and take care to bring it back to its bed in the cowshed every night.

She and her brothers were coming home from school through a big storm of wind and rain. The rain was like a big grey striped sheet in front of them, and they were walking with their heads down. The raindrops fell on their faces, they shut their eyes, they couldn't pull out their pocket handkerchiefs to dry them. The drops were falling from the bottom of their coats into their shoes. When a blast of wind came they had to stop and hold on to each other. It was a long mile. Their mother came to meet them about halfway with coats, but there was no point in putting them on. "Now, to the fire there, and drop every stitch on the floor." It was so hard to take the stockings off because they had stuck to the skin with the rain. Their mother took a towel and dried them in front of the blazing fire; the steam rose from their bodies. How nice the heat was after the harsh wetness on their skins. Their mother handed them warm underclothes from the small oven, and put their best outfits on them. Then the bowls of hot soup at the table.

       ■   ■   ■

She was going to the mountain again. She had decided to do this before going to see her mother and father. How nice it would be to see them again, have a chat by the fire, and be able to tell them about those cursing boys. She could feel confident with her parents, and not like a "shapeless little baggage". She searched for the path but could not see it. The only thing to do was walk through the heather. There were no sheep on the mountain either, so it wasn't strange that there was no sheep path. The house was still there, with two eyes by this time. She had forgotten to bring a present for her parents. She went to the house to ask Leusa Parri for brewer's barm to make barley bread. By the time she went there, someone else was living there, an Englishwoman, who didn't know what brewer's barm was. She turned her back and banged the gate. She went to the stile, longing to see the other valley. Most of the houses were gone and a large factory stood in the middle of the valley. She hurried from the stile and ran to the quarry tip. There was no noise of a load falling from the top of the tip. The scraps of slate looked old, as if they'd been thrown there years ago, sticking to each other. There were a few sprouts of mountain fern looking more lonely than ever. The sea in front of her was as always unchanged. She remembered how the teacher in school would tell the story of Math and Gwydion who lived at the seaside, how they would change things with their magic wands. A pity they weren't there now to change the mountain to the way it was long ago. She decided to go see the stream below the road. There, meandering through the water, was one lonely trout, turning the water into small waves over the white gravel. She gazed at him a long time; then she burst out singing at the top of her voice:

*"In the river's cold stream, little trout,
You go frisking about."*

Then she found herself sobbing as she looked at the trout. In coming up from the stream, she stumbled and fell. Her knee was bleeding and painful. She thought for a moment that she could never walk to her old home. She found that she could, by hobbling. After getting to the road she saw a gang of loutish boys with long filthy hair coming, just like the schoolboys who'd cursed at her. She walked as close to the dyke as she could, but they came nearer the dyke, and one of them said:

"Shove her against the wall, damn her, an old thing like this shouldn't be allowed to live."

"You'll do no such thing," said the voice of a man behind them, "go home where you belong. Now, my girl, walk ahead, and I'll walk behind you."

She was pleased that someone had called her "girl", at her age.

"There you are," the man said, when they came to the village, "you'll be all right now."

There were houses, houses everywhere. At last, she saw her old home hiding itself between two houses.

She knocked lightly on the door of the portico, and put her head into the kitchen before she shut it. Suddenly the pain left her knee. The kitchen was as if there were a layer of mist over it, her father and mother were like shadows in the middle of it. Their faces were the colour of grey-green putty, their cheeks hillocks and hollows, their chins and their hooked noses almost touching each other. They looked like cartoons of themselves. Yet she was able to recognize them. The fire was low in the grate.

"Here she's come at last," her father said.

"She's been a very long time," her mother said, "when I told her to hurry."

"I came as soon as I could. There were boorish old boys on the road."

Neither of the two took notice of that.

"The food's been awaiting you for years," her mother said. "We'll eat now."

There was cold meat, bread-and-butter, and tea, but there was no taste to any of them. Bit by bit the mist cleared, and as the kitchen became brighter, the couple's faces became more natural: the hollows rose. A flush came to her father's cheeks; her mother's face turned naturally pale. Their noses came back to their former shape. The houses around the house went out of sight. The field became visible, with the tree and the hen and the chicks. A cheerful fire came into the grate and lit up the entire kitchen. The father was smiling happily; a blue tenderness came into the eyes of the mother.

"Leave that old meat," she said, "I have a dough cake."

She drew a plate from the small oven, swimming in butter.

The daughter clapped her hands.

"Like long ago. Do you have brown sugar?"

"There it is on the table."

"Oh, it's good. Do you remember my kitten walking into your dough cake?"

"Yes," and the mother laughed. "There's only remembering now."

"Yes."

She was on the brink of talking about those boys and their filthy language, but she was so happy that she decided not to say anything for fear of spoiling the talk.

"Do you remember, dad, the pigs escaping from their sty in the middle of the night in a big wind in mid-winter, and you running after them to the meadow in your drawers?"

The three of them laughed uncontrollably.

Do you remember? Do you remember? and she was on the brink of asking Where are . . . ? Where are . . . ? Where are the others?

But why should she spoil this joy?

"Where's your pipe, dad?"

"I haven't had a smoke for years. I haven't any tobacco."

She had cigarettes in her bag, but what would her mother say if she took them out? She had a proper tongue. But giving pleasure to her father was more important than being scolded for a secret sin.

"Here," she said, "put two of those in your pipe."

The mother smiled.

"I'll take one too," she said. "I remember how my aunt would come over and smoke a pipe."

"What next?" Annie said to herself, in an amazement that was close to fear; she took one too.

And there they were, the three of them smoking, so happy, so happy. Where were the others? Where were the others? No, she didn't want to ask. Light blue smoke was curling up into the air. The sun went out of sight. It began to be night. Their eyelids began to fall over their eyes, as on a statue. The three of them went to sleep.

Tomorrow and Tomorrow

The moon was shining through the bedroom window and laying the pattern of its square panes on the floor and on the coverlet. Within the frame of one square on the bed was Nanw Prisiart's face, with its hooked nose almost meeting its pointed chin. The flesh of the face was like the outer rind on suet. Winds had been beating on it for close to a century.

Outside in the whiteness, a cock was crowing from a nearby garden, his note striking the clear evening as hard as a bullet from a gun. The moon and the cock were bothering Nanw Prisiart, and the pain in her stomach even more. She was certain she was going to die, and just as certain it was the new potatoes and the fresh buttermilk she'd eaten before coming to bed that were the cause of the pain. But she couldn't do anything but lie still and think. She wasn't able to get up and pound the wall for Lias, next door, her nephew. She didn't want to die, she'd never been able to come to terms with Death, though she'd seen everybody in her family buried before her. While there were new potatoes and buttermilk and an appetite for them, life had savour.

She was trying to think, but it was only brief thoughts like little lights in a tunnel that would come, and they were going out almost before she saw them. But one lingered longer than the others, Lias and the new potatoes.

He had brought her the new potatoes and the fresh buttermilk straight from the churn earlier that evening, and had said something, had warned her that she wasn't to eat them that evening, or had directed her to eat them, she couldn't remember which. He had told her to do it, or not to. Whichever, what she'd done was eat them. And this was the result.

Then another little light came from the darkness of her mind: of course, without a doubt, he'd told her to eat them, her nephew had, she could see now, so that she would die, and so that he would get the hundred pounds that she'd left him in her will. A pity she'd ever told him about the money and that he was the one to have it. It was in an impulsive outburst she'd told him about her will, hoping that he would stop shuffling around her so much. She could understand someone shuffling and wagging his tail hoping to get something, not knowing he was going to get it. But here he was, having had the assurance and still coming in and out with his "Have something else, auntie?" Fidgeting around her like a sieve of maggots. It wasn't possible to take a hot egg from the fire in the house without Lias poking his nose inside.

And now here he had told her without an if or an unless to eat the new potatoes and the fresh buttermilk, so that she would go, for sure. If so, he was as much a murderer as anyone who put a tuck-knife in someone's body. Who would have thought it of Lias with his little eyes smiling through his spectacles at eighteen, like a child orphaned on the parish?

Wait now, how old was Lias anyway? Somewhere between thirty and fifty. Meri, his mother, would have been over a hundred. No, indeed, he had said that he'd arrived at the promised age on his last birthday, whenever that was. But he still had the same face, a child's face, but his back was crooked. It was as he was washing the floor for her she saw that. What need there was of washing the floor, Lias alone would know. But she had her bellyful of him every hour of the day, whether it was on his knees washing the floor with one buttonless leather strap of his braces sticking up, like a one-eared pig, or washing dishes like some old Meri Jên, with "What else can I do for you, auntie?", and all for the sake of a hundred pounds.

Oh, gracious! the pain in her stomach! She'd rather see Lias' face than his back this minute anyway, if she could only have a sip of water.

And there was that cock again, crowing at night. Someone was going to die. But someone was always going to die, and if a cock were an omen, not a single cock would ever get to shut his eyes. A pity Lias was so hypocritical too; he was quite obliging. Better than her children or her children's children. Was that a verse from the Bible or something that was true today?

No, Lias was an old bachelor; her sister Meri's child. Ann was her brother John's child, about the same age as Lias, and she never came near her, because Lias had told her about the will. And there was another one then, a daughter of Ann's, Olwen, a middle-aged person, and then a daughter of hers with an odd name to her, a name she could never say, something like "beery"—beer, bare, yes, Beryl, a fairly young girl, and she had a baby. Oh, the people there were in the world, and all of them related to her.

And now she remembered Beryl, the little jade! Maybe she was the one had brought the potatoes and the buttermilk. She wouldn't be surprised. This Beryl was constantly back and forth at the house looking sulky as a mule, especially if her old, old aunt were in pretty good spirits, with a lively look on her. Lias looked like a harried buck every time this Beryl would come and put her baby's pram inside the front door. He'd stare at the mark of the wheels on the clean floor. She was fond of Lias when he would scowl at Beryl.

Oh, yes, she could still hear a few things, and she'd heard this old girl, the baby's mother, say once that it was high time for "this old woman" to die and get out of the way, no, she'd said something else, yes, that was it, "It's high time for this bloody old woman to get out of the way, so someone young could have her house, instead of young people raising their children all over other people's houses." How was it possible for her, Nanw Prisiart, who'd been raised with her head on Victoria's knee, to know what "bloody" was? She knew what a woman with blood in her was, and she knew what bludgers were. They were people who had no fear, people who had guts. And Lias had given her a proper answer, "Now, don't you go using a word like that in front of auntie even though she doesn't hear" (but she'd heard the both of them), "and auntie has more need of a house than you. You can't toss her into the workhouse, and who's going to look after her?" Playing false, he was, thinking about the money. But, at the time, his falseness was a pleasing thing.

Why didn't Beryl's husband put up a house for her on the mountain, the way people did years ago, a squatter's hut, but nobody was satisfied with a house like that now. There must be a bathroom, for goodness' sake, so women and men could see their naked bodies, the bold old things! And this old girl was afraid even to open her bodice to show her breast to the flames of the fire. She'd rather nurse the baby with old tinned food from a bottle. And she was very particular about the time. The baby had to have his food to the second, or the world would be at an end and the people would perish.

A flash from the tunnel once more, with the pain a bit better. Huw, her husband, dead scores of years ago, and she couldn't remember his face, just one thing, how he'd raise one eyebrow higher than the other in talking, like a pot-hook, and after living with him for all those years, she couldn't remember how many, but it was a very long time. But she remembered deciding to start saving the hundred pounds, and she was glad—something saved up and kept, not lost or forgotten, like playing marbles long ago. Not herself, but the children: John, Meri, Margiad, Guto, and—and—a great other lot, collecting a pouchful of marbles every season, and then hiding them for the season with the drawstring pulled tight. Real misers.

And keeping the flat stone too because it was a good one for scattering the marbles everywhere at the first shot.

And she had a hundred pounds in a pouch; no, in the bank, that big place in town with the smooth-mannered, hard-hearted men. Meri's pouch in the cupboard. Her husband Huw had told her when she began saving it that she was saving it for someone else to squander, and perhaps damning his soul. But there was a tang in saving as in food, and Lias wasn't likely to damn his soul. It was a puny, niggardly little old soul he had, and the devil wouldn't offer a penny for it.

Oh, here came the pain again, and it was soulless Lias who'd told her to drink the fresh buttermilk. And that cock. A dandy-cock in the rain, that was Lias. A pity he wouldn't come at cock-crow, so that he couldn't say it was she who'd got him out of bed. Beryl was getting up every four hours for the baby like the watch. But she, Nanw Prisiart, wasn't a baby, but a woman in her own place and her right mind and she had a hundred pounds in the cupboard of the smooth-mannered man in town.

And here came more light from the tunnel. What good was the hundred pounds to her? She didn't want to play marbles or buy a new hat ever again. She'd bought a lot of hats a little while back, because every one of them was making her look old. And all she did was stand at the front door in them. A godly person, but quite upright, that was Huw. And he'd said when she was a young girl that she was so pretty, if she were dressed in rawhide, she'd still be pretty. The best thing, of course, would be to give the hundred pounds to Lias, lest he try again to murder her, and so that he'd leave her alone. She meant to go to the bank tomorrow and take out the hundred pounds and give it to Lias. No, she could put a cross and Lias would go. She hoped that she'd see tomorrow. Oh the pain! She had to knock the wall for Lias. Where was the stick? Here it was, and Oh, what a blessing, here it was feeling better as she was turning on her side and knocking. Thank goodness, she was better again. But Lias would be here in two minutes with his "What's wrong, auntie dear?" and talking and talking, gabble gabble gabble. But never mind, she would see tomorrow, and go down to the larder, no, to the back kitchen, it was her mother had a larder, and have new potatoes and fresh buttermilk again, and it was worth putting up with Lias' hypocrisy for that.

Oh! Winni! Winni!

A December morning in a cellar in town; the gas light hissing every minute like a snake; the sound of people walking on the pavement outside and banging the grating like a child banging one note on a piano all day long; with Winni trying to please her mistress by cleaning the flues of the big old double-oven stove. It would have been easier to do if Robert, the four-year-old child, would stay with his mother on the floor above. But he insisted on being there with Winni, and there was the same amount of soot on both their faces by now. Her mistress wanted to have her stove perfectly heated for the big Christmas cooking. When she was asked by her mistress to do it, Winni had half refused.

"Why don't you ask that Mrs. Jones who comes here to clean on Friday morning to do it?"

"Now, Winni, that isn't the way to speak. Say 'Mrs. Jones,' not 'that Mrs. Jones who comes here to clean'. You know her very well by now."

"There are hundreds of Mrs. Joneses living in this town."

"Yes, but only one who comes here to clean."

"Who's going to show me how to do it?"

"Like this, look."

And her mistress took hold of one of the flues with her fingertips and pulled it out.

"You must put a brush up this hole, as far as you can, and the soot will come down that way."

She only pointed to "that way", having soiled her fingers.

"And then take the soot outside and pour it into the dust-bin."

Here she was, morning having come, with Winni not much wiser after the pointed directions of her mistress, following her fancy with the brush, with her arm often following the brush further than there was need and coming out the same hue as the brush. But the soot had come down smoothly like black flour, plenty of it, and come out, and come out low enough for Robert to dirty his hands in it. After taking the soot outside, she was now blackleading the stove; her face was a lather of sweat, and from pushing away the lock of hair that persisted in falling into her eyes her face was like a Negro's.

That was how her mistress saw her when she came down to see if she had finished. When she saw Winni and the boy, she stood in the door and fretted: "W—ell," under her breath. She snatched the boy up and took him upstairs, screeching, leaving Winni to cope the best she could. Winni wanted to escape somewhere, even to Lisi Jên. But she kept on, boiled water on the gas stove; washed herself and used the water to wash the hearth-stone, hoping that it would take more time for Robert to wash himself upstairs than it took her. She boiled more water while she lit the fire, and washed the kitchen floor: she swept the kitchen and put the matting back. She put on a clean apron and sat on the chair to think.

Which was best, to scrape soot from a big old stove or to live with Lisi Jên in a slovenly kitchen? A year ago she'd been shivering at school in a cold room with a smoky stove that wouldn't draw. This stove was drawing properly now, anyway, the wood crackling in its bosom and the flames rushing up the chimney. There was one other choice she had, to roam the mountain; but she couldn't do that now, when the mist would shroud her head, dripping dew on the locks of her hair, with the bogs sucking at her clogs. There was no cotton grass stirring or heather blossoms, or staghorn moss to pull. London wouldn't be any better; there were dark cellars and gas and stoves there.

The trials of life were closing about her. But she remembered a bright little place, Elin Gruffydd's kitchen; and Sionyn too with his filthy pinafore, flinging things into the fire and running out to the dung-pit with a crust in his hand. No one was running to wash him when he fell into the dung-pit.

In the midst of her reflections her mistress came down. She looked around the kitchen, but she didn't say anything about the lustre of the stove or about the tidiness.

"You must begin fixing dinner now, Winni."

"The stove isn't heated up yet."

"It will be, by the time you peel the potatoes and wash the cabbage, and you can start the meat in the other stove. We'll have fruit instead of pudding today."

There was no peace to be had for thinking about mist or rain, or blue sky or sun, or flowers or moss. She set about it once again, and her heart rose as she looked at the clean kitchen and knew that it was thanks to her. She would have liked to sit in the kitchen all afternoon with her hands folded, do nothing but look at it and think about this Christmas at home. That would have given Begw pleasure; she had a home worth looking forward to spending the day in. But Twm, her father, would stay in bed to recover after drinking the night before; Lisi Jên would fret making dinner, with her husband's cap on her head and a filthy old apron around her waist. But Winni wouldn't have to work, if she herself didn't want to. That was one advantage of having a sluttish tapeworm as a stepmother.

In the afternoon she couldn't muse in her clean kitchen either; she had to take Robert for a walk, do errands, come back to make tea and supper, and then iron until bedtime. Her master brought the supper dishes from upstairs on a tray, and unlike his wife, expressed his appreciation on seeing such a clean kitchen. That was enough for Winni to live on until Christmas; a spur in her to grind the suet, clean the fruit, wash the furniture and wax it.

The evening before Christmas, when Winni stepped over the threshold, all these things had been done, and she had half a crown in her hand, her master's Christmas present, the only half-crown she'd ever held in her hand and known that it was hers. Her father had insisted on having all her November wages without so much as giving her a pocket handkerchief. She was nicely tired; she could sleep on Lisi Jên's hard chaff-bed. Before clapping the door shut, she looked warily to the left and to the right for fear her father would be loitering about. She knew that he and his friends would have come down to the town tonight to drink. She walked proudly and anxiously to a toy shop to buy a present for Sionyn, and she found, in the midst of the dolls and the little horses, a little mule shaking his head, just like the rhyme that she'd recited many a time to her half-brother to keep him quiet, and he'd always shout "Again".

> "The mule, he lifts his head
> Up towards heaven,
> And the people shout with joy,
> Hallelujah, Amen."

On coming out, she put the change in her pocket handkerchief, her only purse; but she didn't know a pair of eyes was looking greedily at her from the other side of the street. The next minute a hand was snatching the handkerchief from her; it was her father's hand: she couldn't do anything but open her mouth in surprise. When she realized what had happened she began running after him, thinking to hit him, but she heard Elin Gruffydd's voice telling her to try and please her mistress, and if she should come to know that she'd been scuffling with her father on the street, she could never go back, or to another place either. When she realized the depth of her disappointment, she burst out sobbing. When she saw people beginning to gather around her she ran down the street and dried her tears on the sleeve of her coat. Then she walked without stopping, with every step on the pavement calling for revenge on her father. With the eighteen pence in change she had intended to buy a pocket handkerchief for Begw and a purse for herself, to keep the few pennies she was hoping to have some day. A man from the same district came towards her—she knew him well by sight, but she didn't know his name.

"What's wrong, Winni?"

And she told him her troubles.

"Here," he said, and put a shilling in her hand, "you can buy something with that; run before the shops close."

And she went, and bought Begw a pocket handkerchief for threepence, a little purse for herself for six, and put the threepence change in the purse, and the purse safely in the pocket of her frock. The man was waiting when she came out of the shop.

"I'll go with you to the brake," he said. "It isn't fitting for a girl of your age to go home in that drunken brake. I came to town to see my sister who's ill, and I see a chance to be carried home."

"Thank you, with all my heart, and don't mention to my father that you gave me anything."

"No danger of my doing that."

Some of her disappointment was eased. Her heart warmed towards people like this man, her master, and Begw's family.

The brake with its horses was standing like a dark whale in a lonely corner of the Square, with only the driver's hat in sight, his head having sunk into his collar.

"A cold evening," he said, through the collar of his topcoat.

The men came from the taverns skimble-skamble; some of them swaying like ships sailing on a raging sea. One tried to get into the driver's seat and fell in trying. Someone lifted him up and set him there. One tried to come and sit beside Winni and put his hand around her waist. And she gave him a push so that he fell neatly on the opposite seat, and the friend who'd helped her came to sit beside her. It was enough that their knees were bumping each other, without stinking breath being near her face. Her father was with the drunkest of them, and he went to sleep with his chin on his breast.

As she left the town with its lights a depression came over Winni again. The lights of the town were sad things; they were there to light the way for the feet of people who were hurrying home from meetings; they showed people's faces as pale, as though they'd just been crying, or as if they were longing, like herself, for something they couldn't have. It's true that some people would laugh and fool about under the lights, sweethearts, but she had to pass them to go into the house and fix supper, not stay with them. They were sadder now as she looked at them on the way, from the brake at the top of the wooded hill, as though they weren't lit for anyone but themselves in their loneliness.

The borderline of the Menai Straits had vanished, making the land one dark blue patch. As she looked to the hills where her home was, the lights there were still sadder, like corpse candles, or "false lights", as the children of the district called them, with a veil of mist over them.

Some of the men would burst into song at times, "My granny's old walking-stick", "The little thatched cottage", and "A memory comes before my eyes". Then they'd quiet down, shutting their eyes: some threw up under their feet. And the horses kept walking and trotting, with the driver's back moving side to side like a brisk clock pendulum to measure the rhythm of the journeying. Nothing else, on an occasional quiet part of the journey, until a burst of singing would come again, with Winni looking at it all as if she were sitting on a bench in a foreign country.

After thanking her benefactor again, Winni quickly left the brake and went to Elin Gruffydd's house, her father being too tipsy to take notice of her. She went in to welcoming light, and "How are you, Winni?" The first thing she did was fall into a chair and cry. Begw was the first to run to her. When Winni raised her head, she saw a neat table with supper on it; Robin and John Gruffydd sitting at it, and Elin Gruffydd standing by the baby's cradle rocking it. The story was told once more; these listeners understood, and showed it by shaking their heads and exclaiming.

"Come to the table, Winni, and have a bite of food," Elin Gruffydd said, "and John can go to escort you home."

"I don't want to go home."

"You'd better go, that will be best," the father said, "or your father will come here to raise a row, and it will be easier for you to go home tonight than tomorrow. Remember that Sionyn will be waiting for you."

Winni cheered up somewhat.

"And you're coming here to tea tomorrow," Elin Gruffydd said, "and bring Sionyn with you."

She expressed her thanks, and took out the pocket handkerchief and gave it to Begw.

"Oh, thank you very much," and Begw ran to the drawer to fetch toffee for Winni.

Winni gave Begw the handkerchief like a woman giving a gift to a child, and Begw presented her with the toffee as a mortal would to a god.

"You shouldn't spend money on Begw," the mother said.

"You've all been so kind, I don't know how to thank you for the toffee, Begw. I'll chew it in bed tonight."

When John Gruffydd and Winni arrived at Twm's house, he and Lisi Jên were eating their supper of sausage, the frying pan on the hob not put away. Twm began roaring.

"Oh, that's where she's been, yes. Why the devil don't you mind your own business?"

"That's what I'm doing, Twm, it's my business and everybody else's if I see someone being wronged. This child isn't getting fair play. You haven't given her a halfpenny of her wages, and here you steal her bit of a 'Christmas box'."

"I had a perfect right to both, she's my child."

"No one would think that from the way you're treating her."

"You and your wife meddle too much for anyone else to get a chance to do anything for her."

"You're putting the cart before the horse, Twm. I don't know what shape she'd have been in going into service, if it weren't for Elin tidying her up."

Through all this Lisi Jên was enjoying her supper without taking her eyes off it, like a person sleeping through thunder and lightning. After John Gruffydd left, Winni went to bed, without anyone offering her supper. She discovered a piece of ribbon in a drawer in the bedroom: she fastened her purse with it and tied it around her neck. Wonder of wonders, Lisi Jên had put clean clothes on the bed. She scrunched up beside Sionyn, and put a piece of Begw's toffee in her mouth. She went to sleep sighing, but she could sleep without being pestered by fleas.

Sometime in the night Sionyn woke up.

"Hi, Winni, I want a present."

He thumped Winni for fear she hadn't heard.

"Who told you you were going to get a present?"

"Mam."

"Where did she think I'd get money to buy a present for anyone?"

No answer.

"No one can buy something with nothing. Go to sleep."

And he began to cry.

"Go to sleep. Perhaps fairy folk will have brought you something by the morning. I know they've come."

Winni awoke before daylight came. She thought that the only thing she could do to kill the time before she could go to Elin Gruffydd's house was work. She began to think of her own mother, and how happy she used to be on Christmas morning, allowed to get up in her nightgown to have a cup of tea and toast with her mother by the fire, with Twm in bed then as he'd be today for sure, taking it easy after the previous night's spree. But she didn't care about that at the time; her mother was there, pretty and clean and a shelter for her from any blow, no matter how poor they were because of Twm's squandering. That sun had risen again in her life, at Begw's house, and her place in town was safe for her if she could keep on as she was doing, and her master had praised her today.

On thinking of that she had an idea. She got hold of an old skirt and bodice of Lisi Jên's and a coarse apron: she lit a candle; she went to the kitchen and took up the ashes that hadn't been taken up for three days; she cleared the ashes from the bakehole in the oven, too, which had been there since the last baking day. She took the ashes out to be sifted in the starry darkness. She blackleaded the grate; she went to the cowshed to fetch a heather faggot and lit a fire. She boiled water and washed the floor and the floor of the milkshed. She dusted the furniture and polished it as well as she could after her stepmother's neglect. How shining her mother had kept it! But now she wasn't as depressed as when she was in bed. She went to look for a cloth and put it on the table, it was shabby enough. But sooner than eat by candlelight, she cleaned the glass chimney of the lamp, glass that the smoke of a crooked wick had blackened. She cut the wick evenly—no wonder the kitchen was like a cellar when she entered the house last night. She cleaned the glass until it was as bright as one of Elin Gruffydd's, which were bright enough to make a chapel cheerful.

And then, in the comparative peace of the kitchen, she sat down at the table and enjoyed a cup of tea and a slice of bread-and-butter: she was a little eight-year-old girl again having breakfast with her mother. But before she was completely finished, Sionyn came from the bedroom and shouted rudely,

"I want a present."

There's a lot of his father in this little bully, Winni thought. She gave him the mule and let him play on the hearth. Then she made a fire under the oven, ready to make dinner, without being quite certain that there was meat. But she remembered seeing a parcel under her father's arm last night. She peeled the carrots and the potatoes. The meat was beginning to sizzle when Lisi Jên got up shortly after nine. Winni's energy was running like a torrent of hot water through her body.

"You're making dinner very early," was Lisi Jên's first remark.

"We'll have it over with first thing. I don't know if you have pudding."

"I made some yesterday."

Lisi Jên enjoyed her breakfast to the last crust before putting the pudding on to boil again and before dressing Sionyn.

Twm got up by dinner time, half-dressed, with a slovenly old handkerchief around his neck. He frowned at the dinner as though he'd just quarrelled with it. He tossed an occasional remark to his wife as he dug into the food.

"And you've become too much of a lady about the town there to talk to your father," was his first greeting to Winni, "and wearing your best frock to dinner."

"Yes, and I want to be more of a lady if being a good-for-nothing is anything like this."

"Who is it raised you, I wonder?"

"Not you, you . . . you scoundrel."

"Leave him alone," Lisi Jên said, "or we'll have nothing but squawking all day long. Winni's the one made the dinner," to her husband.

"A proper job for her; an honour for her to be able to look after her father."

There was such a diabolical brutish look on him at that moment that his daughter would have liked to throttle him, and squeeze his flesh until it was in shreds like the rotten potatoes boiled for the pigs. But just as in town, something—perhaps going to Begw's house for tea—made her hold back. That would have spoiled her tea for her.

It was no surprise to Elin Gruffydd to see Winni and Sionyn there before the others came from the Literary Meeting. She remembered that Winni wouldn't go to the festival after her mother died. Literary Meeting was a thing to grow up with, for years. Sionyn had brought his mule with him and that kept him quiet until tea-time, so that he wasn't bothering Begw's youngest brother.

"I've made another frock for you, Winni, from the end of a piece I bought very cheap at the Goat. You'll wear this one to rags if you don't have another for a change."

"Oh, how pretty, Elin Gruffydd," Winni said as she gazed at the red frock she'd put on, "I can't ever thank you enough. I'll keep it on to have tea."

"You'll need to have a coat for next winter as well, but it's Lisi Jên should buy that from your wages."

"Yes, it's hard to know what to do. Dad was there when I got them the last time, and I'd have been in trouble if I hadn't given them to him."

"It isn't my place to interfere; if I bought you clothes from your wages, Twm would be bad-mouthing me at the quarry. And you know what that would be like. He might as well stand at a stall on the Square, and bad-mouth me from there. Can't you speak to your master and your mistress, they could refuse to give the wages to your father?"

"I'll try."

The others came into the house from the meeting and ran to the fire to get warm, with Begw looking admiringly at Winni's new frock.

"Oh, you're pretty, Winni."

"It's thanks to your mother."

The tea was very plain; only bread-and-butter and jam and home-made currant bread, *bara brith,* with thick butter on it; but it was a feast to Winni, having it like this at a clean table with everyone in good humour. She was ashamed of Sionyn's frock and coat, though she'd ironed them before starting out; before that they'd been in wrinkles as though dogs had been lying on them.

"How are things going in town, Winni?" Begw asked.

"Oh, the place is fine, plenty of style, plenty of carrying food upstairs, and plenty of work with the little boy."

"He'll grow, and summer will come."

Winni began to laugh.

"You know, here's a strange thing."

She stopped.

"Do you know what mince pies are?"

"No," the mother said, "it was at farms I was in service."

"Well, you make a crust like apple tart, but you put it on little tins instead of a plate, and put this mince meat in the middle. And while mistress was making the mince meat with apples, suet, raisins, and things like that, I asked her where the meat was, and mistress had a good laugh. There isn't any meat in it."

"Is it something good?" Robin asked.

"Capital."

She began laughing again.

"I was thinking of Lisi Jên, the greatest slut, and she can make a capital pastry crust. Isn't it a strange thing that feckless people can do some one thing properly?"

Everybody laughed.

"Well, it so happened I'd watched Lisi Jên making crust. Twm Ffinni Hadog, in spite of his name, likes apple tart better than anything, and I've learned to make crust. Mistress praised me."

"You can make some for me the next time."

"Yes, if I'm still in the town."

"Aren't you happy there, Winni?"

"Oh yes," she said, reflecting.

Sionyn began making noises about going home, and the smile left Winni's face.

"Look," Elin Gruffydd said, "run home with him, and come back to supper. It's a sure thing that he won't go with any of us."

Winni cheered up once more, and she was in high spirits when she returned. She had begun by now to have a taste of talking to grown-up people, when they were good listeners. Begw was far away from her, in a different world, a child's world still. She was feeling she was a woman by now, and if Begw had been asked she would have said this wasn't the same Winni who had preached eloquently on the mountain; stealing her bread-and-butter from her basket and dancing barefoot. She'd tamed down since then. But she'd grow to Winni's age herself one day, and get to be her equal. At this time all she could do was listen in admiration. To the others, Winni was beginning to rise from the dung-pit.

"You were asking just before," Winni said as she enjoyed her supper of cold beef, pickled onions, and cold Christmas pudding, "if I was happy in my place. Yes, but that's a very bothersome old house there, having to take every meal upstairs, and there's no bathroom there. So I'm forced to carry water up to the room where they live when they wash all over. They're saying that they'd like to build a house outside of town, but this is handy to the shop."

She began to laugh, laugh so much that Begw began laughing with her, because she knew there was something funny to come.

"What do you suppose, mister is washing mistress all over in this bath; I'd be ashamed for anyone to see me stark naked like that . . ."

Elin Gruffydd began to perspire and look at Robin, and a fearful and expectant nervousness took hold of Begw. Elin Gruffydd interrupted Winni.

"They tell me that your mistress is a very delicate woman, has a lot of rheumatics, that's why, to be sure."

John Gruffydd stuck his beak in.

"Were there many in the brake last night?"

"It was full, and everybody had been drinking except me and that man who gave me a shilling."

"Yes, Elis Ifans y Wern; he found a text for a sermon, for sure."

"Do you know Guto Sboncyn?" Winni asked.

"Yes, very well."

"Guto Grasshopper, my father calls him, when he has something very bad to say about him. He was there. He hasn't one tooth in his head; and when he was setting out to sing and raised his head, you could see to the bottom of his belly. Afterwards, he'd quiet down and close his eyes; and then he was looking just like a graven image, asleep."

It was the word "graven" made Elin Gruffydd change the conversation.

"Do you go to Sunday School, Winni?"

"Yes, every Sunday, but I have to hurry home to make tea, so I don't get to see much of the girls in the class. They're a mixture, servant girls from the country like me and town girls. You should hear the town girls talk with a silly old accent, and they don't know anything of their Bible; they'd be talking about their sweethearts all through the lesson if they had a chance. But I don't want to talk about the town, this is where I am tonight. Tomorrow night the feet will be tramping overhead."

She became sad once more, and sighed.

She didn't see her father after going home or before setting off next day. He was enjoying a quarter-shift in bed—less money for Lisi Jên at the end of the month. Lisi Jên would suffer one day, Winni thought, but she had got up to make breakfast for her. Sionyn was in the land of enchantment.

In this grey good-for-nothing morning, just before the dawn came up, a morning that couldn't raise anyone's hopes, on her way down to town, Winni looked forward to the future. She meant to make her fortune; her purse was tied around her neck, with threepence in it: Elin Gruffydd's new frock in a parcel under her arm, and the memory of the happy time yesterday with Begw's family in her heart.

Notes

For readers who may wish the information, I have listed the Welsh title, book, and date of publication for each story. I have not thought it necessary to trace the initial publication of stories in periodicals. The years in the headings of Parts II and VI refer to the range of dates of book publication.

INTRODUCTION

I have drawn for information and quotations upon Kate Roberts' autobiography, *Y Lôn Wen* (Denbigh: Gwasg Gee, 1960); her reminiscences for the radio series *Y Llwybrau Gynt*, published in *Atgofion, Cyfrol 1* (Nant Peris: Gwasg Tŷ ar y Graig, 1972); her interviews with Saunders Lewis, published in *Crefft y Stori Fer* (Denbigh: Y Clwb Llyfrau Cymraeg, 1949), with J. E. Caerwyn Williams in *Ysgrifau Beirniadol III* (Denbigh: Gwasg Gee, 1967), and with Gwilym Rees Hughes in *Barn* 139 (May 1974); and Emyr Humphreys' dramatization of her life, *The Triple Net* (London: Channel 4 Television, 1988). For insight as well as information and quotations, I am indebted to Walter Allen, *The Short Story in English* (Oxford: Oxford University Press, 1981); Pennar Davies, "The Short Stories of Kate Roberts," in *Triskel One* (Llandybie: Christopher Davies, 1971); John Rowlands' essay in *Profiles* (Llandysul: Gomer Press, 1980); R. M. Jones, "Storiau Cynnar Kate Roberts," in his *Llenyddiaeth Gymraeg 1902–1936* (Llandybie: Cyhoeddiadau Barddas, 1987); and especially Derec Llwyd Morgan's excellent monograph, *Kate Roberts*, in the Writers of Wales series (Cardiff: University of Wales Press, 1974).

Two of Kate Roberts' novels have been published in English: *Feet in Chains* (1936), translated by John Idris Jones (Cardiff: John Jones, 1977), and *The Living Sleep* (1956), translated by Wyn Griffith (Cardiff: John Jones, 1976). A selection of her earlier stories was published in translations by several hands under the title *A Summer Day* (Cardiff: Penmark Press, 1946); *Tea in the Heather* has been translated by Wyn Griffith (Ruthin: John Jones, 1968); a selection of the later stories in translations by E. C. Stephens and W. G. Griffith was brought out in a special illustrated limited edition (Y Drenewydd: Gwasg Gregynog, 1981).

"Fellowship meeting": in the chapter of her autobiography titled "Culture and the Chapel," Kate Roberts gave some details of what the *seiat,* fellowship meeting, involved. "We went to the seiat every week. We didn't learn a verse [from the Bible] for the Wednesday evening seiat, but many verses, and the heads [key points] of the sermon on the previous Sunday, or observations from it." She notes that the children were given the "heads" in a small book "on Monday night or Tuesday, and we had to learn them thoroughly before Wednesday night. I don't know what would have happened to us if we'd spoken our verses as feebly and ineptly as the children of the present day do. I fear we would have been afraid to face our homes that evening. I don't recall that it was very taxing to learn the verses and the heads of the sermons."

"Literary meeting": Kate Roberts explained in her autobiography that "something like this is called an *eisteddfod* [a literary and musical festival] today, something much smaller. Rhosgadfan and Rhostryfan would join in the festival, and it was held on Christmas afternoon and night and the evening before. What made it important was the great preparing for it, so numerous and so varied were the competitions. Rhostryfan would be like a beehive for about a month before the meeting, when the written examinations, and the oral examinations for the smallest children, were held. Besides these [there were] examinations in sewing, in the Scripture, essays, translating, examinations on books and Welsh literature (the books we were studying at the County School were sometimes combined with these); there were competitions we could do at home as well. All this in addition to the reciting, the singing, the two-person debate. I would never compete in the public things but I competed in the examinations, and I was shameless enough to compete in examinations for some much older than myself. I believe the texts of these examinations were of a very high standard. . . . A number of the poets would go forward to the platform to recite stanzas on matters of the day in the village. . . . Things without much worth, you'll say—no indeed. Stanzas like these about people we knew were the bond of the friendship and the good fellowship that existed in the neighbourhood, and that gave us pride because they had done something. It was there the audience came closest to being part of what was happening on the stage."

I AUTOBIOGRAPHY

"Pictures" and "The Last Picture" are the first and last chapters of *Y Lôn Wen* (Denbigh: Gwasg Gee, 1960), which Kate Roberts subtitled "Part of an Autobiography".

Glasynys: the bardic name of Owen Wynne Jones (1828–70), poet, historical novelist, short story writer, and a native of the same region as Kate Roberts.

Quarry supper: the evening meal, after the quarryman returns home from work.

Gelert, Llywelyn's hound: according to legend, Llywelyn the Great (1173–1240), ruler of North Wales, returned from hunting to find his favorite hound, Gelert, covered with blood; he slew it on the presumption that it had killed his infant son—and then discovered the dog had in fact killed a wolf in safeguarding the boy. The story has no basis in fact; *The Oxford Companion to the Literature of Wales* (Oxford: Oxford University Press, 1986) states that it was invented by an eighteenth-century innkeeper in the village of Beddgelert (Gelert's Grave) to explain the place-name. W. R. Spencer based a poem on the story, and this was set to music by Joseph Haydn.

The Statesman, the Welsh Herald: the *New Statesman* and *Yr Herald Gymraeg* were English and North Welsh newspapers at the turn of the century.

The mountain gate: a gate leading to the open mountainside.

"Jeriwsalem fy ngartref gwiw": presumably a translation of the hymn by Joseph Bromehead, "Jerusalem, my happy home."

Five-stones: in an earlier chapter, Kate Roberts wrote: "I have forgotten something of the game of five-stones though this was my favourite game when I was a child. It was a game for girls, and one without quarrelling or pushing or pulling—one that you could play by yourself. One had to have five stones, the smoother the better. Then place a shawl or an apron on the table. The basic part was easy. You put one stone on the shawl, tossed another stone in the air, and picked up the stone from the shawl as the other was falling into your hand. 'Pick up one', that was called. Then you placed two stones on the shawl, then three, then four, tossing one stone up and gathering up the others. Then, there were harder things to do, like placing four of the stones in a square, tossing one stone up, and while that was in the air, taking your finger and gathering the stones together, one at a time, then collecting the four into your hand as before. I can't remember entirely all of these complexities."

II STORIES (1925–1937)

The Letter: "Y Llythyr," in *O Gors y Bryniau* (Cardiff: Hughes a'i Fab, 1925); hereafter *OGYB*.

Provoking: "Pryfocio," in *OGYB*.

The Widow: "Y Wraig Wddw," in *OGYB*.

Pegging a pig: putting a wooden peg or metal ring in a pig's snout to prevent it from rooting up the ground.

Old Age: "Henaint," in *OGYB*.

The Ruts of Life: "Rhigolau Bywyd," in *Rhigolau Bywyd* (Aberystwyth: Gwasg Aberystwyth, 1929); hereafter *RhB*.

The Maid of Eithinfynydd: Y Fun o Eithinfynydd (1897), a popular novel by Mary Oliver Jones, which Kate Roberts in an interview remembered as making an impression on her in her youth.

The *Red Echo: Yr Eco Goch*, a weekly newspaper.

Association: the quarterly meeting of Welsh Presbyterians.

'Steddfod: Eisteddfod, a literary and musical festival. The National Eisteddfod is held annually in a different town, alternating between North and South Wales; there are also regional festivals of the same kind.

The Loss: "Y Golled," in *RhB*.

Between Two Pieces of Toffee: "Rhwng Dau Damaid o Gyfleth," in *RhB*.

November Fair: "Ffair Gaeaf" (literally "Winter Fair"), a market fair held early in November. See the later story with this title.

Indian rock: hard crystal candy.

Y Bardd Crwst: the bardic name of Abel Jones (1830–1901), a popular itinerant ballad-singer born in Llanrwst. The name had associations with his birthplace and also suggested something like "the Pennyloaf Poet."

Sisters: "Chwiorydd," in *RhB*.

The Victory of Alaw Jim: "Buddugoliaeth Alaw Jim," in *Ffair Gaeaf* (Denbigh: Gwasg Gee, 1937); hereafter *FfG*. This story, like two others in Kate Roberts' third collection, is set in South Wales during the depression of the 1930s. "In Wales there was a decline in the metallurgical and coal industries, as well as a shut-down of the busy export ports along the southern coast. The numbers employed in coal-mining alone fell from 270,000 in 1920 to 128,000 by 1939. . . . The standard of living fell, nutritional deficiencies marred the health of more than one generation and a culture of unemployment settled on south Wales, a region of which the rate of long-term, mass unemployment exceeded that for any other part of Britain" (*Oxford Companion*, p. 143). The name "Alaw Jim" means "Jim's Melody"; such names are given to racing dogs, as they are to racehorses.

The Quilt: "Y Cwilt," in *FfG*.

Red-Letter Day: "Diwrnod i'r Brenin," in *FfG*.

The Last Payment: "Y Taliad Olaf," in *FfG*.

November Fair: "Ffair Gaeaf," in *FfG*.

The Bardd Crwst: see the note under "Between Two Pieces of Toffee."

The Condemned: "Y Condemniedig," in *FfG*.

Protest March: "Y Gorymdaith," in *FfG*.

"Hunger Marches, in which unemployed workers called on the Government to improve their conditions, were a feature of life in south Wales during the 1920s and 1930s. . . . The last march, which took place in 1936, was backed by a united front of Socialists and Communists, who co-operated to an extent without precedent" (*Oxford Companion*, p. 274). The "Means Test" was an inquiry into the financial resources of an applicant for assistance.

III   GOSSIP ROW. STRYD Y GLEP (DENBIGH: GWASG GEE, 1949)

Enoc Huws: the title character of a well-known novel by Daniel Owen (1836–95).

Llyn y Fan: The Faerie Lady of Llyn y Fan Fach, a lake near Llanddeusant, Carmarthenshire, married a farmer's son who swore he loved her, but she warned that she would return to the lake if he struck her "three causeless [i.e., unjustified] blows." After he struck her for the third time, when she laughed at a funeral, she explained that she had laughed with joy because the dead man was now freed from worldly cares, and she returned to the lake.

"I put my hope": a famous line from a poem by the fifteenth-century devotional poet Siôn Cent.

IV TEA IN THE HEATHER. TE YN Y GRUG (DENBIGH: GWASG GEE, 1959)

Grief. "Gofid."

Children's Treasury: *Trysorfa'r Plant*, a popular magazine for children published by the Calvinistic Methodists and edited by the minister Thomas Lewis from 1862 to 1911.

The Spout: "Y Pistyll."

Death of a Story: "Marwolaeth Stori."

Tea in the Heather: "Te yn y Grug."

"Mister Mostyn has a master now": a proverbial saying. The Mostyns had been a wealthy and powerful family in North Wales since the sixteenth century.

A Visitor for Tea: "Ymwelydd i De."

Charles's Dictionary: a scriptural dictionary in four volumes (1805–11) by the Welsh Methodist scholar Thomas Charles.

Escape to London: "Dianc i Lundain."

Becoming Strangers: "Dieithrio."

The Card Christmas: "Nadolig y Cerdyn."

V DARK TONIGHT. TYWYLL HENO (DENBIGH: GWASG GEE, 1962)

The title of the story comes from an anonymous ninth-century poem, "Stafell Cynddylan," one of a group of poems in which the speaker is Heledd, the last survivor of the royal family of seventh-century Powys, as she mourns for the destruction of her home and the deaths of her brothers—in particular, Cynddylan—in battle near the site of modern Shrewsbury. Kate Roberts' narrator refers to and quotes from the poem at several points in the story. The most relevant stanzas—from my translation in *The Earliest Welsh Poetry* (New York: St. Martin's Press, 1970)—are the following:

> *The hall of Cynddylan is dark tonight,*
> *No fire, no pallet.*
> *I'll keen now, then be quiet.*

> *The hall of Cynddylan is dark tonight,*
> *No fire, no candle.*
> *Who but God will keep me tranquil?*

> *The hall of Cynddylan is dark tonight,*
> *No fire, no bright gleaming.*
> *For your sake my heart's aching.*

> *The hall of Cynddylan is dark tonight,*

No fire, no singing.
My cheeks are worn from weeping.

The hall of Cynddylan is dark tonight,
No fire, no household.
Free flow my tears where night falls.

The hall of Cynddylan, the sight stabs me,
No rooftop, no fire.
Dead my lord, myself alive.

The hall of Cynddylan hurts me each hour:
Gone the great assembly
I once saw at your hearthside.

Cynghanedd: the intricate consonantal harmony within the line which is a feature of poems in the Welsh "strict meters."

Gwilym Hiraethog: the bardic name of William Rees (1802–83), poet and journalist.

The Steddfod compositions: the winning poems from the National Eisteddfod (see note under "The Ruts of Life"), held early in August, are published annually.

Williams Pantycelyn: William Williams (1717–91) of Pantycelyn, the farm in Carmarthenshire where he was raised, is the most famous of the Welsh Methodist hymnists.

The Barnyard Trio: students from the University College of North Wales, Bangor, who sang popular songs in the late 1940s.

G.E.C.: the results of the examinations for the General Education Certificate, taken at age sixteen, published annually.

The Plum Tree: Y Goeden Eirin (1946), a collection of short stories by John Gwilym Jones in which the emphasis is on the oddities of human psychology as these are revealed by the "stream of consciousness" in diverse characters.

Siôn Cent: see note under *Gossip Row.*

Goronwy Owen (1723–69): the most gifted Welsh poet of the earlier eighteenth century.

Teddy Boys: the name given rebellious British youths in the early 1960s who imitated Edwardian dress and hairstyles.

Morgan Llwyd: seventeenth-century Puritan preacher and writer, whose *Book of the Three Birds* (1653) consists of dialogues among the Eagle, the Raven, and the Dove. Politically, the birds stand for the civil power, the Royalists, and the Puritans; religiously, they represent the seeker for salvation, the reprobate, and the saint. In the final section of the book, a discussion between the Eagle and the Dove on the nature of the devout life, Morgan Llwyd draws upon his own religious experience. The richness of imagery and rhythms make it one of the classics of Welsh prose.

Dr. Thomas Parry: the book in question is presumably his literary history, *Hanes Llenyddiaith Gymraeg* (1945).

"Oh how sweet is hidden manna": a quotation from a hymn by William Williams Pantycelyn.

R. Williams Parry (1884–1956): poet who won the Chair at the National Eisteddfod in 1910 with his *Yr Haf* (Summer), an *awdl*, or strict-meter ode. It was included with other poems in his collection of 1924, from which the sonnet "Dinas Noddfa" (City of Refuge) comes. The following translation is from my *Twentieth Century Welsh Poems* (Llandysul: Gwasg Gomer, 1982; Chester Springs, Pa.: Dufour, 1982):

> *When the Stars send their tremor through your blood*
> *Shaking your fixed beliefs like forest leaves;*
> *When the Night tries the earth of which you're made*
> *And its terror probes your substance to the core;*
> *Or when you hear the sad rhyme of the Sea*
> *Darkly chanting its entrancing moan,*
> *And the Wind that comes and goes beside your door*
> *Hoarse through the trees, and lisping through the rushes;*
> *Follow the wise, and raise yourself a fort*
> *Where you find refuge from their strong oppression,*
> *Lord of your emptiness, and architect*
> *Of your own heaven. Or else follow him*
> *When he builds a temple, not the work of hand,*
> *Surpassing Nature's secret and beyond.*

"Oh blessed will be the shouting": misquotation of a hymn by Thomas Levi, substituting "shouting" for "singing."

VI STORIES (1964–1981)

Cats at an Auction: "Cathod mewn Ocsiwn," in *Hyn o Fyd* (Denbigh: Gwasg Gee, 1964).

Buying a Doll: "Prynu Dol," in *Prynu Dol* (Denbigh: Gwasg Gee, 1969); hereafter *PD*.

Flowers: "Blodau," in *PD*.

Ann Griffiths (1776–1805): Methodist hymnist who ranked with William Williams Pantycelyn. Her birthplace at Dolwar Fach, in Montgomeryshire, became a center for Methodist preaching after her conversion in 1796.

Teddy Boy: see note under *Dark Tonight*.

The Journey: "Y Daith," in *PD*.

The Battle of Christmas: "Brwydro efo'r Nadolig," in *PD*.

Two Old Men: "Dau Hen Ddyn," in *PD*.

The Treasure: "Y Trysor," in *Gobaith* (Denbigh: Gwasg Gee, 1972); hereafter *G*.

Family: "Teulu," in *G*.

Thomas John Cilgerran: a nineteenth-century Evangelical preacher who pictured eternal damnation in terms of a clock in Hell tolling "Forever! Forever!"

Hope: "Gobaith," in *G*.

Return: "Dychwelyd," in *G*.

Math and Gwydion: magicians in the medieval Welsh stories usually known as *The Mabinogion*.

Tomorrow and Tomorrow: "Yfory ac Yfory," in *Yr Wylan Deg* (Denbigh: Gwasg Gee, 1976).

Oh! Winni! Winni!: "O! Winni! Winni!," in *Haul a Drycin* (Denbigh: Gwasg Gee, 1981).

DATE DUE

OCT 08 '95			

HIGHSMITH   45230